THE LILY AND THE LION

Maurice Druon was a French resistance hero, a Knight of the British Empire and a holder of the Grand Croix de la Légion d'Honneur. He was also a member of L'Académie française and a celebrated novelist, best known for his series of seven historical novels under the title of *The Accursed Kings*, which were twice adapted for television. A passionate Anglophile, he was a great expert on all things English, including its medieval history, which provides great inspiration for the series. His many and diverse fans include George R.R. Martin, Nicolas Sarkozy and Vladimir Putin.

BY MAURICE DRUON

The Accursed Kings

The Iron King
The Strangled Queen
The Poisoned Crown
The Royal Succession
The She-Wolf
The Lily and the Lion
The King Without a Kingdom

THE LILY AND THE LION

Book Six of The Accursed Kings

MAURICE DRUON

Translated from French by
Humphrey Hare

HarperCollins*Publishers*

HarperCollins*Publishers*
1 London Bridge Street
London SE1 9GF

www.harpercollins.co.uk

First published in Great Britain by Rupert Hart-Davis 1961
Arrow edition 1988

This paperback edition 2015

4

A catalogue record for this book is
available from the British Library

ISBN: 978-0-00-749136-0

Printed and bound in Great Britain by
Clays Ltd, St Ives plc

MIX
Paper from
responsible sources
FSC www.fsc.org FSC C007454

'History is a novel that has been lived'
E. & J. DE GONCOURT

'It is terrifying to think how much research
is needed to determine the truth of even
the most unimportant fact.'
STENDHAL

Foreword

GEORGE R.R. MARTIN

Over the years, more than one reviewer has described my fantasy series, A Song of Ice and Fire, as historical fiction about history that never happened, flavoured with a dash of sorcery and spiced with dragons. I take that as a compliment. I have always regarded historical fiction and fantasy as sisters under the skin, two genres separated at birth. My own series draws on both traditions ... and while I undoubtedly drew much of my inspiration from Tolkien, Vance, Howard, and the other fantasists who came before me, A Game of Thrones and its sequels were also influenced by the works of great historical novelists like Thomas B. Costain, Mika Waltari, Howard Pyle ... and Maurice Druon, the amazing French writer who gave us the The Accursed Kings, seven splendid novels that chronicle the downfall of the Capetian kings and the beginnings of the Hundred Years War.

Druon's novels have not been easy to find, especially in English translation (and the seventh and final volume was never translated into English at all). The series has twice been made into a television series in France, and both versions are available on DVD ... but only in French, undubbed, and without English subtitles. Very frustrating for English-speaking Druon fans like me.

The Accursed Kings has it all. Iron kings and strangled queens, battles and betrayals, lies and lust, deception, family rivalries, the curse of the Templars, babies switched at birth, she-wolves, sin, and swords, the doom of a great dynasty ... and all of it (well, most of it) straight from the pages of history. And believe me, the Starks and the Lannisters have nothing on the Capets and Plantagenets.

Whether you're a history buff or a fantasy fan, Druon's epic will keep you turning pages. This was the original game of thrones. If you like *A Song of Ice and Fire*, you will love *The Accursed Kings*.

George R.R. Martin

Author's Acknowledgements

I AM most grateful to Georges Kessel, Pierre de Lacretelle and Madeleine Marignac for the invaluable help they have given me in the writing of this book; and to the authorities of the Bibliothèque Nationale and the Archives Nationales for their indispensable aid in research.

Contents

Part I: The New Kings

Part II: The Devil's Game

Part III: Decline and Fall

Part IV: The War-Brand

Epilogue: 1354–62

The Characters in this Book

THE HOUSE OF FRANCE:

The King: PHILIPPE VI OF VALOIS, great-grandson of
Saint Louis, nephew of Philip the Fair, eldest son of
Count Charles of Valois and his first wife, Marguerite
of Anjou-Sicily, aged 35.*

The Queen: JEANNE OF BURGUNDY, called the Lame,
grand-daughter of Saint Louis, sister of Duke Eudes IV
and of the late Queen Marguerite of Burgundy,
aged 33.

Their Eldest Son: JEAN, Duke of Normandy, the future
King JEAN II, the Good, aged 9.

The Dowager Queens: JEANNE OF EVREUX, daughter of
Louis of France, Count of Evreux, and niece of Philip the
Fair, third wife and widow of King Charles IV, the Fair,
aged about 25.

JEANNE OF BURGUNDY, called the Widow, daughter of

---

* Ages are given as in the year 1328.

Mahaut of Artois and wife of the late King Philippe V, the Long, aged 35.

THE HOUSE OF ENGLAND:

The King: EDWARD III PLANTAGENET, son of Edward II and Isabella of France, aged 16.

The Queen: PHILIPPA OF HAINAUT, second daughter of Count Guillaume of Hainaut and Jeanne of Valois, aged 14.

The Queen Mother: ISABELLA OF FRANCE, widow of Edward II, daughter of Philip the Fair, aged 36.

The King's Relatives: HENRY, called Wryneck,* Earl of Leicester and Lancaster, aged 47.

EDMUND, Earl of Kent, uncle of King Edward III, aged 27.

THE HOUSE OF NAVARRE:

The Queen: JEANNE OF NAVARRE, daughter of Louis the Hutin and Marguerite of Burgundy, granddaughter of Philip the Fair, heiress to the Kingdom of Navarre, aged 17.

The King: PHILIPPE OF FRANCE, Count of Evreux, son of Louis of France and husband of the above, aged about 21.

THE HOUSE OF HAINAUT:

GUILLAUME, called the Good, Sovereign Count of HAINAUT, Holland and Zeeland, father of Queen Philippa of England.

JEANNE OF VALOIS, Countess of Hainaut, wife of the above and sister of King Philippe VI of France.

JEAN OF HAINAUT, younger brother of Count Guillaume.

---

* Wrongly called 'Crouchback' in *The She-Wolf of France*.

THE HOUSE OF BURGUNDY:

EUDES IV, Duke of BURGUNDY, brother of the late Queen
Marguerite of Burgundy and of Queen Jeanne the Lame,
a Peer of France, aged about 46.

JEANNE OF BURGUNDY, his wife, daughter of King
Philippe V, the Long, granddaughter of Mahaut of Artois,
aged 19.

THE HOUSE OF ARTOIS:

MAHAUT, Countess of ARTOIS, widow of Count Othon IV
of Burgundy, mother of the Queen Dowager Jeanne the
Widow and grandmother of Duchess Jeanne of Burgundy,
a Peer of France, aged 59.

ROBERT OF ARTOIS, Count of Beaumont-le-Roger, Lord of
Conches, a nephew of the above, cousin and brother-in-
law of King Philippe VI, a Peer of France, aged 41.

JEANNE OF VALOIS-COURTENAY, half-sister of King
Philippe VI, wife of Robert of Artois, but always known as
the Countess of BEAUMONT, aged 24.

PEERS, PRELATES AND DIGNITARIES OF
THE HOUSE OF FRANCE:

LOUIS I, Duke of BOURBON, Great Chamberlain of France,
grandson of Saint Louis, son of Robert of Clermont, a
Peer of France.

LOUIS OF NEVERS, Count of Flanders, a Peer of France.

GUILLAUME DE TRYE, Duke-Archbishop of Reims, a
Spiritual Peer.

JEAN DE MARIGNY, Count-Bishop of Beauvais, younger
brother of Enguerrand de Marigny, a Spiritual Peer.

GAUCHER DE CHÂTILLON, Count of Porcien and Lord of
Crèvecoeur, Constable of France 1302–1329.

RAOUL DE BRIENNE, Count of Eu, Constable on the decease of the above.

HUGUES, Count de BOUVILLE, ex-Chamberlain to Philip the Fair.

JEAN DE CHERCHEMONT, Chancellor in 1328.

GUILLAUME DE SAINT-MAURE, Chancellor from 1329.

MILLE DE NOYERS, ex-Marshal of France, President of the Exchequer, President of Parliament.

ROBERT BERTRAND, called the Knight of the Green Lion, and MATHIEU DE TRYE, Marshals of France.

BÉHUCHET, an Admiral.

JEAN THE FOOL, a dwarf.

LORDS, PRELATES AND DIGNITARIES OF
THE HOUSE OF ENGLAND:

ROGER MORTIMER, eighth Baron Wigmore, first Earl of March, ex-Justiciar of Ireland, the lover of Isabella, the Queen Mother, aged 42.

WILLIAM DE MELTON, Archbishop of York, Primate of England.

HENRY DE BURGHERSH, Bishop of Lincoln, Chancellor and Ambassador.

ADAM ORLETON, formerly Bishop of Hereford, now of Worcester, and later of Winchester, Treasurer and Ambassador.

JOHN, Baron MALTRAVERS, Seneschal of England, aged about 38.

WILLIAM, Baron MONTACUTE, first Earl of SALISBURY, Councillor and Ambassador, later Lord Warden of the Cinque Ports and Marshal of England, aged 27.

GAUTIER DE MAUNY, Equerry to Queen Philippa.

JOHN DAVERILL, Governor of Corfe Castle.

WILLIAM ELAND, Governor of Nottingham Castle.

THE PRINCIPAL LAWYERS AND ACTORS IN
   THE ARTOIS CASE:

PIERRE DE VILLEBRESME, the Commissioner.

PIERRE TESSON, a notary.

JEANNE DE DIVION, ex-mistress of the late Bishop Thierry
   d'Hirson.

BEATRICE D'HIRSON, niece of Bishop Thierry, Lady-in-
   Waiting to the Countess Mahaut of Artois.

GILLET DE NELLE, Valet to Robert of Artois.

MARIE LA BLANCHE, MARIE LA NOIRE and JEANNETTE
   DESQUESNES, servants of Jeanne de Divion.

PIERRE DE MACHAUT, a witness.

ROBERT ROSSIGNOL, a forger.

MACIOT L'ALLEMANT, a Sergeant-at-Arms.

SIMON DE BUCY, the King's Attorney.

THE EMPEROR OF GERMANY:

LOUIS V OF BAVARIA.

THE KING OF BOHEMIA:

JOHN OF LUXEMBURG, son of the Emperor Henry VII
   of Germany.

THE KING OF NAPLES:

ROBERT OF ANJOU-SICILY, called the Astrologer, uncle of
   King Philippe VI of France.

THE KING OF ARAGON:

ALFONSO IV.

THE KING OF HUNGARY:

LOUIS I, the Great.

THE POPES:

JOHN XXII, formerly Cardinal Jacques DUÈZE, BENEDICT
    XII (from 1334), formerly Jacques FOURNIER, called the
    White Cardinal.

JAKOB VAN ARTEVELDE, leader of the Flemish League.

COLA DI RIENZI, Tribune of Rome.

SPINELLO TOLOMEI, a Sienese banker.

JEAN I, THE POSTHUMOUS, called GIANNINO, son of
    Louis X, the Hutin, and Clémence of Hungary, pretender
    to the throne of France.

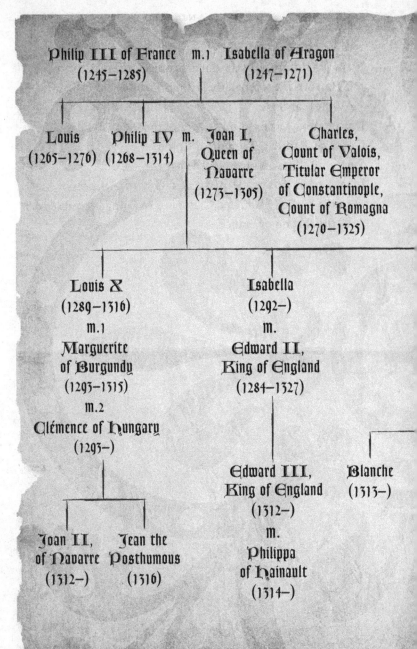

Philip III of France (1245–1285) m.1 Isabella of Aragon (1247–1271)

Louis (1265–1276)

Philip IV (1268–1314) m. Joan I, Queen of Navarre (1273–1305)

Charles, Count of Valois, Titular Emperor of Constantinople, Count of Romagna (1270–1325)

Louis X (1289–1316) m.1 Marguerite of Burgundy (1293–1315) m.2 Clémence of Hungary (1293–)

Isabella (1292–) m. Edward II, King of England (1284–1327)

Edward III, King of England (1312–) m. Philippa of Hainault (1314–)

Blanche (1313–)

Joan II, of Navarre (1312–)

Jean the Posthumous (1316)

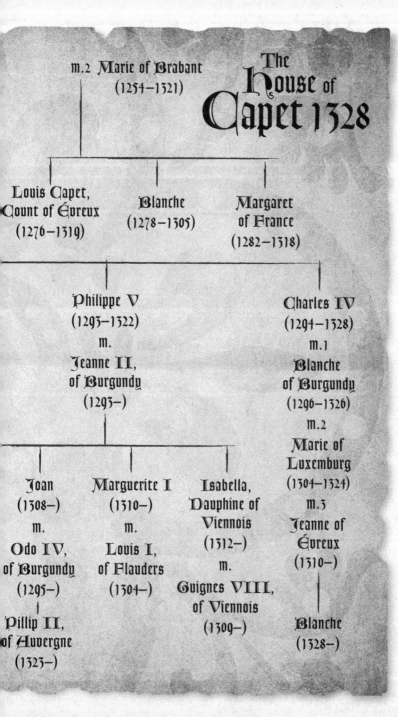

The House of Capet 1328

m.2 Marie of Brabant
(1254–1321)

Louis Capet,
Count of Évreux
(1276–1319)

Blanche
(1278–1305)

Margaret
of France
(1282–1318)

Philippe V
(1293–1322)
m.
Jeanne II,
of Burgundy
(1293–)

Charles IV
(1294–1328)
m.1
Blanche
of Burgundy
(1296–1326)
m.2
Marie of
Luxemburg
(1304–1324)
m.3
Jeanne of
Évreux
(1310–)

Joan
(1308–)
m.
Odo IV,
of Burgundy
(1295–)
|
Pillip II,
of Auvergne
(1323–)

Marguerite I
(1310–)
m.
Louis I,
of Flauders
(1304–)

Isabella,
Dauphine of
Viennois
(1312–)
m.
Guignes VIII,
of Viennois
(1309–)

Blanche
(1328–)

NORTH
KINGDOM of ENGLAND
ENGLISH CHANNEL
Cherbourg
Brittany
Le Mans
Anjou
Poitou
Saintonge
BAY of BISCAY
Bordeaux
Gascony
Bearn

NORTH SEA

Calais

Flanders

Artois

Crécy

Somme R.

Amiens

Coucy

Normandy

Evreux

Paris

Champagne

Chartres

Seine R.

Reims

Meuse R.

Orléans

Loire R.

Dijon

Touraine

Berry

KINGDOM of FRANCE

Burgundy

Poitiers

Bourbon

Limoges

Lyon

Dauphiny

Guyenne

Avignon

Toulouse

Languedoc

Foux

MEDITERRANEAN SEA

The Lily and The Lion

Mahaut, Countess of Artois, was in a very bad temper all the way home.

'Did you hear what that great fool we're unlucky enough to have for King said? He expects me to give up Artois, just like that, and merely to please him! The very idea of making that great foul Robert my heir! My hand would wither away before it signed a thing like that! They've clearly been accomplices in roguery for a long time past and owe each other a lot! And to think that if it weren't for my having cleared the path to the throne . . .'

'Mother . . .' Jeanne murmured in a low voice.

If she had dared to say what she thought and had not been afraid of a savage rebuff, Jeanne would have advised her mother to accept the King's proposals. But it would have done no good.

'He'll never get me to agree to that,' repeated Mahaut.

Though she did not know it, she had signed her death-warrant; and her executioner was sitting opposite her in the litter, looking at her through her dark lashes.

PART ONE

THE NEW KINGS

I

The January Wedding

FROM BOTH SIDES of the river and from every parish in the city, from St Denis, St Cuthbert, St Martin-cum-Gregory, St Mary Senior and St Mary Junior, from the Shambles and from Tanner Row, the people of York had been flowing for the past two hours in a continuous stream towards the huge but still-unfinished Minster that brooded heavily over the city.

The crowd completely blocked the two winding streets of Stonegate and Deangate which led into the yard. Boys, who had found perches above the crowd, could see nothing but a sea of heads covering the whole area. Burgesses, tradesmen, matrons with their numerous broods, cripples on crutches, servants, apprentices, hooded monks, soldiers in shirts of mail and beggars in rags were all crowded as close together as the stalks in a truss of hay. The light-fingered pickpockets were reaping a year's harvest. Faces filled the upper windows like so many bunches of grapes. The damp, cold, misty twilight that enveloped the great building and the crowd standing in the mud seemed scarcely that of noon. It was as if the gathering was pressing close together for warmth.

It was January 24th, 1328, and, in the presence of William de Melton, Archbishop of York and Primate of England, King Edward III, who was not yet sixteen, was marrying his cousin, Madam Philippa of Hainaut, who was barely more than fourteen.

There was not an empty seat in the cathedral. They had all been reserved for the high dignitaries of the kingdom, members of the upper clergy and Parliament, the five hundred invited knights and the hundred tartan-clad Scottish nobles, who had come south to ratify the Peace Treaty. Soon the solemn mass would be celebrated, sung by a hundred and twenty choristers.

Now, however, the first part of the ceremony, the marriage proper, was taking place outside the south door of the cathedral in view of the people, according to the ancient rite and peculiar custom of the archdiocese of York, as a reminder that marriage was a sacrament between husband and wife, affirmed by mutual vows taken in public, to which the priest was merely a witness.

The mist had stained the red velvet of the canopy over the door with patches of damp, it had condensed on the bishops' mitres, and had bedraggled the fur about the shoulders of the royal family assembled round the young couple.

'Here I take thee, Philippa, to my wedded wife, to have and to hold, at bed and at board . . .'[1]*

Coming from the King's young lips and beardless face, his

---

* The numbers in the text refer to the Historical Notes at the end of the book.

4

voice was surprisingly powerful, clear and vibrantly intense. Isabella, the Queen Mother, was struck by it, and so were Messire Jean of Hainaut, the bride's uncle, and the others standing near, such as Edmund, Earl of Kent, and Wryneck, Earl of Lancaster, Chief of the Council of Regency and the King's tutor.

The barons had heard their new King speak with such unexpected force only once before – on a day of battle in the last Scottish campaign.

'... for fairer for fouler, for better for worse, in sickness and in health ...'

The whispering of the crowd gradually subsided; silence spread like a circular ripple and the royal young voice rang out above those thousands of heads, audible almost to the far end of the yard. The King slowly recited the long vow he had learned the previous day; but he might have been inventing it afresh, so clearly did he articulate each phrase and lend each word grave and profound significance. It was like a prayer said once, and destined to last a lifetime.

The boyish figure seemed endued with the mind of a man supremely sure of the vow he was taking in the face of Heaven, of a prince conscious of the part he had to play between his people and his God. The new King was taking his family, his friends, his great officers of State, his barons, his prelates, his people of York and, indeed, of all England, to witness the love he was vowing to Madam Philippa.

Prophets burning with the zeal of God and leaders of nations who are imbued with some unique conviction can infect the crowd with their faith. A public affirmation of love also has this power, and can make everyone share one man's emotion.

There was not a woman in the crowd, whatever her age, whether she was newly married, was deceived by her husband, was a widow, a virgin or a grandmother, who did not feel herself at that moment to be standing in the bride's place; and there was not a man who did not identify himself with the young King. Edward III was uniting himself to every woman among his people; and it was his whole kingdom that was taking Philippa to wife. The dreams of youth, the disillusionments of maturity, and the regrets of old age were all centred on the young couple – heartfelt offerings. And, when darkness fell in the ill-lit streets, the eyes of betrothed couples would glow brighter in the night, and husbands and wives, who had been long at enmity, would reach for each other's hands when supper was done.

From the beginning of time people have crowded to the weddings of princes, in order to enjoy a vicarious happiness which, when seen in the highest, must seem perfect.

'. . . till death us do part . . .'

There was a lump in every throat; a vast, sad, almost reproachful sigh rose from the crowd. At such a moment, there should be no mention of death. Surely this young couple could not be mortal or subject to the common lot?

'. . . and thereto I plight thee my troth . . .'

The young King heard the people sigh, but he did not look at them. His pale blue, almost grey eyes, their long lashes raised for once, were gazing at the chubby, freckled little girl, wrapped in veils and velvets, to whom he was making his vows.

Indeed, Madam Philippa was not at all like a princess in a fairy story; she was not even very pretty, for she had the heavy features, short nose and freckles of the Hainauts. Nor was she endowed with any particular grace of movement; yet she had an attractive simplicity and made no attempt to assume an air of majesty, which would certainly not have become her. Without her royal adornments, she would have looked no different from any other red-headed girl of her age; there were hundreds like her in every one of the northern kingdoms. But this merely increased her popularity with the crowd. Though she was the elected of Fate and of God, she was essentially no different from the women over whom she was to reign. Every stout, red-headed girl felt that she had, somehow or other, been personally complimented and honoured.

Trembling with emotion, Philippa screwed up her eyes as if unable to bear the intensity of her bridegroom's gaze. All that was happening to her was so incredibly wonderful: the coronets about her, the mitres, the knights, the ladies she could see within the cathedral, row on row of them behind the candles, like souls in Paradise, and all the populace there below her! Indeed, she was to be Queen and, what was more, Queen by a love-match.

Oh, how she would cherish, serve and adore her fair and handsome prince, who had such long eyelashes and such slender hands, and who had come so miraculously to Valenciennes twenty months ago with his exiled mother, seeking help and refuge. Their parents had sent them out to play in the garden with the other children; and they had fallen in love. And now that he was King, he had not forgotten her. How happy she would be to devote her life to him. Her one fear was that she was not beautiful enough to please him for ever, nor clever enough always to be a help to him.

'Madam, put out your right hand,' said the Archbishop.

Philippa at once put out her little dimpled hand from her velvet sleeve, holding it firmly, palm upwards, fingers spread.

To Edward it seemed an exquisite rose-tinted star.

From a salver held out to him by another prelate, the Archbishop took the flat gold ring, encrusted with rubies, which he had previously blessed, and handed it to the King. The ring felt damp to the touch, as did everything else in the mist. The Archbishop gently drew their hands together.

'In the Name of the Father,' said Edward, placing the ring just over the tip of Philippa's thumb, 'in the Name of the Son, in the Name of the Holy Ghost,' he said, as he moved it to her fore and middle fingers. And then, as he slipped it home on the fourth finger, he said: 'Amen!'

Philippa was his wife.

Queen Isabella, like every mother at her son's wedding, had tears in her eyes. Though she was making a great effort to pray God to grant her son happiness, she could not help thinking of herself; and she suffered. It had become increasingly clear during these last few days that she would no longer take first place in her son's heart and house. Not, of course, that she had much to fear from this little bundle of embroidered velvet who, at this very instant, was become her daughter-in-law; her authority over the Court could not be challenged, nor indeed her supremacy in beauty. Straight and slender, her fine golden tresses, framing her face, which was still so clear-complexioned, Isabella at thirty-six looked scarcely thirty. She had spent much time that morning before the looking-glass, while donning her crown for the ceremony, and had left it reassured. Yet today she was no longer the Queen but the Queen Mother. How quickly it had happened.

How odd that twenty stormy years should be resolved like this.

She thought of her own wedding, exactly twenty years ago, on a late January day like this. It had taken place at Boulogne in France and there had been a mist then too. She also had believed, as she made her heartfelt vows, that her marriage would be happy. But she had not known to what kind of man she was being married in the interests of the State. How could she have known that her reward for love and devotion would be humiliation, hatred and contempt, that she would be supplanted in her husband's bed, not indeed by mistresses, but by scandalous and avaricious men, that her marriage portion would be ravished from her, her lands confiscated, that to save her life she would have to go into exile, raise an army to reconquer her position, and in the end order the murder of Edward II, who that day had slipped the wedding ring on to her finger? How lucky young Philippa was to be not only married but loved.

First love is the only pure and happy one. If it goes wrong, nothing can replace it. Later loves can never attain to the same limpid perfection; though they may be as solid as marble, they are streaked with veins of another colour, the dried blood of the past.

Queen Isabella turned to look at her lover Roger Mortimer, Baron of Wigmore, who owed it as much to her as to himself that he was now master of England and governed in the name of the young King. Stern-featured, his eyebrows forming a single line, he stood with his arms crossed over his sumptuous robe; he met her eyes, but his held no kindness.

'He knows what I'm thinking,' she thought, 'But why does

he always make one feel that it's a crime to stop thinking of him even for an instant?'

She knew his jealous nature so well; and she smiled at him conciliatingly. What more could he want than he already had? She lived with him as if they were man and wife, even though she was Queen and he married; and she had compelled the kingdom to accept the fact of their love. She had seen to it that he had complete power; he appointed his creatures to every post; he had acquired all the fiefs of Edward II's old favourites; and the Council of Regency obeyed his decrees and merely ratified his wishes. He had even persuaded Isabella to issue the order for her husband's death. It was due to him that she was called the She-wolf of France! How could he expect her not to think of it on this wedding day, particularly since the executioner was present? The long, sinister face of John Maltravers, lately promoted Seneschal of England, seemed to be hanging over Mortimer's shoulder as if to remind her of the crime.

Isabella was not the only person who resented John Maltravers' presence. He had been the late King's warder, and his sudden elevation to the post of Seneschal made it only too obvious for what services he was being rewarded. To those, and there were many, who were now almost certain that Edward II had been murdered, his presence was embarrassing, for they felt that the father's murderer would have done better to keep away from the son's wedding.

The Earl of Kent, the dead man's brother, turned to his cousin Henry Wryneck and whispered: 'It seems as if to kill a king entitles one to rank with his family now.'

Edmund of Kent was shivering. He thought the ceremony too long and the York rite too complicated. Why could the marriage not have been celebrated in the chapel of the Tower of London, or in some other royal castle, instead of making a public show of it? He felt uneasy under the eyes of the crowd; and the sight of Maltravers made it worse.

Wryneck, his head tilted towards his right shoulder – the infirmity which gave him his nickname – muttered: 'The easiest way to become a member of our house is by sinning. Our friend is proof of it. Be quiet, he's looking at us.'

By 'our friend' he meant Mortimer, and it showed how much the feeling had changed since he had disembarked, eighteen months before, in command of the Queen's army and been welcomed as a liberator.

'After all, the hand that obeys is no worse than the head that commands,' thought Wryneck. 'And no doubt Mortimer – and Isabella too – are guiltier than Maltravers. But we must all share some of the guilt; we all put our hands to the sword when we turned Edward II off the throne. It could end in no other way.'

In the meantime, the Archbishop was presenting the young King with three gold pieces bearing on one side the arms of England and Hainaut, and on the reverse a semy of roses, the emblematic flowers of married happiness. These gold pieces were the marriage deniers, symbols of the dowry in revenues, lands and castles, which the bridegroom was giving his bride. An accurate inventory of these gifts had been made, and this somewhat reassured Messire Jean of Hainaut, the bride's uncle, to whom fifteen thousand livres were still owing for the pay of his knights during the campaign in Scotland.

'Kneel at your husband's feet to receive the deniers, Madam,' the Archbishop said.

The people of York had been waiting for this moment,

wondering whether the local rite would be observed to the end, and whether it was as valid for a queen as it was for a subject.

But no one had foreseen that Madam Philippa would not only kneel but also, in the excess of her love and gratitude, embrace her husband's legs and kiss the knees of the boy who was making her his Queen. This chubby Flemish girl could find means of showing the impulses of her heart.

The crowd cheered enthusiastically.

'I'm sure they'll be very happy,' said Wryneck to Jean of Hainaut.

'The people will love her,' Isabella said to Mortimer, who had moved closer to her.

The Queen Mother felt the cheers like a wound because they were not for her. 'Philippa is the Queen now,' she thought. 'My day is over. Yet, perhaps, I shall now get France . . .'

For a courier, with the lilies on his coat, had galloped into York the week before with the news that her last brother of France, King Charles IV, lay dying.

2

Travail for a Crown

CHARLES IV, THE FAIR, had fallen ill on Christmas Day. At Epiphany the physicians and apothecaries tending him had to admit that he was dying. What had caused the fever that consumed him, the tearing cough that shattered his emaciated chest, the blood that he spat? The physicians impotently shrugged their shoulders, It was the curse, of course: that curse which had fallen on all Philip the Fair's heirs. And what medicines could operate against such a curse as that? Both the Court and the people were convinced there was no need to look elsewhere.

Louis the Hutin had died at the age of twenty-seven, murdered, as everyone knew, even though the Countess Mahaut of Artois had been exculpated at a public trial. Philippe the Long had died at twenty-nine through having drunk water from a well in Poitou that had been poisoned by the lepers. Charles IV had lived to the age of thirty-three; but this was the limit. It was a known fact that the accursed could never live longer than Christ.

'It's up to us, Brother, to seize the reins of government and to hold them with a firm hand,' said the Count of Beaumont, Robert of Artois, to his cousin and brother-in-law, Philippe of Valois. 'And this time,' he added, 'we won't let my Aunt Mahaut beat us to it. Anyway, she has no more sons-in-law to push.'

They, at least, both enjoyed the best of health. Robert of Artois, now forty-one, was still the same colossus who had to bend his head to pass through doorways and could overturn an ox by seizing it by the horns. A master of legal procedure, of intrigue and of chicane, he had shown his ability during these last twenty years both in his lawsuit over Artois and in the war in Guyenne, among much else. It had been due to him that the scandal of the Tower of Nesle had come to light. And it was also thanks to him that Lord Mortimer and Queen Isabella had been enabled to take refuge in France, where they had first become lovers, to raise an army in Hainaut, rouse all England and turn Edward II off his throne. Nor, when he went in to dinner, did it embarrass him in the least that his hands were stained with the blood of Marguerite of Burgundy. In recent years, his voice had been more frequently heard in the Council of the weak Charles IV than the Sovereign's.

Philippe of Valois was six years his junior and nothing like so clever. But physically he was tall, strong, wide-chested, and he moved well; he seemed to be almost a giant when Robert was not by; and he had a splendid knightly presence which was much in his favour. Moreover, he inherited the reputation of his father, the famous Charles of Valois, who had been the most turbulent and adventurous prince of his time, a pretender to phantom thrones and a supporter of unrealized crusades, yet a great warrior, whom Philippe did his best to emulate in prodigality and magnificence.

Though Philippe of Valois' talents had not as yet made any particular mark on Europe, everyone had confidence in him. He was a brilliant performer in tournaments, which were indeed his passion; and the valour he displayed there was not negligible.

'Philippe, I'll make you Regent,' Robert of Artois was saying, 'that's what I want, and I promise to do it. Regent, and very possibly King, if God so wills, provided my niece,[2] who's pregnant to her back teeth, doesn't have a son in a couple of months' time. Poor Cousin Charles! He won't see the child he so longed for. And, even if it's a boy, you'll still have the Regency for twenty years. And in twenty years . . .'

He emphasized his thought with a wave of the arm, which seemed to include every possible hazard: infant mortality, hunting accidents, the impenetrable designs of Providence.

'And you, as the good friend I know you to be,' went on the giant, 'will see to it that I get back my County of Artois, of which Mahaut, thief and poisoner that she is, has been so unjustly possessed since the death of my noble grandfather, as well as the peerage that goes with it. Just think, I'm not even a peer of France! Absurd, isn't it? It makes me ashamed for my wife, who is after all your sister.'

Philippe nodded his head, lowering that great nose of his, and blinking his eyes in agreement.

'Robert, justice shall be done you, if I am ever in a position to see to it. You can count on my support.'

The best friendships are based on mutual interest and common plans for the future.

Robert of Artois, who shrank from nothing, undertook to go to Vincennes and make it clear to Charles the Fair that his days were numbered and that certain arrangements must be made: the peers must be summoned at once, and Philippe of Valois recommended to them as Regent. Indeed, so as to make his selection inevitable, why should Charles not confide the administration of the kingdom to Philippe at once, delegating all powers to him?

'We are all mortal, every one of us, my dear cousin,' said Robert, who was himself bursting with health, as he entered the dying man's room, shaking the bed with his heavy tread.

Charles IV was in no condition to argue; indeed, he was relieved that someone else should shoulder his responsibilities. His only concern was to cling on to life, and it was slipping between his fingers.

Thus Philippe of Valois was endued with the sovereign power and was able to summon the peers.

Robert of Artois began campaigning at once. He went first to his nephew of Evreux, a young man of twenty-one, who had great charm but lacked enterprise. He was married to the daughter of Marguerite of Burgundy, Jeanne la Petite, as she was still called, though she was now seventeen. She had been set aside from the succession to the throne of France at the death of the Hutin.

Indeed, the Salic Law had been promulgated on her account, and all the more readily adopted because her mother's misconduct cast a serious doubt on her legitimacy. In compensation, and to appease the House of Burgundy, she had been recognized as heiress to the Kingdom of Navarre. There had, however, been no untoward haste in keeping this promise and the last two Kings of France had remained also Kings of Navarre.

Had Philippe of Evreux borne any resemblance to his uncle, Robert of Artois, he would have seized this splendid opportunity for chicanery on the largest possible scale by contesting the Law of Succession and claiming the two crowns in his wife's name.

But Robert of Artois, who had a great ascendancy over him, would very soon have disabused him of pretensions to being a competitor.

'You shall have Navarre which is your due, my dear nephew, as soon as my brother-in-law of Valois becomes Regent. I have insisted on it as a family matter and as a condition for giving Philippe my support. You shall be King of Navarre! It's not a crown to be despised and, for my part, I advise you to put it on your head just as soon as you can, and before anyone else comes along to dispute it. Between ourselves, your wife would have a better claim to it if her mother had kept on the right side of the blanket. There's going to be a scramble for power, and you had best make sure of support: you have ours. And don't go listening to your uncle of Burgundy; he'll simply persuade you to do something silly for his own ends. Philippe will be Regent; base your plans on that.'

In return for abandoning Navarre, Philippe of Valois could already therefore count on two votes.

Louis of Bourbon had been made a duke a few weeks before and had received the County of La Marche[3] as an apanage. He was the eldest member of the family. If the question of the Regency became dangerously controversial, the fact that he was Saint Louis' grandson might well enable him to sway several votes. In any case, his views were bound to carry weight with the Council of Peers. He was not only lame but a coward; and it would require more courage than he possessed to enter the lists against the powerful Valois clan. Moreover, his son had married a sister of Philippe of Valois.

Robert gave Louis of Bourbon to understand that the sooner he promised his support, the earlier would all the lands and titles he had accumulated as a time-server during the previous reigns be guaranteed to him. He now had three votes.

The Duke of Brittany had hardly arrived from Vannes, and his trunks were not yet unpacked, when Robert of Artois called on him.

'You agree on Philippe, don't you? He's so pious and loyal, we can be sure he'll make a good king – I mean a good regent!'

Jean of Brittany was bound to support Philippe of Valois. After all, he had married one of Philippe's sisters, Isabella. It was true she was dead, but he could hardly do other than be loyal to her memory. To lend weight to his overtures, Robert brought along his mother, Blanche of Brittany, the Duke's elder sister. She was very old and small and wrinkled; but though her mind was far from lucid, she invariably agreed with everything her giant of a son said. Jean of Brittany was more concerned with the affairs of his duchy than with those of France. Since everyone seemed so much in favour of Philippe, why not?

It became a campaign of brothers-in-law. Reinforcements were called up in the persons of Guy de Châtillon, Count of Blois, who was not a peer, and Count Guillaume of Hainaut, who was not even French, because they had both married sisters of Philippe. The great Valois connexion was already beginning to look like the true family of France.

Guillaume of Hainaut was at this very moment marrying off his daughter to the young King of England; there appeared to be no disadvantage in this. Indeed, it might well prove a useful match. But he had been well advised to be represented at the wedding by his brother Jean instead of going himself, for it was here, in Paris, that events of real importance were under way. Guillaume the Good had long desired the lands of Blaton, an inheritance of the Crown of France forming an enclave within his estates, to be ceded to him. If Philippe became Regent, he should have Blaton for some merely symbolic *quid pro quo*.

As for Guy of Blois, he was one of the last barons to have the right to mint his own coinage. Despite this right, he was disastrously short of money and crippled with debts.

'My dear Guy, your right to mint will be bought back from you by the Regency. It shall be our first care.'

Robert had done some very sound work in a remarkably short time.

'You see, Philippe,' he said to his candidate, 'how useful the marriages your father arranged are to us now. People say that a lot of girls are a misfortune to a family; but that wise man, may God keep him, knew very well how to use all your sisters.'

'Yes, but we shall have to complete the payment of the dowries,' Philippe replied. 'Only a quarter of what is due has been paid on several of them.'

'My dear wife Jeanne's to start with,' Robert of Artois reminded him. 'But when we have control of the Treasury . . .'

The Count of Flanders, Louis of Nevers, was more difficult to win over. For he was not a brother-in-law and wanted something more than mere lands or money. His subjects had driven him out of his county and he demanded that it should be reconquered for him. The price of his support was a promise of war.

'Louis, my cousin, Flanders shall be restored to you by force of arms, we give you our word!'

Upon which Robert, who thought of everything, hurried off to Vincennes once again in order to press Charles IV to make his will.

Charles was merely the shadow of a king now, and was coughing up what remained of his lungs.

Yet, dying though he was, his mind was obsessed by the thought of the crusade that his uncle, Charles of Valois, had put into his head. The crusade had been abandoned; and then Charles of Valois had died. Could it be that his disease and the pain he was suffering were a punishment for having failed to keep his oath? His red blood staining the sheets reminded him that he had not taken up the cross to deliver the land in which our Lord had suffered his Holy Passion.

In an attempt to win God's mercy, Charles IV therefore insisted on recording his concern for the Holy Land in his will: 'For my intention,' he dictated, 'is to go there during my lifetime and, if that proves impossible, fifty thousand livres shall be allotted to the first general expedition to set out.'

This was not at all what was required of him, nor indeed that he should encumber the royal finances, which were urgently needed for more pressing matters, with such a mortgage. Robert was furious. That fool Charles was being stubborn to the last!

Robert merely wanted him to leave three thousand livres each to Chancellor Jean de Cherchemont, Marshal de Trye and Messire de Noyers, the President of the Exchequer, on account of their loyal services to the Crown – and, incidentally, because they sat on the Council of Peers by right of their appointments.

'What about the Constables?' murmured the dying King.

Robert shrugged his shoulders. Constable Gaucher de Châtillon was seventy-eight years old, deaf as a post, and so rich he did not know what to do with his money. You did not develop a sudden love of gold at his age. The Constable's name was crossed out.

On the other hand, Robert proved most helpful to Charles in the matter of appointing executors, for this would establish a sort of order of precedence among the great men of the realm. Count Philippe of Valois headed the list, then came Count Philippe of Evreux, and then Robert of Artois, Count of Beaumont-le-Roger, himself.

Having dealt with the will, Robert now turned his attention to the spiritual peers.

Guillaume de Trye, Duke-Archbishop of Reims, had been Philippe of Valois' tutor; and Robert had had his brother, the Marshal, put into the royal will for three thousand livres, which he made ring to good effect. There would be no difficulties in that direction.

The Duke-Archbishop of Langres had long been a supporter of the Valois, as had also Jean de Marigny, Count-Bishop of Beauvais, who had even betrayed his brother, the great Enguerrand, to serve the hatreds of the late Monseigneur Charles of Valois.

There remained the Bishops of Châlons, Laon and Noyon;

and these, it was known, would follow Duke Eudes of Burgundy.

'As for the Burgundian,' cried Robert of Artois, with a wide sweep of his arms, 'he's your affair, Philippe. I can do nothing with him; we're at daggers drawn. After all, you married his sister and you must be able to bring some pressure to bear on him.'

Eudes IV was no diplomatic genius. But he remembered the lessons he had learned from his mother, Agnes of France, the last surviving daughter of Saint Louis, who had died the preceding year, and how the determined old woman had succeeded in negotiating, during Philippe the Long's regency, the reuniting of the County of Burgundy and the duchy. Eudes had then married Mahaut of Artois' granddaughter, who was twenty-seven years younger than himself, but he no longer complained of this now that she was nubile.

The question of the Artois inheritance was the first subject he discussed with Philippe of Valois, when they were closeted together on his arrival from Dijon.

'It is quite understood, of course, that at Mahaut's death, the County of Artois goes to her daughter, Queen Jeanne the Widow, with remainder to the Duchess, my wife, is it not? I must make a point of this, Cousin, for I well know Robert's pretensions to Artois; he has proclaimed them enough!'

These great princes were as bitter in defence of their right of inheritance to a quarter of the kingdom as were the daughters-in-law of the poor in squabbling over cups and sheets.

'Judgement has twice been given assigning Artois to the Countess Mahaut,' replied Philippe of Valois. 'Unless any new facts come to light supporting Robert's claim, Artois will go to your wife, Brother.'

'You see no impediment?'

'None at all.'

And thus the loyal Valois, the gallant knight, the hero of tournaments, had now given two contradictory promises.

Nevertheless, honest in his duplicity, he told Robert of Artois of his conversation with Eudes, and Robert wholly approved it.

'The main thing,' he said, 'is to acquire Burgundy's vote. What does it matter that he should feel secure in a right which is not his anyway? New facts, you said? Very well, we'll produce some, and I won't make you break your word. Don't worry, it's all for the best.'

They had now merely to wait for one last formality – the King's death. It was to be hoped it would not be long delayed, for this splendid conjunction of princes in support of Philippe of Valois might not endure.

The Iron King's last son died on the eve of Candlemas, and the news of his death spread through Paris the next morning, together with the odour of the hot flour of pancakes.

Robert of Artois' plans seemed to be working perfectly when, on the very morning the Council of Peers was to be held, a thin-faced, tired-eyed English bishop arrived in a mud-stained litter to urge the claims of Queen Isabella.

3

A Corpse in Council

THERE WERE NO BRAINS in the head now, no heart in the breast, nor entrails in the stomach. He was a hollow king. But, indeed, there was little difference between Charles IV alive and now that the embalmers had done their work. He had been a backward child, whom his mother had called 'the Goose', a cuckolded husband, and an unsuccessful father, for he had vainly, if stubbornly, endeavoured to assure the succession by marrying three times; he had also been a weak prince, first subject to an uncle and then to cousins, indeed but a fleeting incarnation of the royal entity.

On the state bed, at the far end of the great pillared hall of the Castle of Vincennes, lay his corpse, clothed in an azure tunic, a royal mantle about its shoulders and the crown on its head.

By the light of the massed candles, the peers and barons gathered at the other end of the hall could see the gleam of the corpse's boots of cloth of gold.

Charles IV was presiding over his last Council, which was

known as 'the Council in the King's Chamber', for he was deemed to be ruling still. His reign would end officially only on the following day, when his body was lowered into the tomb at Saint-Denis.

Robert of Artois had taken the English bishop under his wing, while they waited for the latecomers.

'How long did it take you to get here? Twelve days from York? You can't have wasted much time saying masses on the way, Messire Bishop. You've made as much speed as a courier! Did your young King's wedding go off well?'

'I expect so. I was unable to take part in it, for I was already on my way,' replied Bishop Orleton.

And was my Lord Mortimer in good health? Lord Mortimer was a good friend, and had often mentioned Monseigneur Orleton who had organized his escape from the Tower of London. It had been a great exploit on which Robert complimented the Bishop.

'Well, you know, I welcomed him to France,' he said, 'and provided him with the means of returning somewhat better armed than he had arrived. So we are each responsible for half the business.'

And how was Queen Isabella, his dear cousin? Was she as beautiful as ever?

By his idle chatter Robert was deliberately preventing Orleton from mingling with the other groups, speaking to the Count of Hainaut or the Count of Flanders. He knew Orleton well by reputation and he mistrusted him. Was not this the man whose turbulent career had stirred all England, who had been sent by the Court of Westminster on embassies to the Holy See, and who was the author, so at least it was said, of the famous letter with the double meaning – '*Eduardum occidere nolite . . .'* – by which Queen Isabella and Mortimer had hoped to avoid suspicion of having ordered the murder of Edward II?

While the French prelates had all donned their mitres for the Council, Orleton was merely wearing a violet silk travelling-cap with ermine earlaps. Robert noted this with satisfaction; it would diminish the English bishop's authority when his turn came to speak.

'Monseigneur of Valois will be voted Regent,' he whispered to Orleton, as if confiding a secret to a friend.

Orleton made no reply.

At last the one missing member of the Council, for whom they had all been waiting, arrived. It was the Countess Mahaut of Artois, the only woman to be present. Mahaut had aged; she leaned on a stick and seemed to move her massive body with difficulty. Her hair was quite white and her face a dark red. She included all the company in a vague greeting and, when she had sprinkled the corpse with holy water, seated herself heavily beside the Duke of Burgundy. She seemed to be panting for breath.[4]

The Archbishop and Primate, Guillaume de Trye, rose, turned towards the royal corpse, slowly made the sign of the cross, and then stood for a moment in meditation, his eyes raised towards the vault as if seeking Divine inspiration. The whisperings ceased.

'My noble lords,' he began, 'when there is no natural successor upon whom the royal power can fall, that power returns to its source which lies in the assent of the peers. Such is the will both of God and of Holy Church, which sets an example by electing the sovereign pontiff.'

Monseigneur de Trye spoke well and with a preacher's fine

eloquence. The assembled peers and barons had to decide on whom they would confer temporal power in the kingdom of France, first for the exercise of the Regency and then, for it was only wise to look to the future, for the exercise of kingship itself, should the most noble lady, the Queen, fail to give birth to a son.

It was their duty to appoint him who was the best among equals, *primus inter pares*, and also nearest in blood to the Crown. Was it not in similar circumstances in the past that the temporal and spiritual peers had entrusted the sceptre to the wisest and strongest among them, the Duke of France and the Count of Paris, Hugues I, the Great, founder of the glorious dynasty?

'Our dead Sovereign, who is still with us this day,' continued the Archbishop, slightly inclining his mitre towards the catafalque, 'wished to direct our choice by recommending to us, in his will, his nearest cousin, that most Christian and most valiant Prince, who is in every way worthy to govern us and lead us, Monseigneur Philippe, Count of Valois, Anjou and Maine.'

The most Christian and most valiant Prince, who felt his ears buzzing with emotion, was uncertain what attitude to adopt. Modestly to lower his long nose might imply that he doubted both his capacity and his right to rule. But to hold it up proudly and arrogantly might prejudice the peers against him. He therefore sat perfectly still, not even a muscle of his face twitching, with his eyes fixed on his dead cousin's golden boots.

'Let each of us consult his conscience,' concluded the Archbishop of Reims, 'and give his counsel for the general good.'

Bishop Orleton got quickly to his feet.

'I have already consulted my conscience,' he said. 'I have come here to represent the King of England, Duke of Guyenne.'

He had considerable experience of meetings of this kind, where the decisions to be taken had been secretly arranged beforehand, but where everyone nevertheless hesitated to be the first to speak. He was quick to take advantage of it.

'In the name of my master,' he went on, 'I am to declare that the person most nearly related to the late King Charles of France is his sister, Queen Isabella, and that the Regency should therefore be vested in her.'

With the exception of Robert of Artois, who was expecting something of the sort, the Council was for a moment utterly astounded. No one had considered Queen Isabella during the preliminary negotiations, nor had anyone for an instant imagined that she would make a claim. They had quite forgotten her. And now here she was emerging from the northern mists through the voice of a little bishop in a fur cap. Had she really any rights? They all looked questioningly at each other. If strict considerations of lineage were to be taken into account, it was clear that she had undoubted rights; but it seemed sheer folly to claim them.

Five minutes later, the Council was in considerable confusion. They were all talking at once and at the tops of their voices, paying no heed to the presence of the dead King.

Had not the Duke of Guyenne, in the person of his ambassador, forgotten that women could not reign in France, in accordance with the law that had been twice confirmed by the peers in recent years?

'Is that not so, Aunt?' Robert of Artois asked maliciously,

reminding Mahaut of the time when they had been violently opposed over the Law of Succession which had been promulgated in favour of Philippe the Long, the Countess' son-in-law.

No, Bishop Orleton had forgotten nothing; in particular, he had not forgotten that the Duke of Guyenne had been neither present nor represented – no doubt because he had been deliberately informed too late – at the meetings of the peers at which the extension of the so-called Salic Law to the Crown had been so arbitrarily decided, and that in consequence he had never ratified the decision.

Orleton had none of the unctuous eloquence of Monseigneur Guillaume de Trye; he spoke a rather rough and somewhat archaic French, for the French used as the official language of the English Court had remained unaltered since the Conquest, and it might well have raised a smile in other circumstances. But he was adept at legal controversy and never at a loss for a retort.

Messire Mille de Noyers, who was the last surviving jurisconsult of Philip the Fair's Council and had played his part in all the succeeding reigns, had to come to the rescue.

Since King Edward II had rendered homage to King Philippe the Long, it was evident that he had recognized him as the legitimate king and had therefore, by implication, ratified the Law of Succession.

Orleton did not see the matter in that light. Indeed, it was not so, Messire! By rendering homage, Edward II had merely confirmed that the Duchy of Guyenne was a vassalage of the Crown of France, which no one denied, though the terms of this vassalage still remained to be defined after more than a hundred years. But this was irrelevant to the validity of the procedure by which the King of France had been chosen. And, in any case, what was the question in dispute, was it the Regency or the Crown?

'Both, both at once,' said Bishop Jean de Marigny. 'For, as Monseigneur de Trye so rightly said: it is wise to look to the future; and we do not want to be confronted with the same problem again in two months' time.'

Mahaut of Artois was trying to get her breath. Ah, how infuriating this ill-health was, and the singing in the head that prevented her thinking clearly. She disapproved of everything that was being said. She was opposed to Philippe of Valois because to support Valois meant supporting Robert; she was opposed to Isabella whom she had long hated because, in the past, Isabella had denounced her daughters. After a while, she managed to intervene in the discussion.

'If the crown could go to a woman, it would not be to your Queen, Messire Bishop, but to none other than Madame Jeanne la Petite, and the Regency should be exercised by her husband, Messire of Evreux here, or her uncle, Duke Eudes, here beside me.'

There were signs of excitement on the part of the Duke of Burgundy, the Count of Flanders, the Bishops of Laon and Noyon, and even in the attitude of the young Count of Evreux who, for an instant, thought: 'Why not, after all?'

It was as if the crown were hovering uncertainly between floor and ceiling, while several heads were outstretched to receive it.

Philippe of Valois had long abandoned his noble calm and was making signs to his cousin of Artois. Robert rose to his feet.

'Really!' he cried, in a voice that made the candles flicker round the catafalque. 'Everyone here today seems to be denying his past. It would appear that my beloved aunt, Dame Mahaut, is prepared to recognize the rights of Madame of Navarre' – he looked at Philippe of Evreux and emphasized the word 'Navarre' to remind him of their agreement – 'those very rights she was instrumental in wresting from her in the past; while the noble English Bishop seems to be basing his argument on the Act of a king whom he first helped to turn off his throne and then sent home to God with his blessing! Really, Messire Orleton, a law cannot be made and remade every time it is applied, and to suit every party. Sometimes it will serve one party, sometimes another. We love and respect Madame Isabella, our cousin, whom many of us here have helped and served. But her demand, which you have pleaded so well, is clearly inadmissible. Is that not your opinion, Messeigneurs?' he concluded, turning to his supporters for approval.

His speech was received with approbation, in particular by the Duke of Bourbon, the Count of Blois and the spiritual peers of Reims and Beauvais.

But Orleton had not yet shot his bolt. Given that this was a question not only of the Regency but also, eventually, of the Crown itself, given that women could not reign in France, then so as not to reopen the question of a law that already had precedents in its application, he would put forward a claim, not in the name of Queen Isabella, but in that of her son, King Edward III, who was the only male descendant in the direct line.

'But if a woman cannot reign, she clearly cannot transmit the succession!' said Philippe of Valois angrily.

'And why not, Monseigneur? Are not the Kings of France born of woman?'

This retort raised several smiles. Tall Philippe had his back to the wall. After all, was the little English Bishop so very far wrong? The rather doubtful precedent that had been pleaded at Louis' death gave no guidance on this particular point. And since three brothers had reigned consecutively and failed to produce sons, should not the crown go to the son of the surviving sister, rather than to a cousin?

The Count of Hainaut, who till now had been whole-hearted in his support of Valois, began to reflect and to envisage unexpected prospects for his daughter.

The old Constable Gaucher, whose eyelids were as wrinkled as those of a tortoise, was cupping his ear with his hand, for he was hard of hearing, and asking his brother-in-law, Mille de Noyers: 'What's that? What's that they're saying?'

The discussion was becoming complicated and it irritated him. On the question of women succeeding, his views had remained unchanged over the last twelve years. Indeed, it was he who had proclaimed the right of male succession and had persuaded the peers to it by his celebrated apophthegm: 'The lily cannot become a distaff; and France is too noble a kingdom to be handed over to a woman.'

Orleton continued his speech in an endeavour to move his hearers. He invited the peers to take this opportunity, which might not occur again for centuries, to unite the two kingdoms under the same sceptre. He spoke with profound conviction: let them have done with incessant quarrelling, ill-defined terms of homage, wars in Aquitaine that impoverished both their nations, and let them dissolve the useless rivalry in trade which created such continual problems in Flanders. He wanted to see one single people on both sides of the Channel. Was not the whole English nobility of French stock? Was not the French language common to both Courts? Had not many French lords inherited estates in England and had not English barons lands in France?

'Very well, if that's the case, give us England, we shan't refuse it,' said Philippe of Valois sarcastically.

The Constable Gaucher was listening to the explanations his brother-in-law was shouting in his ear, and his face suddenly grew dark. What was that? The King of England claiming the Regency and the crown to follow? Was this to be the result of all the campaigns he had fought beneath the harsh Gascony sun, of all the expeditions through the northern mud against those wicked Flemish drapers, who were invariably supported by England, of the deaths of so many valiant knights and the expenditure of so much treasure? Was it all to come merely to this? What nonsense!

He did not get to his feet, but in a deep, old voice that was hoarse with anger, he cried: 'Never shall France belong to the Englishman! This is no question of male or female, or whether the crown can be transmitted through the womb! But France shall not go to the Englishman because the barons won't have it! Come on Brittany! Come on Blois! Come on Nevers! Come on Burgundy! Do you mean to say you're prepared to listen to this sort of thing? We've a king to bury, the sixth I've seen die in my lifetime, and each one of them had to raise an army against England or those whom England supported. The man who rules France must be of French blood. And let's have no more of this nonsense; it's enough to make my horse laugh!'

He had called on Brittany, Blois and Burgundy in the voice

he was accustomed to use in battle to rally the leaders of banners.

'I give my counsel, in right of being the oldest member present, that the Count of Valois, who is nearest to the throne, be Regent, Guardian and Governor of the realm.'

And he raised his hand to show that he was casting his vote.

'He's quite right!' Robert of Artois said quickly, raising his great paw and looking round at Philippe's supporters to make sure they followed his example.

He was almost sorry he had had the old Constable cut out of the royal will.

'Agreed!' said the Dukes of Bourbon and Brittany, the Counts of Blois, Flanders, and Evreux, the bishops, the great officers of State, and the Count of Hainaut.

Mahaut of Artois caught the Duke of Burgundy's eye, saw he was about to raise his hand, and hastily approved so as not to be the last. But the look she gave Eudes signified: 'I'm voting for your choice. But you'll support me, won't you?'

Orleton's was the only hand not raised.

Philippe of Valois suddenly felt utterly exhausted. 'It's all right, it's all right,' he thought. He heard Archbishop Guillaume de Trye, his old tutor, say: 'Long life to the Regent of the Kingdom of France, both for the good of the people and for that of Holy Church.'

The Chancellor, Jean de Cherchemont, had already prepared the document which was to embody the Council's decision. He had only to insert the Regent's name. He wrote in a large hand: 'The most powerful, most noble and most dread Lord Philippe, Count of Valois.' Then he read out the Act which not only assigned the Regency, but declared that, if the child to be born was a girl, the Regent was to become King of France.

All present appended both their signatures and private seals to the document. All, that is, except the Duke of Guyenne in the person of his representative, Bishop Orleton, who refused, saying: 'One has nothing to lose by defending one's rights, even if one knows one cannot succeed. But the future is long and lies in God's hands.'

Philippe of Valois went over to the catafalque and gazed at his cousin's corpse, at the crown upon the waxen brow, the long gold sceptre lying on the mantle and the golden boots.

They thought he was praying, and his act earned their respect.

Robert of Artois went to him and whispered: 'If your father can see you at this moment, the dear man must be delighted ... There are only two months to wait.'

4

The Makeshift King

PRINCES OF THAT TIME always had to have a dwarf. Poor people almost considered it a piece of good fortune to bring one into the world; they were sure of being able to sell him to some great lord, if not to the king himself.

A dwarf was generally looked on as ranking in the order of creation somewhere between a man and a domestic animal; he was animal because you could put a collar on him, rig him out in grotesque clothes like a performing dog, and kick his backside with impunity; on the other hand, he was human in so far as he could talk and submitted voluntarily to his degrading role for food and pay. He had to clown to order, skip, cry and play the fool like a child, even when his hair had turned white with advancing years. His lack of inches was proportionate to his master's greatness. He was bequeathed like any other piece of property. He was the symbol of the 'subject', of nature's subordinates, expressly created, so it seemed, to be a living witness to the fact that the human race was composed of different species, of which some had absolute power over the rest.

Abasement nevertheless brought certain advantages, for the smallest, weakest and most deformed in the community were among the best-fed and the best-clothed. Moreover, the dwarf was permitted, indeed commanded, to say things to the masters of the superior race that would not have been tolerated from anyone else.

The mockery and even the insults that every man, however devoted he may be, occasionally addresses to his superior in his thoughts were vented, as it were by delegation, in the traditional and often singularly obscene familiarities of the dwarf.

There are two kinds of dwarfs: the long-nosed, sad-faced hunchback, and the chubby, snub-nosed dwarf with the body of a giant supported on tiny, rickety legs. Philippe of Valois' dwarf, Jean the Fool, was of the second kind. His head barely reached to the height of a table. He wore bells on his cap, and silk robes embroidered with a variety of strange little animals.

One day he came skipping and laughing to Philippe and said: 'Do you know what the people call you, Sire?' They call you "the Makeshift King".'

For on Good Friday, April 1st, 1328, Madame Jeanne of Evreux, Charles IV's widow, had been brought to bed. Rarely in history had the sex of a newborn child created such excitement. When it was known to be a girl, everyone recognized it as a sign of God's will, and there was great relief.

The peers had no need to reconsider the choice they had made at Candlemas; they assembled at once and unanimously, except for the representative of England who objected on principle, confirmed Philippe in his right to the crown.

The people also heaved a sigh of relief. The curse of the Grand Master Jacques de Molay seemed exhausted at last. The Capet line, at any rate in its senior branch, was now extinct. During the last three hundred and forty-one years it had given France fourteen successive kings, though the last four had reigned for no more than fifteen years between them. In any family whether rich or poor, the absence of male heirs is considered, if not a disaster, at least a sign of inferiority, In the case of the royal house, the inability of Philip the Fair's sons to produce male descendants was looked on as a punishment. But now there was going to be a change.

Sudden fevers seize on peoples, and their cause must be sought in the movements of the planets since no other explanation can be found for them. How else account for such waves of hysterical cruelty as the crusade of the *pastoureaux* or the massacre of the lepers? How account for the tide of delirious joy that accompanied the accession of Philippe of Valois?

The new King was tall and endowed with the majestic physique so essential to the founder of a dynasty. His elder child was a son, already nine years old and seemingly robust; he had also a daughter, and it was known (Courts make no secret of these things) that he honoured his tall, lame wife almost every night with an enthusiasm the years had in no way abated.

He had a loud and resonant voice, unlike his cousins, Louis the Hutin, and Charles IV, who had stuttered; nor was he inclined to silence as had been Philip the Fair and Philippe V. There was no one who could oppose him, no one who could be put up against him. Amid the general rejoicing, who in France was going to listen to a few lawyers paid by England to draw up objections, which they did without much conviction?

Philippe VI ascended the throne with the consent of all.

And yet he was King only by a lucky chance; he was a nephew and a cousin of kings, but there were many such; he was simply a man who had been luckier than his relations. He was not a king born of a king to be king; he was not a king designated by God and received as such, but a 'make-shift' king, who had been made when one was needed.

Yet the popular nickname in no way detracted from the loyalty and rejoicing; it was simply one of those ironical phrases the populace so often uses to mask its emotions and make itself feel that it is on close and familiar terms with power. When Jean the Fool told Philippe about it, he received a kick that sent him flying across the flagstones. He had, nevertheless, uttered the word that was the key to his master's destiny.

For Philippe of Valois, like every *parvenu*, was determined to show that he was worthy, by his own innate distinction, of the elevated position to which he had attained, and his behaviour therefore tended to an exaggeration of all that might be expected of a king.

Since the King exercised sovereign powers of justice, he sent the treasurer of the last reign to the gallows within three weeks of his accession. Pierre Rémy had been accused of embezzlement on a large scale. A Minister of Finance suspended from the gibbet was invariably popular with the crowd. France believed she had a just king.

By both duty and office the Prince was defender of the Faith. Philippe issued an edict increasing the penalties for blasphemy and enhancing the powers of the Inquisition. As a result, the higher and lower clergy, the minor nobility and the parish bigots were all reassured: they had a pious king.

A sovereign owed it to himself to recompense services rendered; and a great many services had been rendered Philippe to assure his election. On the other hand, the King must not make enemies of the officials who had been attentive to the public interest under his predecessors. As a result, nearly every dignitary or royal officer was retained in his position, while new posts were created or those already existing duplicated to find places for the supporters of the new reign. Every application put forward by the great electors was granted. Moreover, the Valois household, which was itself of royal proportions, was superimposed on that of the old dynasty; and there was a great distribution of profitable offices. They had a generous king.

A king was also in duty bound to bring his subjects prosperity. Philippe VI hastened to reduce and indeed in some cases to suppress altogether the taxes Philippe IV and Philippe V had imposed on trade, public markets and foreign business, taxes which it was said hindered enterprise and commerce.

And what could make a king more popular than to stop the plaguing by tax-gatherers? The Lombards, who had lent his father so much money and to whom he himself still owed enormous sums, blessed him. It occurred to no one that the fiscal policy of the previous reigns had produced long-term effects and that, if France was rich, if the standard of living was higher than anywhere else in the world, if the people wore good sound cloth and often fur and if there were baths and sweating-rooms even in hamlets, all these things were due to the previous Philippes, who had established order in the realm, the unification of the currency and full employment.

And then a king must also be wise, the wisest man among his people. Philippe began to adopt a sententious tone and, in that fine voice of his, to utter weighty aphorisms in which could be distinguished something of the manner of his old tutor, Archbishop Guillaume de Trye.

'Action should always be based on reason,' he would say whenever he was at a loss.

And when he made a mistake, which was often enough, and found himself in the unhappy position of having to countermand what he had ordered the day before, he would declare superbly: 'Reason lies in developing one's ideas.' Or again: 'It is better to be forearmed than forestalled,' he would announce pompously, though throughout the twenty-two years of his reign he was to be constantly at the disadvantage of having to face one disagreeable surprise after another.

No monarch ever uttered so many platitudes with so grand an air. When people supposed he was thinking, he was in fact merely pondering a sentence that would seem like thought; his head was as empty as a nut in a bad season.

Nor was it to be forgotten that a king, a true king, must be valiant, chivalrous and gallant. And, indeed, Philippe had no aptitude for anything but arms – not for war, it must be admitted, but for jousts and tournaments. He would have excelled in training young knights at the Court of a minor baron. But, being a sovereign, his house began to look like a castle in the romances of the Round Table, which were much read at the time and had taken firm hold of his imagination. Life was a round of tournaments, festivals, banquets, hunts and entertainments, followed by more tournaments amid a flurry of plumed helms and horses more richly caparisoned than were the women.

Philippe applied himself with great devotion to affairs of State for an hour a day, either on his return, drenched with sweat, from jousting or on emerging from a banquet with a full stomach and a cloudy mind. His chancellor, his treasurer and his innumerable officers made his decisions for him or went to take orders from Robert of Artois. Indeed, Robert governed far more than the Sovereign.

No difficulty arose without Philippe appealing to Robert for advice, and the Count of Artois' orders were obeyed with confidence, for it was known that any decree of his would be approved by the King.

This was how things stood, when the crowds began to gather towards the end of May for the coronation, at which Archbishop Guillaume de Trye was to place the crown on his former pupil's head, and the festivities were to last for five days.

The whole kingdom seemed to have come to Reims; and not only the kingdom but a great part of Europe, for there were present the superb, if impecunious, King John of Bohemia, Count Guillaume of Hainaut, the Marquess of Namur, and the Duke of Lorraine. During the five days of feasting and rejoicing, there were a lavishness and an expenditure such as the burgesses of Reims had never seen before, and it was they who had to foot the bill for the festivities. Though they had grumbled at the cost of the previous coronation, they now gladly supplied two or three times as much. It was a hundred years since there had been such drinking in the Kingdom of France. There were even horsemen serving drinks in the courts and squares.

On the eve of the coronation, the King dubbed Louis of Nevers, Count of Flanders, knight with great pomp and ceremony. It had been decided that the Count of Flanders was to carry Charlemagne's sword at the coronation and hand it to the King. The Constable, whose traditional privilege it was, had oddly enough consented to surrender it. But it was necessary that the Count of Flanders should be a knight; and Philippe VI could hardly have found a more signal means of showing his gratitude for the Count's support.

Nevertheless, at the ceremony in the cathedral next day, when Louis of Bourbon, the Great Chamberlain of France, had shod the King with the lily-embroidered boots, and then proceeded to summon the Count of Flanders to present the sword, the Count made no move.

'Monseigneur, the Count of Flanders!' called Louis of Bourbon once again.

But Louis of Nevers stood still in his place with his arms crossed.

'Monseigneur, the Count of Flanders,' repeated the Duke of Bourbon, 'if you be present, either in person or by representative, I call on you to come forward to fulfil your duty. You are hereby summoned to appear under pain of forfeiture.'

There was an astonished silence beneath the great vault and there was fear, too, reflected on the faces of the prelates, barons and dignitaries; but the King seemed quite unconcerned and Robert of Artois, his head thrown back, appeared to be deeply engaged in watching the play of sunlight through the windows.

At last the Count of Flanders moved from his place, came to a halt in front of the King, bowed and said: 'Sire, if Louis of

Nevers had been called, I would have come forward sooner.'

'What do you mean, Monseigneur?' replied Philippe VI. 'Are you not Count of Flanders?'

'Sire, I bear the name but do not enjoy its benefit.'

Philippe VI, looking as kingly as possible, drew himself up, turned his long nose towards the Count, and said calmly with a blank stare: 'What is this you're telling me, Cousin?'

'Sire,' replied Louis of Nevers, 'the people of Bruges, Ypres, Poperinghe and Cassel have turned me out of my fief and no longer consider me to be their count and suzerain; indeed, the country is in such a state of rebellion that I can scarcely go to Ghent even in secret.'

Philippe of Valois slapped the arm of the throne with his wide palm in a gesture he had unconsciously adopted from having seen his uncle, Philip the Fair, the incarnation of majesty, make use of it so often.

'Louis, my dear cousin,' he said – and his stentorian voice seemed to roll out of the choir and over the congregation – 'we look on you as Count of Flanders and, by the holy anointing and sacrament we receive today, promise that we shall know neither peace nor rest till you are restored to the possession of your county.'

Louis of Nevers fell on his knees and said: 'Sire, I thank you.'

The ceremony then proceeded.

Meanwhile Robert of Artois was winking at his neighbours, and they at once realized that the scene had been previously arranged. Philippe VI was keeping the promises Robert had made on his behalf to assure his election. And, indeed, Philippe of Evreux was that very day wearing the crown of King of Navarre.

As soon as the ceremony was over, the King summoned the peers and the great barons, the princes of his family, and the lords who had come from beyond the boundaries of his realm to attend his coronation and, as if the matter could not suffer an hour's delay, consulted with them as to the timing of an attack on the Flanders rebels. A valiant king was in duty bound to defend the rights of his vassals. A few of the more prudent spirits, in view of the fact that the season was already far advanced and that there was a risk of not being ready till the winter – they still remembered Louis the Hutin's 'Muddy Host' – counselled him to postpone the expedition for a year. But the old Constable Gaucher cried shame on them: 'For him who has the heart to fight the time is always ripe!'

He was now seventy-eight and eager to command his last campaign; and it was not for shuffling of this sort that he had agreed to surrender Charlemagne's sword.

'And the English, who are at the back of the rebellion, will be taught a lesson,' he muttered.

After all, in the romances of chivalry you could read of the exploits of eighty-year-old heroes still capable of unhorsing an enemy in battle and cleaving his helm to the skull. Were the barons to show less valour than this aged veteran who was so impatient to set off to war with his sixth king?

Philippe of Valois rose to his feet and cried: 'Whoever loves me well will follow me!'

It was decided to mobilize the army at the end of July and, as if by chance, at Arras. It would give Robert an opportunity to sow a little discord in his Aunt Mahaut's county.

They moved into Flanders at the beginning of August.

The fifteen thousand citizen soldiers of Furnes, Dixmude, Poperinghe and Cassel were commanded by a burgess named

Zannequin. Wishing to show that he knew the proper usages, Zannequin sent the King of France a challenge praying him to fix the day of battle. But Philippe felt nothing but contempt for this clodhopper who assumed the manners of a prince and made answer that since the Flemish had no true leader, they would have to defend themselves as best they could. Then he sent his two marshals, Mathieu de Trye and Robert Bertrand, who was known as 'the Knight of the Green Lion', to burn the country round Bruges.

The marshals were highly congratulated when they returned; everyone was delighted to see flames rising from poor people's houses in the distance. The knights discarded their armour and wearing sumptuous robes visited each other's tents, dined in pavilions of embroidered silk, and played chess with their friends. The French camp looked just like King Arthur's in the picture books, and the barons thought of themselves as Lancelot, Hector or Galahad.

And so it happened that the valiant King, who preferred to be forearmed rather than forestalled, was at dinner when the fifteen thousand Flemish attacked his camp, carrying banners on which they had painted a cock and written:

Le jour que ce coq chantera
*Le roi trouvé ci entrera.**

In a very short time they had ravaged half the camp, cut the ropes supporting the pavilions, upset the chessboards, overset the banqueting tables and killed a good number of lords.

---

* The Makeshift King will enter here the day this cock crows.

The French infantry fled; in their panic they never stopped to draw breath till they had reached Saint-Omer forty leagues to the rear.

The King had barely time to don a surcoat bearing the arms of France, cover his head with a basinet of white leather and jump on his charger to try and rally his heroes.

Both sides in this battle committed grave errors through vanity. The French knights had despised the commonalty of Flanders; but the Flemish, to show they were as much warriors as the French lords, had equipped themselves with armour to attack on foot.

The Count of Hainaut and his brother, Jean, whose lines stood a little apart, were the first to get to horse and disorganize the Flemish attack by taking the enemy in the rear. Then the French knights, rallied by the King, hurled themselves on the foot-soldiers, who were so heavily overburdened by their arrogant equipment, overset them, trampled them down and massacred them. The Lancelots and Galahads were content to club and slash, leaving it to their men-at-arms to finish off the wounded with daggers. Those who tried to flee were tumbled over by the charging horses; and those who offered to surrender immediately had their throats cut. The Flemish left thirteen thousand dead on the field, a fabulous heap of flesh and steel; grass, armour, man and beast were all sticky with blood.

The Battle of Mont Cassel, which had begun in so disastrous a way, ended in total victory for France. People talked of it as another Bouvines.

But the real victor was not the King, nor even the old Constable Gaucher, though he had shouted the names of his banners loudly enough, nor Robert of Artois, though he had fallen on the enemy ranks like an avalanche. The man who had saved the day was Count Guillaume of Hainaut. But it was Philippe VI, his brother-in-law, who reaped the glory.

So powerful a king as Philippe could not tolerate any omission on the part of his vassals. He therefore sent a summons to the King of England, Duke of Guyenne, to come to render homage to him without delay.

There are no advantageous defeats, but there can be disastrous victories. Few days in France's history have cost her so dear as Cassel, for it gave currency to a number of false ideas, such as that the new King was invincible, and that foot-soldiers were worthless in war. The defeat of Crécy, twenty years later, was the consequence of this illusion.

In the meantime, the commanders of banners and the bearers of lances, even to the youngest squire, looked down from their saddles in contempt at the inferior species who fought on foot.

That autumn, towards the middle of October, Madame Clémence of Hungary, the unlucky Queen who had been Louis the Hutin's second wife, died at the age of thirty-five in the Temple, where she lived. She left so many debts that, a week after her death, everything she possessed, rings, crowns, jewels, furniture, linen and plate, even her kitchen utensils, were auctioned on behalf of her Italian creditors, the Bardi and the Tolomei.

Old Spinello Tolomei, now very fat and lame, one eye open and the other shut, attended the sale. Six goldsmith-valuers, commissioned by the King, had fixed the reserves. Everything Queen Clémence had been given during her one year of illusory happiness was dispersed.

For four successive days the auctioneers, Simon de Clokettes, Jean Pascon, Pierre de Besançon and Jean de Lille, were to be heard crying: 'A fine gold hat,[5] containing four balas rubies, four large emeralds, sixteen small balas rubies, sixteen small emeralds and eight Alexandraian rubies, six hundred livres! Sold to the King!'

'A ring, with four cut sapphires and one cabochon, forty livres! Sold to the King!'

'A ring, with six oriental rubies, three cut emeralds and three emerald brilliants, two hundred livres! Sold to the King!'

'A silver gilt bowl, twenty-five goblets, two platters and a dish, two hundred livres! Sold to Monseigneur of Artois, Count of Beaumont!'

'A dozen silver-gilt goblets, enamelled with the arms of France and Hungary, a great silver-gilt salt supported by four monkeys, four hundred and fifty livres! Sold to Monseigneur of Artois, Count of Beaumont!'

'A gold-embroidered purse, sewn with pearls, containing an oriental sapphire, sixteen livres! Sold to the King!'

The Bardi company bought the most expensive lot: a ring containing Clémence's largest ruby, which was estimated to be worth one thousand livres. They did not, however, have to pay for it, since it would be placed against her account with them, and they were sure of being able to resell it to the Pope who, having long been in their debt in the past, was now fabulously rich.

Robert of Artois, as if to prove that he was not solely concerned with goblets and drinking-vessels, acquired a Bible in French for thirty livres.

The chapel vestments, tunics and dalmatics were bought by the Bishop of Chartres.

A goldsmith named Guillaume le Flament acquired the dead Queen's eating-utensils for a modest price; among them was a fork, the first ever to be made in the history of the world.

Her horses went for six hundred and ninety-two livres. And Madame Clémence's coach together with that of her ladies-in-waiting were also auctioned.

And when at last everything was removed from the Temple, people had the feeling that an ill-omened house had been shut up.

Indeed, it seemed, that year, as if the past were wiping itself out of its own accord to make way for the new reign. The Bishop of Arras, Thierry d'Hirson, Countess Mahaut's chancellor, died in the month of November. He had been the Countess' adviser for thirty years, her lover too, for that matter, and had served her in all her intrigues. Mahaut was become very lonely now. Robert of Artois had a priest called Pierre Roger, who was a supporter of the Valois party, appointed to the diocese of Arras.[6]

Things were going against Mahaut, while Robert seemed to be prospering in every way; his influence was continually increasing, and he was rising to the highest honours.

In the month of January, 1329, Philippe VI made the County of Beaumont-le-Roger a peerage; at last Robert was a peer of France.

Since the King of England delayed coming to render homage, it was once again decided to seize the Duchy of Guyenne. But before the threat was put into execution, Robert of Artois was sent to Avignon to obtain the intervention of Pope John XXII.

Robert spent two delightful weeks on the banks of the

Rhône. For Avignon, to which flowed all the gold of
Christendom, had become, for anyone who enjoyed high
living, gambling and beautiful courtesans, an enchanted
city over which ruled an ascetic, octogenarian pope withdrawn into the problems of the Beatific Vision. The new
peer of France had several audiences with the Holy Father;
a banquet was given in the pontifical palace in his honour,
and he enjoyed much learned conversation with a number
of cardinals. Nevertheless, loyal to the avocations of his turbulent youth, he also frequented persons of more doubtful
standing. Wherever Robert happened to be, he did not need
to lift a finger to attract loose women, wicked men and
fugitives from justice. If there was but one receiver of stolen
goods in a town, in the first quarter of an hour Robert
had found him out. The monk expelled from his order for
causing scandal, the priest guilty of larceny or violating his
oath, were inevitably to be found in his anteroom in search of
his support. He was often saluted in the street by persons
of sinister appearance and he would try vainly to recollect in
what brothel of what town he had run across them. There
was no doubt that he was trusted by the underworld, and the
fact that he had become the second prince in the kingdom
made no difference.

His old valet, Lormet le Dolois, was too old now to make
long journeys and had not accompanied him to Avignon.
But a younger man, Gillet de Nelle, who had been trained
in the same school, was charged with Lormet's duties. It
was, indeed, Gillet who discovered for Monseigneur Robert a
certain Maciot l'Allemant, a native of Arras and unemployed
sergeant-at-arms, who would stick at nothing. Maciot had
known Bishop Thierry d'Hirson well; and Bishop Thierry,

during his last years, had had a mistress called Jeanne de Divion, who was at least twenty years younger than himself. She was complaining bitterly of the way Countess Mahaut had been treating her since the Bishop's death. Would Monseigneur like to see this Dame de Divion?

Not for the first time, Robert of Artois concluded that there was much to be learned from people of bad reputation. No doubt there were safer hands than Sergeant Maciot's into which to confide one's purse, but the man clearly had much interesting information. Wearing a new suit of clothes and mounted on a good horse, he was sent north.

When he returned to Paris in March, Robert of Artois was in high good humour, prophesying that there would soon be interesting news in the kingdom. He mentioned that royal documents had been stolen by Bishop Thierry on Mahaut's behalf. And a woman with veiled face came frequently to see him in his study where he held long and secret conferences with her. As the weeks went by, he seemed ever happier and more confident, and foretold the imminent confusion of his enemies with increasing assurance.

In the month of April the English Court, yielding to pressure from the Pope, sent Bishop Orleton to Paris once again, with a train of seventy-two persons, lords, prelates, lawyers, clerks and servants, to negotiate the form the homage was to take. Indeed, it was nothing less than a treaty which had to be agreed.

The affairs of England were not going too well. Lord Mortimer had not increased his prestige by compelling Parliament to sit under the menace of his troops. He had been forced to suppress an armed rebellion of the barons under the leadership of Henry Wryneck, Earl of Lancaster, and he was finding great difficulty in governing the country.

At the beginning of May, gallant old Gaucher de Châtillon died in his eightieth year. He had been born in the reign of Saint Louis, and had been Constable for twenty-seven years. His determined voice had often affected the results of battles and had frequently prevailed in the King's Council.

On May 26th young King Edward III, having borrowed, as his father had done before him, five thousand livres from the Lombard bankers to cover the cost of the journey, took ship at Dover to come and render homage to his cousin of France.

Neither his mother Isabella nor Lord Mortimer accompanied him, for they were afraid the power might pass into other hands in their absence. The sixteen-year-old King, under the tutelage merely of two bishops, set out to confront the most imposing Court in the world.

For England was weak and divided, while France was a whole. There was no more puissant nation in Christendom; prosperous, populous, rich in industry and agriculture, governed by a powerful civil service and an active nobility, her lot seemed enviable indeed. While her makeshift king, who had now been reigning for a year during which he had achieved success after success, was the most envied of all the kings in the world.

5

The Giant and the Mirrors

He wanted not only to show himself off but to see himself too. He wanted his beautiful wife, the Countess, his three sons, Jean, Jacques and Robert, of whom the eldest, who was now eight, already gave promise of growing into a tall, strong man, to admire him; and he wanted his equerries and his servants, all the staff he had brought from Paris with him, to see him in his splendour. But he wanted also to be able to admire himself with his own eyes.

For this purpose, he had sent for all the mirrors that happened to be in the baggage of his suite, mirrors of polished silver, circular as plates, hand-mirrors, mirrors of glass backed by tin-foil and set in octagonal frames of silver-gilt, and he had had them hung side by side on the tapestry in his room.[7] The Bishop of Amiens would no doubt be delighted to find his fine figured tapestry torn by nails. But what did that matter? A peer of France could permit himself that much. Monseigneur Robert of Artois, Lord of Conches and Count of Beaumont-le-Roger, wanted to see himself wearing his peer's robes for the first time.

He turned first one way and then the other, advanced and retreated a couple of steps, but could see his reflection only in fragments, split up into pieces like a figure in a church window: on the left, the gold hilt of his long sword and, a little higher to the right, part of his chest where his silk surcoat showed his embroidered arms; here the shoulder to which the great peer's mantle was fastened with a glittering clasp, and there, near the ground, the fringe of the long mantle falling on the gold spurs; and then, crowning it all, the great peer's coronet with eight identical fleurons, set with the rubies he had bought at the late Queen Clémence's sale.

'Well, I'm worthily apparelled,' he said. 'It would be a great pity if I were not a peer, for the mantle suits me well.'

The Countess of Beaumont, also wearing state robes, did not altogether seem to share her husband's satisfaction.

'Are you quite sure, Robert,' she asked anxiously, 'that this woman will arrive in time?'

'Of course, of course,' he replied. 'Even if she doesn't come this morning, I shall make my claim, and present the papers tomorrow.'

The only drawback to Robert's costume was the heat of early summer. He was sweating under the cloth-of-gold, the velvet and the thick silk, and though he had taken a hot bath that morning he was beginning to give off a smell like a wild beast.

Through the window, which was open on to a bright and sunny sky, the cathedral bells could be heard ringing a full peal, drowning the clatter in the town of the trains of the five kings and their Courts.

For, indeed, on this June 6th, 1329, there were five kings in Amiens. No chancellor could remember such a gathering.

To receive the homage of his young cousin of England, Philippe VI had invited his relations and allies, the Kings of Navarre, Bohemia and Majorca, as well as the Count of Hainaut, the Duke of Athens and all the peers, dukes, counts, bishops, barons and marshals.

There were six thousand French horsemen and six hundred English. Charles of Valois would not have disowned his son, nor indeed his son-in-law, Robert of Artois, had he been able to see such an assembly.

The new Constable, Raoul de Brienne, had had to organize the billeting as his first duty. He had done it well, but had lost half a stone in the process.

The King of France and his family were occupying the Bishop's Palace, of which a wing had been allotted to Robert of Artois.

The King of England had been installed in the Malmaison,[8] and the other kings in various burgesses' houses. The servants slept in the passages, the grooms camped outside the town with the horses and baggage-trains.

An enormous crowd had come in from the immediate countryside, the neighbouring counties, and even from Paris. The less fortunate slept under porches.

While the chancellors of the two kingdoms were arguing once more about the terms of the homage, since even after so much negotiation no precise formula had yet been established, the whole nobility of Western Europe spent six consecutive days in jousting and tournament, being entertained by masks, jugglers and dances, and feasting spendidly from noon to starlight in the palace gardens.

Market-gardeners,[9] punting their flat-bottomed boats through the narrow canals into Amiens, were bringing irises, buttercups, hyacinths and lilies to the water-market. These were spread in the streets, courtyards and halls through which the kings passed. The town was saturated with the scent of crushed flowers, of pollen sticking to men's boots, and it mingled with the strong odours of the horses and the crowds.

And the food, the wine, the meat, the spices and the cakes! Pigs, sheep and bullocks were being driven in continuous procession to the slaughterhouses which were working night and day; trains of wagons brought the palace kitchens bucks, stags, wild boar, roe-deer, and hares; sturgeon, salmon and mullet from the sea; pike, bream, tench and crayfish from the rivers; and poultry and game of all kinds, fine capons, fat geese, resplendent pheasants, swans, pale herons and peacocks with tails full of eyes, Barrels of wine were on tap everywhere.

Anyone who wore a lord's livery, down to the most junior lackey, put on an air of importance. The prostitutes were in a frenzy. The Italian merchants had gathered from the ends of the earth for this fabulous fair organized by the King. The façades of the houses were hidden by the silks, brocades and tapestries hanging gaily from the windows.

There were too many bells and fanfares, too much shouting, too many palfreys and dogs, too much food and drink, too many princes and pickpockets, too many whores, too much luxury, too much gold, and too many kings. It made one's head spin.

The kingdom was intoxicated by the sight of its own power, as Robert of Artois was intoxicated by his reflection in the mirrors.

Lormet, his old valet, who in spite of a new livery was spending his time grumbling amid the general rejoicing –

largely because Gillet de Nelle was becoming too important in the household and because there were too many new faces about his master – came in and murmured: 'The lady you were expecting has arrived.'

Robert turned quickly.

'Show her in,' he said.

He winked meaningly at the Countess, and waving his arms drove everybody towards the door, shouting: 'Get out, all of you! Form up in procession in the courtyard.'

For a moment he stood alone by the window, looking out on the crowd which had gathered in front of the cathedral to watch the great go in; a cordon of archers was finding some difficulty in controlling it. The bells above were still pealing; the scent of hot pancakes suddenly floated up to him from a stall; all the neighbouring streets were full of people; and the Hoquet Canal was so crowded with boats that the glimmer of the water was scarcely visible.

Robert of Artois felt triumphant, and he would feel even more so shortly, when he went up to his Cousin Philippe in the cathedral and uttered certain words that would make the assembled kings, dukes and barons start in surprise. None would emerge as happy as he went in; and this would be particularly true of his dear Aunt Mahaut and the Duke of Burgundy.

He would certainly be wearing his peer's robes for the first time to advantage! Twenty years and more of stubborn struggle would receive their reward today. And yet, behind his pride and joy, he felt a sense of regret. What could be the cause of it when fate was smiling on him and all his hopes were coming true? Then suddenly he knew: it was the smell of pancakes. A peer of France, who was about to claim the county of his ancestors, could not go down into the street wearing his coronet with eight fleurons and eat a pancake. A peer of France could not loiter about the streets, mingle with the multitude, tweak a girl's breast, and go brawling through the night in company with half a dozen whores, as he used to do when he was poor and twenty. Yet his nostalgia reassured him. 'Anyway,' he thought, 'the life's not dead in me yet!'

His visitor was standing shyly by the door, not daring to disturb the thoughts of a lord in so splendid a coronet.

She was a woman of about thirty-five, with a triangular face and high cheekbones. The hood of her travelling-cloak revealed plaited tresses, and her full, rounded bosom heaved beneath her white linen bodice as she breathed.

'By God, the Bishop had good taste!' thought Robert, when he turned and saw her.

She bent a knee in a curtsy. He held out his huge gloved hand with its ruby rings.

'Give them to me,' he said.

'I haven't got them, Monseigneur,' she replied.

There was a sudden change in Robert's expression.

'Do you mean to say you haven't got the papers?' he cried. 'You promised me to bring them today!'

'I've come straight from the Château d'Hirson, Monseigneur. I went there yesterday with Sergeant Maciot. We opened the iron wall-safe with skeleton keys.'

'Well?'

'Someone had been there before us. It was empty.'

'What splendid news!' cried Robert, who had turned rather pale. 'You've been trifling with me for a whole month. "Monseigneur, I can give you the deeds that will put you in possession of your county! I know where they are. Give me an estate and an income, and I'll bring them to you next week . . ." And then that week goes by, and then another . . . "The Hirson family are in the château; I can't go there when they're in residence . . ." "I've now been there, Monseigneur, but the key I had with me was not the right one. Have a little patience . . ." And now, on the very day I've got to produce the two documents to the King . . .'

'The three documents, Monseigneur: the marriage contract of your father, Count Philippe, the letter from Count Robert, your grandfather, and Monseigneur Thierry's letter . . .'

'Very well then! The three of them! And now you come here and say foolishly: "I haven't got them; the safe was empty!" Do you expect me to believe you?'

'Ask Sergeant Maciot, who went with me! Don't you realize, Monseigneur, that I'm even more distressed than you are?'

There was a wicked and suspicious glint in Robert's eyes. 'Tell me, La Divion', he said in a different tone of voice, 'are you by any chance trying to double-cross me? Is this an attempt to extract more money from me, or have you betrayed me to Mahaut?'

'How can you even think of such a thing, Monseigneur?' she cried on the verge of tears. 'All my difficulties and my poverty are due to the Countess of Mahaut who stole every-thing my dear Seigneur Thierry left me in his will. I wish Madame Mahaut all the harm you can do her. Just think, Monseigneur, I was Thierry's mistress for twelve years. Many people cut me because of it, but after all a bishop's a man like another! People are so unkind . . .'

She began telling Robert her story all over again, though

he had already heard it three times at least. She talked quickly; her eyes, beneath her straight brows, had the curious inward look of the utterly self-centred, of people whose thoughts are entirely and unceasingly concentrated on their own affairs.

She could obviously expect no help from her husband, whom she had left to go and live with Bishop Thierry. She realized that on the whole her husband had been very accommodating, perhaps because he had early ceased to be a man (Monseigneur would understand what she meant). It was to save her from poverty and in gratitude for all the happy years she had given him that Bishop Thierry had put her down in his will for several houses, a sum in gold and an annuity. But he had been afraid of Madame Mahaut and had felt obliged to appoint her his executrix.

'She always disliked me, because I was younger than she was, and because Thierry in the past – he told me so himself – had been compelled to pleasure her. He was well aware that she would treat me badly when he was no longer there to protect me, and that the Hirsons, who are all against me – particularly Beatrice, Madame Mahaut's lady-in-waiting, who is the worst of the lot – would contrive to throw me out of the house and deprive me of everything due to me . . .'

Robert had ceased to listen to her interminable complaints. He put his heavy coronet down on a chest and scratched his red head in thought. His splendid scheme was falling to the ground, for it was entirely dependent on the production of the documents. 'Just one convincing little document, Brother, and I shall at once order a review of the judgements of 1309 and 1318,' Philippe VI had said. 'But you must realize that I can do nothing without that, however great my wish to serve you, or I shall be breaking my word to Eudes of Burgundy, with all the consequences that you can imagine.' And it was no small document, but the highly important papers Mahaut had stolen so as to be able to lay her hand on the Artois inheritance that he had boasted of being able to produce!

'And in a few minutes' time,' he said, 'I have to be in the cathedral for the homage.'

'What homage?' asked La Divion.

'The King of England's, of course!'

'Oh, so that's why the town's so crowded I could scarcely push my way through.'

So this fool of a woman saw nothing, heard nothing and knew nothing, so busy was she with her own ridiculous little concerns!

It occurred to Robert that he had perhaps been unwise to credit this woman's tale; he began to doubt whether the documents, the safe at Hesdin and the Bishop's confession had ever existed outside her imagination. And was Maciot l'Allemant also a dupe, or had he connived with her?'

'Tell the truth, woman! You've never seen these documents!'

'But I have, Monseigneur!' cried La Divion, pressing her hands to her prominent cheeks. 'It was at the Château d'Hirson, the day Thierry fell ill, before he had himself carried to his Hôtel d'Arras. "My Jeannette, I want to forearm you against Madame Mahaut, as I forearmed myself," he said. "The documents she stole from the archives in order to rob Monseigneur Robert were not destroyed as she believes. Those from the Paris archives were burnt in her presence; but the duplicates from the Artois archives" – these are Thierry's very words, Monseigneur – "I have always kept here, though I told her they had been destroyed too, and I have added a letter in my own hand to them." Then Thierry took me to the safe concealed in the wall of his study, and gave me the documents to read. They all had seals on them; and I could hardly believe my eyes when I saw what villainy had been done. There were also eight hundred livres in gold in the safe. And he gave me the key in case anything happened to him . . .'

'And when you went to Hirson the first time?'

'I mixed up the keys. I think I must have lost the right one. I really do seem to have the most extraordinary bad luck. And once things start going wrong . . .'

She was off again. But Robert felt she was speaking the truth; people did not invent such a stupid story when they set out to deceive. He would have strangled her with pleasure could it have served any useful purpose.

'My going there must have given the alarm,' she added. 'They found the safe and forced the locks. I'm sure it was that Beatrice . . .'

Lormet put his head in at the door. Robert waved him away.

'But after all, Monseigneur,' Jeanne de Divion said, as if she were trying to make amends for her failure, 'don't you think the documents could be easily reproduced?'

'Reproduced?'

'After all, we know what they said! I can repeat Monseigneur Thierry's letter almost word for word . . .'

Vague of eye and waving a finger in emphasis, she began reciting:

'"I feel greatly guilty that I have for so long concealed the fact that the right to the County of Artois belongs to Monseigneur Robert by the agreements made at the marriage

63

of Monseigneur Philippe of Artois and Madame Blanche of Brittany, which were drawn up in duplicate and sealed. Of these deeds I hold one copy, and the other was subtracted from the archives of the Court by one of our great lords . . . I have always intended that, after the death of Madame the Countess at whose desire and on whose orders I have acted, should God call her to Himself before me, restoration should be made to the said Monseigneur Robert of the deeds I have in my possession . . ."'

La Division might lose keys, but she could remember a once-read text. There were no doubt minds made that way. And now she was suggesting to Robert, as if it were the most natural thing in the world, that he should commit forgery. She obviously had no sense whatever of right and wrong, could make no distinction between the moral and the immoral, the permissible and the forbidden. Morality was what happened to suit her. Robert, during the course of his forty-two years, had committed almost every conceivable crime. He had killed, lied, denounced, pillaged and raped. But he had not yet been a forger.

'There is also the old bailiff of Béthune, Guillaume de la Planche, who must remember things that could help us, for he was Monseigneur Thierry's clerk at the time.'

'Where is this old bailiff?' Robert asked.

'In prison.'

Robert shrugged his shoulders. Things were going from bad to worse. He had made a grave mistake to be so hasty. He ought to have waited until he had the documents actually in his hands before giving so many assurances. On the other hand, the King himself had advised him to make use of the occasion of the homage.

Old Lormet put his head in at the door again.

'All right, I'm coming,' Robert said impatiently. 'There's only the square to cross.'

'The King's making ready to go down,' Lormet said reproachfully.

'Very well, I'm coming.'

When all was said and done, the King was his brother-in-law and, what was more, only King because he, Robert, had so desired it. How hot it was! He felt the sweat running down under his peer's robes.

He went to the window, and looked out at the cathedral and its two asymmetrical, fretted towers. The sun was shining at an angle on the great rose window. The bells were still pealing and drowning the noise of the crowd.

The Duke of Brittany, followed by his suite, was mounting the steps to the central porch.

Twenty yards behind him, the lame Duke of Bourbon followed, two pages carrying the train of his mantle.

Behind them again, came Mahaut of Artois' retinue. She had good reason to walk with so firm a step today! Taller than most men, her face crimson, she was acknowledging the greetings of the people with slight but imperious inclinations of the head. There went a criminal, a liar, a poisoner of kings, and a thief who had stolen documents from the royal archives. And now, on the very point of confounding her, of being victorious at last, after twenty years of effort, he was going to be compelled to renounce his triumph. And why? Because a bishop's concubine had lost a key!

Was there not justification for using base means against the base? Should one be over-nice about the means one employed to bring about the triumph of right?

And, after all, when you came to think of it, if Mahaut did possess the documents from the safe at Château d'Hirson – even if she had not immediately destroyed them, which she probably had – she could certainly never produce them or allude to their existence, since they were proof of her guilt. If similar documents were produced in evidence against her, she would be caught. It was a pity he had not the whole day in front of him in which to think it over and get more information. He had to make his mind up within the hour, and entirely on his own.

'I'll see you again, woman; but not a word to anyone,' he said.

Forgery was undoubtedly a serious risk.

He picked up his huge coronet and put it on his head. With a glance at the many mirrors that reflected him split into some thirty separate fragments, he set out for the cathedral.

6

Homage and Perjury

'A KING'S SON CANNOT kneel to a count's son!' said the sixteen-year-old Sovereign. He had thought of this formula entirely on his own, and insisted on it to his counsellors, so that they in turn should insist on it to the French jurisconsults.

'Really, my Lord Orleton,' said young King Edward III, when they arrived in Amiens, 'last year you came over to maintain that I had a greater right to the throne of France than my cousin of Valois. Do you now suggest that I should throw myself to the ground at his feet?'

Like so many boys whose parents have lived dissolute and irregular lives, Edward III, now that he was on his own for the first time, was determined to act on sound and sensible principles. During his six days in Amiens, he had insisted that the whole question of the homage be reconsidered.

'But my Lord Mortimer is most anxious to maintain peace with France,' said John Maltravers.

'My lord,' Edward interrupted him, 'you are here to guard me, I believe, not to advise.'

He could not conceal his dislike of the long-faced Baron

who had been not only his father's jailer but undoubtedly also his murderer. To have to submit to Maltravers' surveillance and indeed his spying, for that was what it amounted to, annoyed Edward very much. He went on:

'My Lord Mortimer is our great friend, but he is not the King, and it is not he who is to render homage. And my Lord Lancaster, who by virtue of presiding over the Council of Regency is alone in a position to take decisions in my name, gave me no instructions before I left as to the nature of the homage I should render. I refuse to render the homage of a liegeman.'

The Bishop of Lincoln, Henry de Burghersh, Chancellor of England, who was also of Mortimer's party, but less under his thumb and certainly more intelligent than Maltravers, could not but approve the young King's concern to defend his dignity and the interests of his realm, in spite of the difficulties it created.

For not only did the homage of a liegeman oblige the vassal to present himself with neither arms nor crown, but also to take the oath on his knees, which implied that the vassal was, as his first duty, the suzerain's man.

'As his first duty,' Edward emphasized, 'and therefore, my lords, if it so happened that, while we were making war in Scotland, the King of France summoned me to a war of his own in Flanders, Lombardy or elsewhere, I should have to abandon everything to join him, failing which he would have the right to seize my duchy. I cannot have that.'

Lord Montacute, who was one of the barons of Edward's suite, developed a great admiration for his young sovereign's precocious wisdom and no less precocious firmness. Montacute himself was twenty-eight.

'I think we shall have a good king,' he said. 'It is a pleasure to serve him.'

From then on he was always by Edward's side, lending him counsel and support.

In the end, the young King had his way. Philippe of Valois' advisers also wanted peace and, above all, to bring the negotiations to a conclusion. The important thing was that the King of England had come. They had not assembled the whole kingdom and half Europe merely to afford them the spectacle of the negotiations ending in failure.

'Very well, let him render merely simple homage,' said Philippe VI to his chancellor, as if it were of no greater significance than a decision about some dance figure, or tournament entry. 'I think he's quite right; in his place, I should no doubt do the same.'

And so it was that Edward III advanced up the cathedral, which was packed with lords right into the side chapels, wearing his sword, his royal mantle, embroidered with leopards, which fell in long folds from his shoulders, and his crown. His fair eyelashes were lowered and excitement had enhanced the usual pallor of his face. The heavy adornments made his extreme youth all the more striking. He looked like an archangel; and all the women felt their hearts go out to him, indeed fell in love with him on the spot.

Two English bishops and ten barons walked behind him.

The King of France, his mantle embroidered with lilies, sat enthroned in the choir, a little higher than the kings, queens and sovereign princes about him, whose crowns formed a sort of pyramid. He rose with majestic courtesy to receive his vassal, who came to a halt three paces from him.

A great ray of sunlight was shining through a window

and touching them as if it were a sword from Heaven.

Messire Mille de Noyers, the Chamberlain, a master of Parliament and a master of the Exchequer, stepped forward from the crowd of peers and great officers and took up his position between the two sovereigns. He was a grave-looking man of about sixty, who seemed not the least impressed either by his state robes or by the part assigned him. In a loud, clear voice he said: 'Sire Edward, the King, our Master and most puissant Lord, does not receive you here in testimony of all the rights he holds by law in Gascony and Agenais, as King Charles IV held them by law, and which are not included in the homage.'

Then Henry de Burghersh, Edward's chancellor, stepped forward to stand beside Mille de Noyers and replied: 'Sire Philippe, our Lord and Master, the King of England, or any other for him or by him, renounces none of the rights he holds in the Duchy of Guyenne and its appurtenances, and declares that the King of France acquires no new rights whatsoever by this homage.'

These were the highly ambiguous formulas that had been agreed upon; they defined nothing, they settled nothing. Each word had a double meaning.

The French wanted it understood that the borderlands, which had been seized in the previous reign during the campaign commanded by Charles of Valois, were to remain directly attached to the Crown of France. This was a confirmation of the *de facto* position.

On the English side, the phrase 'any other for him or by him' was an allusion to the King's minority and to the existence of the Council of Regency; but the 'by him' might in the future equally well apply to the Seneschal of Guyenne or any other royal lieutenant. As for the expression 'no new rights', it could be taken to signify the ratification of the rights already acquired, including those granted by the treaty of 1327. But it was not said explicitly.

These declarations, like every treaty of peace or alliance between nations throughout history, depended for their application entirely on the good or bad will of the Governments concerned. For the moment, the fact that the two princes had come face to face was evidence of a mutual desire to live in amity.

Chancellor Burghersh unrolled a parchment to which was attached the seal of England and read out in the vassal's name:

'"Sire, I become your man of the Duchy of Guyenne and its appurtenances, which I claim to hold from you as Duke of Guyenne and Peer of France in accordance with the Treaties of Peace made between your predecessors and ours, and because of what we and our ancestors, Kings of England and Dukes of Guyenne, have done in the name of the said duchy for your predecessors, the Kings of France."'

Then the Bishop handed Mille de Noyers the parchment he had just read. It had been much shortened in the drafting when the liegeman's homage was cut out.

Mille de Noyers said in reply: 'Sire, you become the man of my Lord the King of France for the Duchy of Guyenne and its appurtenances which you recognize that you as Duke of Guyenne and Peer of France hold from him, and in accordance with the Treaties of Peace made between his predecessors, Kings of France, and yours, and because of what you and your ancestors, Kings of England and Dukes of Guyenne, have done for his predecessors, Kings of France, in the name of the said duchy.'

All this would furnish splendid matter for dispute on the day the two countries fell out.

Then Edward III said: 'In truth.'

And Mille de Noyers replied with these words: 'The King, our Sire, receives you, subject to the protestations and reservations above stated.'

Edward stepped forward three paces to his suzerain. He took off his gloves and handed them to Lord Montacute. He reached out his slender white hands and put them in the large palms of the King of France. Then the two kings kissed.

It was remarked that Philippe VI did not need to bend down far to reach his young cousin's face. The chief difference between them lay in Philippe's robustness which made him seem so imposing. But there could be no doubt that the King of England, who was still growing, would develop into a fine figure of a man.

The bells in the higher tower began pealing again. Everyone was pleased. Peers and dignitaries nodded to each other in satisfaction. King John of Bohemia, behind his handsome auburn beard that spread down across his chest, looked noble and thoughtful. Count Guillaume the Good and his brother Jean of Hainaut exchanged smiles with the English lords. Truly it was a good deed that had just been done.

What was the use of quarrelling, growing angry, threatening, bearing plaints to Parliament, confiscating fiefs, besieging towns, fighting to the death with great waste of gold, toil and the blood of knights, when with a little goodwill on all sides such admirable agreement could be reached?

The King of England took his place on the throne prepared for him a little below that of the King of France. It remained now only to hear mass.

Yet Philippe VI seemed still to be waiting for something. He turned to the peers who were sitting in the stalls and looked for Robert of Artois, whose coronet stood out higher than all the rest.

Robert's eyes were half shut. Though it was pleasantly cool in the cathedral, he was wiping the sweat from his brow with his red-gloved hand. His heart was beating very fast at this moment. He had not realized that the dye was running from his glove and there was a bloody streak across his face.

Suddenly he left his stall; he had made up his mind.

'Sire,' he cried, coming to a halt in front of Philippe's throne, 'since all your vassals are here assembled . . .'

A few moments before, Mille de Noyers and Bishop Burghersh had spoken in clear firm voices, audible throughout the great building. But when Robert spoke he made them sound like birds twittering.

'. . . and since everyone has a right to your justice,' he went on, 'it is justice I come to ask of you.'

'Monseigneur of Beaumont, my cousin, who has done you wrong?' Philippe VI asked gravely.

'I have been wronged, Sire, by your vassal Dame Mahaut of Burgundy who by guile and felony has sequested the title and possession of the County of Artois which is mine by right of inheritance from my ancestors.'

But a voice, very nearly as loud, was heard shouting from the stalls. 'This was bound to happen sooner or later'

It was Mahaut of Artois.

The congregation showed some surprise perhaps, but no very great astonishment. Robert was following the precedent of the Count of Flanders at the coronation. It seemed to have become customary for a peer who thought himself wronged to bring his complaint forward on these solemn occasions; and it was obviously done with the King's prior consent.

Duke Eudes of Burgundy looked inquiringly at his sister, the Queen of France, who gazed back at him and with a movement of her open hands gave him to understand that she was as much surprised as he was and knew nothing of the matter at all.

'Cousin,' said Philippe, 'can you produce documents in evidence to prove your rights?'

'I can,' Robert said firmly.

'He can't, he's lying!' cried Mahaut, who now left the stalls and came to stand beside her nephew in front of the King.

How alike Robert and Mahaut were. They were wearing identical coronets and robes; they were both equally angry, and the blood was mounting in their bull-necks. Mahaut, too, was wearing the great, gold-hilted sword of a peer of France on her Amazonian flank. They could have looked no more alike had they been mother and son.

'Aunt,' said Robert, 'do you deny that the marriage contract made by my noble father, Count Philippe of Artois, appointed me, his first-born, heir to Artois, and that you took advantage of my being a child to dispossess me after my father's death?'

'I deny every word of it, you wicked nephew! How dare you try to disgrace me?'

'Do you deny there was a marriage contract?'

'I deny it!' shouted Mahaut.

There was an angry murmur throughout the cathedral, and old Count de Bouville, who had been Chamberlain to Philip the Fair, was distinctly heard to utter a scandalized 'Oh!' Though it was not everyone who had as good reason as

Bouville, who had been Curator of Queen Clémence's stomach at the time of the birth of Jean I, the Posthumous, to know Mahaut of Artois' remarkable capabilities in the realms of perjury and crime, it was quite obvious that she was flagrantly denying the evidence. A marriage between a son of the House of Artois, a prince of the fleur de lis,[10] and a daughter of the House of Brittany would most certainly not have been arranged without a contract ratified both by the King and the peers of the time. Duke Jean of Brittany, though he had been a child at the time of the marriage, remembered it perfectly and was telling his neighbours so. This time Mahaut had gone too far. It was one thing to plead, as she had done in two lawsuits, the ancient custom of Artois, which was in her favour owing to the premature death of her brother, but it was quite another to deny that there had been a marriage contract. She merely succeeded in confirming everyone's suspicions; and, in particular, that she had done away with the documents herself.

Philippe VI turned to the Bishop of Amiens.

'Monseigneur, please bring the Holy Gospels and hand them to the plaintiff.'

He paused for a moment, then added: 'And also to the defendant.'

And when it was done, he said: 'My cousins, do you agree to maintain your statements by swearing on the Holy Gospels in the presence of ourself, your suzerain, and in the presence of the Kings, our cousins, and all your peers here assembled?'

Philippe looked really majestic as he said this, and his young son, Prince Jean, who was ten years old, gazed at him wide-eyed and open-mouthed, lost in admiration of his father. But the Queen of France, Jeanne the Lame, had a wicked, indeed a cruel line each side of her mouth, and her hands were trembling; while Mahaut's daughter, the Dowager Queen Jeanne, the widow of Philippe the Long, a thin, dried-up woman, had gone as pale as her white dowager's robe. And no less pale were Mahaut's granddaughter, the young Duchess of Burgundy, and her fifty-year-old husband, Duke Eudes. They looked as if they would have liked to rush forward and stop Mahaut taking the oath. There was a great silence and everyone was watching.

'I agree!' said Mahaut and Robert together.

'Take off your gloves,' said the Bishop of Amiens.

Mahaut's gloves were green, and the heat had made their dye run too. And when the two huge hands were stretched out towards the Holy Book, one was as red as blood and the other green as gall.

'I swear,' said Robert, 'that the County of Artois is mine and that I shall produce documents in evidence to establish my right to it.'

'My fine nephew,' cried Mahaut, 'do you dare swear that you have ever seen or possessed such documents?'

Face to face, grey eyes staring into grey eyes, their big square chins almost touching, they defied each other.

'Bitch,' thought Robert, 'so it really was you who stole them!' And since in such circumstances decision is vital, he said in a clear voice: 'I swear it. But do you, my fine aunt, dare swear that these documents have never existed, and that you have never had knowledge or possession of them?'

'I swear it,' she replied with an assurance equal to his own, and she gazed at him, returning hate for hate. Neither of them had gained any advantage over the other. The balance was in equilibrium, the false oaths they had compelled each other to take weighing equally in the opposite scales.

'Commissioners will be appointed tomorrow to make inquiry and enlighten my justice. Whoever has lied will be punished by God, whoever has sworn the truth shall be established in his right,' said Philippe, signing to the Bishop to take the Gospels away.

God does not need to intervene directly to punish perjury, and the heavens may remain dumb. The wicked bear within themselves the seeds of their own misfortunes.

PART TWO

THE DEVIL'S GAME

I

The Witnesses

A GREEN PEAR, STILL NO larger than a man's thumb, was hanging from the espalier.

There were three people sitting on a stone bench: old Count de Bouville, whom the others were questioning, was in the middle, on his right was the Chevalier de Villebresme, the King's commissioner, and on his left the notary Pierre Tesson, who was recording his deposition.

Notary Tesson was wearing a clerk's cap on his huge domed head, and his straight hair hung down from beneath it; he had a pointed nose, a curiously long and narrow chin, and his whole profile looked rather like the moon in its first quarter.

'Monseigneur,' he said with great respect, 'may I read your evidence over to you?'

'Do so, Messire, do so,' replied Bouville.

And his hand moved fumblingly to the little, hard green pear. 'The gardener ought to have that branch fastened back,' he thought.

The notary leaned over the writing-board on his knee and began reading. '"On the seventeenth day of the month of June in the year 1329, We, Pierre de Villebresme, Chevalier ..."'

King Philippe VI had allowed no delay. Two days after the oaths had been taken in Amiens Cathedral, he had appointed a commission of inquiry; and less than a week after the Court's return to Paris, the investigation had begun.

'"... and We, Pierre Tesson, Notary to the King, have come to take the evidence of ..."'

'Master Tesson,' said Bouville, 'are you the same Tesson who was formerly attached to the household of Monseigneur of Artois?'

'The same, Messire ...'

'And you are now Notary to the King? Splendid, splendid, I congratulate you ...'

Bouville sat up a little straighter and clasped his hands across his round paunch. He was wearing a worn velvet robe, old-fashioned and rather too long, which dated from the days of Philip the Fair. He now used it in his garden.

He was twiddling his thumbs, three times one way, three times the other. It was going to be a warm, fine day, but there was still a trace of the cool of the night about the morning.

'"... have come to take the evidence of the high and mighty Lord, Count Hugues de Bouville, and have heard it in the garden of his town house, situated not far from the Pré-aux-Clercs ..."'

'The neighbourhood has changed a great deal since my father built this house,' said Bouville. 'At that time, there were barely three houses between the Abbey of Saint-Germain-des Prés and Saint-André-des-Arts: the Hôtel de Nesle, on the river-bank, the Hôtel de Navarre, which stood back a little, and the house of the Counts of Artois, which they used as a country residence, since there were only fields and water-meadows round it. Look how it's all been built up! All the new rich have come to set themselves up in the district; and now the roads have become streets. In the old days I could see nothing but trees beyond my wall; today, with such sight as is still left in me, I see nothing but roofs. And the noise! Really, the noise in this district these days! You might think you were in the heart of the Cité. Had I even a few more years to live, I'd sell this house and build another elsewhere. But in the circumstances there's no question of that . . .'

And his hand reached out to the little green pear again. The time that must elapse till it grew ripe was all he could hope for now. He had been losing his sight for many months past. Trees, people, the world were visible to him only through a sort of wall of water. He had been active and important, had travelled, had sat on the Royal Council, and had taken part in great events; and now he was drawing to his end in his garden, his mind slow and his sight confused. He was lonely and almost forgotten, except when younger men needed to refer to his memories.

Master Pierre Tesson and the Chevalier de Villebresme exchanged a glance. They were bored. The old Count de Bouville was not an easy witness, for his mind wandered constantly off the point. Yet he was far too old and far too distinguished for one to be sharp with him. Tesson went on:

'". . . and he declared to us in person that which is recorded below, in particular: that when he was Chamberlain to our Sire Philip IV, before the latter became King, he had knowledge of the marriage contract between the late

Monseigneur Philippe of Artois and Madame Blanche of Brittany, and that he had the said contract in his hands, and that the said contract declared in precise terms that the County of Artois would devolve by right of inheritance to the said Monseigneur Philippe of Artois and, after him, to his heirs male, the issue of the said marriage . . .'"

Bouville waved a hand.

'I did not assert that. I had the contract in my hands, as I have told you, and as I told Monseigneur Robert of Artois himself, when he came to visit me the other day, but in all conscience I have no memory of having read it.'

'But why, Monseigneur, would you have had the contract in your hands if it was not to read it?' asked the Chevalier de Villebresme.

'To take it to my master's chancellor for sealing; and I very well remember that the contract was sealed by all the peers, of which my master Philip the Fair was one, in his capacity as heir to the throne.'

'This must be recorded, Tesson,' said Villebresme: 'all the peers applied their seals. Though you did not actually read the document, Monseigneur, you were nevertheless aware that the inheritance of Artois was assured to Count Philippe and his heirs male?'

'I have heard it said,' replied Bouville, 'but I cannot go further than that.'

The way young Villebresme was trying to make him say more than he knew rather irritated him. Why, the fellow hadn't even been born, nor, if it came to that, had his father even thought of begetting him, when the facts he was inquiring into had occurred. These junior Crown officials were all over-zealous in their new duties. But one of these days they too would be old and lonely, and sitting by an espalier in their garden. Yes, Bouville remembered the terms of Philippe of Artois' marriage contract. But when had he first heard them spoken about? Was it at the time of the marriage itself, in '82, or when Count Philippe died, in '98, from wounds received in the Battle of Furnes? Or, again, was it after old Count Robert II had been killed at the Battle of Courtrai, in 1302, having survived his son by four years, which fact had given rise to the lawsuit between his daughter Mahaut and his grandson the present Robert III?

Bouville was being asked to give a precise date to a memory which might well relate to almost any time in a period of over twenty years. And it was not only Tesson and this Chevalier de Villebresme who had come to pick his brains, but Monseigneur Robert of Artois himself, courteously and respectfully, it must be admitted, but nevertheless talking loud and walking restlessly up and down the garden, crushing the flowers beneath his boots!

'Very well, we will make the necessary correction,' said the notary, turning to his manuscript: '". . . and that he had the said contract in his hands, but only for a short while, and remembers also that it was sealed with the seals of all the peers; and the Count de Bouville has also declared to us that he heard tell at that time that the said contract stated in precise terms that the County of Artois . . ."'

Bouville nodded agreement. He would have preferred that 'at that time' be suppressed; the phrase 'heard tell at that time . . .' had been introduced by the notary into his evidence. But he was tired of struggling. And did one little phrase matter all that much?

'". . . would devolve to his heirs male of the said marriage;

and he has also certified that the contract was placed in the archives of the Court, and also believes it certain that it was later subtracted from the said archives by wicked contrivance on the orders of Madame Mahaut of Artois . . ."'

'I didn't say that either,' Bouville remarked.

'You didn't say it in that form, Monseigneur,' replied Villebresme, 'but it emerges from your deposition. Let us go back to what you do certify. In the first place, the marriage contract existed. Secondly, you saw it. Thirdly, it was placed in the archives . . .'

'Sealed with the seals of the twelve peers . . .'

Villebresme exchanged a weary glance with the notary.

'Sealed with the seals of the peers,' he repeated to conciliate the witness. 'You also certify that the contract excluded the Countess Mahaut from the inheritance, and that it disappeared from the archives, so that it cannot be produced at the lawsuit Monseigneur Robert of Artois is bringing against his aunt. Who do you think subtracted it? Do you think King Philip the Fair gave the order?'

It was a cunning question; for it had often been whispered that Philip the Fair had given a partial judgement in favour of the mother-in-law of his two youngest sons. People would be pretending next that it was Bouville himself who had been ordered to see that the documents disappeared!

'Messire, do not associate the memory of my master King Philip the Fair with so villainous a deed,' he replied with dignity.

The bells of Saint-Germain-des-Prés rang out above the roofs and the trees. It occurred to Bouville that it was the hour at which he was brought a bowl of curds; his doctor had advised him to take them three times a day.

'In that case,' went on Villebresme, 'it is clear that the contract was subtracted without the King's knowledge. And who could have any interest in doing that except the Countess Mahaut?'

The young commissioner tapped the stone bench with the tips of his fingers; he was rather pleased with his argument.

'Oh, of course,' said Bouville, 'Mahaut is capable of anything.'

Bouville required no convincing on that point. He knew Mahaut to be guilty of two crimes which were far more serious than the mere stealing of documents. She had undoubtedly killed King Louis X; and, under his very eyes, she had killed a five-day-old child whom she believed to be the little posthumous King – and she had done these things in order to retain her County of Artois. It seemed almost silly to be so scrupulous about one's evidence if it were going to benefit her. She had most certainly stolen her brother's marriage contract, which she now had the face to deny on oath had ever existed. What a horrible woman she was! Because of her, the true heir of the Kings of France was growing up in a little Italian town far from his own realm, in the house of a Lombard merchant, who believed him to be his son. But one must not think of that. Bouville had once confessed the secret, which he alone knew, to the Pope. But he must never think of it now, for it might lead him into indiscretion. Oh, if only these officials would go away!

'You're quite right, let what you have written stand,' he said in a rather quavering voice. 'Do I have to sign?'

The notary handed Bouville the pen. But Bouville could scarcely see the edge of the paper. His signature overran the document. They heard him murmur: 'God will certainly see to it that she expiates her sins before he hands her over to the Devil's care.'

The notary sanded his signature and put the paper and writing-board into his black leather bag; then the two officials rose to take their leave. Bouville saluted them with his hand, without rising. By the time they were ten paces off they had become no more than vague shadows dissolving behind a wall of water.

The old Chamberlain rang a little handbell beside him to ask for his curds. His thoughts were disturbing. How could his venerated master, King Philip the Fair, have given judgement about Artois and yet forgotten the marriage contract he had once sealed? How could he have failed to be aware that the document had disappeared? Ah, well, even the best of kings did not do only good deeds . . .

Bouville determined to go one day soon to visit the banker Tolomei; he would ask for news of Guccio Baglioni and the child – quite casually, of course, simply as a polite inquiry during the course of conversation. Old Tolomei hardly ever moved from his bed these days. With him it was his legs that had failed him. Life was like that: in one man the ears grew hard of hearing, in another the eyes grew dim, and in a third the limbs lost the power of movement. One thought of the past in terms of years, but one no longer dared think of the future except in terms of months or weeks.

'Shall I still be alive by the time this fruit is ripe, shall I be here to pluck it?' Count de Bouville wondered as he gazed at the pear on the espalier.

Messire Pierre de Machaut, Lord of Montargis, was a man who never forgave an injury, even to the dead. The death of his enemies was not enough to allay his resentments.

His father, who had held a high post at the time of the Iron King, had been relieved of it by Enguerrand de Marigny, and the family fortunes had thereby gravely suffered. The fall of the all-powerful Enguerrand had been a personal revenge for Pierre de Machaut; the greatest day in his life was still that on which, as an equerry to King Louis the Hutin, he had led Monseigneur de Marigny to the gallows. Led, of course, was not to be taken too literally: accompanied had been nearer the mark; and not in the first rank either, but lost amid a great number of dignitaries who were all more important than he was. Nevertheless, as the years passed, these lords had died off one after the other, and whenever Messire Pierre de Machaut told of that memorable progress, he moved himself one place forward in the procession.

In the early days he had been content to defy Messire Enguerrand, as he stood in the tumbril, with his eyes, thereby giving him to understand that anyone, however exalted his rank, who injured a Machaut was bound to be overtaken by disaster.

Later on, he began to gild his memories of the occasion and to assert that Marigny, during the course of his last journey, had not only recognized him but had said sadly: 'Oh, Machaut, it's you! Yours is now the triumph. I have done you a wrong and I repent it.'

And now, fourteen years later, it appeared that as Enguerrand de Marigny went to his execution he had spoken only to Pierre de Machaut; and on the way from prison to Montfaucon had told him everything about the state of his conscience.

Pierre de Machaut was a little man, with grey eyebrows

that met above his nose and a stiff leg from a fall in a tournament. He still had his armour carefully greased, though he would never wear it again. He was as vain as he was resentful, and Robert of Artois, who had twice taken the trouble to visit him to hear his account of the celebrated progress of Messire Enguerrand's tumbril, was well aware of it.

'Splendid! Just tell that to the King's commissioners, who will visit you to take evidence about my case,' Robert had said. 'Information from so valiant a man as yourself is of the utmost importance. It will enlighten the King in giving justice and he will be immensely grateful to you, and so shall I. Have you ever been granted a pension for you and your father's services to the realm?'

'Never.'

That was most unjust. When so many intriguers, bourgeois and *parvenus* had succeeded in getting on to the Court pension list during these last reigns, how could anyone of such distinction as Messire de Machaut have been forgotten? It must of course, have been deliberately contrived by Countess Mahaut, who had always been hand in glove with Enguerrand de Marigny.

Robert of Artois would give his personal attention to the matter. It was iniquitous.

He had been so successful that when the Chevalier de Villebresme, attended as usual by Tesson the notary, called on the former equerry, Machaut showed as much zeal in giving his evidence as the commissioner did in questioning him.

The evidence was taken down in a neighbouring garden, for all depositions had by law to be made in the open air and in an open space.

Listening to Pierre de Machaut, you might have thought

that Marigny's execution had taken place the day before yesterday.

'And so you, Messire,' said Villebresme, 'were close to the tumbril when the Sire Enguerrand was taken down from it by the gallows?'

'I got up into the tumbril,' replied Machaut, 'and, on the orders of King Louis X, I inquired of the condemned man whether he wished to confess to his crimes of government before he came face to face with his Maker.'

It had, in fact, been Thomas de Marfontaine who had been charged with that duty, but Thomas de Marfontaine had been dead for a long time now.

'And Marigny continued to protest his innocence of all the crimes he had been accused of at his trial; nevertheless, he admitted – and these, his actual words, make his knavery apparent – having "sometimes acted illegitimately for legitimate ends". I asked him what illegitimate acts he meant, and he told me of many, for instance that he had dismissed my father, the Lord of Montargis, in order to give his post to a relative, and that he had removed the late Count of Artois' marriage contract from the royal archives in order to benefit Madame Mahaut and her daughters, the King's daughters-in-law.'

'Oh, he was responsible for that, was he? He actually admitted it,' cried Villebresme. 'This is most important. Put it down Tesson, put it down!'

The notary needed no encouragement, he was busily scratching away. What a splendid witness the Sire de Machaut was.

'And do you know, Messire,' asked Tesson, 'whether the Sire Enguerrand was paid for the theft?'

Machaut hesitated a moment, his grey eyebrows contracted in a frown.

'Most certainly he was,' he replied. 'I asked him if it was true that he had received, as was being said, forty thousand livres from Madame Mahaut for having enabled her to win her case before the King. And Enguerrand bowed his head. It was both in assent and shame. He said: "Messire de Machaut, pray to God for me." It was clearly a confession.'

And Pierre de Machaut folded his arms with an air which was at once contemptuous and triumphant.

'This makes the whole thing perfectly clear,' said Villebresme with satisfaction.

Tesson was busy dotting the i's and crossing the t's of the deposition.

'Have you heard many witnesses so far?' Machaut asked.

'Fourteen, Messire, and we still have twice as many to hear,' said Villebresme. 'But there are eight of us commissioners and two notaries to do the work.'

2

The Plaintiff Conducts the Inquiry

MONSEIGNEUR OF ARTOIS' study was decorated with four big religious frescoes. The painting was rather flat and ochre and blue were the dominant colours. They depicted four tall figures of saints, 'to inspire confidence' as the master of the house put it. On the right, Saint George was killing the dragon; opposite, Saint Maurice, the other patron saint of knights, was wearing a breastplate and an azure surcoat; on the far wall, Saint Peter was hauling his abundant nets from the sea; and on the fourth wall Saint Mary Magdalene, the patroness of female sinners, was wearing nothing but her long golden hair through which her thighs were shamelessly visible. This was the wall towards which Monseigneur Robert's glance most frequently turned.

The beams in the ceiling were also painted in ochre, yellow and blue, with here and there the coats-of-arms of Artois, Beaumont and Valois. The room was furnished with tables covered with brocades, chests on which were scattered rich weapons and heavy candelabra of gilded iron.

Robert rose from his huge chair and handed the text of the depositions he had been reading to the notary.

'Excellent, first-rate documents,' he said; 'particularly the evidence of the Sire de Machaut which looks quite spontaneous, and supports the Count de Bouville on every point. You're clearly a clever man, Tesson, a master of chicanery, and I don't regret having promoted you to your present position. Behind that starveling face of yours there's more guile than in the empty heads of many Masters of Parliament. It must be admitted that God has given you plenty of room in which to lodge your brain.'

The notary smiled obsequiously and bowed his huge head; it was covered with a cap that looked like a big black cabbage. Monseigneur of Artois' mocking compliments might well mean a promise of preferment.

'Is that the whole harvest? Or have you any other news for me today?' Robert asked. 'How far have we got with the former bailiff of Béthune?'

Litigation can become as great a passion as gambling. Robert of Artois was utterly immersed in his lawsuit; his every thought and action were related to the case. Throughout this fortnight his one desire in life was to procure witnesses. He could think of nothing else from dawn to dusk, and even at night he would awaken, his dreams broken into by some sudden inspiration, and ring for his valet Lormet, who came grumbling and sleepy only to be asked: 'You old snorer, didn't you mention the other day a certain Simon Dourin or Dourier, who was a clerk to my grandfather? Do you happen to know if the man's still alive? Try to find out tomorrow.'

At mass, which he attended every day for propriety's sake, he caught himself out praying God to grant him success in his case. But the transition from prayer to scheming came naturally to him, and during the lesson he would be thinking: 'What about that Giles Flamand, who was at one time an equerry to Mahaut and whom she sacked for some mis- demeanour? He might perhaps give evidence on my behalf. I must remember that.'

Never before had he been so assiduous in attending the King's Council, where his advice was much listened to. He went every day to the palace and seemed to be devoting himself to the business of the realm; but, in fact, he did so only to maintain his influence over his brother-in-law Philippe VI, and by making himself indispensable see that people of his own choosing who were likely to be useful to him were appointed to vacant places. He paid particular attention to legal matters in the hope that they might suggest some manoeuvre to him. He scorned everything else.

That in Italy the Guelphs and Ghibellines should still be massacring each other, that Azzo Visconti should have had his uncle, Marco, assassinated and have barricaded himself into the city of Milan against the troops of the Emperor, Louis of Bavaria, and that Verona, Vicenza, Padua and Treviso should have denied the authority of the French-protected Pope – these things Monseigneur of Artois knew and heard, but they made no impression on him.

And when he learned that in England the Queen's party was in difficulties, and that Roger Mortimer's unpopularity was increasing every day, Monseigneur of Artois merely shrugged his shoulders. He was not interested in England, nor in the fact that the wool merchants of Flanders were entering into increasingly close trade relations with the English companies.

But if it was a question of Master Andrieu de Florence, the Canon-Treasurer of Bourges, being given an ecclesiastical preferment, or of the Chevalier de Villebresme being nominated to the Exchequer, these were matters of importance and could brook no delay. The fact was that Master Andrieu, like the Chevalier de Villebresme, was one of the eight commissioners appointed to investigate the Artois case.

Robert had himself suggested the names of the commissioners to Philippe VI. Indeed, he had almost selected them personally. 'Suppose we appointed Bouchart de Montmorency? He has always served us faithfully. Or Pierre de Cugnieres. There's a sensible man everyone respects.' And it was the same for the notaries, of whom Pierre Tesson had been attached first to the Hôtel de Valois for twenty years and then to Robert's household.

Never before had Pierre Tesson felt so important; nor had he ever been treated with such friendly condescension, presented with so many lengths of stuff for dresses for his wife and so many little purses of gold for himself. Nevertheless, he was tired; Robert harassed his employees, and his extraordinary vitality was very exhausting.

Monseigneur Robert seemed almost always to be on his feet, pacing up and down his study between the frescoes of the saints; and Master Tesson could not sit uninvited in the presence of so great a personage as a peer of France. But notaries are in the habit of working sitting down, and Master Tesson suffered greatly from having to support his black leather bag, for he dared not put it down on the brocades. As he extracted documents from it one after the other, he feared that by the time the case was over he would have a stiff back for the rest of his life.

'I have seen the old bailiff Guillaume de la Planche,' he replied to Robert's inquiry; 'at the moment he's a prisoner in the Châtelet. The Dame de Divion had already been to see him; and he has testified as we expected. He requests you not to forget to speak to Messire Mille de Noyers about a pardon. Things look serious for him and he's in grave danger of being hanged.'[11]

'I'll see he's released; let him sleep sound. What about Simon Dourier, have you taken his evidence?'

'I have not actually taken his evidence yet, Monseigneur, but I've approached him. He's prepared to declare to the commissioners that he was present on the day in 1302 when your grandfather, Count Robert II, dictated the letter shortly before his death confirming your right to the inheritance of Artois.'

'Excellent, excellent!'

'I have also promised him that you will take him back into your house and give him a pension.'

'Why was he sacked?' Robert asked.

The notary bent his arm in a gesture of putting money into his pocket.

'To hell with that!' cried Robert. 'He's an old man now and has had time to repent. I'll give him a hundred livres a year, lodging and clothes.'

'Manessier de Lannoy will confirm that the stolen documents were burned by Madame Mahaut. His house, as you know, was on the point of being sold to pay his debts to the Lombards; he's most grateful to you for having kept a roof over his head.'

'I'm a kind man; it's not sufficiently well known,' said Robert. 'But what about Juvigny, Enguerrand's former valet?'

The notary bowed his head in failure.

'I can get nothing out of him,' he said; 'he absolutely refuses; he pretends he doesn't know or can't remember.'

'What!' cried Robert. 'I myself went to the Louvre, where he enjoys a pension for doing damned little, and had a talk with him. You mean to tell me he refuses to remember? See to it that he's put to the question. The sight of the pincers may well encourage him to tell the truth.'

'Monseigneur,' replied the notary sadly, 'the accused can be tortured, but not witnesses as yet.'

'Well, you can at least let him know that unless his memory comes back to him, I'll have his pension stopped. I may be kind, but it's all the more reason that people should help me.'

He picked up a bronze candelabra, which must have weighed all of fifteen pounds, and tossed it from one hand to the other as he walked up and down. The notary thought how unjust it was of God to give so much strength of muscle to people who used it merely for their own pleasure, and so little to poor notaries who had to carry heavy leather bags.

'Are you not afraid, Monseigneur, that if you cut off his pension, he'll manage to get it back from Countess Mahaut?'

Robert came to a halt.

'Mahaut?' he cried. 'She can't do anything now; she's afraid, she daren't show her face. There's been no sign of her at Court recently. She's keeping quiet, and she's shaking in her shoes, because she knows she's lost.'

'God willing, Monseigneur, God willing! We shall win, of course; but there are still a few little difficulties . . .'

Tesson hesitated to go on, not from fear of what he had to say, but because of the weight of his bag. It meant standing for another five or ten minutes.

'I have been informed,' he went on, 'that our inquiry agents in Artois have been followed, and that our witnesses have been visited by others besides our own people. There has also been a certain amount of coming and going of messengers recently between Madame Mahaut's house and Dijon. Couriers wearing the Burgundy livery have been seen going in at her door.'

Mahaut was clearly trying to reinforce her alliance with Duke Eudes. But what support had the Burgundy party at Court? There was Queen Jeanne the Lame's of course, which was far from negligible.

'But I have the King on my side,' said Robert, 'and the bitch will lose, Tesson, I can promise you that.'

'All the same, we shall have to produce the documents, Monseigneur. Mere statements can always be countered by other statements. And the sooner we can do it the better.'

He had excellent personal reasons for stressing it. A notary might make his fortune by tampering with witnesses, not to speak of extorting evidence by threats and bribes, but he also ran the risk of the Châtelet and even of the wheel. Tesson had no wish to exchange places with the former bailiff of Béthune.

'You shall have your documents! You shall have them, I tell you! Do you think laying one's hands on them is as easy as all that? By the way, Tesson,' Robert went on, suddenly pointing to the black leather bag, 'you have noted in Count de Bouville's deposition that the marriage contract was signed by twelve peers. Why did you record that?'

'Because the witness said so, Monseigneur.'

'Yes, I see. That's very important,' Robert said thoughtfully.

'Why, Monseigneur?'

'Why? Because I'm waiting for the copy of the contract from the Artois archives. It's to be handed over to me, and at a very high price too. If the names of the twelve peers aren't there, it obviously won't be authentic. Who were the peers at that time? The dukes and counts are easy enough, but who were the spiritual peers? You see how careful one's got to be?'

The notary gazed at Robert with mingled anxiety and admiration.

'Do you realize, Monseigneur, that if you were not so great a lord, you would have made the best notary in the kingdom? I intend no offence, Monseigneur, no offence!'

Robert rang to have his visitor shown out.

Hardly had the notary gone, when Robert left the room by a door opening in Mary Magdalene's stomach – a little decorative fantasy which gave him much pleasure – and hastened to his wife's apartments. Having sent away her ladies-in-waiting, he said: 'Jeanne, my dear countess, tell La Divion to stop work on the marriage contract: it must include the names of the twelve peers of the year '82. Do you happen to know who they were? No, nor do I! How can we find out without arousing suspicion? What a lot of time wasted!'

The Countess of Beaumont looked up at her husband with her splendid, calm blue eyes. She was smiling a little. Her giant was uneasy again. She said quietly: 'At Saint-Denis, my dear, at Saint-Denis, in the abbey registers. The names of the peers are bound to be there. I'll send Brother Henry, my confessor; he can pretend he's engaged on some piece of historical research.'

Robert's broad face expressed at once tenderness, gratitude and a certain amusement.

'Do you realize, my dear,' he said, bowing with rather over-elaborate grace, 'that if you were not so great a lady, you would have made the best notary in the kingdom?'

They smiled at each other, and the Countess of Beaumont, who had been born Jeanne of Valois, read in Robert's eyes a promise that he would visit her bed that night.

3

The Forgers

WHEN A MAN SETS out on the path of deception, he always thinks the journey will be short and easy. The first obstacles are surmounted without difficulty and indeed with a certain pleasure. But soon the forest thickens and the way becomes uncertain, branching off into many a track that gets lost in a bog. He stumbles at each step, flounders, sinks into the mire. He grows angry and exhausts himself in vain attempts to find his way; but each attempt turns out to be merely one imprudence the more.

At first sight, the forging of an old document appears to be a comparatively simple matter. You merely require a piece of parchment that has been turned yellow in the sun and rubbed with ash, the hand of a suborned clerk, and a few seals applied to silk laces. None of these should need much time or expenditure.

And yet Robert of Artois had temporarily been compelled to stop the work on his father's marriage contract. Nor was this due only to the search for the names of the twelve peers:

the contract had to be drawn up in Latin, and there were few clerks who still knew the formulas used in princely marriage contracts in old days. Queen Clémence of Hungary's former almoner, who was knowledgeable in these matters, was taking his time in supplying the proper opening and closing phrases; and he could not be pressed for fear of arousing his suspicions.

There was also the matter of the seals.

'Have them copied from the old seals by a die-sinker,' Robert said.

But the die-sinkers were sworn men. And, when asked, the Court die-sinker declared it to be impossible to copy a seal with precision; no two dies were ever completely identical, and a seal impressed with a false die could readily be detected by an expert; moreover, the original dies were always destroyed at their owners' deaths.

Robert had therefore to procure old deeds with the seals he required, detach them – which was far from easy – and transfer them to the forged document.

Robert told La Divion to concentrate her efforts on a document which was simpler to manufacture but of no less importance.

On June 28th, 1302, before leaving to join the Army in Flanders, where he had died from twenty lance-thrusts, old Count Robert II had put his affairs in order and confirmed in a document the dispositions he had made bequeathing the County of Artois to his grandson.

'And it is true, every single witness will confirm it!' Robert told his wife. 'Simon Dourier even remembers which of my grandfather's vassals were present, and of which bailiwicks the seals were attached. We're doing nothing more than establishing the truth!'

Simon Dourier, who had been notary to Count Robert II, provided the general tenor of the document in so far as he could remember it. The writing was done by one of the Countess of Beaumont's clerks, called Dufour. But Dufour's text had too many erasures, and his hand might well be recognized.

La Division went into Artois to take the text to a certain Robert Rossignol, who had been clerk to Thierry d'Hirson; he recopied the document, not with a goose-quill, but with a bronze pen, the better to disguise his writing.

Rossignol, who was promised as a reward the price of a journey to Santiago de Compostela, to which he had vowed to make a pilgrimage if he recovered from an illness, had a son-in-law called Jean Oliette, who was something of an expert in detaching seals. The family was clearly most resourceful. Oliette showed La Division how to set about it.

She returned to Paris and was immediately closeted with Madame de Beaumont and a servant, Jeannette la Mesquine.[12] The three women, with the help of a hot razor, and a horsehair steeped in a liquor that prevented its breaking, set about detaching the wax seals from old documents. They first split the seal in half; then they heated one half and reapplied it to the other over the silk lace or the parchment appendix of the forged document; and finally they heated the edge of the wax a little to remove the traces of the cut.

Jeanne of Beaumont, Jeanne de Division and Jeanne la Mesquine treated more than forty seals in this manner, never working twice in the same place, but sometimes hiding in a room in the Hôtel d' Artois, sometimes in the Hôtel de l'Aigle, or again in various country houses.

Robert would sometimes come to see how they were getting on.

'So my three Jeannes are hard at it!' he would say good-humouredly.

Of the three, the Countess of Beaumont was by far the cleverest.

'A woman's fingers are fairy fingers,' Robert would say, courteously kissing his wife's hand.

But it was not only a matter of being able to detach seals; the right seals had to be procured.

There was little difficulty in finding Philip the Fair's seal, for there were many royal decrees available. Robert got the Bishop of Evreux to send him a document concerning his lordship of Conches on the plea that he needed to consult it. He never returned it.

In Artois, La Division set her friends Rossignol and Oliette, and also two servants, Marie the White and Marie the Black, to seek out old seals of bailiwicks and lordships.

They had soon acquired all the necessary seals save one, the most important of all, that of the late Count Robert II. This might seem absurd, but the fact was that all the family documents were in the Artois archives under the guardian-ship of Mahaut's clerks, and Robert, who had been a minor at the time of his grandfather's death, possessed none at all.

Through a cousin, La Division approached a man called Ourson the One-Eyed, who owned a trade-licence issued by the late Count and sealed with his seal 'in token of good faith'. He was prepared to part with it for three hundred livres. The Countess of Beaumont had told La Division that the document must be acquired no matter what the cost. But La Division had nothing like that sum of money in Artois; and Messire Ourson the One-Eyed was suspicious and refused to part with his licence merely on a promise.

Lacking the necessary resources, La Divion remembered she had a husband living quietly in the castellany of Béthune. He had never shown any sign of jealousy even when Bishop Thierry was alive. She decided to go to see him. There were already too many people in the secret. But what was she to do? Her husband refused to lend the money; but he consented to part temporarily with a good horse he had ridden in tournaments, and Messire Ourson agreed to accept it as security. La Divion also left with him such pieces of jewellery as she had with her.

La Divion was certainly doing her best! Time, trouble, intrigue and travel – she spared herself none of them. Nor was she economical of her powers of persuasion. She was, too, being particularly careful not to mislay things, and she always slept with her keys under her pillow.

Slitting the late Count Robert's seal with a razor was an anxious process. To think that a single seal could cost three hundred livres! And if it happened to break, how could another be obtained?

Monseigneur Robert was becoming rather impatient. The witnesses had all been interrogated; and the King kept asking him, though still with no more than friendly interest, if the documents to whose existence he had sworn would soon be available.

Two days more, one day more – and Monseigneur Robert's impatience would be satisfied.

4

The Guests at Reuilly

DURING THE SUMMER, whenever the cares of State and the anxieties of his lawsuit left him the time, Robert of Artois liked to spend the weekends at Reuilly, a castle belonging to his wife through her Valois inheritance.

He enjoyed the freshness of the woods and the fields that lay about the castle, and it was here that he kept his hawks. He had a large household, for many young nobles, before attaining to knighthood, took service with Robert as equerries, cupbearers, or gentlemen of the bedchamber. If you failed to get a place in the King's household, you got your influential relatives to recommend you to the Count of Artois, and having been accepted you tried to distinguish yourself by your zeal. To hold the bridle of Monseigneur's horse, hand him his leather hawking-glove, serve him at table, or tip the ewer of water over his powerful hands before meals, was to advance yourself a little in the hierarchy of the State; while to shake his pillow to awaken him in the morning, was almost like shaking God's own pillow itself, since

Monseigneur, as everyone knew, ruled the roost at Court.

On this Saturday at the beginning of September, Robert had invited a number of friends to Reuilly; among them were the Sire de Brécy, the Chevalier de Hangest, who was a member of Parliament, the Archdeacon of Avranches, and the old Count de Bouville, who was half blind, and for whom he had sent a litter. He had organized hawking for those who liked getting up early in the morning.

His guests were now, however, assembled in the Justice Room. Robert himself, dressed in country clothes, was sitting relaxed in his great chair. His wife, the Countess of Beaumont, was also present, as was the notary Tesson, who had placed his writing-board and pens on a table.

'My good lords, my friends,' he said, 'I have requested your company so that you may give me your counsel.'

People are always flattered by being asked for their advice. The noble young pages were offering the guests pre-prandial drinks, aromatic wines, and handing round peeled and sugared almonds in silver-gilt dishes. They were taking care to be precise and silent in their duties, and were watching the proceedings with wide-eyed attention for they were garnering memories. In after years they would say: 'I was present that day at Monseigneur Robert's; the Count de Bouville was there, and he had been Chamberlain to King Philip the Fair . . .'

Robert was talking quietly and seriously: a certain Dame de Divion, whom he scarcely knew, had come to him with a document, which she had acquired among others from Bishop Thierry d'Hirson, whose mistress she had been, he added lowering his voice. La Divion wanted money for it, of course – all these women were the same. But the document appeared to be of some importance and, before acquiring it, Robert wished to make sure that he was not being imposed on, that the document was genuine, could be put in as evidence in his lawsuit, and that it was no forgery fabricated simply to extract money from him. He therefore wanted his friends, who were wiser and cleverer than he was in such matters, to examine it.

From time to time Robert glanced at his wife for reassurance as to the effect he was producing. Jeanne encouraged him with an almost imperceptible nod of the head. She admired her husband's remarkable astuteness and his ability to appear ingenuous in order to deceive. He was pretending to be uneasy and suspicious. But there was no doubt that his guests would approve so evidently authentic a document; and once they had approved it, they would certainly not go back on their opinion, and the news would spread through Court and Parliament that Robert possessed proof of his rights.

'Bring in this Dame de Divion,' said Robert, looking severe.

Jeanne de Divion came in looking very shy and provincial. The triangle of her face with its dark and shadowed eyes was framed in a linen wimple. She had no need to pretend to be nervous; she was so.

She drew a roll of parchment from a cloth bag. There were several seals depending from it. She handed it to Robert, who unrolled it, looked at it for a moment and passed it to the notary.

'Examine the seals, Master Tesson.'

The notary checked that the seals were properly attached to the silk laces and bent his huge black cap and crescent profile over the vellum.

'It is without doubt the seal of your grandfather, the late Count, Monseigneur,' he said with conviction.

'Have a look at it, my good lords,' said Robert.

They passed the document from hand to hand. The Sire de Brécy confirmed that the seals of the bailiwicks of Arras and Béthune were genuine. The Count de Bouville held the parchment close to his dim eyes; he could see nothing but a green blur at the bottom of the document and, as he felt the smooth wax with his finger, there were tears in his eyes and he murmured: 'Ah, the green seal of my good master, Philip the Fair!'

Everyone was much moved and for a moment they all fell silent out of respect for the old servant of the Crown's long memories. The young pages would not forget that moment.

La Division, who was standing to one side against the wall, exchanged a discreet glance with the Countess of Beaumont.

'Now read it to us, Master Tesson,' Robert ordered.

The notary resumed the parchment and began:

'"We, Robert of France, Peer and Count of Artois . . ."'

It was the usual opening formula; the guests listened calmly.

'". . . hereby, declare in the presence of the Lords of Saint-Venant, Saint-Paul, Waillepayelle, knights, who will seal this with their seals, and in that of Master Thierry d'Hirson, my clerk . . ."'

One or two of those present glanced at La Division, who bowed her head.

'Very, very clever to have mentioned Bishop Thierry,' thought Robert; 'it will help to support the evidence as to the part he played; it all fits in very well.'

"'... that on the occasion of the marriage of our son, Philippe, we settled our county upon him, reserving to ourselves the right to its enjoyment during our lifetime, and that our daughter, Mahaut, consented to this and renounced her rights to the said county . . .'"

'But this is of capital importance!' cried Robert. 'It's a great deal more than I ever expected! No one ever told me that Mahaut had actually given her consent! You see what a villain she is, my friends! Go on, Master Tesson.'

The guests were much impressed. They nodded their heads and looked at each other. It was undoubtedly a most important document.

"'... and now that God has summoned to himself our dear and beloved son, Count Philippe, we pray our Lord the King, if we should suffer God's will in the wars, graciously to see that the heirs of our son be not disinherited . . .'"

The heads all nodded in dignified approval; the Chevalier de Hangest, who was a member of Parliament, spread wide his hands and, turning to Robert, seemed to be saying: 'Monseigneur, your case is won.'

The notary concluded, "'... and we have sealed this with our seal, in our Hôtel d'Arras, this twenty-eighth day of June in the year of grace 1322.'"

Robert could not repress a start. The Countess of Beaumont turned pale. La Divion felt as if she were dying with her back to the wall.

Nor were they alone in having heard the words 1322. The guests turned in surprise to the notary, who was looking rather panic-stricken.

'Did you say 1322?' asked the Chevalier de Hangest. 'Surely you must mean 1302, the year of Count Robert's death?'

Master Tesson wished he could plead that his reading was at fault; but the text was there, under his eyes, and bore only too clearly the date 1322. They would most certainly ask to examine the document again. How could it have happened? Oh, how angry Monseigneur Robert would be! And what a business he, Tesson, had allowed himself to get mixed up in! The Châtelet, that's where it would all end for him, in the Châtelet!

He did what he could to repair the disaster. 'It's not very well written,' he stuttered. 'Oh, yes, of course, it's 1302 that's meant . . .'

And he quickly dipped his pen in the ink and corrected the figure to the right date.

'Have you the right to make such a correction?' said the Chevalier de Hangest, sounding rather shocked.

'Certainly, Messire,' said Tesson; 'there are two dots under the date and it is the usual practice for a notary to correct ill-written words under which dots have been placed.'

'That's perfectly correct,' the Archdeacon of Avranches confirmed.

But the incident had destroyed all the good impression the reading of the document had made.

Robert summoned a page, whispered to him to hurry dinner along, and then did his best to start the conversation going again.

'Well, Master Tesson, so in your view the document is genuine?'

'Certainly, Monseigneur, certainly,' Tesson replied quickly.

'And what do you think, Messire Archdeacon?'

'I think it perfectly genuine.'

'You ought perhaps,' said the Sire de Brécy in a friendly

way, 'to have it compared with other of the late Count of Artois' documents drawn up in the same year.'

'And how do you suppose I can do that, my dear friend,' replied Robert, 'when my Aunt Mahaut has them all in her archives? I believe the document to be genuine. You can't invent a thing like that! I didn't know the facts myself, in particular that Mahaut had renounced her rights.'

At that moment there was a sound of horns in the courtyard. Robert clapped his hands.

'They're announcing the water, Messeigneurs! Let us go and wash our hands, and then to dinner.'

Robert was walking up and down the Countess' room in a fury, making the boards tremble beneath his feet.

'And you read it! And Tesson read it! And La Division read it! And none of you had the wit to see this frightful mistake which endangers our whole plan.'

'But you read the document yourself over and over again, my dear,' the Countess replied calmly, 'and you seemed delighted with it.'

'Yes, of course I read it! And I didn't see the mistake either! To read something to yourself and to read it aloud are two quite different things. Besides, how should I possibly imagine that anyone could make such a ridiculous mistake as that! That fool of a notary! And that other fool who wrote the document! What's he called? Rossignol? He pretends he's capable of writing a document, extracts more money from you than it would take to build a house, and then he can't even put the right date on it. I'll have that Rossignol seized, and whipped till he bleeds!'

'You'll have to fetch him from Santiago de Compostela

to which he's gone on pilgrimage at your expense, my dear.'

'Well, when he comes back then!'

'Aren't you afraid he may talk a bit too much during the whipping?'

Robert shrugged his shoulders.

'It's damned lucky it happened here and not while the document was being read out to Parliament! You must keep a closer watch on the other documents, my dear, and make sure there are no more errors of that kind.'

Madame de Beaumont thought it unfair that her husband's anger should fall on her. She was as much concerned at the mistake as he was, and just as sorry for it, but after all the trouble she had gone to, and with her hands flayed from cutting the wax of so many seals, she thought Robert might really exercise a little self-control and not blame her.

'After all, Robert,' she said, 'why are you so determined on this lawsuit? What's the point of running all these risks, and making me and so many members of your household run them too? We shall end only by being convicted of perjury and forgery.'

'This is not perjury! And it's not forgery either!' Robert shouted. 'I am going to bring the real and hidden truth out into the light of day!'

'Very well, it's the truth,' she said; 'but you must admit that the truth in this instance makes no very handsome appearance. In this guise, there is a grave risk that it will not be recognized! You've already everything you could possibly want, my dear. You're a peer of the realm, the King's brother-in-law through me, and all-powerful in the Council; your revenues are enormous, and the dowry and inheritance

I brought you make you the envy of all. Why not leave Artois alone? Don't you think we've already staked enough on a gamble that may cost us so dear?'

'My dear, your argument is all wrong and I'm surprised to hear you talking like this when you're usually so sensible. I may be the premier baron of France, but I'm a baron without lands. My little County of Beaumont, which was given me only in compensation, is a domain of the Crown. I have no power over it and am merely handed the revenues. I have been made a peer because, as you have just said, the King is your brother. It may well be that God will give him long to reign over us, but no king is eternal. We have seen enough of them die in our time! Suppose Philippe died, would I be given the Regency? If that wicked lame woman, his wife, who hates us both, became Regent with the support of Burgundy, what power would I have? Would the Treasury even continue to pay me my revenues? I have no ruling powers, nor power to administer justice; I have no great vassals who are really mine; I have no lands from which to draw men of my own who owe me complete obedience and whom I can place in jobs. Who are the men in high positions today? Men from Valois, Anjou, Maine, the fiefs and apanages of your father, Charles. Where do I find my own servants? Among them. I repeat, I have nothing of my own. I cannot raise enough banners to make people tremble before me. Real power lies only in the number of castellanies one commands and from which one can raise fighting men. My fortune depends on myself alone, on the strength of my arm and the place I occupy in the Council; my credit is founded merely on favour, and favour lasts only as long as God wills. We have sons – think of them, my dear. And since we cannot yet tell whether they have inherited my brains, I should much like to leave them the coronet of Artois, which is after all their just inheritance.'

Never had he expressed his real thoughts at such length. The Countess of Beaumont forgot her irritation of a moment before and saw her husband in a new light. This was not the cunning giant who delighted in intrigue, the bad hat capable of every kind of roguery, the seducer of women, whether noble, bourgeoises or servant girls, but a true great lord talking logically about the basis of his power. When, in the past, Charles of Valois had negotiated for a kingdom, an emperor's crown or sovereign alliances for his daughters, he used to justify his actions with similar arguments.

A page knocked at the door: the Dame de Division was urgently demanding an interview with the Count.

'What the hell does she want now? Isn't she afraid I'll strangle her? Send her in.'

La Division came in, looking very pale. She had just heard that her two servants in Artois, Marie the White and Marie the Black, who had helped her buy the seals for the forged document, had been arrested by the Countess Mahaut's sergeants-at-arms.

5

Mahaut and Beatrice

'To HELL WITH THE lot of you and may the Devil burn your guts!' cried Countess Mahaut. 'What's the use of my having those two women arrested, if they're immediately set free again? We could have got all the information we want out of them.'

The Countess Mahaut was at her Château of Conflans on the Seine, by Vincennes, and she had just heard that La Division's two servants, who had been arrested by the bailiff of Arras on her orders, had been set free. She was furiously angry and, for the moment, 'the lot of you' at whom she was directing her curses was represented by Beatrice d'Hirson, her lady-in-waiting. The fact was that the bailiff of Arras was Beatrice's uncle, a younger brother of the late Bishop Thierry.

'The servants were released on an order from the King presented by two sergeants-at-arms, Madame,' Beatrice replied calmly.

'To hell with that! What the Devil does the King care about two servants employed in a kitchen in an Arras suburb? They were released on orders from Robert who went to the King to demand their freedom. Did anybody even take the names of the sergeants and make sure they really were the King's officers?'

'Their names are Maciot l'Allemant and Jean Le Servoisier, Madame,' replied Beatrice still quite unmoved.

'Two of Robert's sergeants-at-arms! I know that Maciot l'Allemant; he's the man my scoundrel of a nephew employs on all his wicked work. Besides, how did Robert know that two of La Divion's servants had been arrested?' Mahaut asked, looking suspiciously at her lady-in-waiting.

'Monseigneur Robert has a considerable intelligence system in Artois; you know that, Madame.'

'I can only hope,' said Mahaut, 'that he has found no recruits to it among the people about me. In any case, to serve me ill is to betray me! I'm betrayed on all sides. Since Thierry's death, one might well suspect that you're none of you loyal to me any more. You're ungrateful, all of you! And when I think how generous I've been! For fifteen years I've treated you as my own daughter.'

Beatrice d'Hirson lowered her long black lashes and stared vaguely at the flagstones. Her smooth, amber-complexioned face and the well-marked curve of her lips betrayed no expression of any kind whatever, neither humility, nor rebellion, though there was perhaps something a little false about the lowered lashes concealing her eyes.

'Your Uncle Denis, whom I made my treasurer to please Thierry, robs me right and left. Where are the accounts for the produce of my cherry orchard which he sold this summer on the Paris market? I'll have his accounts audited one of these days. You've got everything, lands, houses and castles, all bought out of the money you make out of me. And then your fool of an Uncle Pierre, whom I made bailiff because I thought he was too stupid to be anything else but loyal to me, can't even keep the doors of my prisons shut! People just walk out as they please, as if they were inns or brothels!'

'How could my uncle disobey the King's order, Madame?'

'What did that whore's servants have to say for themselves during the two days they were in jail? Were they made to talk? Did your uncle put them to the question?'

'But Madame,' said Beatrice in her drawling voice, 'he could hardly do that without a legal order. Look what happened to your bailiff of Béthune.'

Mahaut brushed the argument aside with a wave of her huge hand.

'None of you serve me loyally any more,' she said, 'and, if it comes to that, you've always served me ill, the lot of you!'

Mahaut was growing older. Age had left its mark on that giant body of hers; there was a rough white down on her cheeks which grew empurpled at the least cross; and the blood mounting from chest to throat sometimes looked like a red bib. She had been seriously ill several times during the last year. It had been a disastrous time in every way.

Since the perjury at Amiens and the commission of inquiry had been set up, her temper had been appalling. Her mind was becoming senile and she began to lump all her troubles indiscriminately together. If a frost came to spoil the roses she grew by the thousand in her gardens, or some mechanical fault affected the hydraulic machines that supplied the water for the artificial cascades at her Château d'Hesdin, her fury fell like a hurricane on gardeners, mechanics, pages and Beatrice alike.

'And those paintings, completed scarcely ten years ago!' she would cry, pointing to the frescoes in the gallery at Conflans. 'Forty-eight livres parisis I paid that painter your Uncle Denis summoned from Brussels. He guaranteed he'd use only the best colours![13] Not ten years ago, and look at them now! The silver on the helmets is tarnished already and at the bottom the paint's peeling off the wall! Do you call that sound honest work?'

Beatrice was bored. Mahaut's suite was numerous enough but it consisted entirely of people older than Beatrice. At the moment Mahaut was keeping herself rather aloof from the Court of France, which was entirely subject to Robert's influence. In Paris and at Saint-Germain the Makeshift King was continually holding tournaments, festivals and banquets in honour of the Queen's birthday, the departure of the King of Bohemia, or for no reason at all, except his own pleasure. Mahaut scarcely went to Court at all and, when she did, it was to put in only a brief appearance because her rank as a peer of the realm obliged her to do so. She was no longer of an age to dance, nor of a humour to watch others enjoying themselves, particularly at a Court where she was treated so ill. She no longer even cared to stay in Paris, in her house in the Rue Mauconseil; she lived in retirement within the walls of Conflans, or at Hesdin which she had restored after Robert's devastation of it in 1316.

Tyrannical, now that she no longer had a lover – the last had been Bishop Thierry d'Hirson whom she had shared with La Division, which was why Mahaut hated the woman so much – and fearful of being suddenly taken ill in the night, she insisted on Beatrice sleeping at the farther end of her room, where the atmosphere was stagnant with the accumulated odours of age, medicaments and food. For Mahaut ate as much as ever, and was liable to be seized with a monstrous hunger at any hour of the day or night. The hangings and carpets smelt of venison, jugged hare, and garlic broth. Frequent fits of indigestion obliged her to call in physicians, apothecaries and surgeon-barbers; and potions and infusions of herbs followed the spiced meats. Ah, indeed, where were the good times now, the days when Beatrice had assisted Mahaut to poison kings?

Beatrice herself was beginning to feel that time was passing. Her youth was over. She was thirty-three, the age at which every woman, even the most perverse, knows she has reached a watershed in life, and begins to think of the past with nostalgia and of the future with anxiety. But Beatrice was still beautiful; she found proof of it in men's eyes, her favourite mirrors. But she knew, too, that she no longer had quite that perfect golden-fruit complexion which had made her so attractive at twenty; her dark eyes, which showed almost no white between the lashes, were less brilliant when she awakened in the morning; and her hips were spreading a little so that she had to alter her dresses. The day had come when she could not afford to waste time.

But how could she escape to meet a lover when Mahaut insisted she should sleep in her room? How could she go at midnight to some secret house to attend a black mass and enjoy the spice of pleasure in the practices of the sabbath?

'What are you dreaming about?' the Countess asked sharply.

'I'm not dreaming, Madame,' she replied, gazing at Mahaut

with her liquid eyes. 'I'm merely thinking you might find someone who would serve you better than I do. I'm thinking of getting married.'

It was a sly threat and its effect was immediate.

'And a fine match you'd be!' cried Mahaut. 'Ah, the man who takes you for wife will have done well for himself! He'll have to go searching the beds of all my equerries for your maidenhead, and then search them again for his horns!'

'At my age, Madame, and as you've kept me unmarried to serve you, a maidenhead is more of a misfortune than a virtue. In any case, it's a great deal commoner than are the houses and property I shall bring my husband.'

'If you keep them, my girl! If I let you keep them! For they've been shorn from my back!'

Beatrice smiled and once again veiled her dark eyes with her lashes.

'Oh, Madame,' she said sweetly, 'you surely wouldn't take back your presents from someone who has served you in all the secret things we have done together?'

Mahaut looked at her with hatred. 'The bitch has a hold over me,' she thought.

Beatrice knew very well when it was necessary to remind Mahaut of the royal corpses that lay between them, of the Hutin's sugared almonds, of the poison on the lips of little Jean I; and she knew very well, too, how the scene would end: there would be a rush of blood to the Countess' face and the red bib would rise in her bull-neck.

'You shan't marry! Just look at the harm you're doing me by arguing, and content yourself with that!' said Mahaut, collapsing into a chair. 'The blood's making my ears sing. I shall have to be bled again.'

'Don't you think, Madame, that it's because you eat so much you have to be bled so often?'

'I shall eat what I please,' shouted Mahaut, 'and when I please! I don't need a fool like you to tell me what's good for me. Go and get me some English cheese! And some wine! Hurry!'

There was no English cheese left in the larder; the last consignment was finished.

'Who's eaten it? I'm being robbed! Bring me a pie then!'

'All right, you shall have a pie! Stuff yourself and die!' thought Beatrice, as she set down the dish.

Mahaut seized a large slice and bit into it. A sudden crack rang through her head, but it was not caused by the crust; a front tooth, rotten at the neck, had broken.

Mahaut's bloodshot grey eyes opened a little wider, and an expression of astonishment swept over her face. The slice of pie in one hand, and a glass of wine in the other, she sat with her mouth open, the half-broken tooth sticking out horizontally from her lip. She put down the glass, painlessly pulled out the broken tooth, and stared at it in childish horror. With the tip of her tongue she probed the gap in her jaw, the rough, sore surface of the root. She had lost many teeth, including all her back teeth, but never in this way. They had disintegrated bit by bit and caused abscesses, till the rotten teeth had been extracted, cloves being inserted into her gums. But this time it was a front tooth, a piece of herself; she had been accustomed to seeing it; and now, suddenly, it had gone. The little piece of yellow ivory held in her fat fingers seemed the very symbol of old age. She heard a gasp from Beatrice and looked up. Her lady-in-waiting was standing there with arms akimbo and shoulders shaking, unable to contain her laughter.

Quickly, before Beatrice could escape, Mahaut slapped her face hard, twice. Beatrice's laughter ceased abruptly; her long lashes parted to reveal a wicked glint in her dark eyes, but it lasted only a second.

That night, as Beatrice helped the Countess to undress, peace seemed to have been restored between them. Automatically running her tongue over the stump the surgeon-barber had filed down, Mahaut reverted to her obsession and said: 'Don't you see why I was so anxious those two women should be questioned? I'm convinced La Divion is helping Robert to forge documents, and I want him to be caught red-handed.'

But Beatrice, now that she had been slapped, had other plans.

'May I make a suggestion, Madame? Will you listen to it?'

'Of course, my girl, speak out, speak out! I'm quick to anger and have a ready hand; but I trust you, you know that.'

'Well, Madame, the difficulties all arise out of my Uncle Thierry's will, and the fact that you've refused to pay over to La Divion the moneys he left her. She's a wicked woman, of course, and doesn't deserve it. But you've made an enemy of her, and there can be no doubt that she was told certain secrets by my uncle which she's now selling to Monseigneur Robert. It was certainly lucky I was able to empty the safe at Hirson in which my uncle kept some of your papers. Think of the use that wretched woman could have put them to. If you'd given her a little money and some lands her lips would have been sealed.'

'Yes, indeed,' said Mahaut, 'I may have made a mistake there. But you must admit she's only a whore who went and took her pleasure between a bishop's sheets and then got herself put into his will as if she were a legal wife. All the same, I may well have made a mistake.'

Beatrice was helping Mahaut to take off her shift. The giantess had her huge arms raised above her head, revealing the sorry white hair in her armpits. There was a hump of fat at her neck, as on the withers of an ox. Her breasts were heavy, monstrous, pendulous.

'She's old,' thought Beatrice, 'and she's going to die – but the question is when? Till her dying day I shall have to dress and undress her hideous body and spend all my nights with her. And what will happen to me when she's dead? No doubt Monseigneur Robert will win his case with the King's support. Mahaut's household will be dispersed.'

When Mahaut had put on her nightgown, Beatrice said: 'If you offered to pay La Divion the legacy she's claiming, and even perhaps a little more, you'd win her over to your side and, if she's been wickedly intriguing with Monseigneur Robert, you'd find out what they've been doing and thereby gain the advantage.'

'You may be right,' said Mahaut. 'It's well worth spending a thousand livres for my county, even if they're the wages of sin. But how can I approach the whore? She lives in Robert's house, and he no doubt has her closely watched – and probably sleeps with her, too, for that matter, for he's always lacked taste. If she's approached he must not be allowed to get wind of it.'

'I'm quite prepared to undertake it, Madame. I'll go and see her and have a talk with her. After all, I'm Thierry's niece; he might easily have asked me to help her in some way.'

Mahaut gazed attentively at the calm, almost smiling face of her lady-in-waiting.

'You're running a considerable risk,' she said. 'If Robert ever came to hear of it . . .'

'I know, Madame, I know the risks I'm running; but they don't frighten me,' said Beatrice, as she drew the embroidered coverlets over the Countess.

'You're a good girl,' said Mahaut. 'I hope your cheek isn't smarting too much?'

'It is, Madame; but, as always, it's at your service.'

6

Beatrice and Robert

LORMET OPENED THE tradesmen's door to her, as if she were merely a second-hand clothes-dealer or a seamstress come to deliver an order. Indeed, dressed in a light cloak of grey cloth, of which the hood covered her hair, Beatrice d'Hirson looked like any ordinary bourgeoise.

She recognized Monseigneur of Artois' valet at once, for he was the man who served his master in his secret enterprises; but she showed no surprise, nor did she on being led across the two courtyards, past the kitchens, and up towards the private apartments.

Lormet went first; he was rather short of breath these days, and every now and then looked back over his shoulder, to glance suspiciously at her. She was decidedly too beautiful and, as she followed him with a smooth, swaying step, she seemed not in the least intimidated.

'What are Mahaut's people doing here?' Lormet wondered disapprovingly. 'What has this bitch come to cook up on our stoves? Ah, Monseigneur Robert is very imprudent to let her in! Madame Mahaut knows how to set about things; she's certainly sent him a good-looker!'

They passed through a corridor with an arched roof, a hanging tapestry and a low door that opened on well-oiled hinges. Beatrice saw the three walls frescoed with Saint George, his lance in rest, Saint Maurice leaning on his sword and Saint Peter hauling in his nets.

Monseigneur Robert was standing in the middle of the room, his legs wide apart, his arms akimbo, and his chin resting on his collar.

Beatrice lowered her long lashes, and felt a delicious tremor of mingled fear and pleasure.

'I don't suppose you expected to see me,' said Robert of Artois.

'Oh, yes, Monseigneur,' Beatrice replied in her drawling voice, 'it was you I came in the hope of seeing.'

For the last week, she had been sending her emissaries openly enough to La Divion and the whole household must have known what was going on.

Nevertheless Robert seemed rather surprised.

'Well, what have you come for? To tell me of the death of my Aunt Mahaut?'

'Oh, no Monseigneur!' said Beatrice. 'Madame Mahaut has merely lost a tooth.'

'That's good news anyway,' said Robert, 'but it hardly seems worth a visit. Has she sent you with a message? Does she realize she's lost her case and does she want to negotiate with me? Because I shall not do so!'

'Oh, no, Monsiegneur, Madame Mahaut has no thought of negotiating because she knows she's going to win.'

'Does she, indeed! And against fifty-five witnesses all of

whom are prepared to swear to the thefts and frauds she has committed!'

Beatrice smiled.

'Madame Mahaut will have at least sixty witnesses, Monseigneur, to prove that yours are lying, and they will have been just as well paid too.'

'Oh, so that's it, is it? You've gained entry here to beard me, have you? Your mistress' witnesses will count for nothing against mine, because mine will be supported by documentary evidence which I shall produce!'

'Oh, really, Monseigneur?' said Beatrice, her voice hypocritically respectful. 'So Madame Mahaut was wrong, was she? She was so surprised to hear that members of your household had recently been searching Artois for old seals.'

'They've been looking for seals,' said Robert irritably, 'because my new chancellor is trying to lay his hands on all old documents so as to put some sort of order into my archives.'

'Oh, really, Monseigneur' said Beatrice.

'How dare you question me? I'm asking you what the devil you're doing here Have you come to bribe my people?'

'There's no need to do that, Monseigneur, since I have reached your presence.'

'Well, what do you want?' he shouted.

Beatrice glanced round the room. She noticed the door she had come in by, which opened in Mary Magdalene's stomach. She laughed lightly.

'Does every woman you receive come in through that cat's hole?'

The giant was becoming slightly unnerved. That drawling, ironical voice, that quick laugh, those dark eyes which sparkled momentarily and were then extinguished behind the long curving lashes, all rather disturbed him.

'Take care, Robert,' he said to himself, 'she's a famous whore and has certainly not been sent to see you for your good!'

He had known Beatrice for many years. Nor was it the first time she had exercised her fascination on him. He remembered the night at the Abbey of Châlus when, on coming from a late council with Charles IV about the affairs of England, he had found Beatrice waiting for him in the cloisters of the guesthouse. And there had been other occasions, too. At every meeting she had gazed into his eyes in just this way, had swayed her hips and made her bosom heave. Robert was not the man to be fettered by constancy; a tree trunk clothed in a skirt would have made him turn aside. But this woman, who was hand-in-glove with Mahaut, had always made him prudent.

'Slut though you may be, my dear, you're probably well-informed. My aunt thinks she'll win her case; but you see further than she does, and you're already pretty certain she'll lose it. Favourable winds are going to cease blowing towards Conflans and it's high time to make your peace with Monseigneur Robert, who has been so slandered and wronged, and whose hand will be very heavy on the day of vengeance. Isn't that it?'

He was as usual pacing up and down. He was wearing a short tunic that seemed moulded to his body; the huge muscles of his thighs stretched tight the stuff of his hose. From behind her lashes Beatrice watched him, her eyes moving from his red hair to his shoes.

'How heavy he must be!' she thought.

'But, I can tell you, my favour is not to be gained merely with a smile,' Robert went on. 'Unless, of course, you're in desperate need of money and have a secret to sell me? I'm generous to those who serve me, but pitiless to those who try to cross me.'

'I have nothing to sell you, Monseigneur.'

'In that case, Demoiselle Beatrice, if I may give you a word of warning, it will be in your best interests to steer clear of the doors of my house, whatever pretext you may have for entering them. My kitchen is carefully guarded. My dishes and my wine are tasted.'

Beatrice passed the point of her tongue across her lips as if she were savouring some delicious wine.

'He's afraid I'll poison him,' she thought.

She was enjoying herself even though she was frightened. And to think that Mahaut believed she was spending her time trying to win over La Divion! Beatrice felt she was holding a number of deadly, if invisible, strings in her hand. She had merely to pull the right ones.

She pushed her hood back, untied the laces at her throat and took off her cloak. Her thick dark hair was plaited into tresses about her ears. Her shot-silk dress, cut very low in the bodice, generously revealed the swelling of her breasts. Robert, who had a taste for luxuriant women, could not help thinking Beatrice had gained in beauty since their last meeting.

Beatrice spread her cloak on the flagstones so that it made a half-circle. Robert looked at her in surprise.

'What are you doing?'

She made no answer, but took three black feathers from her bag and placed them on top of the cloak, crossing them so as to make a little star; then she turned round, describing an imaginary circle with her forefinger, and muttered some incomprehensible words.

'What are you doing?' Robert repeated.

'I'm casting a spell on you, Monseigneur,' she said calmly, as if it were the most natural thing in the world, or at any rate the most natural thing for her.

Robert roared with laughter. Beatrice looked at him and then took his hand as if to draw him into the circle. Robert withdrew his hand.

'Are you afraid, Monseigneur?' said Beatrice with a smile.

What an advantage women had! No lord could have dared to tell Count Robert of Artois that he was afraid without a huge fist crashing into his face, or a twenty-pound sword slitting open his skull. And here was a mere vassal, a mere woman of the bedchamber, who came wandering into his house, had herself introduced into his presence, took up his time with her nonsense – 'Mahaut has lost a tooth. I have no secrets to sell you!' – put her cloak down on his floor and then had the nerve to tell him to his face that he was afraid.

'You've always seemed to be afraid of having anything to do with me,' Beatrice went on. 'When long ago you first came to Madame Mahaut's house and told her that her daughters were to be indicted – do you remember? – you even seemed to be frightened of me then. And often since then, too, for that matter. No, Monseigneur, don't let me think you're frightened of me!'

Robert was on the point of ringing for Lormet to turn the impertinent woman out. It was certainly what he ought to do. But behind her on the wall was Mary Magdalene, her rounded thighs emerging from her hair.

'What do you think you're doing with that cloak, the circle and the three feathers?' he asked. 'Raising the Devil?'

'Yes, of course, Monseigneur,' said Beatrice.

He shrugged his shoulders at such nonsense and, merely for the fun of it, stepped into the circle.

'And now it's happened, Monseigneur, just as I said! Because you're the Devil yourself!'

What man could resist such a compliment? Robert laughed long and delightedly. He seized Beatrice's chin between finger and thumb.

'Do you realize I could have you burned as a witch?'

'Oh, Monseigneur!'

She stood very close to him, her face turned up towards his huge chin. It bristled with red hairs. She could smell his scent of a hunted boar. She was intoxicated by danger, desire, Satanism and the fact of her betrayal.

She was a whore, a true whore, just the sort Robert liked. 'What danger can she be to me?' he thought.

He seized her by the shoulders and drew her to him.

'He's Madame Mahaut's nephew, and he'll do her all the harm he can,' Beatrice thought breathlessly, her mouth to his.

7

Bonnefille House

WHEN BISHOP THIERRY D'HIRSON was still alive, he had owned a house in the Rue Mauconseil in Paris, close to the Countess of Artois' and he had enlarged it by buying a house from a neighbour, Julien Bonnefille. Beatrice had inherited the house and now suggested to Robert of Artois that they should met there.

The prospect of having an affair with Mahaut's lady-in-waiting, so close to Mahaut's own town house and, what was more, in a house that had been paid for with Mahaut's money, excited Robert's sense of comedy. Every now and then Fate provided a joke of this kind.

At the start, however, Robert was very cautious indeed. He also owned a house in the same street and, though he did not live in it, there was at least some excuse for his presence in the neighbourhood; nevertheless, he preferred not to go to Bonnefille House till after dark. In the crowded, narrow streets of the districts by the Seine, a nobleman like Robert could not pass unnoticed, for his height was so conspicious and he was accompanied by an escort. He therefore waited for darkness to fall. Gillet de Nelle and three footmen, selected from among the strongest and most discreet, always went with him. Gillet was in command of the guard, and the three strong-armed bruisers were stationed at the doors of Bonnefille House, where they did their best to look as if they were casual loiterers.

On his first visits Robert refused to drink the spiced wine Beatrice offered him. 'The wench may have been ordered to poison me,' he thought. He was reluctant to take off his surcoat, which was lined with thin chain mail, and throughout their pleasure he kept an eye on the chest on which his dagger lay.

Beatrice was amused by his fears. It delighted her that a little bourgeoise from Artois, who was still unmarried at over thirty and had been tumbled in so many beds, could frighten a colossus like Robert, who was so powerful a peer of France.

Indeed, for her, too, the adventure had all the spice of perversity. Not only was it taking place in the house of her uncle, the Bishop, but with Madame Mahaut's mortal enemy. Beatrice had continually to invent new lies to account for her absence. La Division was being difficult, she said; she would not give in all at once; it would be madness to hand her a large sum of money in return for which she would no doubt merely tell lies; it was wiser to keep in constant touch with her, extract the account of wicked Monseigneur Robert's intrigues little by little, the names of his accomplices, and then verify what she said by seeing the Sieur Juvigny at the Louvre, or Michelet Guéroult, notary Tesson's assistant. Oh, it was certainly a most complicated business and required both time and money. 'I think I really must give the clerk a piece of stuff for his wife; it may induce him to talk. Will you authorize me to take two livres, Madame?'

And how amusing it was to look Madame Mahaut straight in the eye, smile at her and think: 'Less than twelve hours ago, I was giving myself naked to Messire, your nephew!'

Now that she saw her lady-in-waiting taking so much trouble in her service, Mahaut chid her less, indeed showed her affection once more and made her presents. For Beatrice, on the other hand, there was an exquisite and double pleasure to be derived from deceiving Mahaut and subjugating Robert at the same time. For a man was not subjugated merely by an hour in the same bed with him, any more than a wild beast was mastered by being bought and kept in a cage.

Mere possession is not power.

You are not master of a wild beast till you have trained it to lie down at the sound of your voice, retract its claws, and need no bars but your eyes.

For Beatrice, Robert's suspicions were so many claws to be filed. In all her career as a huntress she had never before had the opportunity to trap so great a quarry, and one whose vicious nature was a byword. Robert of Artois' name was on the point of being used to frighten children.

The day Robert accepted a goblet of red wine from her hand, Beatrice knew she had won her first victory. 'I might have poisoned it,' she thought, 'and he would have drunk it.'

And the day he fell asleep, like the ogre in the fable, she felt she had achieved a real triumph. The giant had a line about his neck where the robe or breastplate ended; the brick of his face tanned by the open air ceased: and below was white, freckled skin, while his shoulders were covered with red hairs like pig's bristles. This line seemed to Beatrice positively to invite the axe.

His copper-coloured hair, which was curled and hung in ringlets over his cheeks, had been pushed aside to reveal a small, childish, delicately-shaped ear, which was rather touching. 'You could stick a bodkin into that ear till it reached the brain,' thought Beatrice.

A few minutes later Robert woke up with a start and looked anxiously about him.

'Well, Monseigneur, I didn't kill you,' she said with a laugh. Her laughter revealed dark red gums.

As if in gratitude, he took her again. He had to admit that she made an admirable partner, inventive, practised, yielding, never sullen, and crying her pleasure aloud. Robert, who had had every sort of skirt in his time, silk, linen and cotton, and believed himself a master in lechery, had to confess that he had met his match.

'If you learnt such things at the sabbath, my dear,' he said, 'we ought to send more virgins to it!'

For Beatrice often talked to him of the sabbath and the Devil. Deliberate of movement, drawling of voice, and seeming so soft and languorous, she revealed true violence only in bed, while her speech became rapid and animated only when she talked of demons and sorcery.

'Why have you never married?' Robert asked her. 'You must have had offers from many men, particularly if you allowed them such a foretaste of marriage.'

'Because marriages are made in church, and I hate the Church.'

Kneeling on the bed, hands on knees, a dark shadow in the hollow of her thighs, and her eyes wide, Beatrice said: 'You see, Monseigneur, the priests and popes of Rome and Avignon don't teach the truth. There is not one God; there are two, the god of light and the god of darkness, the prince of Good and the prince of Evil. Before the creation of the world, the inhabitants of darkness rebelled against the inhabitants of light, and the vassals of Evil, in order to exist, for Evil is death and annihilation, devoured part of the principles of Good. And then, since the two forces of Good and Evil were in them, they were able to create the world and engender mankind in whom the two principles are not only mingled but in perpetual conflict, though Evil is predominant, because it is the natural element of their origin. And it is evident that these two principles exist, since man and woman exist, diversely made, like you and me,' she went on with a lustful smile. 'And it is Evil that arouses our lust and draws us together. And therefore people who have a stronger disposition towards Evil than towards Good must honour Satan and make a pact with him, if they are to be happy and successful. For them the Lord of Good is the enemy.'

This strange philosophy, redolent of sulphur, and confected from ill-digested scraps of Manichaeanism and corrupt elements, ill-transmitted and ill-understood, of the doctrines of the Cathars, was at that time a great deal more widespread than the rulers realized. Beatrice was far from being exceptional; but for Robert, who had never come across these ideas before, she opened the door to a world of mystery; and he was fascinated, moreover, to hear a woman talk of such things.

'You're a great deal more intelligent than I thought. Who taught you all this?'

'The former Templars,' she said.

'Oh, the Templars! They certainly knew a great deal.'

'You destroyed them.'

'Not I, not I!' cried Robert. 'It was Philip the Fair and Enguerrand, Mahaut's friends. Charles of Valois and I were against suppressing them.'

'They have remained powerful through magic; all the misfortunes that have beset the kingdom since their suppression have been due to the pact they made with Satan, because the Pope condemned them.'

'Oh, the misfortunes of the kingdom!' said Robert, far from convinced. 'Have not many of them been due to my aunt rather than to the Devil? After all, it was she who murdered my cousin, the Hutin, and his son after him. Didn't you lend a hand there yourself?'

He often returned to the question, but Beatrice always managed to avoid it. Sometimes she smiled vaguely as if she had failed to hear him; or, again, she would answer off the point.

'Mahaut doesn't know that I've made a pact with the Devil. She would certainly dismiss me if she did.'

And she would hastily branch off into her favourite subjects again: the black mass, the enemy and negation of the Christian mass, which had to be celebrated at midnight in a cellar, and preferably near a cemetery; the two-faced idol they worshipped; and the black host consecrated by uttering the name of Beelzebub thrice. The officiant should preferably be an unfrocked priest or a renegade monk, and that was why so many of them were former Templars.

'The God above is bankrupt; he promises happiness and pays the creatures who serve him with nothing but misfortune; one should obey the god below. Listen, Monseigneur, if you want the Devil's support for the documents in your case, pierce their corners with a red-hot iron and let the hole show traces of fire. Or, again, mark each page with a little cross in ink, the upper branch shaped like a hand. I know exactly how to do it.'

But Robert did not entirely believe in all this; and though she knew better than anyone that the documents he claimed to possess must be forgeries, he refused to agree to anything of the kind.

'If you want to obtain complete power over an enemy and bring him to disaster through the Devil's will,' she told him one day, 'you must rub his armpits, the back of his ears and the soles of his feet with an unguent made of fragments of the host, the powdered bones of an unbaptized child, the semen of a man that has been spread on the back of a woman during the black mass, together with the woman's menstrual blood.'[14]

'It would not make me feel so safe,' Robert said, 'as a little rat or vermin poison administered to a certain enemy of mine.'

Beatrice pretended not to have heard him. Yet the very idea sent the blood coursing through her veins. She knew she must give Robert no immediate answer, that he must not be allowed to know that she had in fact already consented. What better pact could there be to link two lovers for ever than participation in crime?

She was in love with him, and did not realize that, in trying to trap him, she herself had been caught in the snare. She existed only for the hours they could spend together, and then lived on the memory of their last meeting and in the expectation of the next, waiting to feel once again his fifteen stone crushing her, and to smell the zoo-like odour that emanated from him, particularly when he was making love, and hear that wild beast's growl she could draw from his throat.

There are many more women with a taste for monsters than one is apt to think. The Court dwarfs, Jean the Fool and his colleagues, were well aware of it; they could not satisfy all their conquests. Even the victim of some accidental peculiarity becomes an object of curiosity often leading to desire; a one-eyed knight, for instance, merely for the fascination of raising his black patch. And Robert, in his way, was a sort of monster.

The autumn rain was falling on the roofs. And Beatrice was amusing herself chasing the rumblings of his gigantic stomach with her fingers.

'In any case, Monseigneur,' she said, 'you have no need of help to get what you want; you require no instruction in the sciences. You're the Devil I've summoned up in you. The Devil who does not know he is the Devil.'

Satiated, he was staring dreamingly up at the ceiling, listening to her.

The Devil had flaming eyes, huge claws on his fingers to lacerate people's flesh, a forked tongue, and breath like that of a furnace. But the Devil might also perhaps have the weight and smell of Robert. She was really in love with Satan. She was the Devil's woman and no one would separate her from him.

One night, when Robert of Artois returned from Bonnefille House, his wife handed him the notorious marriage contract, completed at last except for the seals.

Robert read it through, went over to the hearth, and

casually thrust the poker into the fire. When the point was red hot, he made a hole with it in one of the leaves of parchment, which sizzled.

'What are you doing, my dear?' asked Madame de Beaumont.

'I'm merely making sure it's good-quality parchment,' he said.

Jeanne of Beaumont looked at her husband for a moment, then said gently, almost maternally: 'Really, Robert, you ought to get your nails cut. What's this new fashion you've adopted of wearing them so long?'

8

Return to Maubuisson

IT MAY WELL HAPPEN that a plot, which has been hatching for a long time, is in fact compromised from the start by some failure in reasoning.

Robert suddenly realized that the ballistas he had mounted so carefully might well break at the very moment of firing, because he had neglected an essential spring.

He had certified to his brother-in-law, the King, and solemnly sworn on Holy Writ, that his titles of inheritance existed; he had had documents forged to resemble as nearly as possible those that had disappeared; he had suborned innumerable witnesses to establish the validity of the documents. It seemed likely that he had enough support for his case to be accepted without argument.

But there was one person who knew without a shadow of doubt that his documents were forgeries; and this was Mahaut of Artois, since she had herself burned the real documents, first those she had stolen through Enguerrand de Marigny from the Paris archives some twenty years ago, and then, more recently, the copies found in Thierry d'Hirson's safe.

Moreover, though a forgery may be accepted as authentic by people who are favourably disposed and who have never seen the original, this is far from the case with someone who is aware that falsification has taken place.

Of course Mahaut could not declare: 'These documents are forged because I have burnt the originals'; but, knowing they were forged, she would do her best to show them up; one could be sure of that. Though it had failed, the arrest of La Division's servants was warning enough. There were too many people involved in the forgery, and someone was bound to betray it either from fear or in the hope of reward.

If some error had crept in, like the unfortunate '1322' in place of '1302' in the letter read at Reuilly, Mahaut would certainly not fail to dicover it. The seals might appear perfect, but Mahaut would demand a minute examination. More-over, the late Count Robert II, as was the usual practice of princes, always had the name of the clerk who had written it mentioned in an official document. But, of course, there could be no question of it in a forgery. The omission might well pass in a single document, but could it do so in the three that were to be presented? Mahaut would merely open the Artois archives and say: 'Compare them. Can you find among all the documents bearing my father's seal a single one in which the clerk's hand resembles the writing of these?'

Robert had come to the conclusion that the forged documents, which for him had acquired all the value of authenticity, could not be used until the person who disposed of the originals had also been disposed of. In other words, he could win his case only on condition that Mahaut was dead.

This was no longer merely a wish, it had become a necessity.

'Should Mahaut happen to die,' he said to Beatrice one day, with a pensive air, his hands clasped behind his head, his eyes staring up at the ceiling in Bonnefille House, 'should she die, I could take you into my household as my wife's lady-in-waiting. Since I would then have acquired the inheritance of Artois, people would think it quite normal that I should take over certain members of my aunt's household. I should then always have you near me.'

It was a coarse bait, but presented to a greedy fish.

Beatrice could think of no more delightful prospect. She could imagine herself living in Robert's house, hatching her plots, first as his secret, then as his official mistress, for these things are always accepted in time. Besides, who could tell? Madame de Beaumont, like everyone else, was not immortal. Of course, she was seven years younger than Beatrice, and seemed to enjoy excellent health, but what a triumph it would be for an older woman to supplant a younger. It might well be that a properly managed magic spell might make a widower of Robert within the next few years. Love neither reasons nor sets bounds to the imagination. There were times when Beatrice dreamed of herself as the Countess of Artois, dressed in peeress' robes.

And suppose the King, as might also happen, should die, and Robert became Regent? There were women in every century who rose from lowly birth to the highest rank through the desire they were able to arouse in a prince, and because they had both physical graces and mental abilities which made them superior, by natural right, to all others. The Empresses of Rome and Constantinople, so the troubadors related, had not all been born on the steps of the throne.

Among the great of this world a woman rose quickest by lying on her back.

Before permitting herself to be hooked, Beatrice allowed just enough time to elapse to make sure of the fisherman. Robert had to pledge himself to the hilt before he could convince her, promise over and over again that he would take her into the Artois household, guarantee the position and prerogatives she would enjoy, as well as the precise lands he would give her. At last she was prepared to admit that she might be able to find a magician who, by making a proper waxen likeness, piercing it with needles and uttering the right spells, could destroy Mahaut. Nevertheless, Beatrice still made a pretence of being hesitant and having scruples. Was not Mahaut her benefactress and indeed that of the whole Hirson family?

Gold necklaces with jewelled clasps began to adorn Beatrice's neck; Robert was beginning to learn the methods of gallantry. As she played with a jewel he had given her, Beatrice said that the surest and most rapid method of casting a successful spell was to take a child less than five years old, make it swallow a white host, cut the child's head off, dip a black host in its blood and then, by some subterfuge or other, persuade the victim to eat it. There would be little difficulty in finding a child of the right age. Many a poor family, over-burdened with brats, would be prepared to sell one, and there was no need to divulge the purpose for which it was required.

Robert made a wry face; the scheme involved too many complications for an uncertain result. His preference was for administering good, sound poison, which would do the job.

In the end Beatrice seemed to give way for love of the devil she adored, and from impatience to go to live in the Hôtel d'Artois, where she could see him several times a day. She would do anything for him. But, in fact, she had already been in possession of a sufficient quantity of white arsenic to exterminate the whole district for a week, when Robert thought he was persuading her at last by getting her to accept fifty livres with which to buy some.

It was now merely a question of waiting for the right opportunity. Beatrice told Robert that Mahaut was surrounded by physicians, who were hurriedly summoned at her slightest indisposition; while the kitchens were under constant surveillance and the cupbearers attentive to their duties. It was no easy undertaking.

And then, suddenly, Robert changed his mind. He had had a long audience with the King, who had just received the report from the commissioners who had worked so diligently to the plaintiff's directions. More than ever convinced that his brother-in-law was in the right, Philippe VI's one desire was to serve him. To avoid a lawsuit, of which the result must be a foregone conclusion, but which was bound to create a considerable scandal to the disadvantage both of the Court and the kingdom, he had decided to summon Mahaut and persuade her to surrender Artois.

'She'll never agree,' said Beatrice, 'and you know it as well as I do, Monseigneur.'

'Anyway, let's try it, If the King does manage to make her see reason, it will be by far the best way, won't it?'

'No; poison is the best way.'

An amicable solution would not suit Beatrice at all for it would mean a postponement of her becoming a member of Robert's household. She would have to go on being the Countess' lady-in-waiting till Mahaut died, and only God knew when that would be. It was therefore she who now wanted to bring matters to a head; all the obstacles and difficulties she had raised herself no longer frightened her now. As for a suitable opportunity, there were many every day, for instance when she brought the Countess Mahaut her medicines and infusions.

'But the King has summoned her to Maubuisson in three days' time,' Robert went on.

Eventually the lovers agreed that, if Mahaut fell in with the King's proposal that she should give up Artois, she would be allowed to go on living; but, if she refused, Beatrice would poison her that very same day. What better opportunity could there be? If Mahaut were taken ill after dining with the King, who would dare suspect him of murdering her or, if they did suspect it, dare voice their suspicions?

Philippe VI had suggested to Robert that he should be present at the interview of conciliation; but Robert had refused.

'Sire, my brother, your words will carry more weight if I am not present; Mahaut hates me so much that the mere sight of me would be more inclined to make her stubborn than accommodating.'

He believed this to be true, but he also wanted to establish an alibi.

Three days later, on October 23rd, Countess Mahaut was jolting along the road to Pontoise in her great gilded litter, painted with the arms of Artois. Her only surviving daughter, Queen Jeanne, Philippe the Long's widow, was with her. Beatrice was sitting opposite her mistress on a tapestry-covered stool.

'What sort of proposal do you think the King is going

to make, Madame?' Beatrice asked. 'If it's a question of a compromise, I hope you'll refuse it, if you'll forgive my offering advice. I shall soon have all the proof we need against Monseigneur Robert. La Division is prepared to give us evidence to confute him.'

'Why don't you bring this Divion to see me? You seem to be on very good terms with her, and yet I've never set eyes on her,' said Mahaut.

'It's impossible, Madame; she's in fear of her life. If Monseigneur Robert got to know of it, she would most certainly not hear mass the next morning. I can only persuade her to come to see me at night at Bonnefille House, and then she always has an escort of footmen to guard her. But you must refuse, Madame, absolutely refuse!'

The widowed Jeanne, dressed in white, was silently watching the landscape go by. It was not till the steep roofs of Maubuisson appeared above the autumn woods in the distance that she said: 'Do you remember, Mother, fifteen years ago?'

Fifteen years ago, dressed in sackcloth and with her head shaven, she had screamed her innocence along this very road from the black tumbril taking her to Dourdan. In a second black tumbril, her sister Blanche and her cousin, Marguerite of Burgundy, were on their way to Château Gaillard. Fifteen years ago!

She had been pardoned and had recovered her husband's affection. Marguerite was dead, and Louis X was dead. Jeanne had never questioned Mahaut about the circumstances surrounding Louis the Hutin's and little Jean I's deaths. And then Philippe the Long had become King and reigned for six years, after which he too had died. Jeanne could not believe she was the same woman who had suffered that appalling day at Maubuisson fifteen years ago. After all, she had eventually been crowned Queen of France at Reims; and now here she was travelling in her mother's litter. Indeed, her mother, who was so imposing and autocratic, was the only constant thing in her life; she had always submitted to her domination and ever since childhood had been frightened of speaking to her.

Mahaut was also remembering the past.

'It's all been that wicked Robert's fault,' she said, 'It was he who conspired with that bitch Isabella. I'm told affairs are not going too well at the moment either for her or that Mortimer whose whore she is. They'll all be punished one day!'

They were all three lost in their own thoughts.

'And now I've got long hair again; and wrinkles too for that matter!' murmurered the widowed Queen.

'You shall have Artois, my girl,' said Mahaut, tapping her knee.

Beatrice was looking out at the passing countryside and smiling at the clouds.

Philippe VI received Mahaut courteously, but also with a certain haughtiness of speech as befitted a king. He desired peace between his great barons. The peers, who were the supports of the Crown, must give no example of discord or sharp practice to the people.

'I have no intention of being biased by what may have happened in previous reigns,' Philippe said, as if he were casting a veil of indulgence over Mahaut's past actions. 'I must take my stand on the present. My commissioners have completed their task; and I cannot conceal the fact, Cousin, that the witnesses are very far from being in your favour. What's more, Robert is on the point of producing his documents.'

'The witnesses are bribed and the documents forged,' Mahaut muttered.

Dinner was held in the great hall, where once Philip the Fair had pronounced judgement on his three daughters-in-law. 'It must be in everyone's thoughts,' the Dowager Queen Jeanne said to herself and she could summon up no appetite. In fact, apart from her mother and herself, no one was thinking of that long ago event of which nearly all the witnesses were dead. After dinner one old equerry might perhaps say to another: 'Do you remember, Messire, how we were standing by Monseigneur Charles of Valois, and now Madame Jeanne has come back here as Dowager Queen ...' But a moment later he would be thinking of something else.

We are all apt to fall into the error of assuming that other people think we are as important as we do ourselves; but unless there is some particular reason for their remembering it, others forget what has happened to us very quickly; and, even if they have not forgotten, their memories attach much less weight to it than we are inclined to believe.

Had the meeting taken place elsewhere, Mahaut might perhaps have been more amenable to Philippe VI's proposals. He was a monarch who always wanted to be the arbiter, and was therefore constantly in search of compromise. But Mahaut's old hatreds were all revived by Maubuisson and she was in no mood to yield. She would have Robert convicted of forgery and prove that he was a perjurer. She could think of nothing else.

She made up for having to measure her words by eating enormously, engulfing everything that was put before her, and draining her goblet as soon as it was filled. The combination of wine and anger turned her face purple. The King was actually suggesting that she should hand over her county to Robert for a payment of forty thousand livres a year in compensation.

'I can guarantee,' Philippe said, 'that I shall get your nephew to agree to the proposal.'

But Mahaut was thinking: 'If Robert has got his brother-in-law to make me this proposal, it must be because he is not very sure of his titles and with his usual cunning would prefer to pay an annual rent of forty thousand livres than produce his forged documents.'

'I refuse, Sire, my cousin,' she said, 'to despoil myself in this way; and since Artois is mine, your justice will let me keep it.'

Philippe lowered his long nose and looked up at her. Her stubbornness might be due simply to pride, or it might be fear that by yielding she would be admitting the accusations against her. But Philippe, in his desire for a compromise, had an alternative solution: Mahaut should keep her county, title, rights, and peer's coronet for her lifetime, but would sign a deed to be ratified by the peers, in the King's presence, making her nephew Robert heir to Artois. She could really have no objection to this arrangement; her only son had died young; her daughter enjoyed a royal dowry; and her grand-daughter had acquired, through marriage, the huge Duchy of Burgundy. Could Mahaut really want more? In this way Artois would go back one day to the natural heir.

'Had your brother, Count Philippe, not died before your father, you cannot deny, Cousin, that your nephew would be in possession of the county today. This way both your honours will be safe, and it seems to me that I am resolving your differences most justly.'

Mahaut set her jaw and shook her head in refusal.

Philippe VI showed some irritation and hastened the service of dinner. If Mahaut was going to treat him like this and offend him by refusing to accept his arbitration, let her have her lawsuit and let the result be on her own head!

'I am not inviting you to stay the night, Cousin,' he said, as soon as they had washed their hands; 'I do not believe a stay in my Court would be agreeable to you.'

This was a clear sign of his disfavour.

Before taking the road, Mahaut went for decency's sake to shed a tear or two at the tomb of her daughter, Blanche, in the abbey chapel. She had stated in her will that she wished to be buried there herself.[15]

'Maubuisson,' she said, 'is not a place that has brought us much luck. But to lie there dead, what does it matter?'

She was in a very bad temper all the way home.

'Did you hear what that great fool we're unlucky enough to have for King said? He expects me to give up Artois, just like that, and merely to please him! The very idea of making that great foul Robert my heir! My hand would wither away before it signed a thing like that! They've clearly been accomplices in roguery for a long time past and owe each other a lot! And to think that if it weren't for my having cleared the path to the throne . . .'

'Mother . . .' Jeanne murmured in a low voice.

If she had dared to say what she thought and had not been afraid of a savage rebuff, Jeanne would have advised her mother to accept the King's proposals. But it would have done no good.

'He'll never get me to agree to that,' repeated Mahaut.

Though she did not know it, she had signed her death-warrant; and her executioner was sitting opposite her in the litter, looking at her through her dark lashes.

'Beatrice,' said Mahaut suddenly, 'help me to unlace. My stomach's swollen.'

Her anger had upset her digestion. They had to stop the litter so that Madame Mahaut might relieve herself in a neighbouring field.

'I shall give you some quince paste tonight, Madame,' said Beatrice.

Night had fallen by the time they reached the Rue Mauconseil in Paris. Mahaut's stomach was still rather upset, but she was feeling better. She took a little supper and went to bed.

9

The Wages of Sin

BEATRICE WAITED TILL ALL the servants were asleep. She then went to Mahaut's bed, and raised the tapestry curtain that was drawn close at nights. The night-light hanging from the ceiling gave a faint blue glow. Beatrice was in her nightdress and was holding a spoon in her hand.

'Madame, you've forgotten to take your quince paste.'

Mahaut was sleepy, her mind was confused with anger and fatigue, and she merely said: 'Oh, yes. You're a good girl to have remembered it.'

And she swallowed the spoonful.

Two hours before dawn she awakened her household with a great clamour of shouting and bell-ringing. They found her vomiting into a basin held by Beatrice.

Summoned at once, Thomas de Miesier and Guillaume de Venat, her physicians, inquired about the previous day's menu, insisting on a detailed account of everything the Countess had eaten. They had little difficulty in diagnosing a serious attack of indigestion, complicated by a flux of blood caused by anger.

Barber Thomas was sent for and bled the Countess for his usual fee of fifteen sols; also Dame Mesgnière, the herb woman from Petit Pont, who administered a clyster of an infusion of herbs.[16]

Beatrice, on the pretext of going to fetch an electuary from Master Palin, the spice-maker, escaped during the course of the evening to meet Robert at Bonnefille House, only three doors away from Mahaut's.

'It is done,' she said.

'Is she dead?' cried Robert.

'Oh, no, she's going to suffer a long time yet,' said Beatrice with a glint in her dark eyes. 'But we shall have to be careful, Monseigneur, and not see each other too often just at present.'

It took Mahaut a month to die.

Night after night, dose by dose, Beatrice hastened her to the tomb; and she was able to do so all the more easily because Mahaut trusted no one but her, and refused to take medicine from any hand but hers.

After the vomiting, which lasted three days, she was attacked by a sort of catarrh of the throat and chest and could not swallow without great pain. Her physicians declared she had caught a chill during her indigestion. Then, when her pulse began to weaken, they thought she had been bled too much; and then her skin broke out into spots and boils all over her body.

Attentive, thoughtful, always at hand, her manner as calm and smiling as any patient could wish, Beatrice took great delight in watching the loathsome progress of her handiwork. She scarcely ever went to see Robert; but the daily problem of which dish or medicine to lace with poison afforded her pleasure enough.

When her hair started falling out in grey tufts like musty hay, Mahaut realized she was dying.

'I've been poisoned,' she said in her agony.

'Oh, Madame, Madame, don't say such a terrible thing,' Beatrice replied. 'Your last dinner before being taken ill was at the King's.'

'That's just what I'm thinking,' said Mahaut.

She was still difficult and hot-tempered, inclined to rate her physicians and call them donkeys. She showed no sign of desiring the consolation of religion, and was more concerned with the affairs of her county than with those of her soul. She dictated a letter to her daughter. 'Should I die, I command you to go to the King at once and insist on rendering homage for Artois before Robert can attempt anything . . .'

The pain she was suffering never for an instant made her think of the agonies she had inflicted on others in the past; she remained hard and self-centred to the end, and even the approach of death aroused in her no urge to repentance, no sign of human compassion.

Nevertheless, she thought it desirable to confess to killing two kings, crimes she had never admitted to her ordinary confessors. For this purpose she summoned an obscure Franciscan; and when the monk emerged, pale and shaken, from her room, he was immediately arrested by two sergeants-at-arms, who had orders to take him to the Château d'Hesdin. Mahaut's instructions were misunderstood. She had ordered the monk to be imprisoned in Hesdin till after her death; but the Governor of the castle thought it was the monk's death that was in question and promptly had him thrown into an *oubliette*. It was Countess Mahaut's last crime, though for once an involuntary one.

In the end the sick woman was seized with appalling cramps, which first attacked her toes, then her calves and then her forearms. Death was rising towards the heart.

On November 27th couriers left for the Convent of Poissy where Jeanne the Widow was staying, and for Bruges to warn the Count of Flanders. Three more were sent off at intervals during the course of the day to the King at Saint-Germain, where he was in company with Robert of Artois. Each courier to Saint-Germain seemed to Beatrice to be bearing Robert a loving message: the Countess had received the last sacraments; the Countess could no longer speak; the Countess was expiring.

Finding herself alone for a moment with the dying woman, Beatrice bent over the bald head, and the pustulous face, of which the whole life seemed now centred in the eyes, and said very softly: 'You have been poisoned, Madame – by me. Because of my love for Monseigneur Robert.'

At first the dying woman looked incredulous, then the incredulity turned to hatred. Dying as she was, her last emotion was a desire to kill. Oh, why should she regret any of her actions? Surely she had been right to be wicked, since the world was so full of wicked people! But even now, at the last moment, it never occurred to her that she was being paid the wages of sin in her own coin. Hers was a soul beyond redemption.

When her daughter arrived from Poissy, Mahaut pointed to Beatrice with a stiff, cold finger that had lost almost all power of movement. Her lips stirred but no sound came. She died in the effort to speak.

At the obsequies, which took place on November 30th at Maubuisson, Robert looked thoughtful and depressed, which surprised everyone. An air of triumph, it was thought, would have been more in keeping with his character. Yet his attitude was not feigned. When an enemy you have fought for twenty years dies, you feel a sense of loss. Hatred is one of the stronger links, and when that link is broken, a certain melancholy results.

Obedient to her mother's last wishes, Queen Jeanne the Widow next day asked Philippe VI to hand over to her the government of Artois. Before doing so, Philippe had a frank talk with Robert.

'I can do no other than defer to your Cousin Jeanne's request. By the various contracts and judgements she's the legitimate heiress. But this decision is merely provisional and for form's sake until some agreement is reached or the case is heard. You must make your application to me as soon as possible.' This Robert immediately did, in the following letter:

'My very dear and dread lord, since I, Robert of Artois, your humble Count of Beaumont, have long been disinherited despite all right and reason, and by means of malice, fraud and guile, of the County of Artois, which belongs to me and should belong to me for many good and just reasons, which have recently come to my knowledge, I hereby request that you will listen to my cause ...'

The first time Robert went back to Bonnefille House again, Beatrice thought she would be regaling him by giving an hour-by-hour account of Mahaut's last moments. He listened without a word and showed no pleasure at the recital.

'One might think you were sorry for her,' she said.

'Not at all, not at all,' replied Robert deep in thought. 'She has paid for her crimes.'

His mind was already on the next fence.

'Now I can be a lady-in-waiting in your household. When are you going to take me into your house?'

'When I have Artois,' Robert replied. 'You must arrange to take service with Mahaut's daughter. I shall have to get her out of the way next.'

Madame Jeanne the Widow, enjoying a consideration such as she had not known since the death of her husband, Philippe the Long, and free at last, at the age of thirty-seven, from her mother's stultifying domination, set out in state to take possession of Artois and halted for the night at Roye-en-Vermandois. She asked for a goblet of claret. Beatrice d'Hirson sent Huppin, the cupbearer, to fetch one. Huppin was more attentive to Beatrice's bright eyes than he was to his duties: for four weeks past he had been pining for love of her. It was Beatrice who handed the goblet to the Queen. This time she was in a hurry and so used salts of mercury instead of arsenic.

Madame Jeanne's journey ended there.

Those present at the Dowager Queen's deathbed stated that she was taken ill about the middle of the night, that the venom was trickling from her eyes, mouth and nose, and that her body was stained all over with white and black patches. She lasted only forty-eight hours, having survived her mother by no more than two months.

Then the Duchess of Burgundy, Mahaut's granddaughter, laid claim to the County of Artois.

PART THREE
DECLINE AND FALL

I

The Phantom Bait

THE MONK SAID HIS name was Thomas Dienhead. He had a low forehead beneath a narrow ring of brown hair, and he kept his hands hidden in his sleeves. His Dominican's habit was a dirty white. He looked furtively about him and asked three times whether 'my lord' was alone, and if anyone could overhear them.

'Go on, speak up, man,' said the Earl of Kent, lying back in his chair, and swinging his leg with a hint of impatience.

'My lord, our good Sire, King Edward II is still alive.'

Edmund of Kent seemed less surprised than might have been expected, in the first place because he was not the man to show his feelings, and in the second because this staggering news had already reached him a few days before by another emissary.

'King Edward is being kept secretly in Corfe Castle,' the monk went on, 'I have seen him and have come to tell you.'

The Earl of Kent got to his feet, stepped over his greyhound, went to the leaded window and stared out at the grey sky above his Manor of Kensington.

Kent was twenty-nine, and no longer the slender young man who had commanded the English troops in the disastrous war in Guyenne in 1324, and who had been besieged in La Réole by his Uncle Charles of Valois to whom he had had to surrender for lack of reinforcements. But though he had filled out a little, he was still as fair and pale as ever, had still that slightly haughty and abstracted air, which concealed a tendency to reverie rather than real thought.

In fact, he had never heard anything so surprising in his life. Was it really possible that his half-brother, Edward II, whose death had been announced three years ago, whose tomb was in Gloucester, and the names of whose assassins were now currently known throughout the kingdom, could be alive? Were his imprisonment in Berkeley Castle, his atrocious murder, the letter from Bishop Orleton, the guilt of Queen Isabella, Mortimer and Seneschal Maltravers, and the hurried burial, nothing but rumours put about by those who had an interest in spreading the belief that the King was dead and then exaggerated by popular imagination?

It was the second time in less than a fortnight that someone had come to tell him the news. The first time he had refused to believe it. Now he was beginning to wonder.

'If the news is true, it may well lead to many changes in the kingdom,' he said, as if to himself rather than to the monk.

During the last three years England had begun to awaken from her dreams. Where were the liberty, the justice and the prosperity the people had believed Queen Isabella and the great Lord Mortimer were bringing them? Of the hopes and confidence that had been placed in them, nothing remained now but disillusionment.

What was the point of dethroning, plundering, imprisoning and – so, at least, it had been believed till today – murdering the weak Edward II, who was ruled by such despicable favourites, if it was merely to replace him by a king who was a minor, still weaker therefore than his father had been, and deprived of all power by his mother's lover?

What was the point of having beheaded the Earl of Arundel, beaten Chancellor Baldock to death and quartered Hugh Despenser, when Lord Mortimer ruled just as autocratically, taxed the country as stringently, oppressed, insulted and terrified, and would brook no opposition to his authority?

At least Hugh Despenser, vicious and greedy though he had been, had had certain weaknesses, due to his feminine nature, on which it was possible to prevail. He would yield to fear or money. But Roger Mortimer was violent and inflexible. The She-wolf of France, as the Queen Mother was called, had a wolf for lover.

Power soon corrupts those who seize it in disregard of the public weal.

Brave, heroic even, famous for his unparalleled escape, Mortimer during his exile had been the incarnation of any unhappy people's aspirations. It was remembered that he had conquered the Kingdom of Ireland for the English Crown, but it was forgotten that he had done so for his own ends.

Indeed, Mortimer had never thought of the nation as a whole, nor of the needs of its people. He had become the champion of the popular cause merely because that cause had, at a given moment, coincided with his own. But he had represented the grievances of only a small part of the nobility and had been obsessed by an impatient longing for power. When he became master of England, he behaved as if the whole country had passed into his personal service.

In the first place, he had appropriated to himself almost a quarter of the realm on becoming Earl of March, a title and a fief he had created entirely for his own benefit. Hand in glove with the Queen Mother, he behaved like a king, and as if the young Sovereign were merely his heir.

When, in October 1328, Mortimer had demanded of Parliament, then meeting at Salisbury, that his elevation to the peerage be confirmed, Henry Wryneck, Earl of Lancaster, the senior member of the royal family, had absented himself. At the same session, Mortimer had surrounded Parliament with his armed forces to make sure his wishes were carried out. Pressure of this kind has never been appreciated by Parliaments.

Almost inevitably, the coalition that had once been formed to destroy the Despensers began rallying again about the same princes of the blood. Henry Wryneck and the Earls of Norfolk and Kent, the young King's uncles.

Two months after the Salisbury affair, Wryneck, taking advantage of Mortimer's and Isabella's absence, summoned a number of bishops and barons to a secret meeting at St Paul's in London, in order to raise an armed rebellion. But Mortimer had spies everywhere; and before the coalition could even take up arms, he had sent his own troops to sack the town of Leicester, Lancaster's most important fief. Henry wanted to continue the struggle; but Kent, who thought the rebellion had got off to a bad start, seceded without much credit to himself.

Lancaster had been able to escape the consequences of this

abortive rising with no more than a fine of eleven thousand pounds, which he in fact did not pay, only because he was nominally President of the Council of Regency and the King's guardian, and because, by a logical absurdity, Mortimer needed to maintain the legal fiction of Lancaster's guardianship, in order to be able to condemn his adversaries, such indeed as Lancaster himself, in due legal form for rebellion against the King.

Lancaster himself had been sent to France on the pretext of negotiating the marriage of the young King's sister with Philippe VI's eldest son. This banishment combined prudence with a mark of disfavour; the negotiations were bound to last a long time.

In Lancaster's absence, Kent automatically, indeed almost in spite of himself, became the leader of the discontented party. He was now the centre of the conspiracy, and was anxious to make people forget his defection of the previous year by proving that it had not been due to cowardice.

All these things were vaguely stirring in his mind as he stood at the window of his castle in Kensington. The monk was still standing there, quite motionless, his hands in his sleeves. The fact that he was a Dominican, just like the first emissary who had come to tell him Edward II was still alive, inclined the Earl of Kent to take the news seriously, for the Dominican Order was well known to be hostile to Mortimer.

If the information was true, the accusations of regicide against Isabella, Mortimer and their accomplices naturally fell to the ground. But it might well alter the whole situation in the country.

For the people were now beginning to miss Edward II and, passing from one extreme to the other, were almost ready to make a martyr out of that dissolute prince. If Edward II were still alive, Parliament might well abrogate its previous decisions, declare they had been imposed on it by force, and restore the former Sovereign to his throne.

In any case, what real proof was there of his death? The inhabitants of Berkeley inspecting the corpse? But how many of them had ever seen Edward II before? How could one be sure that they had not been shown the body of another man? No member of the royal family had been present at the mysterious obsequies in Gloucester Abbey; moreover, the body that had been lowered into the tomb in a black-draped coffin had been a month old.

'And so you say, Brother Dienhead, that you have actually seen him with your own eyes?' Kent asked, turning back to the monk.

Thomas Dienhead once again glanced about him like a true conspirator, and replied in a low voice: 'I was sent there by the Prior of my order; I gained the confidence of the chaplain, who insisted I should put on layman's clothes before he would let me in. I spent the whole day hidden in a little building to the left of the guardroom. In the evening, I was taken to the great hall, and there I saw the King dining in considerable state.'

'Did you speak to him?'

'I was not allowed to go near him,' said the monk; 'but the chaplain pointed him out to me from behind a column and said: "There he is."'

Kent fell silent for a moment; then he said: 'Should I require you, can I send for you at the Dominican Monastery?'

'No, my lord; my prior has advised me not to return to there for the moment.'

And he gave Kent an address in London at a priest's house in the neighbourhood of St Paul's.

Kent took out his purse and offered three gold pieces. But the monk refused them; he was not allowed to accept presents.

'For the charities maintained by your order,' said the Earl of Kent.

Brother Dienhead withdrew a hand from his sleeve, bowed very low, and departed.

That very day, Edmund of Kent informed the two principal prelates who had taken part in the abortive conspiracy, Graveson, Bishop of London, and William de Melton, Archbishop of York, who had married Edward III and Philippa of Hainaut.

'I have twice been assured of this and from what seem to be trustworthy sources . . .' he wrote.

The replies were not long delayed. Graveson had received the news with satisfaction and guaranteed his support to the Earl of Kent in any action he thought it proper to undertake; as for the Archbishop of York, Primate of England, he sent his personal chaplain, Allyn, to promise five hundred men-at-arms, and more should they be necessary, to deliver the former King.

Kent then made contact with Lord de la Zouche, and several others, including Lord Beaumont and Sir Thomas Rosslyn, who had taken refuge from Mortimer's vengeance in Paris. For there was once again an exiled party in France.

But what turned the scale was a secret and personal communication from Pope John XXII to the Earl of Kent. The Holy Father, having also heard that King Edward II was still alive, adjured the Earl of Kent to do all he could to deliver him, giving absolution in advance to those who took part in the enterprise 'ab omni poena et culpa.' The Holy Father could have made it no clearer that any means would be permitted, and even threatened the Earl of Kent with excommunication should he neglect to undertake so pious a task.

Nor was this any merely verbal message, but a letter written in Latin for a prelate of the Holy See which, though the signature was somewhat illegible, was supposed to be a faithful record of the words uttered by John XXII in the course of a conversation on the subject.

A mission headed by Chancellor Burghersh, Bishop of Lincoln, had just returned from Avignon, where it had gone to negotiate a possible marriage between Edward III's sister and the heir to the throne of France. The letter had been carried by a member of the Bishop's suite.

Edmund of Kent, who was much stirred by all this, decided to go and check this information for himself, and see what chances there were of the King's escaping.

He summoned Brother Dienhead from the address he had given him, and set out for Dorset with a small but trusty escort. This was in the month of February.

He reached Corfe on a stormy day when squalls from the sea were whipping across the desolate peninsula, and sent for the Governor of the castle, Sir John Daverill, who came to pay his respects at the one inn in Corfe, hard by the Church of St Edward Martyr, the murdered King of the Saxon dynasty.

Daverill was tall, narrow-shouldered, wrinkled of brow and scornful of lip; his courtesy seemed a little off-hand, rather as if this were a waste of time for a busy man; he apologized for being unable to receive the noble lord in the castle. His orders were peremptory.

'Is King Edward II alive or dead?' Edmund of Kent asked.

'I may not tell you.'

'But he's my brother! Is he the man you're guarding?'

'I'm not allowed to tell you. A prisoner has been put in my charge; I may reveal neither his name nor his rank.'

'Will you allow me to interview the prisoner?'

John Daverill shook his head. He was a stone wall, a rock, as impenetrable as the great sinister keep, defended by three large fortifications, that stood on the hill above the slab roofs of the village. There was no doubt that Mortimer chose his servants well.

But there are ways of denying that produce the effect of an affirmative. Would Daverill have been so mysterious, and so inflexible, if it were not the former King over whom he was standing guard?

Edmund of Kent used all his charm, which was considerable, and also other arguments to which human nature is not always insensible. He placed a heavy purse of gold on the table.

'I want the prisoner to be well treated,' he said. 'This is to ease his circumstances; there are a hundred pounds sterling in it.'

'I can assure you he's well treated, my lord,' said Daverill in a low voice that seemed to hint at complicity.

He picked up the purse without apparent embarrassment.

'I would willingly give double the sum,' said Edmund of Kent, 'merely to see him.'

Daverill reluctantly refused.

'You must realize, my lord, that there are two hundred guards in the castle . . .'

Edmund of Kent felt he was being an astute soldier by

making a mental note of this important fact; it would have to be taken into account when planning the escape.

'. . . and if one of them talked, and the Queen Mother came to hear of it, she'd have me beheaded.'

He could not, surely, have betrayed himself more clearly, admitted more overtly that it was King Edward II who lay behind those walls.

'But I can take a message,' Daverill went on, 'because that will be between ourselves.'

Kent was delighted with the rapid progress he had made and at once sat down to write a letter, while the wet gusts of wind made the windows of the inn rattle.

'May it please you, my very dear brother, I write in all loyalty and respect. I pray God with all my heart that you are in good health, for arrangements are being made to deliver you soon from your prison and the misfortunes under which you suffer. Be assured that I have the support of the greatest barons in England and of all their resources both of troops and treasure. You will be King once more; both prelates and barons have sworn it on the Gospels.'

He merely folded the letter and handed it to Daverill.

'I pray you to seal it, my lord,' Daverill said. 'I would prefer not to know its contents.'

Kent sent one of his suite for wax, applied his seal, and Daverill hid the letter under his surcoat.

'A message,' he said, 'will reach the prisoner from outside, and I have no doubt he will destroy it at once. Thus . . .'

And he spread his hands wide in a gesture of obliteration and oblivion.

'If I know anything about men, when the day comes this man will open wide the gates; we shall not even have to fight a battle,' thought Edmund of Kent.

Three days later his letter was in the hands of Roger Mortimer, who read it to the Council at Westminster, and Queen Isabella, turning to the young King, cried dramatically: 'My son, my son, I beseech you to take steps against your most mortal enemy who is trying to make the kingdom believe the fable that your father is still alive, so that he may depose you and take your place. For God's sake give orders for this traitor to be punished before it is too late.'

In fact, orders had already been issued, and Mortimer's men were galloping to Winchester to arrest the Earl of Kent on his way home. But it was not only his arrest Mortimer desired; he wanted a spectacular conviction. There were also special reasons for haste. In a year's time Edward III would have reached his majority; he was showing signs of being impatient to start ruling. Having exiled Lancaster, if Mortimer could eliminate Kent, he would cut off the opposition and prevent the young King escaping from his influence.

On March 19th, Parliament met at Winchester to sit in judgement on the King's uncle.

On being brought from prison, where he had lain for over a month, the Earl of Kent looked thin, haggard and bewildered, and seemed not even to realize what had happened to him. He was clearly not the man to withstand adversity. His haughty nonchalance of manner had gone. On being interrogated by Robert Howel, the Coroner of the Royal Houses, he collapsed, admitting everything, told the story from beginning to end, and gave the names of his informers and accomplices. But who were his informers?

The Dominican Order knew of no brother called Dienhead; he had clearly been invented by the accused in an attempt to save himself. And so also had the letter from Pope John XXII; no member of the Bishop of Lincoln's suite had had any conversation concerning the late King during the embassy to Avignon, either with the Holy Father, or with his cardinals and counsellors. Edmund of Kent kept insisting it was true and felt as if he were going out of his mind. Had he not talked with these Dominicans? Had he not held the letter 'ab omni poena et culpa' in his hand?

In the end Kent realized the terrible trap into which he had been drawn by the phantom bait of the late King. Mortimer and his creatures had organized the whole plot: the false emissaries, the false monks, the forged letter and, falsest of all, Daverill of Corfe Castle! And Kent had fallen into it headlong.

The Royal Coroner demanded the death penalty.

Mortimer was sitting on the front bench of the Lords, and held them all with his eyes; while Lancaster, the one man who would have dared speak up in favour of the accused, was out of the kingdom. Mortimer had let it be known that he would not prosecute Kent's accomplices, whether prelates or no, if Kent himself were condemned. Many of the barons present were compromised in one way or another. They abandoned the accused to the vengeance of the Earl of March. Indeed, he was an expiatory victim.

And though Kent humbly admitted his errors to the House, and offered to go barefoot, wearing only a shirt and with a rope about his neck, to make his submission to the King, the Lords regretfully pronounced the sentence that was expected of them. To quiet their consciences, they whispered to each other. 'The King will pardon him, the King will use his prerogative of mercy.'

It was, in fact, very unlikely that Edward III would have his uncle beheaded for a deed which, though certainly culpable, had been largely occasioned by imprudence and only too obvious provocation.

Many of those who voted for the death sentence did so in the determination of asking for a pardon next day.

The Commons, however, refused to ratify the Lords' sentence; they demanded more information and a further investigation.

But as soon as Mortimer got the vote of the Upper Chamber, he hurried off to the castle, where Isabella was at dinner.

'It is done,' he said; 'we can execute Edmund. But many of our false friends are expecting your son to save him from paying the supreme penalty. I beg you to act first.'

They had been careful to get the young King out of the way for several hours by arranging an official reception for him at Winchester College.

'The governor,' added Mortimer, 'will execute your order, my dear, as if it were the King's.'

Isabella and Mortimer gazed into each other's eyes; this was neither the first crime they had committed, nor their first abuse of power. The She-wolf of France signed the order for the immediate execution of her cousin and brother-in-law.

Edmund of Kent was brought from his dungeon; he was dressed in a shirt and his hands were bound; a small escort of archers led him into the castle's inner courtyard; and there he waited for three hours in the rain while evening fell. Why was he being subjected to this interminable wait before the block? He alternated between wild hope and utter despair. Surely, it could be only because his nephew, the young King, was ordering his reprieve. This hideous waiting must surely be a punishment to inspire him with repentance and also with an appreciation of the quality of the King's mercy. He prayed, and then suddenly began sobbing. His shirt was soaked and he was shivering; the rain trickled over the block and the archers' helmets. Would the torture never end?

The fact was that the whole of Winchester was being searched for an executioner, and none could be found. The city's executioner and his assistants, well aware of how the trial had been conducted and that the King had had no opportunity of issuing a reprieve, obstinately refused to exercise their office on a prince of the blood. They would rather lose their jobs.

Next the officers of the garrison were approached to detail one of their men or ask for a volunteer who would be handsomely rewarded. They refused in disgust. They were prepared to maintain order, mount guard over Parliament, escort the condemned man to the place of execution, but neither they nor their men could be expected to do more.

Mortimer was coldly and furiously angry with the Governor of the castle.

'Is there no forger, brigand or murderer in your prisons, who would purchase his life in exchange? Go on, make haste, if you don't want to end up in jail yourself!'

The dungeons were visited and in the end a man was found; he had robbed a church and was to be hanged the next week. They handed him the axe, but he insisted on wearing a mask.

Night had fallen. By the light of the torches flickering under the rain, the Earl of Kent saw his executioner arrive and knew that the long hours of hope had been no more than a last derisory illusion. He uttered a cry of terror; and they had to force him to kneel at the block.

The amateur executioner was more frightened than cruel, in fact he was trembling even more than his victim. He had no experience in handling an axe. He missed his first blow, and the steel slid off the hair. It took him four further blows, struck into a red, nauseating mass. The old archers standing round vomited.

And so died Edmund, Earl of Kent, a gracious but ingenuous prince, before he reached the age of thirty. And the man who had stolen a ciborium was sent home to his family.

When young King Edward III emerged from a long disputation in Latin about the doctrines of Master Occam, he was told that his uncle had been beheaded.

'With no order from me?' he said in surprise.

He sent for Lord Montacute, who had accompanied him to the homage at Amiens, and on whose loyalty he knew from experience he could rely.

'My lord,' he said, 'you were in Parliament this day. I want to know the truth.'

2

The Axe in Nottingham

A CRIME OF STATE must always have at least the appearance of legality.

The fount of law lies in the sovereign, and sovereignty belongs to the people, who exercise it either through the intermediacy of elected representatives, or by delegation to an hereditary monarch. Sometimes both these forms are combined, as they already were in England.

There could therefore be no legal act in the country which had not the joint consent of monarch and people, whether that consent was tacit or overt.

The execution of the Earl of Kent was legal in form, since the royal powers were exercised by the Council of Regency and, in the absence of the Earl of Lancaster, President of the Council, the power of signing orders devolved on the Queen Mother; but the execution had neither the true consent of Parliament, for it had been sitting under duress, nor the adherence of the King, who had been kept in ignorance of the order issued in his name. Such a deed was bound to be disastrous to its authors.

Edward III did all he could to show his disapproval by insisting that his uncle of Kent's obsequies be worthy of a prince of the blood.[17] Since it was merely a question of a corpse, Mortimer deferred to the young King's wishes. But Edward never forgave him for having taken the life of a member of the royal family without his knowledge; nor could he forget that Madame Philippa had fainted at the brutal announcement of his uncle of Kent's execution, for the young Queen was six months with child and greater tact should have been shown her. Edward reproached his mother and, when she answered irritably that Madame Philippa showed too much sympathy with the enemies of the kingdom and that it required courage to be a queen, Edward replied: 'It is not every woman who has such a stony heart as yours, Madame.'

The incident, however, had no ill-consequences for Madame Philippa, and towards the middle of June she gave birth to a son.[18] Edward III felt that deep, grave, simple joy which every man must feel at the birth of the first child given him by the woman he loves and who loves him. He also felt suddenly more mature as a king. His succession was now safe. His sense of dynasty and of his own place in the line of his ancestors and descendants, though the latter were as yet represented merely by a weak child in a frilly cradle, was constantly in his mind and he began to find the tutelage imposed on him increasingly intolerable.

Nevertheless, he felt certain moral scruples. What good could it do to overthrow the directing clique, if one had no better men to replace it with or better principles to apply?

'Am I fit to govern, and am I old enough to do it?' he often wondered.

His mind had been profoundly affected by the odious examples of his father and mother. His father had been entirely ruled by the Despensers, and his mother was completely under the domination of Roger Mortimer.

His enforced inaction gave him the chance of watching and thinking. Nothing could be done in the kingdom without Parliament giving or being made to give its agreement. The importance gained by this advisory assembly during recent years, when it had met with increasing frequency in all kinds of places and on every sort of occasion, was simply the consequence of bad government, ill-conducted military campaigns, a dissolute royal family and disorders within the realm due to the constant hostility between the central power and coalitions formed by the great feudal barons.

A stop must be put to the expensive journeys by which the Lords and Commons moved from Winchester to Salisbury and then to York, to hold sessions with no other object than to enable Lord Mortimer to make the country feel the weight of his hand.

'When I am really King, Parliament will sit on regular dates, and in London whenever possible. As for the army, it is not the King's army, but consists of the armies of the barons who obey only when it suits them to do so. There must be an army recruited for the service of the realm, and commanded by leaders who hold their power from the King alone. And the law, too, must be concentrated in the hands of the King and everyone must be equal before it. From what they say, there is far greater order in the Kingdom of France. And we must encourage trade, for people are complaining that it suffers from taxes and embargoes on leather and wool which are the wealth of the country.'

These ideas were simple enough, but they were important because they were in a royal mind and they were almost revolutionary at a time of such anarchy, despotism and cruelty as the nations had scarcely known before.

The aggrieved young Sovereign was thinking very much the same thoughts as his oppressed people. He told only a very few intimates of his intentions, his wife Philippa, Guillaume de Mauny, the equerry she had brought with her from Hainaut, and Lord Montacute in particular, who kept him informed of the views of the young lords.

It is often at the age of twenty that a man formulates the principles by which he will live for the rest of his life. Edward III had one great quality for a sovereign: he was without passions or vice. He had had the luck to marry a princess he loved; and he had the luck to remain in love with her. He had the supreme form of pride, in that his position as King seemed perfectly natural to him. He insisted on respect both for his person and his function; but he hated unnecessary pomp, because it was an insult to the poor and contrary to real majesty.

People who had known the Court of France in the old days said he resembled King Philip the Fair in many ways: in feature, pallor of complexion, and in the coldness of his blue eyes when on occasion he raised his long lashes.

Edward was certainly more communicative and enthusiastic than his maternal grandfather. But those who remarked on this had known the Iron King only in his last years, after more than a quarter of a century of power. No one could remember what Philip the Fair had been like at the age of twenty. The blood of France was more apparent in Edward III than that of the Plantagenets, and it seemed as if the real Capet was on the throne of England.

In October of this year, 1330, Parliament was summoned once again, on this occasion to Nottingham. It looked like being a stormy session; most of the Lords could not forgive the execution of the Earl of Kent, which not only weighed heavily on their consciences, but confirmed all their suspicions about the murder of Edward II.

Henry Wryneck, Earl of Lancaster, who was called 'old Lancester' because he was the only member of the royal family who had succeeded in preserving his big lopsided head for fifty years, had at last returned to England, as brave and wise as ever. A disease of the eyes which had threatened him for a long time past had suddenly grown worse and he had become half blind; he had to be led; but the infirmity seemed only to make him the more venerable, and his advice was sought with all the greater deference.

The Commons were concerned because they were to be asked to consent to new subsidies, and to ratify new taxes on wool. But where did all the money go?

How had Mortimer used the thirty thousand pounds of the Scottish indemnity? Had that hard campaign of three years ago been fought for him or for the kingdom? And why had the melancholy Baron Maltravers, over and above his pay as Seneschal, been given a thousand pounds as his salary for guarding the late King, if it was not a payment for murdering him? For in the end things always came out, and Treasury accounts cannot be kept secret for ever. These were the purposes to which the revenues from taxation were put. And Ogle and Gournay, Maltravers' assistants, as well as Daverill, the Governor of Corfe Castle, had all received similar sums.

Mortimer, whose progress along the road to Nottingham was accompanied by so splendid a train that the young King himself seemed merely to be part of his suite, was no longer really supported by more than some hundred partisans, all of whom owed their fortune to him, were powerful simply because they served him, and would be in danger of disgrace, banishment or even death, the moment he fell.

He believed himself obeyed because a network of spies – there was even John Wynyard in the King's entourage – kept him informed of all that was said and so prevented conspiracies. He believed himself powerful because his troops made him feared by the Lords and Commons. But troops may march to another man's orders and spies may betray.

Power, without the consent of those over whom it is exercised, is a fraud that cannot long endure, a delicate balance between fear and rebellion, which may suddenly be overset when enough men become aware that they all think alike.

Riding on a saddle embroidered with gold and silver, surrounded by an escort in scarlet uniforms bearing his pennon on their lances, Mortimer was travelling over a very muddy road.

During the journey, Edward III noticed that his mother seemed ill, that her face was drawn and wan, her eyes tired and less bright than usual. She was riding in a litter and not on her white hackney as she normally did; the litter had to make frequent stops, for its movement made her feel sick. Mortimer's manner towards her seemed at once attentive and embarrassed.

Perhaps Edward would not have noticed these signs so much had he not seen the same in Madame Philippa, his wife, earlier in the year. Besides, servants talk during journeys; the Queen Mother's women gossiped with Madame Philippa's. At York, where they lay for two days, Edward could no longer doubt that his mother was pregnant.

He was overwhelmed with shame and disgust. The jealousy of an eldest son increased his resentment. What had become of that splendid and noble image he had made of his mother in his childhood?

'It was on her account I hated my father, because of the shame he inflicted on her. And now she's disgracing me. At forty she'll be the mother of a bastard who will be younger than my own son.'

As a king, he felt humiliated before his realm, and as a husband before his wife.

In their room in York Castle, unable to sleep, restlessly turning from side to side between the sheets, he said to Philippa: 'Do you remember our wedding here, my love? Oh, what a sad reign I've brought you to!'

Philippa was placid and sensible, and felt less passionate about the matter; nevertheless, her sense of propriety was outraged.

'Such a thing could never happen at the Court of France,' she said.

But this infuriated Edward.

'Oh, my love, what about your cousins of Burgundy who all three deceived their husbands? And what about your poisoned kings?'

It was as if the French dynasty had suddenly become Philippa's own family.

'In France people are more courteous,' replied Philippa, 'less blatant in their desires, less cruel in their rancour.'

'They dissemble better and are more secretive. They prefer poison to steel.'

'You're less civilized here.'

He fell silent. She feared she had offended him, and reached out a soft round arm towards him.

'I love you very much, my sweet,' she said, 'because you're not like them.'

'And it's not only the shame,' Edward went on, 'but the danger, too.'

'What do you mean?'

'I mean that Mortimer is perfectly capable of killing us all, marrying my mother so as to get himself recognized as Regent and then claiming the throne for his bastard.'

'You can't think that; it would be madness!' said Philippa.

Indeed such a plot, which meant the denial of every religious and dynastic principle, would have been quite unthinkable in any firmly established monarchy; but anything was possible, the wildest venture conceivable, in a kingdom that was torn by the struggle between rival factions.

'I shall talk to Montacute about it tomorrow,' said the young King.

When they reached Nottingham, Lord Mortimer showed himself particularly irritable, autocratic and impatient, because John Wynyard, though he had been unable to overhear what was said, had reported to him that there had been much converse between the King, Lord Montacute and several other young lords during the latter part of the journey.

Mortimer began by taking to task Sir Edward Bohun, the Vice-Governor, for the lodging arrangements he had made;

in accordance with custom he had intended to put the great lords in the castle itself.

'By what right,' cried Mortimer, 'have you disposed of these apartments so close to the Queen Mother's without reference to me?'

'I thought, my lord, that the Earl of Lancaster . . .'

'The Earl of Lancaster, and all the rest of them too, must be lodged at least a mile from the castle.'

'And yourself, my lord?'

Mortimer frowned as if he found the question offensive.

'My apartment will be next to the Queen Mother's, and the Constable will hand her the keys of the castle each evening.'

Edward Bohun bowed.

Too many precautions can sometimes be disastrous. Mortimer wished to avoid comment on the Queen Mother's condition; above all, he wanted to isolate the King, but he merely gave the young lords the opportunity to meet and make plans with each other, far from the castle and his spies.

Lord Montacute assembled his most trusted friends, young men between twenty and thirty for the most part: Lords Molins, Hufford, Stafford, Clinton, as well as John Nevil de Horneby and the four Bohun brothers, Edward, Humphrey, William and John, the last of whom was Earl of Hereford and Essex. These young men formed the King's party, and had Henry of Lancaster's blessing, indeed more than his blessing.

As for Mortimer, he was living in the castle with the Chancellor Burghersh, Simon Bereford, John Monmouth, John Wynyard, Hugh Turplington and Maltravers, consulting with them as to how best to counter the new conspiracy he guessed was being hatched against him.

Bishop Burghersh felt the wind was changing and was far

from eager for severe measures; he hid behind his ecclesiastical dignity and advised negotiations. In the past he had been nimble in changing from the Despensers' party to Mortimer's.

'We've had enough of arrests and blood-letting,' he said. 'Perhaps some gratifications in the form of lands, money and honours . . .'

Mortimer silenced him with a glance; his eyes, half-hidden behind the straight line of the lids under the massive brow, could still make people quake.

At that very hour Lord Montacute was having a private conversation with Edward III.

'I beseech you, my noble King,' he said, 'no longer to tolerate the insolence and intrigues of the man who ordered your father's assassination, beheaded your uncle, and corrupted your mother. We have sworn to shed the last drop of our blood to free you from him. We're ready to go to any lengths; but we must act quickly and, to do so, we must be able to enter the castle in large enough numbers, for none of us are lodged in it.'

The young King thought for a moment.

'I know now, William,' he replied, 'how well I love you.'

He did not say 'how well you love me'. His was a truly royal mind, for he never doubted that people would wish to serve him; for him, the important thing was to give his trust and affection to the right people.

'You will go on my behalf to the Constable of the castle, Sir William Eland,' he went on, 'and pray him, on my orders, to obey you in everything you ask of him.'

'May God help our cause, my lord!' said Montacute.

Everything now depended on Eland being won over and being loyal; if he revealed Montacute's plan, the conspirators were lost, and perhaps even the King himself too. But Sir Edward Bohun guaranteed that he would be amenable, if it were only because Mortimer had treated him like a mere servant ever since his arrival in Nottingham.

William Eland did not disappoint Montacute, for he promised obedience to the utmost of his power, and swore to keep the secret.

'Since you are with us,' said Montacute, 'give me the keys of the castle tonight.'

'My lord,' replied Eland, 'you must know that the gates and doors are locked every night and that I have to give the keys to the Queen Mother who sleeps with them under her pillow till morning. And I must also tell you that the usual castle guard has been relieved and replaced by four hundred of Lord Mortimer's personal troops.'

Montacute thought that all his hopes were dashed.

'But I know of a secret entrance leading into the castle from the fields,' went on Eland. 'It's an underground passage dating back to the Saxon kings, who had it made so that they could escape from the Danes when they ravaged the countryside. Queen Isabella, Mortimer, and their people know nothing of this passage, for I have had no occasion to reveal its existence to them. It leads into the very heart of the castle, into the keep,[19] and you can enter by it without a soul being the wiser.'

'How shall we find the entrance in the fields?'

'I shall be with you, my lord!'

Lord Montacute had a second, hasty conversation with the King; then, during the course of the evening, together with the brothers Bohun, the other conspirators and Sir William Eland, he took horse and left the town, openly declaring that they thought themselves in danger in Nottingham.

Their departure, which looked so like flight, was immediately reported to Mortimer.

'They know they've been unmasked and have given themselves away. I shall have them seized tomorrow and brought before Parliament. At least we shall have a quiet night, my dear,' he said to Queen Isabella.

Towards midnight, on the other side of the keep, in a granite-walled room lit only by a night-light, Madame Philippa inquired of her husband why instead of coming to bed he sat on the edge of it, wearing a coat of mail under his royal surcoat and with a short sword beside him.

'Great things may happen tonight,' Edward replied.

Though Philippa looked calm and placid enough, her heart was beating fast; she remembered the conversation they had had in York.

'Do you think they're coming to assassinate you?'

'That may happen, too.'

There was a sound of voices whispering in the next room, and Gautier de Mauny, whom the King had ordered to stand guard in his anteroom, knocked discreetly at the door. Edward went to open it.

'The Constable is here, my lord,' he said, 'and others with him.'

Edward went to Philippa and kissed her forehead; she seized his hands, gripped them for a moment and murmured: 'God keep you!'

Gautier de Mauny asked: 'Am I to come with you, my lord?'

'Bolt the doors behind me and watch over Madame Philippa.'

In the grassy courtyard of the keep the conspirators had

assembled round the well in the moonlight, shadows armed with swords and battle-axes.

The young men had bound rags about their feet; the King had failed to take this precaution and his footsteps were the only ones to echo down the flagstones of the long corridors. Their progress was lit by a single torch.

There were servants sleeping on the floor. If they half-awakened, someone murmured: 'The King,' and they stayed where they were, drew a little closer together and wondered at this passage of armed lords in the night, yet content not to know too much.

There was no trouble till they reached the antechamber to Queen Isabella's apartments, where the six men posted by Mortimer refused them entrance, even though it was the King who demanded it. The battle was brief; and only John Nevil was wounded by a pike-thrust in the arm. Surrounded and disarmed, the guards were made to stand with their backs to the wall. The struggle had lasted no more than a minute, but behind the heavy door they heard the Queen Mother scream and then the bolts being shot home.

'Come out, Lord Mortimer!' Edward ordered. 'Your King has come to arrest you.'

His voice was clear and strong as it was in battle, and also as the crowd at York had heard it on his wedding day.

There was no reply but the sound of a sword grating as it was drawn from the scabbard.

'Come out, Mortimer!' the young King shouted once again.

He waited for another few seconds, then seized a battle-axe from one of the young lords, swung it high and drove it into the door with all his might.

With this axe-blow, he at long last firmly asserted his royal power; it was the end of his humiliations and the curbs on his will; and it was also the freeing of his Parliament, the restoration of honour to the Lords and of law to the realm. It was not on his coronation day that Edward III's reign began, but now, at this moment, when the bright steel bit into dark oak and the noise of splintering wood echoed through the vaults of Nottingham Castle.

Ten other axes attacked the door, and the heavy oak soon yielded.

Roger Mortimer was standing in the middle of the room; he had had time to don his hose; his white shirt was open to the waist and he held a sword in his hand.

His flinty eyes gleamed under his thick eyebrows, his greying, uncombed hair hung down about his rugged face; there was still an impressive strength about him.

Queen Isabella stood by his side, tears pouring down her face. She was shivering with fear and cold; her little naked feet made two white patches on the flagstones. The rumpled bed could be seen in the next room.

The young King's first glance was at his mother's stomach, at its shape as revealed by the nightdress. He would never forgive Mortimer for reducing his mother, who was so beautiful, so gallant in adversity, so cruel in victory and always so royal, to this weeping woman, who stood there groaning and wringing her hands because they had come to take her man from her.

'My son, my son, I beseech you, spare my dear Mortimer!'

She had come forward and was standing between her son and her lover.

'Has he spared your honour?' said Edward.

'Don't hurt his body!' she cried. 'He is a gallant knight and our beloved. Don't forget you owe him your throne!'

The conspirators hesitated. They wondered if there must be a struggle and whether they would have to kill Mortimer under the Queen's very eyes.

'He has had rewards enough for hurrying me to the throne! Go on, my lords, seize him!' said the young King, pushing his mother aside and waving his companions forward.

Montacute, the Bohuns, Lord Molins and John Nevil, his arm bleeding though he paid it no attention, surrounded Mortimer. Two battle-axes were raised above his head, and three swords were held with their points to his chest. Then a hand seized his arm and made him drop the sword he held. He was pushed towards the door. As he crossed the threshold, he turned and said: 'Goodbye, Isabella, my Queen; we have loved one another well!'

And it was true. The greatest, most spectacular and most devastating love of the century, which had started merely as a chivalrous exploit, but had stirred all the Courts of Europe as well as the Holy See, whose passion had assembled a fleet, equipped an army and been consummated in tyranny, bloodthirstiness and power, was now come to its end amid the battle-axes and by the light of a smoky torch. Roger Mortimer, eighth Baron of Wigmore, former Justiciar of Ireland and first Earl of March, was led away to prison, while his royal mistress, clothed only in a nightdress, collapsed at the foot of their bed.

Before dawn broke Bereford, Daverill, Wynyard and Mortimer's other principal supporters had been arrested; Seneschal Maltravers, Gournay and Ogle, Edward II's three murderers, were in flight and being pursued.

In the morning the populace crowded into the streets of Nottingham to shout their joy as the escort went by, taking Mortimer away in chains and a tumbril, the supreme disgrace for a knight. Wryneck, his head resting on his shoulder, was in the front row of the crowd and, even though his tired old eyes could barely see the procession go by, he danced with joy and threw his cap in the air.

'Where are you taking him?' people asked.

'To the Tower of London.'

3

To the Common Gallows

THE RAVENS IN THE Tower live to a great age, to over a hundred they say. The same huge, sly, persistent bird, which seven years ago had tried to peck the prisoner's eyes out through the bars of his dungeon window, had once again taken up its post in front of it.

Were they mocking Mortimer in giving him the same dungeon as before? Where the father had kept him shut up for eighteen months, the son now held him prisoner. It occurred to Mortimer that there must be something in his character, some quality in his nature which made him intolerable to the royal authority, or made that authority unbearable to himself. In any case, a king and he could not live together in the same country, and one or other of them had to die. He had destroyed one king; and now another was going to destroy him. It is a great misfortune to be born with the soul of a king if one is not destined to reign.

And if it was from prudence that he had been put in the same dungeon because the means by which he had escaped from it were known, it was a singularly useless precaution. This time he had no wish to escape.

To Roger Mortimer it seemed that he had died in Nottingham. For men such as he, who are governed by pride and have achieved, if only temporarily, their highest ambitions, downfall is equivalent to death. The true Mortimer was now, and for all human eternity, part of the history of England; the dungeon of the Tower contained no more than the indifferent envelope of his flesh.

Curiously enough, that envelope had fallen at once into its old habits. As when, after an absence of twenty years one returns to the house in which one lived as a child, one's knee of its own volition and by a sort of muscular memory presses against the door that always stuck or one's foot steps farther in on the staircase to avoid the worn edge of a tread, so Mortimer was repeating the physical movements of his previous imprisonment. He could even walk the few steps from the window to the wall in the dark without ever knocking into anything; his first act on entering the dungeon had been to push the stool back into its old place; he recognized at once the familiar sounds of the guard being relieved and the bell tolling for the services in the Chapel of St Peter ad Vincula; and without any conscious thought. He knew the hour at which he would be brought his meals. Nor was the food much better than it had been in the time of the ignoble Constable Seagrave.

Because the barber Ogle had on the previous occasion served Mortimer as a messenger in organizing his escape, he was not allowed anyone to shave him. His beard had a month's growth.

But apart from this everything was the same, even to the

raven which Mortimer in the past had nicknamed Edward. The bird was pretending to be asleep; but every now and then it would open a round eye before darting its great beak through the bars.

Nevertheless, there was one thing lacking: the melancholy conversation of his old uncle, Lord Mortimer of Chirk, who used to lie on the plank bed. Roger Mortimer understood now why the old man had refused to escape with him. It was not through fear of the danger nor through weakness of body; one has always enough strength to set out, even if one must fall by the wayside. It was the feeling that his life was over that had held the old Lord of Chirk back and led him to prefer to await his end on the plank bed.

For Roger Mortimer, who was only forty-five, death would not come of itself. He felt vaguely troubled when he looked towards the centre of the Green, where the block usually stood. But you become accustomed to the nearness of death by a whole series of simple thoughts that add up in the end to no more than a weary melancholy. It occurred to Mortimer that the sly raven would live on after him, and would tease other prisoners; the rats, too, would go on living, those big wet rats that emerged at night from the muddy banks of the Thames to run about the stones of the fortress; and even the flea that was irritating him under his shirt would jump onto his executioner the day of his death and go on living. Every life that is wiped from the world leaves the other lives intact. There is nothing so ordinary as death.

He sometimes thought of his wife, Lady Jeanne, but without nostalgia or remorse. He had kept her sufficiently aloof from politics for there to be no reason for arresting her. She would no doubt be allowed to keep her own property. As for his sons, they would have to suffer their share of the hatred that had brought about his downfall; but since it was improbable that they would ever become men of as great attainment or ambition as himself, what did it matter whether they were Earls of March or not? The great Mortimer was himself, or rather what he had been. He had no regrets either for his wife or for his sons.

As for Queen Isabella, she would die one day, and from that moment there would be no one on earth who had really known him as he was. It was only when he thought of Isabella that he emerged from his contemptuous detachment from life. There was no doubt that he had died at Nottingham; but the memory of those four years of passion was still alive, rather as the hair still obstinately continues to grow after the heart has ceased to beat. Indeed, this was all that remained for the executioner to sever. When his head was separated from his body, the memory of the royal hands clasped about his neck would be annihilated.

As he did each morning, Mortimer had asked the date. It was November 29th. Parliament must therefore have met and he was awaiting the summons to appear before it. He well knew the cowardice of assemblies; and he realized that no one would speak up in his defence; far from it, both Lords and Commons would take hasty vengeance for the fear with which he had inspired them for so long.

In fact, sentence had already been pronounced by Parliament in the session at Nottingham. It was not to an act of justice they were submitting him, but to a necessary imitation of it, a formality, exactly like the sentences he himself had had delivered in the past.

A twenty-year-old king impatient to rule and young lords

impatient for the royal favour required his death so that they might be sure of their power.

'For young Edward, my death is the necessary complement to his coronation. And yet, they will do no better than I did; the people will be no happier under their rule. Where I have failed, who can succeed?' he thought.

What attitude should he adopt during the mockery of a trial? Humble himself, as had the Earl of Kent? Cry *peccavi*, entreat, offer submission with bare feet and a rope about his neck, and admit to his past errors? You had to have a very great desire to live before you could submit yourself to such farcical disgrace. 'I have committed no fault. I was the strongest, and I remained so till others, stronger yet for a moment, brought about my downfall. That is all.'

Should he insult them? Face that Parliament of sheep for the last time and say: 'My lords, I took up arms against Edward II, but though you are sitting in judgement on me today, who among you did not follow me then? I escaped from the Tower of London. My lord bishops, you are sitting in judgement on me today, but who among you did not furnish assistance and money to help me to freedom? I saved Queen Isabella from being murdered by her husband's favourites, I raised troops and armed a fleet to deliver you from the Despensers, I deposed the King you hated and had his son, who is having me judged today, crowned. My lords, earls, barons and bishops, and you, honourable members of the Commons, who among you did not support me in accomplishing these things, and did not applaud me in all I did? Even to the Queen's love for me! You can reproach me with nothing more than having acted on your behalf, and you are merely eager to destroy me so as to be able to expiate in the death of one man events for which you are all responsible.'

Or should he remain silent, refuse to answer questions, defend himself and go to the useless trouble of justifying himself? Let the hounds bay now that they were no longer subject to the whip. 'How right I was to keep them in a state of terror!'

His thoughts were interrupted by the sound of footsteps. 'The moment has come,' he thought.

The door opened and sergeants-at-arms appeared. They stood aside to make way for the Earl of Norfolk, Marshall of England, who was followed by the Lord Mayor and the Sheriffs of London, as well as by a number of delegates from the Lords and Commons. They could not all get into the dungeon and crowded together in the narrow passage.

'My lord,' said the Earl of Norfolk, 'I come in the King's name to read the sentence passed on you three days ago by Parliament assembled.'

They were surprised to see Mortimer smile at the announcement. It was a calm, contemptuous smile, but it was directed at himself rather than at them.

The sentence had been pronounced three days ago, without interrogation, defence or even the prisoner's appearance, while a moment before he had been considering what attitude he should adopt when he was brought before his accusers. A vain anxiety! He was being given a lesson: he might have dispensed with legal formalities in the cases of the Despensers, the Earl of Arundel and the Earl of Kent.

The Crown Coroner began reading out the judgement.[20]

'"In as much as it was ordered by Parliament, sitting in London, immediately after the coronation of our Lord the

King, that the King's Council should consist of five bishops, two earls and five barons, and that nothing might be decided except in their presence, and that the said Roger Mortimer, without regard to the will of Parliament, appropriated to himself the government and administration of the kingdom, appointing and changing as he pleased the officers of the King's household and of the whole kingdom, in order to place his own friends as he felt inclined. . . .'"

Standing with his back to the wall, one hand resting on a window bar, Roger Mortimer gazed out at the Green and seemed scarcely interested.

"'In as much as the father of our King was taken to Kenilworth Castle, by order of the peers of the realm, to be detained there and treated in accordance with his princely dignity, the said Roger ordered him to be refused all those things he required and to be transferred to Berkeley Castle where eventually, on the orders of the said Roger, he was treacherously and ignominiously assassinated. . . .'"

'Get away, you evil bird!' Mortimer cried suddenly, much to everyone's astonishment. The raven had pecked at the back of his hand.

"'In as much as it was forbidden by an Ordinance of the King, sealed with the Great Seal, to enter the Chamber of Parliament, then sitting at Salisbury, in arms under pain of forfeiture, the said Roger and his armed band nevertheless entered it, thus violating the Royal Ordinance . . .'"

This list of crimes was interminable. Mortimer was charged with having organized a military expedition against the Earl of Lancaster; with having placed spies about the young King who had been constrained to 'conduct himself rather as a prisoner than as a king'; with having acquired for his own use, as if they were gifts, numerous estates belonging to the Crown; with having ransomed, despoiled or banished numerous barons who had rebelled against his tyranny, and conspired to make the Earl of Kent believe that the King's father was still alive, 'which decided the said earl to verify the facts by the most loyal and honest means'; with having usurped the royal powers by bringing the Earl of Kent before Parliament and having him put to death; with having misappropriated sums intended for the financing of the war in Gascony, as well as thirty thousand silver marks paid by the Scots in accordance with the Treaty of Peace; with having taken over the Royal Treasury to his own profit and to that of certain members of the Council, with the result that the King was no longer in a position to uphold his rank; and, finally, with having created discord between the King's father and his Queen Consort, 'being therefore responsible for the fact that the Queen never returned to her lord to share his bed, to the great dishonour of the King and the whole realm', and also with having dishonoured the Queen 'by appearing overtly as her notorious and admitted paramour'.

Mortimer, staring at the ceiling and stroking his beard, was smiling again. His whole story was being read over and it was in this strange form that it would go into the archives of the kingdom for ever.

'"And for the above reasons the King referred the matter to the earls, barons and others that they might pronounce just sentence against the said Roger Mortimer; which the members of Parliament, having consulted together, agreed to do, declaring that all the charges enumerated were valid, notorious, and known to all the people, in particular the article touching the death of the King in Berkeley Castle. They have therefore decided that the said Roger, a traitor and an enemy to the King and the realm, shall be dragged upon a hurdle to the place of execution and there hanged . . ."'

Mortimer started. So it was not to be the block after all! He was to be a victim of the unexpected till the end.

"'And also that this sentence shall be without appeal, as the said Mortimer himself decided in the past in the cases of the two Despensers and the late Lord Edmund, Earl of Kent, the King's uncle."'

The clerk ceased reading and rolled up the pages. The Earl of Norfolk, Kent's brother, looked Mortimer straight in the eyes. He had been very much in the background these last few months, but now he had reappeared as the embodiment of legal vengeance. Because of the way he looked at him, Mortimer felt an urge to speak – not for long, but merely to say to the Earl Marshal, and through him to the King, the councillors, the Lords and Commons, the clergy and the people, to all those whom he had held in subjection: 'When a man appears in the realm of England who can do all those things you have just read out, you will submit yourselves to him once again. But I do not think he will appear just yet. It is now time to make an end. Are you taking me to the place of execution at once?'

He seemed still to be giving orders, even the order for his own execution.

'Yes, my lord,' said the Earl of Norfolk. 'We are taking you to the Common Gallows immediately.'

The Common Gallows was where robbers, forgers, panders and other were hanged: it was the gibbet for common criminals.

'Very well, let us go!' said Mortimer.

'You must first be stripped for the hurdle.'

'Very well, strip me then.'

They stripped him of his clothes, leaving him only a cloth about his loins. And, amid his warmly clothed escort, he went out naked into the drizzling November rain. His strong body made a pale patch among the dark cloaks and armour of his guards.

The hurdle was on the Green. It consisted of rough cross-pieces fastened to two runners, and was attached to a horse's traces.

Mortimer glanced at it with a contemptuous smile. What trouble they were taking to humiliate him! He lay down on the hurdle of his own accord and they bound his wrists and ankles to it. They set the horse in motion and the hurdle moved smoothly across the grass of the Green, and then more roughly over the gravel and stones of the road.

The Earl Marshal of England, the Lord Mayor, the sheriffs, the Parliamentary delegates and the Constable of the Tower followed it. An escort of soldiers, pike on shoulder, kept the way open and guarded the procession.

They passed out of the Tower to be greeted by a cruelly hostile crowd, which increased throughout their progress.

When one has looked at men all one's life from a horse's back or a baron's chair, it is strange to see them suddenly from ground-level, their wagging chins, their mouths twisted in shouting, their nostrils agape. Neither men nor women were beautiful seen thus; their faces were grotesque and wicked, frightful gargoyles which one should have trampled down when one was on one's feet! Had it not been for the drizzle falling straight into his eyes, Mortimer could have had an even better look at these faces so full of hate, as he was bumped and jolted along on the hurdle.

Something damp and slimy hit him on the cheek and ran down into his beard; he realized someone had spat at him. Suddenly he felt a sharp, piercing pain run through his body; a cowardly hand had thrown a stone and hit him between the legs. Had it not been for the pikemen, the crowd, which was intoxicated by its own furious howlings, would have torn him to pieces there and then.

He, who six years earlier had been received with acclamations down all the roads of England, was now being dragged between walls of insults and curses. Crowds have two voices, one for hatred and the other for joy; it is one of the great mysteries that many throats shouting in concert can produce such very different sounds.

Suddenly there was silence. Had they reached the gallows already? It was only Westminster and the hurdle was passing under the windows at which the members of Parliament were gathered. They looked silently down on the man, who had held them subject to his will for so many months, being dragged like a felled tree over the cobbles. The established institutions of England had won at last.

Mortimer, his eyes full of rain, was searching for one face. He was hoping that, by a supreme act of cruelty, Queen Isabella had been compelled to watch his torment. He could not see her.

Then the procession turned towards Tyburn.[21] When it reached the Common Gallows, the condemned man was unbound and hastily confessed. For the last time, Mortimer dominated the crowd from the scaffold. He suffered little, for the hangman pulled so hard on the rope that it broke his neck.

That day Queen Isabella was at Windsor, where she was making a slow recovery from having lost both her lover and his child she was expecting.

King Edward informed his mother that he would spend Christmas with her.

A Bad Day

FROM THE WINDOWS OF Bonnefille House Beatrice d'Hirson was watching the rain fall in the Rue Mauconseil. She had been waiting for some hours past for Robert of Artois, who had promised to come that afternoon. But Robert never kept his promises, either in small things or in great, and Beatrice was beginning to think that she was very silly to believe in him.

To a woman waiting for a man, he has every fault. Had not Robert promised, and for nearly a year now, that she would be a lady-in-waiting in his household? At bottom he was much like his aunt; all the Artois were alike. An ungrateful lot! You worked yourself to death in their service, running after suppliers of poisons and casters of spells, committed murder to serve their interests, ran the risk of the gallows or the stake – and all for what? It was certainly not Monseigneur Robert who would have been arrested had Beatrice been caught putting arsenic into Madame Mahaut's medicines, or salts of mercury into the Dowager Queen

Jeanne's wine. 'I don't know the woman!' he would have said. 'Does she dare maintain she was acting on my orders? It's a lie. She was a member of my aunt's household, not of mine. She's obviously saying it to save herself. Send her to the wheel.' And who would hesitate between the word of a peer of France, the King's brother-in-law, and that of an obscure bishop's niece, whose family was no longer even in favour?

'And what have I done it all for?' Beatrice thought. 'Simply in order to wait all alone in my house, to which Monseigneur Robert deigns to pay a visit once a week! He said he would come after vespers; and benediction has already rung. No doubt he's carousing somewhere with a couple of barons he's invited to dinner, and talking of his great exploits, the affairs of the kingdom and his lawsuit, while pinching the maidservants' bottoms. Even La Divion eats at his table now, I hear! And here am I, staring out at the rain. He'll come in late at night, heavy, belching and red in the face; he'll talk nonsense for a moment, collapse on the bed, sleep an hour and leave again. If he comes at all, that is!'

Beatrice was bored, even more than she had been at Conflans during Mahaut's last months. Her affair with Robert was stuck in a bog. She had thought to trap the giant, but it was he who had won the day. Humiliated and unsatisfied, her passion was beginning to change into secret resentment. She seemed always to be waiting for him! Nor could she go out and do a round of the taverns with a friend in search of adventure, because Robert was certain to come when she was out. Besides, he had her watched.

She was well aware that Robert had cooled towards her, and looked on her now merely as an obligation, an accomplice who had to be humoured. Sometimes a fortnight went by without his showing desire for her.

'You won't win in the long run, Monseigneur Robert!' she whispered to herself. In her heart of hearts she was beginning to hate him, because she could not possess him often enough.

She had tried all the best receipts for love philtres: 'Draw some of your blood on a Friday in spring; put it to dry in the oven in a little pot with two hare's testicles and a dove's liver; reduce the whole to a fine powder and make the person on whom you have designs swallow it; and if it has no effect the first time, repeat on three further occasions.'

Or again: 'Go on a Friday morning into an orchard before sunrise and pluck from a tree the finest apples you can find; then write on a small piece of white paper with your blood both your name and surname and below them the name and surname of the person whose love you desire; and endeavour to acquire three of his hairs, which you join with three of yours, and with these bind the little paper on which you have written with your blood; then split the apple in half, remove the pips, and put the paper bound with the hair in their place; and with two little skewers made of pointed twigs of green myrtle, neatly join the two halves of the apple together and place them to dry in the oven so that they become hard and have no moisture, like the dry Lenten apples; then wrap the apple in laurel and myrtle leaves and endeavour to place it under the pillow of the bed in which the beloved person sleeps without his perceiving it; and in a short while he will give you proof of his love.'

But it had been no good. The Friday apples had had no effect. Sorcery, in which Beatrice believed herself infallible, seemed to have no power over the Count of Artois. And yet he was not the Devil, after all, in spite of what she had said to win him.

She had hoped to become pregnant. Robert seemed to be fond of his sons; from pride perhaps, but he was fond of them. They were the only people in the world of whom he spoke at all tenderly. Perhaps he would be fond of a little bastard too. Besides, Beatrice could have made good use of such an event; she could have shown her pregnancy and said: 'I am expecting a child by Monseigneur Robert.' But whether it was the things she had done in the past or the Evil One himself that had made her barren, she had been disappointed in this also. And now Beatrice d'Hirson, the Countess Mahaut's former lady-in-waiting, was reduced to waiting, staring at the rain, and dreaming of revenge.

Robert of Artois arrived late, looking worried and scratching at the stubble of his beard with his thumb. He scarcely glanced at Beatrice, who had been careful to don a new dress, and poured himself out a large goblet of hippocras.

'It's tepid,' he said, making a face, and sinking into a chair which groaned beneath his weight.

Of course it was tepid! The decanter had been standing there for four hours!

'I was expecting you earlier, Monseigneur.'

'No doubt! Important matters detained me.'

'Like yesterday and the day before!'

'You must realize that I cannot be seen entering your house by daylight, particularly at this moment when the utmost prudence is necessary.'

'A splendid excuse! But you shouldn't tell me you're coming in daylight if you intend to do so only by night. But the night, of course, belongs to your wife, the Countess!'

He shrugged his shoulders in exasperation.

'You know very well that I no longer sleep with her.'

'Every husband tells his mistress that, from the greatest in the land to the humblest cobbler, and they are all lying. I wonder if Madame de Beaumont would be so gracious and so kind to you if you never visited her bed. As for the days, Monseigneur is always attending the Privy Council, as if the King held Council from dawn to dusk! Or Monseigneur is hunting, or jousting, or has gone to Conches to visit his estate!'

'Peace, woman!' Robert cried, slapping the table with his hand. 'I've enough on my mind without listening to your nonsense. I've entered my plea at the King's Court today!'

It was December 14th, the day Philippe VI had fixed for the opening of the Artois case. Beatrice knew it, for Robert had told her. But she had forgotten it in her jealousy.

'Has it all gone well?'

'Not altogether,' Robert replied rather gloomily. 'I presented my grandfather's documents, and their authenticity was contested.'

'And, of course, you believed them authentic,' said Beatrice with a malicious smile. 'Who contested them?'

'The Duchess of Burgundy who insisted on the documents being examined.'

'Oh, so the Duchess of Burgundy is in Paris, is she?'

Beatrice's long lashes were raised for an instant and her eyes suddenly glinted, but then the lashes fell and they were concealed once more. Robert was deep in thought and did not notice.

Beating his fists together and thrusting out his jaw, he said: 'She came expressly to do it, with the Duke. Mahaut will wrong me even through her descendants, will she? There's bad blood in that family! All the daughters of Burgundy are whores, thieves and liars! That young Duchess they married off to the fool Eudes, who's old enough to be her grandfather, is only twenty-four. But she's already a bitch, like the rest of her family. They've got Burgundy; what do they want with the county they've stolen from me? But I shall win! I'll raise Artois if necessary, as I did against Philippe the Long, that slut's father. And this time I shan't march on Arras, but against Burgundy, lance in rest!'

For all his boastful talk, his heart was not in it. This was not the sort of anger that brought him shouting to his feet, making the walls shake; it lacked the dramatic fury which he knew so well how to use. And, indeed, what audience had he worth the trouble?

In love, custom eats away a person's character. At first, when the affair is still new, you make an effort because you fear what you do not know. Force is what matters; but when mystery has gone, fear also disappears. Each time you show yourself naked, you lose a little of your power. Beatrice was no longer afraid of Robert.

She no longer feared him because she had seen him asleep so often, and she treated him as no one else would have dared to do.

And it was the same with Robert's feelings towards Beatrice. She had became a jealous and demanding mistress, full of reproaches, like all women when a secret liaison has gone on too long. Her talents as a sorceress no longer amused Robert. Her magic and Satanic practices had become commonplace. He was on his guard against her, but simply from atavistic habit, since it had always been common knowledge that women were liars and deceivers. Since she had begun

MAURICE DRUON

demanding he should pleasure her, it no longer occurred to
him to fear her, forgetting that she had first thrown herself
into his arms merely from a lust for treachery. Even the
memory of their two crimes was losing its power and becoming dimmed by the dust of days, while the corpses of their
two victims were disintegrating in the earth.

They had reached that stage which is all the more dangerous because one no longer believes in danger. Lovers should
remember that when they cease to love they become once
again what they were before. Their weapons are never
destroyed, merely laid aside.

Beatrice watched Robert in silence. His thoughts were far
away, concerned with further machinations by which to win
his case. But when, over a period of twenty years, you have
made use of every available resource, searched into law and
custom, suborned witnesses, forged documents, committed
murder even, and the King is your brother-in-law into the
bargain, and you still cannot carry the day, there is reason
for occasional moments of despair.

Changing her attitude, Beatrice suddenly came and knelt
beside him. She was tender, coaxing, submissive, nestling
consolingly against him.

'When will my dear Monseigneur Robert take me into
his house? When will he make me lady-in-waiting to the
Countess, as he promised? Think how splendid that would
be! I should always be near you, and you could send for me
whenever you liked. I should be able to serve you and watch
over you better than anyone else. When is it to be?'

He could not know how much depended on his answer.

'When I've won my case,' he said, as he always did when
she asked that question.

'At the rate it's going, I shall have to wait till my hair's turned white.'

'When judgement has been given then, if you prefer. I have said it, and Robert of Artois never goes back on his word. But, damn it, have a little patience!'

He now regretted having had to dangle that promise before her. He was utterly determined never to put it into effect. Beatrice in the Hôtel d'Artois? How intolerably troublesome and boring that would be!

She got to her feet and went over to warm her hands at the peat fire burning on the hearth.

'I think I've been patient enough,' she said without raising her voice. 'First it was to be after Madame Mahaut's death; then after Jeanne the Widow's. Well, they're both dead now, and New Year's Eve will soon be sung in the churches. And yet you still won't take me into your house. A promiscuous whore like La Divion, who was my uncle's, the Bishop's, mistress and who has forged such splendid documents for you that a blind man could see they're false, has the right to sit at your table and flaunt herself at your Court . . .'

'Let La Divion alone. You know very well I keep that stupid liar near me only from prudence.'

Beatrice smiled fleetingly. Prudence! So he had to treat La Divion with prudence, had he? And merely because she had heated a few seals. But from her, Beatrice, who had sent two princesses to their graves, he feared nothing and could reward her with ingratitude.

'You've really no cause for complaint,' said Robert. 'You have the best of me. If you were in my house, I'd be able to see you less often and less freely.'

Monseigneur Robert was really very conceited; he talked

of his presence as if it were some sublime gift he deigned to bestow.

'Well, if I have the best of you, why do you delay giving it to me,' replied Beatrice in her drawling voice. 'The bed is ready.'

And she pointed to the open door that led into the bedroom.

'No, my dear; I must go back to the palace to see the King in private to confound the Duchess of Burgundy.'

'Oh, of course, the Duchess of Burgundy!' said Beatrice, nodding her head as if in assent. 'Am I to expect the best of you tomorrow then?'

'Alas, tomorrow I have to leave for Conches and Beaumont.'

'And how long will you stay away?'

'Not long. A fortnight.'

'So you won't be here for the New Year?' she asked.

'No, my beautiful sweet; but I'll make you a present of a fine jewelled clasp to decorate your bosom.'

'I'll wear it to dazzle my menservants, since they're the only people I'm likely to see.'

Robert should have been more on his guard. There are unlucky days. During the hearing, on this December 14th, his documents had been so firmly protested against by the Duke and Duchess of Burgundy that Philippe VI had frowned heavily and gazed anxiously at his brother-in-law. It was no day on which to be casual and offend a woman such as Beatrice by leaving her for a whole fortnight unsatisfied in mind and body. He got to his feet.

'Does La Division go with you in your suite?'

'Yes, my wife has so decided.'

Beatrice's bosom heaved in a sudden gust of hatred, and her lashes made dark shadows on her cheeks.

'In that case, Monseigneur Robert, I shall await you like a loyal and loving servant,' she said, raising a smiling face to him.

Robert kissed her lightly and automatically on the cheek. He laid his heavy hand on her buttocks, held it there for a moment, and then gave her a little, indifferent slap. No, he definitely did not want her any more; and in her eyes that was the worst offence of all.

5

Conches

I<small>T WAS A COMPARATIVELY</small> mild winter that year.

Before daybreak Lormet le Dolois came to shake Robert's pillow. Robert yawned hugely like a wild beast, sprinkled some water on his face from the basin Gillet de Nelle held out to him, and hurried into his hunting-clothes, which were of skins with the fur inside, the only really comfortable kind. Then he went to hear low mass in the chapel; the chaplain had orders to hurry through the office, the Epistle, the Gospel and communion in a few minutes. Robert began tapping his foot impatiently if the chaplain took too long over his prayers; and the ciborium was hardly back in its place before he was out of the door.

He would drink a bowl of hot soup, eat two wings of a capon, or perhaps a piece of fat pork, accompanied by a good goblet of the white wine of Meursault which sharpens the wits, flows like gold in the throat, and reawakens the humours of the body the night has put to sleep. He ate and drank standing. Ah, if Burgundy had produced nothing but its wines, instead of having dukes too! 'Eating in the morning is good for the health,' Robert would say, still chewing as he went to his horse. With hunting-knife at waist, horn over the shoulder, and wolfskin cap pulled down over the ears, he was in the saddle.

The hounds, held back by the whip, gave tongue; the horses pawed the ground, their rumps shivering in the sharp morning air. The standard was flying from the keep, since the Lord was in residence in the castle. The drawbridge was lowered, and hounds, horses, grooms and huntsmen debouched with a great clatter towards the pond that lay in the centre of the town, and then, led by the gigantic baron, set off into the fields.

On winter mornings a thin white mist with a scent of wood-smoke tends to lie over the Ouche countryside. Robert of Artois loved Conches. It was only a small castle, of course, but it was pleasant with its good forests around it.

A pale sun was already dispelling the mist by the time they reached the meeting-place with the hunt servants, who had ringed the woods early with the lyam hounds, picked up spoor and slot, and marked the boughs.

The woods of Conches were full of stags and wild boars. The hounds were well broken in. If the boar could be prevented from stopping to stale, he could be taken in little over an hour. The great, majestic stags, however, provided a longer hunt, since they tended to break cover and run in the open, where the turf flew from under the horses' hooves, till they were brought to bay, stiff, panting, their tongues hanging beneath their great heads, in some lake or swamp.

Count Robert hunted at least four times a week. But his hunting bore no resemblance to the great royal hunts with two hundred lords in the field, where you saw nothing of what was going on and, for fear of losing hounds, hunted the King rather than the stag. Here Robert really enjoyed himself alone with his huntsmen, a few vassals from the neighbourhood, who were very proud to be invited, and his two sons whom he was beginning to instruct in the art of hunting, an accomplishment essential to a knight. He was pleased with his sons, who were now ten and nine years old, and were growing up into strong boys; he superintended their training in arms and at the quintain. How lucky his boys were! Robert had lost his father when still too young.

When the quarry was brought to bay, he dispatched it himself, using his hunting-knife for a stag and a spear for a boar. He showed great dexterity in this and enjoyed putting the steel to the exact spot where he felt it sink with a single thrust into the yielding flesh. Both stag and huntsman would be smoking with sweat; and then the stag would collapse as if struck by lightning, while the man stood unharmed.

On the way home, while he discussed the incidents of the hunt, the villeins in the villages, their clothes in tatters and wearing rags bound about their legs, would come running from their hovels to kiss their lord's spur with mingled dread and ecstasy – a good custom which was dying out in the towns.

As soon as the master returned to the castle, the horn blew for water for the midday meal. In the great hall hung with tapestries bearing the arms of France, Artois, Valois and Constantinople, for the Countess of Beaumont was a Courtenay through her mother, Robert sat down to dinner with a ferocious appetite and ate for three hours on end, teasing his entourage meanwhile. He would send for his master cook, who appeared with his wooden spoon hanging from his belt, to compliment him if the haunch of well-marinated wild pig was properly tender, or to threaten him with the gallows if the hot pepper sauce served with the venison roasted whole on the spit was insufficiently seasoned.

After dinner he would retire for a short siesta, and then return to the great hall to give audience to his provosts and tax-collectors, cast an eye on the accounts, attend generally to the business of his fief and dispense justice. He liked dispensing justice; he enjoyed the sight of envy and fear in litigants' eyes, the deceit, cunning, malice and lies – in fact, to see himself reflected on the lowly scale of the rabble.

He particularly enjoyed cases of wanton wives and cuckolded husbands.

'Bring in the cuckold!' he would order, sitting squarely in his oaken chair.

He would ask the lewdest questions, while the clerks sniggered behind their quills, and the plaintiff became crimson with shame.

Robert had an annoying habit, for which his provosts were always reproaching him, of inflicting only minor sentences on thieves, robbers, coggers, suborners, highwaymen, pimps, panders and roughs, except of course when he himself had suffered by the crime or robbery. He felt a secret and innate sympathy for the malefactors of the world.

By the time justice had been done, evening was beginning to fall. Robert would go down to the baths, which were in a basement room in the keep, and plunge into a tub of hot water perfumed with aromatic herbs that removed fatigue.

He had himself dried and rubbed down like a horse, shaved, combed and curled; and for an hour afterwards he smelt almost human.

The pages, cupbearers and servants had already set the trestle-tables for supper, at which Robert would appear in a huge red-velvet baronial robe lined with fur, embroidered with the gold lilies and the castles of Artois, and reaching to his feet.

The Countess of Beaumont wore a robe of violet silk, lined with miniver and embroidered with 'J' and 'R' (Jeanne and Robert) intertwined in gold and with semy of silver trefoils.[22]

The food was less heavy than at midday, consisting of soups of herbs or milk, a roast peacock or swan garnished with young pigeons, fresh and ripened cheeses, and sweet tarts and cakes which improved the taste of the old wines that were poured from decanters shaped like lions or birds.

The service was in the French manner, that is to say two to a bowl, a man and a woman eating from the same dish, except for the Lord. Robert had his own platter, which he emptied with spoon, knife and fingers, wiping his hands on the table-cloth, like everyone else. He ate the smaller birds bones and all.

Towards the end of supper, the minstrel Watriquet de Couvin was asked to take his short harp and declaim one of the lays of his own composing. Messire Watriquet came from Hainaut; he knew Count Guillaume and the Countess, Madame de Beaumont's sister, well, since he had begun his career at their Court. He now visited all the Valois in turn, for he was much in demand and earned substantial fees.[23]

'Watriquet, give us the lay of the *Ladies of Paris*!' Robert would demand with his mouth full.

It was his favourite; and though he knew it almost by heart, he always wanted to hear it over again, like a child demanding the same story every night and insisting that no detail be omitted. Who would have thought, seeing him at a moment such as this, that Robert of Artois was capable of crime and forgery?

The lay of the *Ladies of Paris* recounted the adventure of two bourgeoises, Margue and Marion, the wife and niece of Adam de Gonesse, who, when on their way to the tripe-seller on the morning of Twelfth Night, had the misfortune to meet a neighbour, Dame Tifaigne, a hat-maker, who persuaded them to accompany her to a tavern where the host, so it was said, gave credit.

The ladies sat down to a meal in the Maillets Tavern and the landlord, whose name was Drouin, served them an excellent repast: claret wine, a fat goose, a large dish of garlic, and hot buns.

At this point in the story, Robert of Artois always began laughing in anticipation, while Watriquet went on:

'*Lors commença Margue à suer*
Et boire à grandes hanapées.
En peu d'heures eurent échappées
Trois chopines parmi sa gorge.
"*Dame, foi que je dois saint Georges,*"
Dit Maroclippe, sa commère.
"*Ce vin me fait la bouche amère;*
Je veux avoir de la grenache,
Si devais-je vendre ma vache
Pour en avoir aux mains plein pot".'

Sitting by the great hearth, where a whole tree trunk was burning, Robert of Artois lay back in his chair and laughed aloud.

This reminded him of his youth spent in taverns, brothels and other places of the sort. In his time he had known so many of these free and easy bitches sitting and drinking so eagerly without their husband's knowledge! At midnight, sang Watriquet, Margue, Marion and the hat-maker, having sampled all the wines from the Artois to the 'Saint-Mélion', and having ordered cakes, biscuits, sweet almonds, pears, gingerbread and nuts, were still in the tavern. Margue suggested going out and dancing. The tavern-keeper insisted they should leave their clothes with him as security before they left. Drunk as they were, they readily agreed. In a second they had discarded their cloaks, dresses, bodices, stays and shifts.

Off they went into the January night, naked as the day they were born, staggering, tripping and singing at the tops of their voices: 'Amour au vireli m'en vois', grazing the walls and holding each other up only to collapse dead-drunk, all three of them, on to a heap of refuse.

Day dawned and doors opened. They were discovered all muddy and bloody, as motionless as 'merdes en la mi-voie'. Their husbands were sent for, who assumed they had been murdered; and the women were carried to the Cemetery of the Innocents, where they were thrown into a common grave.

'L'une sur l'autre, toutes vives;
Or leur fuyait par les gencives
Le vin, et par tous les conduits.'

They awakened only the following night, covered with earth and among the dead, but still not sober. They began to shout in the dark, icy cemetery.

> *'"Drouin, Drouin, où es allé?*
> *Apporte trois harengs salés*
> *Et un pot de vin du plus fort*
> *Pour faire à nos têtes confort;*
> *Et ferme aussi la grand fenestre!"'*

Monseigneur Robert positively howled with laughter. The minstrel Watriquet had some difficulty in finishing his lay for the giant's laughter filled the hall for some minutes on end. Tears in his eyes, he was slapping his ribs. Time and again he repeated: *'Et ferme aussi la grand fenestre!'* His amusement was so contagious that all the household were laughing with him.

'Oh, the hussies! Naked to the winds! *"Et ferme aussi la grand fenestre!"'*

And he roared with laughter again.

By and large, it was a good life at Conches; and was it not true happiness? The Countess of Beaumont was a good wife, the County of Beaumont was a good fine little county, and what did it matter that it was a domain of the Crown since its revenues were assured? But what of Artois? Was Artois really so important after all, was it worth the anxiety, the struggle and the effort? 'Do I really care whether I am buried, when my turn comes, at Conches or at Hesdin?'

But these are the kind of doubts one tends to have after the age of forty, when some business on which one is engaged is turning out badly and one has a fortnight's leisure. Yet one knows only too well, in one's heart of hearts, that this fugitive wisdom will have no effect on one's actions. Nevertheless, tomorrow, Robert would go to hunt the stag in the neighbourhood of Beaumont, and would take the opportunity to inspect the castle there and determine what repairs were needed.

It was on his return from Beaumont with his wife, on the penultimate day of the year, that Robert of Artois found his equerries and servants waiting for him in considerable agitation on the drawbridge of Conches.

During the course of the afternoon, some men had come to arrest Dame de Divion and take her to prison in Paris.

'Arrest her? Who came to arrest her?'

'Three sergeants-at-arms.'

'What sergeants-at-arms? On whose orders?' Robert shouted.

'The King's.'

'Oh, really! And so you let them have their way! You're a lot of fools and I'll have you flogged. Arrest someone in my house? What impudence! Did you see the order?'

'We saw it, Monseigneur,' replied Gillet de Nelle, quaking with fright, 'and we insisted on keeping it. We let them take Madame de Divion only on that condition. Here it is.'

It was indeed a royal order, drawn up in a clerkly hand, but sealed with Philippe VI's seal. It was no mere Chancellory seal, which might well have been explained by some piece of high-level knavery. The wax was impressed with Philippe's private seal, the 'Little Seal' as it was called, which the King carried on his person in a purse, and which was used only by his own hand.

The Count of Artois was not a man much given to anxiety. But that day he knew what fear meant.

6

The Wicked Queen

To ride from Conches to Paris in a single day was a long stage, even for a brilliant horseman with a good horse. Robert of Artois left two of the equerries accompanying him on the road with foundered horses. It was night when he reached Paris but in spite of the late hour the streets were still full of happy crowds seeing the New Year in. Drunkards were vomiting in the shadows outside the taverns; women were reeling arm in arm through the streets, as in Watriquet's lay, and singing at the tops of their voices.

Paying no attention to the rabble, whom his horse sent staggering out of the way, Robert went straight to the palace. The Captain of the guard told him that the King had been there during the day to receive the good wishes of the town-people, but that he had left for Saint-Germain.[24]

So Robert crossed the bridge and went to knock at the gates of the Château, where he had contacts. A peer of France need have no qualms about waking the Governor; but, on being questioned, the Governor asserted that he had received no prisoner by the name of Jeanne de Divion, nor anyone who resembled her description during the last two days.

Anyone arrested on the order of the King could be imprisoned only in the Châtelet or the Louvre; so Robert went to the Louvre; but the Captain of the Louvre gave him the same answer. Where, then, was La Divion? Was it possible that Robert had travelled quicker than the King's sergeants-at-arms, ridden by a different road and thereby got ahead of them? And yet, at Houdin, where he had made inquiries, he had been told that three sergeants-at-arms had passed through several hours before with a woman prisoner. It was all very mysterious.

Robert gave it up and went to his own house, where he slept badly. At dawn he left for Saint-Germain.

There was a white frost over field and meadow; the branches of the trees were bright with rime, and the hills and forests round the Manor of Saint-Germain looked like a landscape of sugar.

The King had just woken up. But, for Robert, all doors were opened to Philippe VI's bedchamber. The King was still in bed, surrounded by chamberlains and huntsmen, to whom he was giving orders for the day's hunting.

Robert hurried in, quickly went down on one knee, rose and said: 'Sire, my brother, take back the peerage you gave me, and my fiefs, lands and revenues, deprive me of their use and profit, and dismiss me from your Privy Council at which I am no longer worthy to appear. I count for nothing now in the realm!'

Opening his blue eyes wide in surprise above his long fleshy nose, Philippe said: 'What's the matter with you,

Brother? What has upset you? What are you talking about?'

'I'm simply stating the truth. I'm saying I no longer count for anything in the realm since the King, without even deigning to inform me, has had a woman living under my roof arrested!'

'Whom have I arrested? Who is she?'

'A certain Dame de Divion, Brother, a member of my household and a woman of the bedchamber to my wife, your sister, whom three sergeants-at-arms arrested on your orders at my Castle of Conches and have taken to prison!'

'On my orders?' said Philippe, in stupefaction. 'But I have given no such orders. Divion? I don't even know the name. In any case, Brother, have the grace to believe me when I say that I would never have anyone arrested under your roof, even if I had reason to do so, without telling you of it and first asking your advice.'

'That is what I would have thought, Brother,' said Robert, 'yet the order is undoubtedly yours.'

And from beneath his surcoat he produced the warrant the sergeants-at-arms had left behind them.

Philippe VI glanced at it, recognized his private seal, and the flesh of his nose turned pale.

'Hérouart, my gown!' he cried to one of his chamberlains. 'And get out, all of you! Hurry! Leave me alone with Monseigneur of Artois!'

Throwing back the gold-embroidered coverlets, he got out of bed, wearing a long white nightshirt. His chamberlain helped him into a furred gown, and went to stoke the fire on the hearth.

'Get out, get out! I said leave me alone.'

Never since he had been in the King's service had Hérouart

de Belleperche been spoken to so roughly, as if he were a mere scullion indeed!

'No, I never sealed this nor dictated anything of the sort,' said the King, when the Chamberlain had gone.

He examined the document with great care, fitted the two pieces of the seal, which had been broken to open the letter, together, and took a crystal magnifying-glass from a drawer in a side table.

'Perhaps someone has counterfeited your seal, Brother,' said Robert.

'It cannot be done. The die-sinkers, as you no doubt know, are skilled in the prevention of forgery. They invariably introduce some tiny, secret, deliberate imperfection, especially in royal seals or in those of great barons. Look at the "I" in my name – do you see the little break in the staff, and the little hollow mark in the foliage of the border?'

'In that case,' said Robert, 'could someone have removed the seal from another document?'

'I know it can be done with a hot razor or by other means. My chancellor has told me so.'

Robert's expression became remarkably ingenuous, as if he were hearing some extraordinary fact for the first time. But his heart began beating rather faster.

'But that cannot be the case,' Philippe went on, 'because to prevent that kind of thing I use my Little Seal only for seals that must be broken; I never apply it to a flat page or a lace.'

He was silent for a moment, his eyes fixed on Robert as if he were asking him for an explanation, though, in fact, he was trying to think of one himself.

'The only possible conclusion,' he said, 'is that someone termporarily stole my seal. But who? And when did they do it? It never leaves the purse at my belt during the day; I put it aside only at night.'

He went to the side table, took a purse of cloth-of-gold from the drawer and felt the contents, then he opened it and took from it a little gold seal, its shaft in the shape of a lily.

'And I always put it on again in the morning.'

He was talking more slowly now, for he had a terrible suspicion. He picked up the warrant and studied it very carefully again.

'I know that hand,' he said. 'It's not that of Hugues de Pommard, nor that of Jacques la Vache, nor that of Geoffroy de Fleury.'[25]

He rang for Pierre Trousseau, the other chamberlain on duty.

'Send me the clerk Robert Mulet, it he's in the house, and if he's elsewhere, find him. Tell him to come here with his pens.'

'Am I not right in thinking,' Robert asked, 'that Mulet is secretary to your wife, Queen Jeanne?'

They had unconsciously reverted to the second person singular they had used in the past, when Philippe was still very far from becoming King, and Robert was not yet a peer, and they were merely cousins and good friends. In those far-off days Monseigneur Charles of Valois had always held Robert up as an example to Philippe, because of his strength, his tenacity, and his good sense in affairs of State.

'Yes, Mulet sometimes works for me and sometimes for Jeanne,' Philippe said evasively to cover his embarrassment.

He realized that the same suspicions had occurred to Robert.

Mulet was in the house and hurried in, carrying his writing-board under his arm. He bowed low to kiss the King's hand.

'Set out your board and write,' said Philippe VI. He at once began to dictate: 'In the King's name, to our loyal and beloved Provost of Paris, Jean de Milon, greetings. We order you to set free . . .'

The two cousins had both drawn near and were reading over the clerk's shoulder. His writing was clearly the same as in the warrant.

'. . . at once the Dame Jeanne de . . .'

'Divion . . .' supplied Robert.

'. . . who is in our prison of . . . Where is she?' Philippe asked.

'Neither in the Châtelet, nor the Louvre,' said Robert.

'In the Tower of Nesle, Sire,' said the clerk, who hoped his zeal and excellent memory would be appreciated.

The two cousins looked at each other and folded their arms with an identical gesture.

'How do you know?' the King asked the clerk.

'Because, Sire, I had the honour of writing your order to arrest the lady three days ago.'

'Who dictated it to you?'

'The Queen, Sire. She told me you had no time to do so and had therefore asked her to do it on your behalf. There were two orders, one for her arrest and one for her imprisonment.'

Philippe had turned very pale; he was both ashamed and furious, and dared not look his brother-in-law in the face.

'The bitch,' Robert thought. 'I knew she hated me, but to go to the lengths of stealing her husband's seal to injure me! How has she managed to be so well informed?'

'Are you going to finish dictating the order, Sire?' he asked.

'Of course, of course,' said Philippe, emerging from his thoughts.

He dictated the last paragraph. The clerk lit a candle at the fire, poured a few drops of red wax on the folded sheet and presented it to the King so that he might himself apply the Little Seal.

Philippe was lost in thought and seemed scarcely to be aware of what he was doing. Robert took the order and rang the bell. Hérouart de Belleperche came into the room. He seemed to be spending his whole time running in and out this morning.

'To the Provost, within the hour, on the King's order,' Robert said, handing him the letter.

'And summon Madame the Queen at once,' Philippe ordered from the farther end of the room.

The clerk Mulet was still waiting, looking from the King to the Count of Artois and wondering whether his zeal was meeting with quite the appreciation he had expected. Robert waved him out of the room.

A minute or two later Queen Jeanne came in with her peculiar lame gait. At every step she took, she seemed to be moving through a quarter of a circle, pivoting on her longer leg. She was slender and facially almost beautiful, though her teeth were already rotting. Her eyes were large, but falsely and deceitfully limpid; she had long fingers that were not quite straight, so that light showed between them when she held them close together.

'Since when, Madame, have you sent out orders in my name?'

The Queen assumed a perfectly calculated expression of innocent surprise.

'An order, my beloved Sire?'

Her voice was low and melodious, with that underlying warmth of affection she was so adept at lending it.

'And since when have you purloined my seal while I'm asleep?'

'Your seal, sweetheart? I've never touched your seal. Which seal do you mean?'

She was silenced by a tremendous slap in the face.

It was a savage and painful blow and Jeanne the Lame's eyes filled with tears; her mouth hung open in surprise and she put her hand to her cheek which was already turning red.

Robert of Artois was surprised too, but he was also delighted. He could never have believed that his Cousin Philippe, whom everyone said was ruled by his wife, could raise his hand to her. 'Has he really become King at last?' Robert wondered.

Philippe of Valois had certainly become a man and, like every husband, whether a great lord or the least of servants, was ready to correct his wife when she lied. He gave her another slap as if the first had made his hand itch for more; and then a hail of blows followed. Jeanne was terrified and put up her hands to defend her face. But Philippe's blows fell wherever they could, from the crown of her head down to her shoulders. And he was shouting: 'It was the other night you played this trick on me, wasn't it? Have you the nerve to deny it, when Mulet has admitted everything? You wicked whore to fondle and caress me, to tell me how much you love me, and then take advantage of my love to make a fool of me and steal my royal seal! Do you realize the crime you've committed, that it's worse than theft? No subject in my realm, however great, shall use another's seal without being flogged.

And you have used mine. You wicked woman, to bring dishonour on me before my peers, my cousin, my own brother! Am I not right, Robert?' he said, interrupting his blows for a moment to seek Robert's approbation. 'How can we govern if our subjects use our seals for their own purposes and issue orders we have never willed? It violates our honour.'

He turned back to his wife, his anger rising again, and cried: 'So this is the use to which you put the Hôtel de Nesle I was weak enough to give you! God knows, you worried me for it enough! Are you as wicked as your sister was, and is that accursed Tower to be the scene of the crime of Burgundy for ever? If you were not Queen and I had escaped the misfortune of marrying you, I'd have you thrown into prison. Since no one else can punish you, I shall do it myself.'[26]

And the blows started raining down again.

'I hope he kills her,' thought Robert.

Jeanne had fallen on the bed, her legs were kicking from beneath her robe, and every blow drew a groan or a scream from her. Then she suddenly turned on him like a cat with her claws out, and began shouting, her cheeks wet with tears: 'Yes, I did it! Yes, I stole your seal while you were asleep, because you're being unjust. I did it to help my brother of Burgundy against this wicked Robert who has always tried to injure us by his guile and his crimes. It was he who plotted with your father to kill my sister, Marguerite.'

'Don't let me hear my father's name in your viper's mouth!' cried Philippe.

Frightened by the anger in her husband's eyes, she fell silent, for he really seemed quite capable of killing her.

Laying a protective hand on Robert of Artois' shoulder, he

said: 'And beware, you wicked woman, of trying to injure my brother who is the greatest support of my throne.'

He went over to the door to tell his chamberlain to cancel the day's hunting, and twenty listening ears retreated hurriedly. Jeanne the Lame was hated by the servants, whom she harassed by her demands on them and reported for the smallest fault; among themselves, they called her 'the Wicked Queen'. The story of the beating she had received would be heard with delight by the whole palace.

Later that morning Philippe and Robert were slowly walking up and down in the garden of Saint-Germain as the frost was melting. His head bowed, the King was saying: 'Is it not a terrible thing, Robert, to have to be on guard against one's own wife, even when one's asleep? What can I do about it? Keep my seal under my pillow? She'd merely slip her hand in and take it, for I'm a sound sleeper. Yet I can't very well shut her up in a convent; she's my wife! There is only one thing I can do and that is no longer to have her sleep with me. The trouble is, I'm in love with her, the bitch! Keep it to yourself, but like everyone else I have enjoyed a few other women. But I've always come back to her with all the greater enthusiasm. However, if she does it again, I shall beat her again.'

At that moment Trouillard d'Usages, Vidame du Mans, and a gentleman of the household, came down the path to announce the Provost of Paris who was just behind.

Trotting paunchily along on his short legs, Jean de Milon looked far from happy.

'Well, Messire Provost, have you released the woman?'

'No, Sire,' replied the Provost, sounding rather embarrassed.

'Why not? Was my order forged? Perhaps you didn't recognize my seal?'

'Not at all, Sire, but before obeying it I wished to speak to you about it, and I am very glad to find Monseigneur of Artois with you,' said Jean de Milon, looking at Robert in some embarrassment. 'The woman has confessed.'

'What has she confessed?' Robert asked.

'To every kind of crime, Monseigneur, forgery, counterfeiting, and other things too.'

Robert managed to maintain his self-control and pretended to take the news as a joke. He shrugged his shoulders and cried: 'Of course, if she's been put to the question, I've no doubt at all that she's confessed to a great deal! If I handed you over to the torturers, Messire de Milon, I guarantee you'd confess to have committed sodomy on me!'

'Alas, Monseigneur,' said the Provost, 'the woman confessed before being put to the question, simply from fear of being put to it. And she named a long list of accomplices.'

Philippe VI stared silently at his brother-in-law. A new suspicion was working in his head.

Robert felt the trap closing in on him. A king who had just beaten his wife, and in the presence of a witness, for having purloined his seal and forged a document, would find it difficult to release an ordinary subject who had committed similar misdeeds, even to please his dearest cousin.

'What do you advise, Brother?' Philippe asked Robert, never taking his eyes off him. Robert realized that his safety depended on his answer. He had to pretend to be honest. And so much the worse for La Divion. He would simply declare everything she had or might say to be shameless lies.

'Your justice, Sire, my brother, your justice!' he cried.

'Keep the woman in prison, and if she has deceived me be sure that I shall ask you to exercise the greatest severity.'

Meanwhile he was wondering. 'Who can have informed the Duke of Burgundy?' But he was immediately aware of the obvious answer. There was only one person who could have informed the Duke of Burgundy, or the wicked Queen herself, that La Divion was at Conches. And that was Beatrice.

It was not until the end of March, when the Seine, swollen by the spring rains, had overflowed its banks and flooded the cellars, that in the neighbourhood of Chatou some watermen fished a sack out of the river containing the body of a naked woman.

Paddling in the mud, the whole population of the village gathered round the macabre find, and the mothers slapped their brats and cried: 'Go on, get along with you; this is no fit sight for you!'

The body was hideously swollen and had the horrible green tinge of advanced decomposition; it must have been over a month in the river. It was clear, nevertheless, that it was the body of a young woman. Her long black hair seemed to be moving because of the bubbles bursting in it. The face had been crushed and lacerated to prevent identification; and there was the mark of a cord round the neck.

The watermen, torn between disgust and a horrible attraction, poked at the obscene body with their boathooks.

Suddenly the water swelling it poured out of the body, which began to move of its own volition, giving a momentary illusion of coming to life again. The women fled screaming.

The bailiff had been sent for and, when he arrived, asked a

few questions, took a look at the dead woman and inspected the objects that had been in the sack with the body. These were drying on the grass and consisted of a goat's horn, a wax figure wrapped in rags and pierced with pins, and a crude pewter ciborium engraved with satanic emblems.

'A witch,' declared the bailiff; 'presumably killed by her fellows after some sabbath or black mass.'

The women crossed themselves. The bailiff detailed a party to go and bury the body at once, together with the wicked objects, in a spinney at some distance from the village. No prayer was said over it.

It had been a well-organized and well-disguised crime, in which Gillet de Nelle had followed the expert advice of Lormet le Dolois; and it had now turned out just as the murderers had intended.

Robert of Artois had avenged Beatrice's betrayal, though this was far from implying that he was being successful on other counts.

Two generations later, the villagers of Chatou would no longer remember why a spinney downstream was called 'The Witch's Wood'.

7

The Tournament at Evreux

ABOUT THE MIDDLE OF May, heralds in the livery of
France, accompanied by trumpeters, appeared in the market-
squares of towns, at the crossroads in villages and at the
entrance gates of castles. The trumpeters sounded their long
instruments from which hung pennons embroidered with
lilies, while the herald unrolled a parchment and proclaimed
in a loud voice:

"'Oyez! Oyez! This is to make known to all princes, lords,
barons, knights and squires of the Duchies of Normandy,
Brittany and Burgundy, of the Counties and Marches of
Anjou, Artois, Flanders and Champagne, and to all others,
whether they be of this kingdom or of any other Christian
kingdom, provided they be not banished or enemies of our
Lord the King, whom God preserve, that on the day of Saint
Lucy, July 6th, nearby the town of Evreux, there will be held
a great festival of arms and most noble tournament, which
will be contested by the noble jousters with light maces
and blunted swords, in appropriate harness, helms, coats of

mail and horse armour, in accordance with ancient custom.

"'And the leaders in this tournament are the most high and mighty princes, my most dread lords, our beloved Sire, Philippe, King of France, the challenger, and the Sire John of Luxemburg, King of Bohemia, the defendant. And by these presents I make known to all princes, lords, barons, knights and squires of the said territories and of all other nations whatsoever, who wish and desire to joust so as to acquire honour, that they should wear the little badges I shall presently give them, so that they may be recognized as jousters, and whosoever desires one may ask for it. And at the said tournament there will be rich and noble prizes presented by the ladies.

"'Moreover, I announce to all princes, barons, knights and squires, who have intention to joust, that you are required to be present at the said place of Evreux and take up your quarters there on the fourth day previous to the tournament. And this I make known by order of my lords, the stewards, and so I crave your pardon.'"

The trumpets sounded again, and the urchins ran beside the herald's escort as far as the outskirts of the town, as he rode on to cry his news elsewhere.

Before dispersing, the villagers said to each other: 'If our lord goes to this tournament, it's going to cost us a pretty penny. He'll take his lady and all his household along. They have all the fun and we have to pay the poll-tax.'

Nevertheless, more than one of them was thinking: 'Suppose the lord took my eldest with him as stableboy, he'd certainly get a good tip, and perhaps even some future employment. I'll talk to the priest and ask him to put in a word for my Gaston.'

For the next six weeks the tournament was the main pre-occupation in every castle. The young dreamed of astonishing the world by their first exploits.

'You're still too young; wait another year! You'll have plenty of opportunity,' the parents replied.

'But the son of our neighbour at Chambray, who's the same age as I am, is going!'

'If the Lord of Chambray has gone out of his mind, or if he can afford to chuck his deniers away, that's his business.'

There were many boys impatient to become orphans.

The old men's memories were stirred. To listen to them, you might have thought that men were stronger, armour heavier and horses faster in their day.

'At the Kenilworth tournament, given by Lord Mortimer of Chirk, the uncle of the man they hanged in London last winter . . .'

'At the tournament at Condé-sur-Escaut, given by Monseigneur Jean d'Avesnes, the father of the present Count of Hainaut. . . .'

They borrowed against the next harvest, mortgaged their woods, and took their silver to the nearest Lombard to pay for plumes for my lord's helm, muslins and silks for my lady's dresses, and caparisons for horses.

The hypocrites complained: 'What an expense and trouble we're being put to! How much pleasanter it would be to stay at home! But we simply must appear at the tournament for the honour of the house. Since our Lord, the King, has sent a herald to the very door of our manor, we should certainly displease him if we failed to put in an appearance.'

Everyone was busy, hammering iron, sewing mail on to leather jerkins, training horses and practising in parks from which the birds fled in terror of the charging knights, the shock of lances going home and the great clashing of swords. Little barons would devote three hours to fitting their basinets.

The local lords organized tournaments at home to get their eyes in. And the older men, puffing into their moustaches, judged the hits as they watched their juniors knock each other down. After which everyone ate a great deal.

These war-like games, taking one barony with another, cost in the end as much as a real campaign.

Finally they all set out. At the last moment grandfather would have decided to come to recapture the atmosphere of his youth, and the fourteen-year-old son would also have got his way: he could serve as a junior squire. The war-horses were led by hand so as not to tire them; robes and armour were packed into travelling-chests and loaded on to mules. The serving-men walked in the dust. On the way they stayed in the guest-houses of monasteries or in the manor of a relative, who was himself going to the tournament. There would be a splendid supper and a skinful of wine; and as dawn broke they would all take the road together.

And so, from halt to halt, the companies grew in numbers till they met the count, whose vassals they were, travelling with a huge train. They would kiss his hand, and exchange a few commonplaces, which would form a subject of conversation for some time to come. The ladies would don a new dress from their travelling-chest and the company would join the count's suite, which already covered a league of road, its banners floating in the spring sunshine.

Mock armies, equipped with lances without points, swords without edge and maces without weight, were crossing the

Seine, the Eure and the Risle, or marching up the banks of the Loire, to take part in a mock war in which there was nothing at stake except personal vanity.

For a week before the tournament there was not an empty room or attic in the whole of Evreux. The King of France was holding his Court in the largest abbey, and the King of Bohemia, in whose honour the tournament had been organized, was lodging with the Count of Evreux, the King of Navarre.

John of Luxemburg, the King of Bohemia, was a most singular prince who was also completely impoverished; he had more debts than lands, and lived at the expense of the French Treasury. It had not, however, occurred to him to appear with a lesser train than his host, from whom he derived such resources as he had. Luxemburg was nearly forty, though he looked ten years younger; he had a spreading, silky, chestnut beard, an amused if rather haughty expression, but a most prepossessing and friendly manner. He was strong, vital, audacious and gay, but also very stupid. Nearly as tall as was Philippe VI, he had a magnificent presence and looked every inch a king as conceived by the popular imagination. He had the gift of making himself liked by all, both princes and commoners; he had even succeeded in being friends with both Pope John XXII and the Emperor Louis of Bavaria, those inveterate enemies, which was remarkable in a fool, for everyone agreed that John of Luxemburg was as stupid as he was attractive.

But stupidity is no bar to enterprise; on the contrary, it tends to conceal difficulties which an intelligent man would consider insuperable. John of Luxemburg had forsaken

Bohemia, where he was bored, to embark on a series of absurd adventures in Italy. 'The struggles of the Ghibellines are destroying the country,' he thought. 'The Emperor and the Pope are quarrelling over republics whose inhabitants are in a state of virtual civil war. Since I'm a friend of both parties, why don't they hand these states over to me, and I'll restore peace to them?' The most astonishing thing about it was that he had very nearly succeeded. For a few months he had been the idol of the whole of Italy, except for the Florentines, who are difficult people to take in, and King Robert of Naples, who soon became concerned at the activities of this embarrassing interloper.

In April, John of Luxemburg had conferred secretly with the Cardinal Legate, Bertrand du Pouget – who, so it was said, was a natural son of Pope John XXII – with the object of settling the fate of Florence, removing the Malatesta from Rimini, and establishing an independent principality of which Bologna would be the capital. But then, somehow or other, though he could never quite understand how it had come about, just when his affairs seemed to be going so well and he was even thinking of replacing his intimate friend, Louis of Bavaria, on the Imperial throne, John of Luxemburg had suddenly found two formidable coalitions ranged against him, in which the Guelphs and the Ghibellines were for once in a way allies, Florence was in league with Rome, and the King of Naples, the Pope's friend, was attacking him from the south, while the Emperor, the Pope's enemy, was attacking him from the north, and the two Dukes of Austria, the Margrave of Brandenburg, the King of Poland and the King of Hungary, were all coming to their support. To a prince who was so generally beloved, and whose only desire had been to bring peace to the Italians, this indeed seemed a most unwarranted situation!

Leaving eight hundred knights under his son Charles to hold the whole of Lombardy, John of Luxemburg, his beard flowing in the wind, had hurried from Parma to Bohemia, which the Austrians had invaded. Falling into the arms of Louis of Bavaria, he had succeeded by means of a great show of affection in clearing up the absurd misunderstanding. The Imperial crown? It would never have occurred to him but for the Pope! And now he had come to see Philippe of Valois to ask him to intervene with the King of Naples, and to provide further subsidies to enable him to pursue his plans for a peaceful kingdom in Italy.

Philippe VI could do no less than organize a tournament in honour of his gallant guest.

Now, therefore, on the plain of Evreux, by the banks of the Iton, the King of France and the King of Bohemia, who were the closest of friends, were preparing to fight a mock war, with more knights under arms indeed than the King of Bohemia's son had at his disposal to keep all Italy at bay.

The lists, that is to say the enclosure in which the tournament was to take place, had been laid out on a wide level plain; they formed a rectangle of three hundred by two hundred feet, were surrounded by an open palisade of pointed stakes, while inside another lower palisade was topped by a stout rail. During the jousting the contestants' servants stood between the two palisades.

Three stands had been erected on the shady side and were covered with awnings and hung with flags; the centre stand was for the stewards, and the other two for the ladies.

The plain all around was covered with the tents of the

squires and grooms, each flying its owner's standard; and people strolled out to admire the war-horses.

The first four days of the meeting were devoted to individual jousts, the private challenges one lord issued another. Some wanted their revenge for a defeat at a previous encounter; others, who had never met before, wished to try their strength; or again two famous jousters would be urged on to compete against each other.

The stands were full or empty according to the reputations of the contenders. If two young squires had succeeded in obtaining permission to enter the lists when they were free in the early morning, there would be merely a few friends and relations. But if there was to be an encounter between the King of Bohemia and Messire Jean of Hainaut, who had come expressly from Holland with twenty knights, the stands were in danger of collapsing. It was then that the ladies would tear a *manche* from their dress to give the knight of their choice; it was a false sleeve as often as not, the silk being attached to the true sleeve by a few easily broken tacks, though not always, since the more forward often delighted in exposing a shapely arm.

There was every kind of person in the stands, and every kind of behaviour. It had been quite impossible to pick and choose among the crowd who made of Evreux a sort of fair of the nobility. There were a number of high-class prostitutes, as splendidly dressed as the baronesses, and often prettier and better mannered, who succeeded in appropriating the best seats, made eyes at the men and provoked them to other tourneys.

The jousters, who were not in the lists, went to sit by the ladies under cover of watching their friends' exploits, and many a flirtation begun there was continued in the evening during the dancing and the merrymaking in the castle.

Messire Jean of Hainaut and the King of Bohemia, invisible behind their armour and their plumes, each bore on the shaft of his lance six silk *manches* like so many hearts transfixed. The jousters had either to unhorse each other or break a lance. They were permitted to aim only at the chest and their shields were curved to deflect the lance-thrust. Stomachs protected by high saddle-bows, heads enclosed in helms with visors down, the contestants charged each other. The spectators in the stands shouted and stamped their feet in their excitement. They were a perfect match for each other, and for a long time to come people would talk of the grace with which Messire of Hainaut had set his lance in rest,[27] and of how the King of Bohemia had sat so straight and firm in the saddle till the two lances bent like bows and snapped.

As for Count Robert of Artois, who had come from nearby Conches, he rode huge Percheron horses and his weight made him a formidable opponent. He wore red armour and a red plume floating from his helm. His lance was also red and he was peculiarly dextrous at plucking his adversary from the saddle at full gallop and making him bite the dust. But Monseigneur of Artois was in an unusally gloomy humour these days and seemed to be taking part in the tournament rather from duty than from pleasure.

In the meantime the stewards, selected from among the most important men in the kingdom, such as the Constable Raoul de Brienne and Messire Mille de Noyers, were busy organizing the final grand tourney.

Between the time spent in arming and disarming, appearing in the lists, discussing the day's exploits, dealing tactfully with disgruntled knights who wanted to fight under one banner rather than another, feasting, listening to minstrels after the feasts, and dancing when the songs were done, the King of France, the King of Bohemia and their counsellors had very little time each day to discuss the affairs of Italy which were, after all, the real reason for the meeting. However, great affairs can of course be settled in a few words if the parties to them are in humour to agree.

Like two real kings of the Round Table, Philippe of Valois, looking magnificent in his embroidered robes, and John of Luxemburg, no less sumptuously clothed beneath his spreading beard, solemnly declared, goblet in hand, their mutual friendship. Such matters as a letter to Pope John XXII or an embassy to King Robert of Naples were decided in haste.

'We must also, my dear Sire, discuss the little matter of the crusade,' Philippe VI would say.

For he was once again taking up that favourite project of his father and his cousin, Charles the Fair. All seemed so well with France, the Treasury so full and the peace of Europe, with the King of Bohemia's help, so well assured, that for the honour and prosperity of Christendom a splendid and glorious expedition against the infidel ought clearly to be set on foot at once.

'Ah, Messeigneurs, they're sounding the horns for water!'

The conference was over. The crusade could be discussed after dinner or tomorrow.

At dinner, there was a great deal of laughter at the expense of the young King of England who had come over three months ago, accompanied only by Lord Montacute and disguised as a merchant, for a secret conference with the King of France.[28] Yes, he was disguised as a merchant, like any

Lombard! And for what purpose? Merely to negotiate a trade agreement about exporting woollens to Flanders! Really, had one ever known a prince to bother about such things before and to do a wool merchant's job, as if he were a common tradesman from a guild or Hanse?

'And so, my friends, since that's what he wanted, I received him as if he were a merchant!' said Philippe of Valois. 'There was no feasting or jousting, merely walks along the rides of the Forest of Halatte; and I gave him a very ordinary little supper.'

Poor Cousin Edward, what ridiculous ideas he had! At this very moment he was organizing a standing army of footmen and introducing compulsory service in his country. What could he hope to gain by that? It was well known – and the Battle of Mont Cassel had given proof of it – that only the chivalry counted in war, and that infantry fled as soon as they saw a breastplate.

'Nevertheless, there seems to be less disorder in England since Lord Mortimer was hanged,' observed Mille de Noyers.

'Order, yes,' replied Philippe VI, 'but only because the English barons are tired of fighting among themselves for the moment. As soon as they've recovered their breath, poor Edward will find out how much use his infantry is against them. And to think the dear boy once thought of claiming the crown of France! Well, Messeigneurs, do you regret not having him for your prince, or do you prefer your "Makeshift King"?' he added gaily, beating himself on the chest.

As they came out of every banquet, Philippe said to Robert of Artois in a low voice, 'Brother, I want to speak to you privately about a most serious matter.'

'Whenever you wish, Sire, my cousin.'

'Well, we'll try to have a talk tonight.'

But at night there was dancing, and Robert made no effort to hasten on the conversation, because he knew only too well what the King had to say to him. Since La Divion's avowals – and she was still in prison – further arrests had been made, including that of the notary Tesson, and the witnesses had all been subjected to a counter-inquiry. It was noticed that Philippe did not ask Robert to be present at his brief conferences with the King of Bohemia, and this could only be interpreted as a sign of disfavour.

The day before the tourney, the King-at-Arms,[29] accompanied by his heralds and trumpeters, went to the castle, the lodgings of the principal lords and to the lists themselves, and proclaimed:

'"Oyez, Oyez, most high and mighty princes, dukes, counts, barons, lords, knights and squires I notify you, on the orders of Messeigneurs the stewards, that each of you should this day bring the helm in which he is to joust, and his banners also, to the house of Messeigneurs the stewards, so that my lords the stewards may apportion them; and when they have done so, the ladies will come to see and inspect them to announce their pleasure; and that will be all for this day, except for the dancing after supper."'

As the helms were brought to the stewards' house by the servants, they were lined up on chests in the cloister, and divided into two teams. They looked like the spoils of some fabulous, decapitated army. So that they could be told apart, the combatants fixed to their helms, above the torse or count's coronet, the strangest and gaudiest emblems: an eagle, a dragon, a naked woman, a mermaid, or a rampant unicorn, as well as long silk streamers in the lord's colours.

During the afternoon, the ladies came to the house, and preceded by the stewards and the two leaders of the tournament, that is to say the King of France and the King of Bohemia, were invited to make a tour of the cloister while the herald stopped before each helm and named its owner:

'Messire Jean de Hainaut . . . Monseigneur the Count of Blois . . . our Lord Philippe, King of Navarre . . .'

Some of the helms were painted, together with the swords and the shafts of the lances, and from this certain nicknames were derived such as the White Knight, the Black Knight and so on.

'Messire the Marshal Robert Bertrand, Knight of the Green Lion . . .'

Then followed a monumental red helm, surmounted by a golden tower: 'Monseigneur Robert of Artois, Count of Beaumont-le-Roger . . .'

The Queen, who was limping along at the head of the procession of ladies, put out her hand as if to touch it. Philippe seized her wrist and stopped her. 'My dear, I forbid you!' he said in a low voice.

Queen Jeanne smiled wickedly.

'It would have been a splendid opportunity,' she muttered to her sister-in-law, the young Duchess of Burgundy, who was standing beside her.

According to the rules of tournament, if a lady touched a helm, the knight to whom it belonged was *recommandé*, which meant that he lost his right to take part. When he entered the lists, the other knights beat him with the shafts of their lances; his horse was taken from him and given to the trumpeters; and he himself was made to sit astride the bar of the palisade that surrounded the lists and was condemned to stay in that ridiculous position throughout the tourney. The disgrace was inflicted on a man who had defamed a lady, or forfeited his honour in some way, such as lending money on usury or committing perjury.

The Queen's behaviour had not escaped Madame de Beaumont, who turned pale. She went to her brother, the King, and reproached him.

'Sister,' replied Philippe with severity, 'you should thank me rather than complain.'

That night, during the dancing, everyone was discussing the incident. The Queen had certainly looked as if she had intended to *recommander* the Count of Artois; and Robert was scowling with fury. He overtly refused to give his hand to the Duchess of Burgundy during the dancing, and then went over to Queen Jeanne, who never danced because of her lameness; he stood before her for a long moment with his arm bent as if inviting her to dance, which was a wicked affront by way of revenge. Both wives tried to catch their husband's eyes; the viols and the harps sounded in an agonized silence. The merest spark would have set the tourney off that night and started the mêlée in the ballroom.

The entrance of the King-at-Arms, escorted by his heralds, come to make another proclamation, was a welcome diversion.

'"Oyez, Oyez, high and mighty princes, lords, barons, knights and squires, who are to engage in the tourney! I am to inform you on the orders of Messeigneurs the stewards that you must be in the ranks, armed and ready to joust, by noon tomorrow, for one hour after noon the judges will cut the cords to begin the tourney, for which there will be rich prizes given by the ladies. I am to tell you further that none must take into the ranks mounted grooms to serve him to a greater number than is hereinafter stated: four for princes, three for counts, two for knights, and one for squires; but as to footmen, each may do as he pleases, in accordance with the stewards' orders. And, may it please you, you will raise your right hands to the saints, and all promise with one voice that in the said tourney none will strike with the point of his sword nor below the belt; and should the helm per-adventure fall from the head of any among you, none shall touch him till his helm has been replaced and laced; and, if any act otherwise, he shall submit to the confiscation of his armour and war-horse, and be banished from all further jousting. And you will swear and promise on your faith and honour.'''

The jousters all raised their hands and cried: 'Yes, yes, we swear it!'

'Have a care tomorrow,' the Duke of Burgundy said to his knights; 'our cousin of Artois may well turn rogue and break his oath.'

Then they set to dancing again.

8

The Honour of a Peer and the Honour of a King

THE JOUSTERS WERE ALL in their tents, each of which had embroidered walls and was surmounted by a banner. They were arming: first the mailed hose to which the spurs were attached; then the plate armour for arms and legs; then the leather hauberk over which the body-armour was placed, a sort of cylinder of steel which was either articulated or of a single piece according to preference; then the leather *cervellière* to protect the head from blows on the helm, and then the helm itself, plumed and surmounted by an emblem, which was laced to the collar of the hauberk by leather laces. Over the armour a brilliantly coloured surcoat of silk was worn; it was long and floating, with huge scalloped sleeves that hung from the shoulders, and the blazon was embroidered on the breast. Finally, the knight was handed his blunted sword and his shield, which might be either a targe or a buckler.

His war-horse was waiting outside, dressed in horse-armour and champing a long-cheeked bit; its forehead was protected by a steel plate to which was affixed, as to the helm of its master, an eagle, dragon, lion, tower or bunch of plumes. Servants held the three blunt lances each jouster was allowed, and the mace which was light enough not to be lethal.

The nobility strolled to and from among the tents, watching the champions being armed and encouraging their friends.

Young Prince Jean, the King's eldest son, stared admiringly at these preparations, while Jean the Fool, who was accompanying him, pulled faces under his fool's cap.

The populace, of which there was a great number, was held back by a company of archers; they were unlikely to see much except dust, since the jousters had been trampling the lists for the last four days, and now the grass was dead and the surface, though it had been watered, had turned to powder.

Before they even got to horse, the jousters were sweating in their harness, for the steel soon became hot under the July sun. They would lose at least four pounds in weight during the course of the day.

The heralds went by shouting: 'Lace your helms! Lace your helms, my lords and knights, and hoist your banners to escort the commander's banner!'

The stands were full and the stewards, among whom were the Constable, Messire Mille de Noyers and the Duke of Bourbon, had taken their places in the centre.

The trumpet sounded; the jousters mounted heavily with the help of their servants and took their places either in front of the tent of the King of France or that of the King of Bohemia. They formed escort in file and rode off towards the lists, every knight accompanied by his standard-bearer. Cords divided the enclosure in half, and the two teams drew up face to face. There was a great fanfare of trumpets and the King-at-Arms came forward to repeat for the last time the rules governing the tourney.

At last he shouted: 'Cut the cords! Cry battle!'

The Duke of Bourbon could never hear this cry without unhappy memories, for it was the cry his father, Robert of Clermont, the sixth son of Saint Louis, used to utter in those fits of madness which suddenly overtook him in the middle of a feast or a royal council. The Duke of Bourbon preferred being a judge to a combatant, for to run away in a tourney was much more difficult than in war. His lameness was a good excuse to stay outside the lists.

The men whose duty it was raised their axes and cut the cords. The standard-bearers shouted their war-cries and broke rank; the mounted grooms, armed with the shortened shafts of lances, some three feet long, lined up against the palisade, ready to go to their masters' help. Then the earth shook beneath the charging hooves of two hundred horses and the mêlée began.

The women were on their feet in the stands, watching the helm of their favourite knight and shouting encouragement. The stewards took careful note of the blows exchanged so as to determine the victors. The clangour of lances, stirrups and armour, of all the mass of steel was deafening; and the dust rose and screened the sun.

In the first charge four knights were thrown from their horses and some twenty broke their lances. In response to shouts emerging from the combatants' visors, servants ran out with fresh lances for the disarmed and to pick up the unhorsed, who were struggling like so many crabs turned over on their backs. One of them had a broken leg and it took four men to carry him from the lists.

Mille de Noyers was sulky and, though a steward, was paying little attention to the performance. As far as he was concerned this was all a waste of time. He had to preside over the Exchequer, see that the decrees of Parliament were put into effect, and superintend the general administration of the kingdom. Yet, to please the King, he had to sit here and watch these yelling horsemen break their ash lances! He made no attempt to hide his feelings.

'These tournaments cost too much; they're an extravagance and the people disapprove of them,' he was saying to his neighbours. 'The King doesn't hear what his subjects are saying in the towns and villages! When he goes by he merely sees people kneeling to kiss his feet; but I hear the reports of the bailiffs and the provosts. It's all useless and arrogant expenditure! And while it's going on, nothing gets done; Ordinances have been waiting to be signed for a fortnight; and Councils are held merely to decide who is to be King-at-Arms or Knight of Honour. The greatness of the kingdom is not measured by mock chivalry. King Philip the Fair knew it well and agreed with Pope Clement to forbid tournaments.'

The Constable Raoul de Brienne, shading his eyes with his hand the better to see the mêlée, replied: 'Of course, you're quite right up to a point, Messire, but you neglect one aspect of tournaments; they're good training for war.'

'What war?' said Mille de Noyers. 'Is anyone going to war with these wedding cakes on their heads, and scalloped sleeves two ells long? Ordinary jousting is good training for fighting. I agree; but a tourney like this, in which a knight no longer wears fighting armour nor carries the full weight, has lost its point. In fact, it does more harm than good, for our young squires, who have never seen service, are led to believe that this is what meeting a real enemy is like and that you attack only when you hear the cry of "Cut the cords!"'

Mille de Noyers could speak with authority, for he had been a marshal of the army at the time his brother-in-law, Gaucher de Châtillon, had been appointed Constable and this young Brienne was still sucking his thumb.

'Nevertheless, it's a good thing our lords should get to know each other for the crusade,' said the Duke of Bourbon as if that settled the matter.

Mille de Noyers shrugged his shoulders. It well became the Duke, that notorious coward, to talk of a crusade!

Messire Mille was tired of conducting the affairs of France under a sovereign whom everyone considered admirable but whom he, with his long experience of power, knew to be largely incapable. It is bound to be wearisome to keep working for ends which no one approves, and Mille, who had begun his career at the Court of Burgundy, was sometimes tempted to return there. It was better to administer a duchy wisely than a kingdom foolishly, and Duke Eudes had been making overtures to him. He now looked for him in the mêlée and saw that he had been unhorsed by Robert of Artois. Mille de Noyers began to take an interest in the tourney again.

While Duke Eudes was being hoisted to his feet by his servants, Robert dismounted and offered to fight his adversary on foot. Mace and sword in hand, the two towers of steel, stumbling a little, advanced on each other and began showering each other with blows. Mille watched Robert of

Artois carefully, prepared to disqualify him at the first foul. But Robert was keeping to the rules, using only the edge of his sword and hitting above the belt. He was hammering at the Duke of Burgundy's helm with his mace and crushing the dragon that surmounted it. And though the mace weighed only a pound, the Duke seemed half stunned, for he was clearly finding some difficulty in defending himself and his sword was slashing the empty air rather than Robert. Suddenly, when trying to make a feint, Eudes of Burgundy lost his balance and fell over; Robert put his foot on his chest and the point of his sword at the lacings of his helm; and the Duke cried 'Mercy!' It was surrender and he had to leave the mêlée. Robert had himself hoisted into the saddle again and galloped proudly past the stands. An enthusiastic lady tore off her sleeve and Robert gathered it on the end of his lance.

'Monseigneur Robert might really be a little less vainglorious these days,' said Mille de Noyers.

'Oh, the King protects him!' said Raoul de Brienne.

'Yes, but how long will it last?' said Mille de Noyers. 'Madame Mahaut seems to have died rather suddenly, and Madame Jeanne the Widow, too, for that matter. And then there's that Beatrice d'Hirson, their lady-in-waiting, who has disappeared, and for whom her family have been searching in vain. The Duke of Burgundy will be wise to have his dishes tasted.'

'You seem to have had a sudden change of heart about Robert. Only a year ago you were a great supporter of his.'

'Last year I had not yet had to look into his case. I've just been conducting the second inquiry.'

'Ah, here's Messire of Hainaut going into the attack,' said the Constable.

Jean of Hainaut, who was second-in-command to the King of Bohemia, was fighting with furious gallantry; there was not an important lord in the King of France's team whom he did not challenge. It was already obvious that he would win the victor's prize.

The tourney lasted a full hour, at the end of which the judges ordered the trumpets to be sounded, the barriers to be opened and the combatants to separate. A dozen knights and squires of Artois appeared however not to have heard the signal and were furiously attacking four Burgundy lords in a corner of the lists. Robert was not among them, but he had undoubtedly inspired the action; and the fight looked as if it might become a massacre. King Philippe VI was obliged to remove his helm and, much to everyone's admiration, go bareheaded, so that he might be recognized, to separate the combatants.

Preceded by heralds and trumpets, the two teams formed up again to leave the lists in procession. Their armour was dented, their surcoats were in rags, the paint was peeling from their arms, their horses were lame and the housings torn. The result of the tourney was one man dead and several crippled for life. Apart from Messire Jean of Hainaut, who had won the Queen's prize, everyone who had taken part received a present as a souvenir, a silver-gilt goblet, or a silver cup or bowl.

Back in their tents, of which the flaps were raised, the lords were being disarmed. Their faces were red, their hands were flayed by the joints in their gauntlets and their legs were bruised. Meanwhile they were talking over the tourney.

'My helm was dented at the very start. That's what put me off!'

'If the Lord of Courgent had not come to your support, you'd have had it, my friend!'

'Duke Eudes couldn't stand up to Monseigneur Robert for long!'

'Oh, yes, Brécy did very well, I must admit!'

Amid laughter, swearing and grunts of fatigue, the combatants went off to the baths that had been set up in a nearby barn. The tubs had been made ready and they got into them in order of precedence, princes, first, then barons, then knights, and last of all the squires. There was a general atmosphere of friendliness and good-fellowship resulting from physical competition, though a few stubborn resentments might have been detected.

Philippe VI and Robert of Artois were in neighbouring tubs.

'A splendid tourney, a splendid tourney!' Philippe was saying. 'Ah, Brother, I must talk to you.'

'Sire, my brother, I'm all ears.'

It was obvious that Philippe was upset by what he had to say. But could there be a better moment to have a heart-to-heart talk with his cousin and brother-in-law, the friend of his youth and manhood, than now when they had been jousting together and the barn was full of shouting knights, clapping each other on the shoulder and splashing water, and the steam rising from the tubs seemed to isolate them?

'Robert, your case is no good because your documents are forged.'

Robert raised his red hair and red cheeks above the edge of the tub.

'No, my brother, they're genuine!'

The King looked depressed.

'Robert, I beseech you, don't be obstinate about it. I've done as much as I can for you, and against the advice of many members of my family and my Council. I've agreed to give Artois to the Duchess of Burgundy only on the condition that your rights are reserved. I've insisted that Ferry de Picquigny, who's devoted to you, should be appointed Governor. I've even offered to buy Artois from the Duchess so that it can be given to you.'

'There's no point in buying Artois from her since it's already mine.'

At such intransigent obstinacy Philippe gave a sign of anger. He shouted to his servant: 'Trousseau! Please bring me some more cold water.'

Then he went on: 'It's the parishes of Artois that refuse to pay the price to change masters; and what can I do? The Ordinance for the opening of your case has been waiting a month; and for a month I've been refusing to sign it, because I don't want my brother to be confronted by a lot of low people who'll sully him with mud which I'm not at all sure he'll be able to wash off. We're all fallible; there's not one of us whose every action has always been praiseworthy. Your witnesses have been bribed or threatened; your notary has talked; the forgers are in jail and have admitted manufacturing the documents.'

'They're genuine,' Robert repeated.

Philippe VI sighed. How difficult it was to save a man from himself!

'I'm not saying, Robert, that you're personally guilty. Nor am I saying, as others are, that you put your hand to these documents yourself. They were brought to you and you believed them to be genuine, but you were deceived.'

Robert sat in his tub and set his jaw.

'It may even be,' Philippe went on, 'that my own sister, your wife, has deceived you. Women sometimes commit these deceits in the belief that they're helping us. They're deceitful by nature. Look at my own wife, who didn't hesitate to purloin my seal.'

'Yes, women are deceitful,' Robert said angrily. 'This whole affair is a women's intrigue, organized between your wife and her sister-in-law of Burgundy. I don't know these vile people whose extorted confessions are being put in evidence against me.'

'I would also like to consider what they're saying about the death of your aunt as mere calumny,' Philippe went on, lowering his voice.

'But she'd dined with you!'

'Her daughter hadn't when she died in forty-eight hours.'

'I was not the only enemy they'd made during the course of their wicked lives,' Robert replied in a tone of assumed indifference.

He got out of the tub and demanded towels to dry himself with. Philippe followed suit. They stood there face to face, naked, their skins pink, their bodies very hairy. Their servants were waiting a few yards away, with their dress clothes over their arms.

'I'm waiting for your answer, Robert,' the King said.

'What answer?'

'That you'll agree to give up Artois, so that I can quash the whole business.'

'And break the promise you made me before you ever became King? Sire, my brother, have you forgotten who got you your throne, rallied the peers to your support and won your sceptre for you?'

Philippe of Valois seized Robert's wrist, looked him straight in the eyes and said: 'If I had forgotten, Robert, do you think I'd be talking to you like this now? For the last time, give it up.'

'Never,' replied the giant, shaking his head.

'You're refusing your King?'

'Yes, Sire, the King I made.'

Philippe let his hands fall.

'If that's the case,' he said, 'and you refuse to save your honour as a Peer, I shall have to look to my honour as a King!'

9

The Tolomei

'FORGIVE MY BEING UNABLE to rise to welcome you properly, Monseigneur,' said Spinello Tolomei rather breathlessly as Robert of Artois was shown in.

The old banker was lying on a bed that had been placed in his private office; a light coverlet revealed the shape of his increasing stomach and narrowing chest. A week's beard on his hollow cheeks looked like a deposit of salt; his mouth had gone blue and seemed to be gasping for air. Paris was stifling in the August afternoon, and the window, open on to the Rue des Lombards, lent no freshness to the room.

There was not much life left in Messer Tolomei's body now, nor in the gaze of his single open eye, which seemed to look out on the world with a weary contempt, as if all the eighty years of his life had been nothing but useless effort.

Round the bed were standing four dark-skinned men, with thin lips and eyes bright as black olives; they were wearing sombre robes and had all assumed the tragic mien with which Italians greet the approach of death.

'My cousins Tolomeo Tolomei, Andrea Tolomei, Giaccomo Tolomei,' said the dying man by way of introduction. 'And then here's my nephew, Guccio Baglioni, whom of course you know.'

At thirty-five Guccio's hair had already gone white at the temples.

'They've come from Siena to see me die, and also for other matters,' said the old banker slowly.

Robert of Artois, wearing travelling-clothes, was leaning a little forward in the chair they had brought up for him, and was gazing at the old man with the deceptive concentration so often to be seen on the faces of people obsessed by grave anxiety.

'Monseigneur of Artois is a friend, I may presume to say so,' Tolomei told his relations. 'Anything that can be done for him must be done; he has often saved us in the past, and our present difficulties are none of his choosing.'

Since the Sienese counsins understood no French, Guccio quickly translated what his uncle had said. The cousins nodded their heads in concert, their expressions grave.

'But if it's money you require, Monseigneur, alas, alas, and despite all my devotion to you, there's nothing we can do. You well know why . . .'

Spinello Tolomei was husbanding his strength and had no need to elaborate the situation. What good would it do to complain about the disastrous situation in which the Italian bankers had been placed during these last months?

In January the King had issued an edict threatening all Lombards with expulsion. This was nothing new; in every reign, when times were hard, the same threat had been held over them and they had been compelled to pay heavily all over again for their right of residence. To compensate their loss, the bankers had merely increased the rate of interest for a year. But this time the edict contained a far more serious clause: all debts owed the Italians by French lords were annulled; and the debtors were absolutely forbidden to pay, even if they had the desire and the ability. The royal sergeants-at-arms were mounting guard at the doors of the banks and turning away honest customers who came to pay their debts. The Italian bankers were naturally much concerned.

'And it's all because the nobility has run too far into debt with these fantastic festivals, these tournaments in which it wants to shine in front of the King. Even under Philip the Fair we were not treated like this.'

'I did my best for you,' Robert said.

'I know, I know, Monseigneur. You have always stood up for our companies. But there it is; and you're in no better favour than we are at the moment. We were hoping that things would come right in the end as they've always done before. But Macci dei Macci's execution is the final blow!'

The old man stared out of the window and fell silent.

Macci dei Macci was one of the greatest Italian financiers in France, and Philippe VI, on Robert's advice, had appointed him to the Treasury at the beginning of his reign. And now he had been hanged without proper trial.

Guccio Baglioni said with latent anger in his voice: 'He was a man who devoted all his time and intelligence to the service of the kingdom. He felt himself to be more French than if he had been born on the banks of the Seine; he even called himself Mache des Mache. Did he profit from his office more than the people who had him hanged? It's always the Italians

266

who are persecuted because they have no means of defending themselves!'

The Italian cousins were catching what they could of the conversation; at the name Macci dei Macci, they raised their eyebrows, closed their eyes and groaned in concert.

'Tolomei,' said Robert of Artois, 'I have not come to borrow money from you, but to ask you to receive some from me.'

Weak though he was, at this statement Messer Tolomei almost sat up in surprise. The Sienese cousins re-opened their eyes, hardly daring to believe they had understood correctly.

'Yes,' went on Robert, 'I want to give you all the cash I possess against letters of credit. I'm going. I'm leaving the kingdom.'

'You, Monseigneur! Has your case gone as badly as that? Has judgement been made against you?'

'It will be within the month. Do you know, banker, how this King treats me even though I'm married to his sister and he would never have been King except for me? He has sent his bailiff of Gisors to blow his horn at the doors of all my castles, at Conches, Beaumont and Orbec, to summon me before his seat of justice at Michaelmas! It's a travesty of justice and the verdict is already decided against me. Philippe has laid all his hounds on me: Saint-Maure his wicked chancellor, Forget his thieving treasurer, Mathieu de Trye his marshal, and Mille de Noyers to give them a line. The very men who are all in alliance against you and have hanged your friend Mache des Mache! It's the Wicked Queen, the lame woman, who has won. Burgundy has vilely gained the day. They've thrown my lawyers and my chaplain into jail, and tortured my witnesses to make them retract. Well, let them condemn me; I shan't be there. They've stolen Artois from me, so let them blackguard me to their heart's content. This kingdom no longer means anything to me, and its King is my enemy; I shall go abroad to do him all the harm I can. Tomorrow I'm going to Conches to send my horses, plate, jewels and arms to Bordeaux, where I shall put them on board a ship for England. They want to seize my body and my goods; but they shan't take me anyway.'

'Are you going to England, Monseigneur?' Tolomei asked.

'I'm going first to ask refuge of my sister, the Countess of Namur.'

'Is your wife going with you?'

'She'll join me later. Well, that's how it is, banker. I want to hand my cash over to you against letters of credit on your branches in Holland and England. And you can keep ten per cent for your trouble.'

Tolomei moved his head a little on the pillow, and began a conversation in Italian with his nephew and cousins of which Robert understood nothing. He heard the words *debito* ... *rimborso* ... *deposito*. Was the Tolomei Company transgressing the royal edict by accepting the money of a French lord? Clearly not, since this was no question of paying a debt but of a *deposito*.

Tolomei turned his unshaven cheeks and blue lips back to Robert of Artois.

'We are going too, Monseigneur; or, rather, they are going,' he said, pointing to his relations. 'They will take with them all we have here. At the moment our companies are not in agreement. The Bardi and the Peruzzi are hesitating; they think the worst is over, and that if they cringe a little ... They're like the Jews, who always have faith in the law and believe they'll be held quit when they've paid up; they pay up and then they're sent to the stake. So, there it is, the Tolomei are leaving. Their departure will cause a certain amount of surprise since they're taking to Italy all the money that has been invested with us; most of it is already on the road. Since the authorities refuse us the payment of our debts, we're removing the deposits.'[30]

The old man's sunken face looked sly for the last time.

'I shall leave nothing in France but my bones, and they're of no great value,' he added.

'France has certainly not treated us well,' said Guccio Baglioni.

'What do you mean? She's given you a son, and that's not too bad!'

'Of course,' said Robert of Artois, 'you've got a son, haven't you? Is he coming on well?'

'Thank you, Monseigneur,' replied Guccio, 'he'll soon be taller than I am; he's fifteen now. But he shows little liking for banking.'

'He'll come to it, he'll come to it,' said the old man. 'Very well, Monseigneur, we accept. Deposit your cash with us; we'll take it out of the country and give you letters of credit for the full amount. We'll take no commission. Ready money is always useful.'

'I'm grateful to you, Tolomei; my coffers will be brought to you tonight.'

'When money takes flight from a kingdom, that kingdom's happiness is measured. You will have your revenge, Monseigneur; I shall not see it, but I tell you, you'll have your revenge!'

Tolomei, who usually kept his left eye shut, now opened

both of them and looked straight at Robert. There was a clear gleam of truth in them at the last. And Robert of Artois suddenly felt moved because an old Lombard, who was soon to die, had looked at him with compassion.

'Tolomei, I have seen brave men in battle fight on to the end; in your own way you are as brave as they.'

The banker's lips parted in a sad smile.

'It is not courage, Monseigneur, very much the contrary. If I were not dealing with banking business, I would be very much afraid at this moment!'

He raised his old hand from the coverlet and signed to Robert to come near.

Robert bent over him, as if to be told a secret.

'Monseigneur,' said Tolomei, 'permit me to bless my last customer.'

And with his thumb he traced the sign of the cross over the giant's head, as Italian fathers do on the brows of their sons when they are about to set off on a long journey.

IO

The Seat of Justice

PHILLIPPE VI, CROWNED AND wearing a royal robe, was
seated on a throne, of which the arms ended in lions' heads,
in the centre of a tiered dais. Above his head were the arms
of France, embroidered on a great silk hanging. From time
to time he leaned to his left towards his cousin, the King
of Navarre, or to his right towards his relative, the King of
Bohemia, to catch their eyes and make sure they realized how
patient and forbearing he had been.

The King of Bohemia was shaking his splendid chestnut
beard in mingled incredulity and indignation. How could a
knight, a peer of France, a prince of the fleur de lis, as was
Robert of Artois, have behaved like this, had a hand in all the
sordid doings that were being read out and compromised
himself with such wicked people?

In the front row of the temporal peers, each of whom had a
shield with his blazon suspended above his seat, was Prince
Jean, the heir to the throne, who was taking his place for the
first time. He was thirteen, unusually tall for his age, had a

very long chin, and looked sulky and stupid. His father had just created him Duke of Normandy.

Beyond him was the Count of Alençon, the King's brother, the Dukes of Bourbon and Brittany, the Count of Flanders and the Count of Etampes. There were two empty seats: those of the Duke of Burgundy, who could not sit since he was a party to the case, and of the King of England, who had not even sent a representative.

Among the spiritual peers were Monseigneur Jean de Marigny, Count-Bishop of Beauvais, and Guillaume de Trye, Duke-Archbishop of Reims.

To lend still greater solemnity to the court, the King had summoned the Archbishops of Sens and Aix, the Bishops of Arras, Autun, Blois, Forez and Vendôme, the Duke of Lorraine, Count Guillaume of Hainaut and his brother, Jean, and all the great officers of the Crown: the Constable, the two marshals, Mille de Noyers, Master of the Exchequer, the Lords of Châtillon, Soyecourt and Garencières, who were members of the Privy Council, and many others. They were grouped in front of the dais along the walls of the great hall of the Louvre in which the hearing was taking place.

Sitting on mats on the ground with their legs crossed were the masters of requests, the counsellors of Parliament, the clerks of justice and the minor ecclesiastics.

Some six paces in front of the King stood the Procurator General, Simon de Bucy, surrounded by the commissioners of Inquiry. For the last two hours he had been reading his speech for the prosecution, the longest he had ever had to make in the whole of his career. He had had to recapitulate the whole history of the Artois affair, whose origins dated back to the end of the previous century, to remind the court of the case in the year 1309, of the judgement given by Philip the Fair, of Robert's armed rebellion against Philippe the Long in 1316, and of the second judgement given in 1318, before dealing with more recent events, the perjury at Amiens, the inquiry, the counter-inquiry, the innumerable depositions, the suborning of witnesses, the forging of documents, and the arrest of the accomplices.

The unbelievable complexity of the facts, as they were now marshalled and brought out into the light of day, made this one of the greatest law cases concerned with an individual the world had ever seen, and for forty years, moreover, it had been intertwined with the history of the kingdom. The audience was at once fascinated and dumbfounded by the Procurator's revelations. So this was the secret life of the great Baron before whom everyone had still been trembling only yesterday, whose friend everyone had tried to become, and whose decisions had ruled France for so long. It was he who had been at the back of the denunciation of the scandals of the Tower of Nesle, the imprisonment of Marguerite of Burgundy, the annulment of Charles IV's marriage, the war in Aquitaine, the cancelling of the crusade, the support given to Isabella of England and the election of Philippe VI! It was he who had been the driving force behind all these events, their mainspring, their governor, and yet throughout had been moved by one sole consideration, one single interest: the inheritance of Artois.

And how many of those present – including the King himself – owed their places, their titles and their fortunes to this perjurer, forger and criminal!

The accused's place in the court was occupied symbolically by two sergeants-at-arms holding up a great silk banner bearing Robert's blazon: 'Azure semy de lis or, a label of four points gules charged on each point with three castles or.'

And every time the Procurator mentioned Robert's name, he turned towards the banner as if indicating the man himself.

He had now reached the matter of Robert's flight.

'Though the summons was properly served by Master Jean Loncle, officer to the bailiwick of Gisors, at all his ordinary domiciles, the said Robert of Artois, Count of Beaumont, has defaulted before our Lord the King and his court of justice, convened this twenty-ninth day of September. Moreover, we have been apprised and had it confirmed to us from many sources that the said Robert has embarked his horses and his treasure in a ship at Bordeaux, and has had his gold and silver currency illegally exported from the kingdom, and that he himself, instead of appearing before the King's court of justice, has fled beyond the frontiers.

'On the sixth day of October, 1331, the woman de Divion, found guilty of numerous crimes both on her own account and in complicity with the said Robert, including forging documents and counterfeiting seals, was burnt at the stake in Paris in the Place aux Pourceaux, and her bones reduced to powder, in the presence of Messeigneurs the Duke of Brittany, the Count of Flanders, the Sire Jean of Hainaut, the Sire Raoul de Brienne, the Constable of France, the Marshals Robert Bertrand and Matthieu de Trye, and Messire Jean de Milon, Provost of Paris, who has reported to the King that the execution has been carried out . . .'

As their names were mentioned, they stared down at the floor. They remembered only too well La Divion screaming at the stake as the flames caught her hempen shirt, the flesh of her legs swelling and bursting in the heat, and how appalling the stench was that the October breeze wafted towards them. This was how the mistress of the late Bishop of Arras had died.

'On the twelfth and fourteenth days of October, Master Pierre d'Auxerre, councillor, and Michel de Paris, bailiff, informed Madame de Beaumont, the spouse of the said Robert, first at Jouy-le-Châtel, then at Conches, Beaumont, Orbec and Quatremares, her ordinary domiciles, that the King summoned him to appear on the fourteenth day of December. Nevertheless, the said Robert, on that date, failed to appear for the second time. In his great mercy, our Lord the King once more adjourned the court till the fifteenth, the Feast of Candlemas, and so that the said Robert might not plead ignorance, the proclamation was read first in the Great Chamber of Parliament, then at the Marble Table in the great hall of the palace, and then taken to Orbec and Beaumont, and later to Conches by the same Masters Pierre d'Auxerre and Michel de Paris, where they were unable to have speech with the Dame de Beaumont, but made proclamation at the door of her chamber, and loudly enough for her to hear them ...'

Every time Madame de Beaumont's name was mentioned, the King passed his hand over his face, and his long fleshy nose seemed to quiver; for she was his sister.

'When the case came before the King's Parliament of Justice on the said date, the said Robert of Artois failed to appear, but was represented by Master Henry, Dean of the Brussels bar, and by Master Thiébault de Meaux, Canon of Cambrai, appearing for him by proxy and with instructions to plead the reasons for his absence. But in view of the fact that the adjournment was for Monday, the fifteenth, at Candlemas, and that the commission of which they were the bearers was for the Tuesday, their submissions were not recognized as valid, and default was for the third time entered against the defendant. Moreover, it is notorious that during this time Robert of Artois endeavoured to take refuge with his sister, Madame the Countess of Namur; but that, our Lord the King having forbidden Madame de Namur to aid or abet this rebel, she forbade the said Robert, her brother, to sojourn in her estates. Upon which the said Robert wished to take refuge with Monseigneur the Count Guillaume in his estates of Hainaut; but on representations from our Lord the King, Monseigneur the Count of Hainaut similarly denied the said Robert asylum. And, then again, the said Robert asked for refuge and asylum from the Duke of Brabant, but on representations from our Lord the King the said Duke, having first made answer that, being no vassal of the King of France, he could receive into his states whom he pleased, ultimately yielded to the remonstrances made to him by Monseigneur of Luxemburg, the King of Bohemia, and responded courteously by exiling Robert of Artois from the duchy.'[31]

Philippe VI kept turning to the Count of Hainaut and the King of Bohemia, making them sad yet grateful little signs of friendship. There was no doubt that Philippe was very unhappy about these proceedings; nor was he alone in being so. However guilty Robert of Artois might be, his friends were horrified at the thought of him moving from little Court to little Court, to be welcomed one day and banished the next, only to journey on and be rebuffed once more. Why had he so obstinately pursued his own downfall, when the

King had shown himself so determinedly clement to the very end?

'Notwithstanding that the inquiry was closed, after seventy-six witnesses had been heard, of which fourteen were detained in the royal prisons, and that the King's justice was sufficiently enlightened thereby and the charges on the indictment clearly proven, our Lord the King, because of his long-standing friendship, made it known to the said Robert of Artois that he was prepared to give him a safe-conduct to return to the kingdom and leave it again, if he so desired, and that he might hear the charges made against him, present his defence, admit his faults and obtain pardon. Yet, the said Robert, far from accepting this offer of clemency, has not returned to the kingdom, but in various places in which he has resided has made contact with all kinds of wicked people, outlaws and enemies of the King, and has informed a great number of persons, who have repeated it, that it is his intention to assassinate by steel or sorcery the Chancellor, the Marshal de Trye and divers councillors of our Lord the King, and finally he has also uttered similar threats against the King himself.'

A murmur of indignation rose on all sides.

'These things being known and notorious, and in view of the fact that the said Robert of Artois has failed once again to answer the summons, though it has been made in proper form, for this eighth day of April, being the Wednesday before Easter, and that we now summon him to appear for the fourth time . . .'

Simon de Bucy paused and made a sign to a sergeant mace-bearer, who cried in a loud voice: 'Messire Robert of Artois, Count of Beaumont-le-Roger, is summoned to appear!'

Everyone turned instinctively to the door as if the accused were really about to appear. There were a few seconds of complete silence. Then the sergeant struck the floor with his mace and the Procurator continued: '. . . and in view of the fact that the said Robert has defaulted, we demand in the name of our Lord the King: that the said Robert be deprived of his titles, rights and prerogatives as a peer of the realm, as well as of all his other titles, lordships and possessions; moreover, that his goods, lands, castles, houses, chattels, rents and perquisites be confiscated and remitted to the Treasury, that they may be disposed of as the King wills; further, that his blazon be destroyed in the presence of the peers and barons, so that it may never more appear on banner or seal, and that his person be banished for ever from the realm, and all vassals, allies, relatives and friends of our Lord the King be forbidden to shelter him; and, finally, we demand that this sentence be cried and proclaimed to the sound of trumpets in the principal centres of Paris and made known to the bailiffs of Rouen, Gisors, Aix and Bourges, and also to the seneschals of Toulouse and Carcassone, that it may be put into execution, by the King's will.'

Master Simon de Bucy fell silent. The King seemed to be dreaming. He glanced round the assembly but his eyes came to rest on no one. Then, bowing his head, first to the right and then to the left, he said: 'My peers, I ask your counsel. Silence means consent!'

No one raised a hand or said a word.

Philippe VI clapped his hand on the lion's head on the arm of the throne and said: 'Judgement is passed!'

The Procurator ordered the two sergeants who were holding up Robert of Artois' blazon to advance to the foot of the throne. The Chancellor Guillaume de Saint-Maure, who was one of those Robert in his exile was threatening with death, stepped forward to the blazon, asked one of the sergeants for his sword, pierced the edge of the stuff, and then slit the blazon in half with a sound of tearing silk.

The peerage of Beaumont was abrogated. The man for whom it had been created, the Prince of France who was descended from King Louis VIII, whose giant strength was legendary and whose intrigues were infinite, was henceforward merely an outlaw. He no longer belonged to the kingdom over which his ancestors had ruled, and nothing within that kingdom belonged to him any more.

For these peers and lords, for all these men whose blazons were an expression not only of their power but almost of their very existence, who flew them on standards from their roofs, from their lances, from their horses, who embroidered them on their own breasts, on the surcoats of their squires and on the liveries of their servants, who painted them on their furniture and engraved them on their plate, marking with them men, animals and everything which in any degree formed part of their power or their wealth, this rending, which was a sort of lay excommunication, was more degrading than the block, the hurdle or the stake. For death effaces crime, and dishonour is extinguished with the dishonoured.

'Still, as long as you're alive, you've never quite lost the day,' thought Robert of Artois, travelling by hostile, foreign roads towards yet greater crimes.

PART FOUR

THE WAR-BRAND

I

The Outlaw

FOR OVER THREE YEARS Robert of Artois prowled round the frontiers of the kingdom like some great wounded beast.

Related to all the kings and princes of Europe, nephew of the Duke of Brittany, uncle of the King of Navarre, a brother of the Countess of Namur, brother-in-law of the Count of Hainaut and the Prince of Taranto, cousin of the King of Naples, the King of Hungary and of many others, he was now, at the age of forty-five, a solitary traveller to whom the doors of every castle were closed. He had sufficient money, thanks to the letters of credit given him by the Sienese bankers; but no equerry ever came to the inn in which he happened to be staying to invite him to dine with the local lord. If there was a tournament in the neighbourhood, the host wondered how he could avoid asking Robert of Artois, the outlaw and the forger, who in the old days would have been put in the place of honour. And the Captain of the town would intimate a cold request from Monseigneur the Suzerain Count that he would move on. For Monseigneur the Suzerain Count, or

Duke, or Margrave, had no desire to quarrel with the King of France and felt no obligations towards a man who was so disgraced that he no longer had either blazon or banner.

And Robert had to continue on his random way, accompanied by his single servant, Gillet de Nelle, who was a bad character and thoroughly deserved to be hanged, though, like Lormet in the past, he was utterly devoted to his master. As a reward Robert gave him that satisfaction which is more precious than high wages: the intimacy of a great lord in adversity. During their wanderings they spent many nights playing dice together at a table in the corner of some wretched tavern. And when they needed women, they would go off together to one of the numerous Flanders brothels, in which there was always a good selection of plump whores.

It was in these places that Robert heard the latest news from France, either from merchants returning from the fairs or from whores who had listened to travellers' talk.

In the summer of 1332 Philippe VI had married his son, Jean, the Duke of Normandy, to the daughter of the King of Bohemia, Bonne of Luxemburg. 'That's why John of Luxemburg had me expelled from the lands of his cousin of Brabant,' Robert thought, 'and this is the price of his intervention.' The celebrations held in honour of the wedding, which took place at Melun, had, so it was said, surpassed in splendour anything seen before.

Philippe VI had taken the opportunity of this great assembly of princes and lords to have the cross solemnly sewn on to his royal robe. For the crusade had now at last been decided on. Pierre de la Palud, the Patriarch of Jerusalem, had preached it in a sermon at Melun, drawing tears from the six thousand wedding guests, of whom eighteen hundred were

German knights. Bishop Pierre Roger had preached it at Rouen, to which diocese he had recently been appointed, after holding those of Arras and Sens. The general expedition was planned to set out in the spring of 1334. A huge fleet was being built in the Provençal ports of Marseilles and Aigues-Mortes. And Bishop Jean de Marigny had already been sent with a challenge to the Sultan of Egypt! But if the Kings of Bohemia, Navarre, Majorca and Aragon, who were living at Philippe's Court, if the dukes, counts and great barons, together with a certain number of knights impatient for adventure, supported the King of France's projects with enthusiasim, the minor provincial nobility, on the other hand, appeared to be showing rather less eagerness to seize the red cloth crosses the preachers handed them and take ship for the sands of Egypt. The King of England was pressing forward with the military training of his people, but was unresponsive to the plan for invading the Holy Land. While old Pope John XXII, who was moreover engaged in a serious quarrel with the University of Paris and Buridan, its rector, about the problems of the Beatific Vision, was turning a deaf ear to the proposal. Indeed, he had only given his approval to the crusade with a bad grace and was even more reluctant to subsidize it. On the other hand, the spice, incense, silk and relic merchants, not to mention the armourers and shipbuilders, were wholly in favour of the expedition.

Philippe VI had already made arrangements for the Regency during his absence by making the peers, barons and bishops take an oath of obedience to his son, Jean, and swear that they would hand over the crown to him without argument if he himself should die beyond the seas.[32]

'It's because Philippe can't be quite sure that his son's

legitimate that he's having him recognized now,' thought Robert of Artois.

His elbows on the table in front of a pot of beer, Robert dared not tell the casual acquaintances who gave him the news that he knew all the great people they talked about; he dared not say that he had jousted against the King of Bohemia, procured Pierre Roger his mitre, dandled the King of England on his knee and dined at the Pope's table. But he noted all they said in the hope of being able to turn it one day to his own advantage.

It was hatred that sustained him. And he would go on hating as long as he lived. Wherever he happened to be, it was hatred that awakened him with the first ray of light filtering through the shutters of his unfamiliar room. Hatred was the salt in his food and the sky above his road.

It is said that a strong man is one who can see his own mistakes. But perhaps they are even stronger who never see them. Robert was one of these. It was not he who had done wrong; but everyone else, the living and the dead, Philip the Fair, Enguerrand, Mahaut, Philippe of Valois, the Duke of Burgundy, and the Chancellor Sainte-Maure. And, as he travelled on, he added more names to the list of his enemies: his sister of Namur, his brother-in-law of Hainaut, John of Luxemburg and the Duke of Brabant.

In Brussels he recruited a shady lawyer called Huy and his clerk, Berthelot; it was with these lawyers that he began collecting a household again.

At Louvain Huy discovered a monk of hideous appearance and dubious life, Brother Henry de Sagebran, who knew more about spells and witchcraft than he did about litanies and works of charity. With the help of Brother Henry de Sagebran, the former Peer of France, remembering the lessons he had learnt from Beatrice d'Hirson, baptized wax dolls in the names of Philippe, Saint-Maure or Mathieu de Trye, and pierced them with needles.

'Pay particular attention to this one and pierce it from the head right down through the body, for its name is Jeanne and she's the Queen of France. She's not really a queen, she's a devil!'

He also procured invisible ink with which to write certain death-dealing formulas on parchment. The parchment, however, had to be placed in the victim's bed. Provided with a little money and many promises, Brother Henry de Sagebran set off for France, like any honest mendicant, with a quantity of these lethal parchments concealed beneath his habit.

In the meantime, Gillet de Nelle had recruited hired assassins, professional thieves and escaped prisoners, low fellows who preferred crime to an honest day's work. And when Gillet had collected a little band of them, and they had received suitable training, Robert sent them into France with orders to operate for preference at the great assemblies and festivals.

'Backs are an easy target for the knife when every eye is on the lists or every ear listening to the crusade being preached.'

Robert had grown thinner on his travels; the crease had sunk deeper into the muscles of his forehead, and his preoccupation with wickedness from morning till night, and even in his dreams, had permanently marked his features. On the other hand, the whole adventure seemed to have rejuvenated him in spirit. He enjoyed the unaccustomed food of these foreign countries, and their women too.

When Liège expelled him, it was not because of his past misdeeds, but because Gillet and he had turned a house leased from a certain Sieur d'Argentau into a haunt of whores and the noise they made kept the whole neighbourhood awake.

There were good days; and bad ones too, such as that on which he learnt that Brother Henry de Sagebran, with his lethal parchments, had been arrested in Cambrai, and another on which one of his hired assassins reported that his comrades had been unable to get farther than Reims and were now languishing in the 'Makeshift' King's prisons.

Then he fell ill as the result of an absurd accident. There was a canal in front of the house in which he was living and water sports were being held. He put his head out of the window and pushed it up to the neck into a fish-trap that was hanging there. He had stuck his head in so firmly that he had a long struggle to get it out and scratched his cheeks on the mesh of the trap. The scratches became infected and fever set in. He was seriously ill for four days and very nearly died.

Disgusted with the Flemish Marches, he went to Geneva. As he was wandering round the lake, he learned of the arrest of his wife, the Countess of Beaumont, and of their three children. As a reprisal against Robert, Philippe VI had not hesitated to imprison his own sister, first in the keep of Nemours and then at Château Gaillard, which had been Marguerite of Burgundy's prison. Burgundy was undoubtedly having its revenge.

Travelling under a false name and dressed like any ordinary bourgeois, Robert left Geneva for Avignon. He stayed there a fortnight, trying to set intrigues on foot for his cause. He found the capital of Christendom more luxurious and dissolute than ever. Ambition, vanity and vice were not here concealed behind tournament armour, but behind the robes of prelates; the insignia of power were not silver harness and plumed helms, but mitres encrusted with precious stones and gold chalices heavier than a king's goblet. The hatreds of the sacristy took the place of challenges in the lists. There was little secrecy in the confessional; and the women were more immoral, unfaithful and venal than elsewhere, since sin could be their only title to fame.

And yet no one was prepared to risk compromising himself for the former Peer of France. People pretended they had hardly known him. Even in this sink of vice Robert was a pariah. The list of his enemies grew longer.

Nevertheless, he found some consolation in learning from the general gossip that his cousin of Valois' affairs were going much less well than might have been supposed. The Church was much perturbed by the crusade. What would happen to the West, left at the mercy of the Emperor and the King of England, when Philippe and his allies had set sail? Suppose the two sovereigns formed an alliance? The expedition had already been postponed for two years. The spring of 1334 had gone by with nothing ready. People were now talking of 1336. Philippe VI had presided in person over a plenary assembly of the doctors of Paris on Mount Sainte-Geneviève and had brandished the threat of a decree of heresy against the aged Pontiff, now ninety, if he refused to retract his theological pronouncements. Everyone was waiting for his death, which month after month was reported to be imminent – but these reports had been current for eighteen years!

'The great thing,' thought Robert, 'is to go on living; if you can last long enough the day will come when you'll win.'

The death of some of his enemies had already given him hope. The Treasurer Forget had died at the end of the previous year; the Chancellor Guillaume de Sainte-Maure was also dead. Jean, Duke of Normandy, the heir to the throne of France, was gravely ill; and even Philippe VI, so it was said, was far from well; perhaps Robert's spells had not been wholly ineffective.

For his return to Flanders he donned the habit of a lay brother; and a very strange brother the giant made, for his cowl stood out above the crowd like a steeple above the houses at its feet. He marched up to abbeys with the stride of a warrior, rang the bell at the gate as if he intended to tear it down, and demanded the hospitality due to a man of God in the tone of voice he would have used to ask a squire to hand him his lance.

As he sat in a refectory in Bruges at the bottom of a long greasy table, bending his head over his bowl and pretending to murmur prayers of which he did not know a single word or listening to the reader in the recess halfway up the wall reading the lives of the saints, his monotonous voice echoing in the vaults of the roof above the heads of the monks, Robert thought: 'Why not finish my days here in the profound peace of the monastic life with its freedom from care, its renunciation, its assurance of refuge, its regular hours, and its end to wandering?'

However turbulent, cruel and ambitious a man may be, he has inevitably been tempted at some time or other to resign it all and seek rest. What was the use of struggles and vain enterprises, when they must all end in the dust of the tomb? Robert thought of it, as five years earlier he had thought of retiring with his wife and sons to the quiet life of a little provincial lord. But these were seldom more than passing thoughts. In any case, they always occurred to Robert too late, indeed at the very moment events were to hurl him back into the vortex of action and battle, his true vocation.

In Ghent, two days later, Robert of Artois made the acquaintance of Jakob Van Artevelde.

Van Artevelde was much the same age as Robert, approaching fifty. He was stout, stocky and square of face; a great eater and drinker, though he held his liquor well. As a young man, he had been to Rhodes with Charles of Valois, had made several other voyages and knew his Europe well. A dealer in honey and a cloth manufacturer on a large scale, he had married as his second wife a woman of noble birth.

Hard, haughty and imaginative, he had first acquired power over his own town of Ghent, which he completely controlled, and then over the principal Flemish communes. When the fullers, cloth merchants, or brewers, whose trades constituted the real wealth of the country, desired to make representations to the Count or the King of France, it was to Jakob Van Artevelde they turned to put forward their petitions and complaints in a strong voice and clear words. He had no title; he was merely Messire Van Artevelde, but everyone bowed before him. He had enemies of course, and went about with an escort of sixty armed servants who waited for him at the doors of the houses in which he dined.

Jakob Van Artevelde and Robert of Artois immediately recognized each other as men of the same kidney: clever, lucid, obsessed with the desire for power and physically brave.

That Robert was an outlaw mattered not in the least to

Van Artevelde; indeed, for the man of Ghent, a former great lord who knew all the intrigues of the Court of France, all the men who held any position there, and yet was hostile to France, might prove a godsend. To Robert, this ambitious bourgeois seemed worth twenty nobles who forbade him their manors. Artevelde was a power among his fellow citizens and he was hostile to the Count of Flanders and therefore to Philippe VI; this was what mattered.

'We do not like Louis of Nevers, and he has succeeded in remaining our count only because the King of France massacred our train-bands at Mont Cassel.'

'I was there,' Robert said.

'He never comes near us except when he wants money to spend in Paris; he refuses to listen to the representations we make; and his idea of governing the country is merely to pass on the oppressive decrees of the King of France. We have just been obliged to expel the English merchants, though we have absolutely nothing against them. The King's quarrels with his cousin of England about the crusade and the throne of Scotland mean nothing to us.[33] And now England, in reprisal, is threatening to cut off the supply of wool. If that happens, our spinners and weavers, not only here but throughout Flanders, will have no alternative but to break up their looms and close their workshops. But on that day, Monseigneur, they will take up arms again; and Hainaut, Brabant, Holland and Zeeland will be with us, for those countries are allies of France merely through the marriages of their princes, but neither by the hearts nor stomachs of the people; and you cannot reign for long over a people you've starved.'

Robert listened attentively to Artevelde's talk. At last he

had met a man who knew his subject, spoke out and seemed
to have real strength behind him.

'If you really intend to rebel again,' said Robert, 'why
don't you make a definite alliance with the King of England?
And why not enter into negotiations with the Emperor of
Germany who, since he's the Pope's enemy, is therefore also
the enemy of France, who holds the Pope in her hand? Your
train-bands are brave, but can only mount minor actions
because they lack cavalry. Give them the support of a corps of
English knights and a corps of German knights and advance
into France through Artois. I guarantee to raise reinforcements for you there.'

He could already see the coalition in being and himself
riding at the head of an army.

'Believe me, Monseigneur, I have thought of it often
enough,' replied Artevelde. 'There would be no difficulty in
entering into negotiations with the King of England and even
with the Emperor Louis of Bavaria, if our bourgeois were
ready to do so. The people in the communes hate Count
Louis, but they still turn to the King of France when they
want justice. They have sworn loyalty to the King of France.
Even when they take up arms against him, he still remains
their master. Besides, through France's clever diplomacy,
our towns have agreed to pay a fine of two million florins to
the Pope if they rebel against their suzerain, and the Pope has
threatened to excommunicate us if we don't pay up. Our
families are afraid of being deprived of priests and masses.'

'What you mean is that the Pope has been obliged to
threaten you with excommunication or ruin to keep your
communes quiet during the crusade. But who can force you
to pay up, when the French army is in Egypt?'

'You know what the common people are like,' said Artevelde; 'they never know their own strength till the moment for using it has passed.'

Robert emptied his great flagon of beer; he was getting to like beer. He was silent for a moment, staring at the panelling. Jakob Van Artevelde had a handsome and comfortable house; the brass and pewter were well polished, and the oak furniture gleamed in the shadows.

'So it's allegiance to the King of France that prevents your making new alliances and taking up arms?'

'Precisely that,' said Artevelde.

Robert had a lively imagination. For the last three and a half years he had been slaking his thirst for revenge with minor draughts such as spells, sorcery, and hired assassins who never reached their intended victims. His hopes had now suddenly taken on a new dimension; a great idea was germinating in his mind, one that was worthy of him at last.

'Suppose the King of England became King of France?' he asked.

Artevelde looked at Robert of Artois with incredulity as if he doubted that he had heard him right.

'I repeat, Messire: Suppose the King of England *was* King of France? Suppose he laid claim to the crown, established his right to it, proved that the Kingdom of France was his, and became your legitimate sovereign?'

'Surely Monseigneur, that is only the wildest of dreams!'

'Not at all!' cried Robert. 'The quarrel has never been decided; the cause has never been lost. When my cousin of Valois came to the throne – that is when I got him his throne and you see how grateful he is to me – the English delegates came over to claim the rights of Queen Isabella and her son

Edward. It's not so long ago; less than seven years. No one would listen to them because no one wanted to listen to them, and I had them escorted back to their ship. You call Philippe "the Makeshift King"; why don't you make another? Suppose the whole case was reopened and you said to your spinners, weavers and merchants, and to the people of your communes: "Your Count holds his rights illegally; it is not to the King of France he owes homage. Your real sovereign is the King in London."'

It was a dream, of course, but it appealed to Jakob Van Artevelde. The wool that came by sea from the north-west, the cloth both coarse and fine that was exported by the same route, the traffic in the ports, all encouraged Flanders to turn its eyes towards the Kingdom of England. The money from tithes and taxes was all that went to Paris.

'Do you really believe, Monseigneur, that anyone in the world can be convinced by what you say and persuaded to take part in such an enterprise?'

'It is enough, Messire, for one person to be convinced: the King of England himself.'

A few days later, with a passport describing him as a cloth merchant, and accompanied by Gillet de Nelle, who for form's sake was carrying a few ells of cloth, Monseigneur Robert of Artois took ship at Antwerp on his way to London.

2

Westminster Hall

ONCE AGAIN, CROWNED AND sceptre in hand, a king was sitting surrounded by his peers. Once again prelates, earls and barons were grouped about his throne. Once again the serried ranks of clerics, doctors, jurists, counsellors and dignitaries stood before him.

But instead of the lilies of France, the leopards of the Plantagenets were embroidered on the royal robes. Nor was it the old stone vaults of the Louvre that echoed the murmur of the crowd, but the splendid oak roof, the huge carved beams, of Westminster Hall. The Parliament of England was in session, and the six hundred knights, squires and sheriffs from town and county covered the big square flagstones of the floor.

Curiously enough, the great assembly had gathered to listen to an address from a Frenchman.

Standing a few paces in front of the throne, halfway up the steps at the end of the hall, his robe scarlet and gold in the light from the great window, Count Robert of Artois was making a speech to the delegates of the people of England.

During the two years that had elapsed since Robert had left Flanders, the wheel of destiny had made a quarter-turn. Moreover, the Pope was dead.

Towards the end of 1334 the now feeble little old man, who, during one of the longest of all pontifical reigns had given the Church both a powerful administration and prosperous finances, had been compelled, as he lay on his deathbed in the green room in his great palace at Avignon, publicly to renounce the only tenets he had ever been able to hold with true conviction. To avoid the schism threatened by the University of Paris, and in pursuance of the orders of the Court of France in whose favour he had settled so many dubious affairs and kept so many secrets, he had to deny his sermons, writings and encyclicals. Master Buridan[34] had dictated to the Holy Father what it was proper to hold in matters of dogma: Hell existed, full of roasting souls, the better to assure authority over their subjects to the princes of this world; Paradise, like any good hotel, was open to every loyal knight who massacred on behalf of his king, as well as to all accommodating prelates who blessed crusades. None of these righteous people had need to wait for the Last Judgement before enjoying the Beatific Vision.

The day after this enforced disclaimer, John XXII died; and there were doctors on Mont Sainte-Geneviève malicious enough to observe: 'At any rate, he must know now if Hell exists.'

The Conclave made ready to assemble, but it was involved in such a maze of rival interests that the election looked as if it might well take longer than ever before, even including the latest of eighteen years ago. France, England, the Emperor, the impetuous King of Bohemia, the erudite King of Naples, the Kings of Majorca and Aragon, the Roman nobility, the Visconti of Milan and the Republics were all exerting influence on the cardinals.

To gain time and not to favour any of these influences, the cardinals, on being locked in, had all decided on the same policy: 'I shall vote for whoever has the least chance of being elected.'

But God works in a mysterious way. The cardinals had agreed so well on the candidate who could not possibly become Pope that their voting papers all bore the same name: Jacques Fournier, the 'White Cardinal' as he was called, since he always wore the Cistercian habit. When the announcement was made, the cardinals, the populace and indeed the Pope-elect were all equally surprised. The new Pope's first utterance to his colleagues was that they had elected an ass.

He was being too modest.

Benedict XII, having been elected by mistake, showed himself to be a pacific pope. His first concern was to stop the bloody struggle that was going on in Italy, and to re-establish concord, if it were possible, between the Holy See and the Empire. And, for a while, it looked as if it might be possible. Louis of Bavaria had responded favourably to the Pope's advances and negotiations were being pursued, when Philippe of Valois had angrily entered the lists. How dared they exclude him, the leading monarch in Christendom, from such important negotiations? Was any influence but his to be allowed to hold sway over the Holy See? Was his dear cousin, the King of Bohemia, to renounce his chivalrous plans for Italy?

Philippe VI ordered Benedict XII to recall his ambassadors

and break off negotiations, under threat of confiscating all the cardinals' property in France.

Then, accompanied by his friend the King of Bohemia, by the King of Navarre and an escort of barons and knights so numerous that it was practically an army, Philippe VI went to spend Easter 1336 in Avignon. He had arranged to meet the Kings of Naples and Aragon there. It was his way of reminding the new Pope of his duty, and making it perfectly clear what was expected of him.

But Benedict XII, in his own peculiar way, showed that he was not such an ass as he pretended to be, and that a king would be well advised to assure himself of the Pope's friendship before undertaking a crusade.

On Good Friday he went into the pulpit to preach on the subject of our Lord's agony, and to give his blessing to the crusade. He could do no less when four crusading kings and two thousand lances were encamped round the town. But on Low Sunday Philippe VI, who had gone to the coast of Provence to inspect his great fleet, was unpleasantly surprised to receive a letter written in elegant Latin relieving him of his vows and oaths. Since there was still a state of war among the Christian nations, the Holy Father could not possibly allow the greatest defenders of the Church to depart for the lands of the infidel.

The Valois crusade came to an end in Marseilles.

The gallant King had been high-handed, but the Cistercian Pope was more high-handed still. For the hand that blessed could also excommunicate; and it was hard to imagine a crusade which was excommunicated before it had even set off.

'Settle your differences with England, my son, and your

difficulties with Flanders; and leave me to settle the difficulties with the Emperor; give me proof that there will be a sound and lasting peace in our countries, and then you may go to convert the infidel to those virtues which you have shown yourself.'

Since the Pope insisted on it, Philippe first set about adjusting his differences with England. But he chose to do so by reminding young Edward of his obligations as a vassal and demanding that he should hand over immediately that felon, Robert of Artois, to whom he was giving asylum. When their pride is wounded, counterfeit great men such as Philippe are apt to seek these contemptible forms of revenge.

By the time the demand for his extradition had been forwarded to London by the Seneschal of Guyenne, Robert had already obtained a solid footing in the English Court. His manners, his innate force and his readiness of speech had already gained him many friends; old Wryneck was full of his praises. The young King had great need of an experienced man who was an expert in French affairs. And who knew them better than the Count of Artois? Since he might be useful, his misfortunes inspired nothing but compassion.

'Sire, my cousin,' he said to Edward III, 'if you consider my presence in your kingdom troublesome or dangerous, hand me over to the hatred of the Makeshift King. I shall not complain, for you have shown me great hospitality; I shall have only myself to blame for having, against all right, given the throne to that wicked Philippe instead of to yourself, whom I then scarcely knew.'

He said this with a deep bow and his hand on his heart.

Edward III answered quietly: 'My cousin, you are my guest, and your counsel is precious to me. If I handed you over to the King of France, I would be the enemy not only of my own honour but of my interest. Moreover, you have been welcomed to the Kingdom of England and not to the Duchy of Guyenne, French sovereignty does not rule here.'

Philippe VI's demand was left unanswered.

And week by week, if not day by day, Robert continued his persuasions. He distilled the poison of temptation into Edward's ear and into those of his counsellors. He would come in and say: 'I salute the real King of France!'

He never missed an opportunity of pointing out that the Salic Law had been invented only for a special occasion and that Edward's right to the crown of Hugues Capet was the better founded. Young Edward was only the latest of the princes on whom Robert had exercised the seductions of his dangerous policies.

When a second demand was made for Robert's extradition, Edward III had responded by giving the exile three castles, a pension of twelve hundred marcs and settling some of his debts with the Lombard bankers.[35]

It was also at this time that Edward gave handsome proofs of his gratitude to his servants. He created his friend William Montacute Earl of Salisbury, and distributed titles and lands to the handful of young lords who had supported him in the affair at Nottingham.

And then, for the third time, Philippe VI sent his Grand Master of the Crossbowmen with an ultimatum to the Seneschal of Guyenne, who was to inform the King of England, that Robert of Artois, the mortal enemy of the Kingdom of France, must be handed over within a fortnight or the duchy would be sequestered.

'That's just what I expected!' cried Robert. 'That fool

Philippe can think of nothing better than to repeat the plan I made, my dear Sire Edward, against your father: first issue an order which is contrary to law, then sequester the duchy in default of its execution, and thereby impose the alternatives of humiliation or war. The difference, however, is that England now has a king who really rules, and France no longer has Robert of Artois.'

He did not add: 'There was then an exile in France playing exactly the same game as I am here, and his name was Mortimer!'

Robert had succeeded beyond his hopes; he was himself becoming the cause of the war he longed to see declared; and in his own person he was now of capital importance. To get the war started, he preached the policy that the King of England should lay claim to the crown of France.

And this was why, on that September day of 1337, he was standing on the steps of Westminster Hall, looking like some huge storm-bird with his wide sleeves spread against the tracery of the great window, and addressing the English Parliament at the King's request. With thirty years' training in public affairs behind him, he was able to speak without documents or notes.

Some of the members had only an imperfect knowledge of French and had to get their neighbours to translate certain passages for them.

As the Count of Artois developed his theme, a deep silence fell over the assembly, broken only by murmurs of surprise at some of the more startling revelations. And, indeed, his speech contained much matter for astonishment. Though the two countries were separated by no more than a narrow arm of the sea, though the princes of the two Courts intermarried, though the barons of England held estates in France and merchants travelled from one land to the other, yet neither nation really knew what was happening in the other.

For instance, the rule that 'France can neither be remitted to nor transmitted by a woman' was not based on ancient custom at all, but merely the result of the whim of a peppery old dotard of a constable twenty years ago when the succession to a king who had been assassinated was in question. Yes, indeed, Louis X, the Hutin, had been assassinated. Robert of Artois not only asserted it but named his murderess.

'I knew her well; she was my aunt, and she stole my inheritance from me.'

Robert spiced his speech with the crimes committed by the French princes and the scandals of the Capet Court. The members of the English Parliament shuddered with horror and indignation, just as if the appalling crimes committed in their own land and by their own Court were of no account.

And Robert pursued his arguments, which were precisely the opposite to those he had once put forward in favour of Philippe of Valois. He managed to do so, however, with just as much conviction.

It was clear, therefore, that at the death of King Charles IV, Philip the Fair's last son, the crown of France, even if one bowed to the French barons' dislike of being ruled by a woman, should in all justice have gone through Queen Isabella to the only male in the direct line.

The great red robe suddenly swirled before the eyes of the startled English as Robert turned to the King. He fell on one knee on the stone floor. 'Should have gone to you, noble Sire Edward, King of England, whom I recognize and salute as the true King of France,' he cried.

There had been no such enthusiasm since the wedding at York. The English were being told that their Sovereign could claim a kingdom twice as large as England and three times as rich. It was as if every man's fortune and worldly dignity had been increased in proportion.

But Robert knew that an audience's enthusiasm must never be given time to lapse. He rose quickly to his feet and began reminding the assembly that, at the time Charles IV's successor was being chosen, King Edward had sent over the famous and much respected Bishop Adam Orleton who, were he not at present in Avignon seeking the Pope's support for the cause, could have borne witness himself to what had happened when he had claimed the King of England's rights.

And was Robert to pass over in silence the part he himself had played in the election of Philippe of Valois? Throughout his life he had found that nothing served him better than calculated candour. He employed it now.

Who was it who had refused to listen to the English Bishop? Who had refused to admit the claims he made? Who had prevented him from presenting his case to the barons of France? Robert beat his chest with his huge fists and cried: 'It was I, my noble lords and squires! It was I, who am standing here before you; I thought I was acting for the best and maintaining peace; and so I chose the part of injustice. And I have not yet fully expiated the crime I committed then, even by all the misfortunes that have since befallen me.'

His voice echoed among the beams and reached the farthest corners of the hall.

Could he have found a more convincing argument? He was accusing himself of having had Philippe VI elected unjustly; he pleaded guilty, but at the same time presented his defence. Before becoming King, Philippe of Valois had promised him an equitable solution to all the outstanding difficulties; a lasting peace would be negotiated, leaving possession of the whole of Guyenne to the King of England; Flanders would be granted certain privileges for the encouragement of trade; and Artois would be restored to himself. He had therefore acted as he did with conciliation in view and for the general good. But here, indeed, was proof that one should never base one's actions on anything but justice; to listen to the false promises of men was clearly disastrous, for today the heir to Artois was an exile, Flanders starving and Guyenne menaced.

Therefore, if they had to go to war, let it not be over vain quarrels about homage, interpretations of sovereignty or definitions of vassalage, but rather for a real, great and true aim: the possession of the crown of France. The day the King of England donned it, there would cease to be any reasons for discord either in Guyenne or Flanders. Nor would there be lacking allies in Europe, among both the princes and the people.

And if noble Sire Edward required him, Robert of Artois, to spill his blood in this great adventure which would change the fate of nations, he was prepared, he cried, his hands reaching out from his velvet sleeves towards the King, the Lords and the Commons, indeed towards the whole of England, to offer it freely.

3

The Defiance at the Tower of Nesle

WHEN IN PARIS ON All Saints' Day Bishop Henry de
Burghersh, the Treasurer of England, escorted by William
Montacute, the new Earl of Salisbury, William Bohun, now
Earl of Northampton, and Robert Ufford, now Earl of Suffolk,
presented Edward III's letters of defiance to Philippe VI, the
King of France laughed as the King of Jericho had laughed
at Joshua.

Could he have heard right? Was young cousin Edward
really claiming the crown of France? Philippe caught the eyes
of his cousins the King of Navarre and the Duke of Bourbon.
They had just come from dinner, and Philippe was in
particularly good humour. His cheeks and long nose turned
slightly pink, and he began laughing again.

Had this bishop, who leaned so majestically on his crozier,
and these three English lords, who stood so stiffly before him
in their emblazoned surcoats, come to make some moderate
announcement, such as their master's refusal to hand over
Robert of Artois, or a protest against the decree for the seizure

of Guyenne, Philippe would doubtless have been angry. But this claim to his crown and kingdom merely turned the embassy into a piece of buffoonery.

Yes, he had heard right: they were claiming that the Salic Law was invalid and that his coronation had been irregular.

'The fact that the peers made me King of their own free will and the Archbishop of Reims crowned me eight years ago is of no importance, I suppose, Messire Bishop?'

'Many of the peers and barons who elected you have since died,' replied Burghersh, 'and many others are now wondering if what they did was approved by God!'

Philippe threw his head back, opened his mouth wide, and laughed aloud.

Had not King Edward recognized him as King when he came to render homage at Amiens?

'Our King was then a minor. The homage he rendered you, which to be valid required the consent of the Council of Regency, was decided merely on the order of the traitor Mortimer who has since been hanged.'

This bishop, who had been appointed Chancellor by Mortimer, had been his chief counsellor, had accompanied Edward to Amiens and had himself read the formula of homage in the cathedral, certainly had his wits about him.

And what was he saying now in those same loud tones? That it was he, Philippe, in his capacity as Count of Valois, who should render homage to Edward. For the King of England was perfectly prepared to recognize the rights of his cousin of France to Valois, Anjou and Maine, and even to his peerage. This was really being too magnanimous!

The King was listening to these ridiculous demands in the Hôtel de Nesle. He had given it to his wife and was spending a day there between visits to Saint-Germain and Vincennes. As minor lords might say: 'We shall sit in the great hall', or 'in the little parrot room', or 'we shall have supper in the green room', so the King would decide: 'Today I shall dine in the Palace of the Cité', or 'in the Louvre', or 'with my son the Duke of Normandy, in the house which belonged to Robert of Artois'.

And so the walls of the old Hôtel de Nesle, and of the still older Tower that could be seen through the windows, were witness to this farce. It would seem that certain places are destined to be the scenes of the tragedy of nations under the guise of comedy. For it had been in this house that Marguerite of Burgundy had deceived the Hutin in the arms of the Chevalier d'Aunay, unaware that her pleasures were to change the whole course of the French monarchy, and now the King of England was presenting his defiance to the King of France, and the King of France was laughing![36]

Indeed, he laughed so much that he felt almost moved to pity, for he recognized Robert's inspiration behind this absurd embassy. The man was clearly mad. He had found another king, younger and more ingenuous, to impress with his gigantic follies. Really, where would he stop? Defiance between kingdoms! Substituting one king for another! Yet, given a certain degree of aberration, you could hardly hold people responsible for absurdities that were part of their nature. If Robert of Artois had appeared at that moment, Philippe would undoubtedly have embraced him and pardoned him.

'Where are you staying, Monseigneur Bishop?' Philippe VI inquired courteously.

'At the Hôtel du Château Fétu, in the Rue du Tiroir.'

'Very well, go home then! Enjoy yourself for a few days in our good city of Paris and then, if you wish, come back to see us again with some more sensible request. For I don't hold this against you. Indeed, to have undertaken such a mission and to have carried it out without laughing, as I have seen you do, is no small feat. I consider you to be the best ambassador to whom I have ever given audience.'

He did not know how right he was. Henry de Burghersh had passed through Flanders on his way to Paris. And there he had held secret conversations with the Count of Hainaut, the King of England's father-in-law, the Count of Gueldre, the Duke of Brabant, the Marquess of Juliers, Jakob Van Artevelde and the aldermen of Ghent, Ypres and Bruges. He had even sent members of his suite to the Emperor Louis of Bavaria. Philippe VI was still in ignorance of certain negotiations that had taken place and of certain agreements that had been reached.[37]

'Sire, I must present you with the letters of defiance.'

'Very well, very well, let's have them,' Philippe said. 'We shall keep these splendid pages by us and read them often. They will serve to cheer us should we be sad. And now you shall be served with something to drink. Your throat must be parched with so much talking.'

He clapped his hands to summon a page.

'God forbid,' cried Bishop Burghersh. 'I should be a traitor if I drank the wine of an enemy to whom I have sworn from the bottom of my heart to do all the harm I can!'

Philippe of Valois started roaring with laughter again. Without another glance at the ambassador and the three English lords, he put his hand on the King of Navarre's shoulder and withdrew with him into his private apartments.

4

Windsor

WINDSOR LIES IN GREEN, rolling, friendly country. The castle seems to envelop the hill rather than crown it, and its plump walls are like the arms of a giantess asleep on the grass.

The country round Windsor is very similar to that of Normandy, or at least to those parts in which lie Evreux, Beaumont and Conches.

On this particular morning Robert was riding slowly along. On his left wrist he was carrying a falcon, its talons sunk into the thick leather of his glove. A single equerry was riding in front of him along the river-bank.

Robert was bored. No decision had been reached about the French war. Towards the end of the previous year the English, as if to confirm the defiance presented at the Tower of Nesle by some war-like act, had merely contented themselves with taking a small island, which belonged to the Count of Flanders and lay off Bruges and L'Eclus. In revenge, the French had come over and set fire to a few towns on the South Coast. The Pope had at once insisted on a truce to the war, which had never in fact been properly begun, and both sides had agreed to it for the strangest reasons.

Philippe VI, though refusing to take Edward's pretensions to the crown of France seriously, had nevertheless been much impressed by a communication he had received from his uncle, King Robert of Naples. This prince, erudite to the point of pedantry, was, together with a Porphyrogenite of Byzantium, one of the only two rulers in the world who deserved the title of 'Astrologer'. He had recently investigated the horoscopes of Edward and Philippe; and so impressed had he been by his findings that he had gone so far as to write to the King of France advising him 'to avoid ever going to war with the King of England, for that King would always be successful in anything he undertook'. Such prophecies cannot be entirely laughed off and, however successful you may be in the lists, you are bound to hesitate before breaking a lance with the stars.

As for Edward III, he seemed a little afraid of his own audacity. For many reasons the dangers involved seemed excessive. He feared his army might prove insufficient both in numbers and in training; he sent embassy after embassy to Flanders and Germany in the hope of cementing the coalition. Henry Wryneck, who was now half blind, advised prudence, unlike Robert of Artois who wanted immediate action. What was Edward waiting for to begin campaigning? Was he going to delay till the Flemish princes he had rallied to his cause had died; till Jean of Hainaut, now exiled from the Court of France, where he had enjoyed so much favour, and living in England again, had lost the strength of his arm and could no longer wield a sword; till the weavers of Ghent and Bruges had grown weary and saw fewer advantages to be derived from the unkept promises of the King of England than from obedience to the King of France? Edward hoped to receive assurances from the Emperor; but the Emperor would certainly not run the risk of being excommunicated a second time before English soldiers were actually on the Continent. There was too much talk, negotiation and procrastination; the real fact was that courage was lacking.

Nevertheless, Robert of Artois seemed to have little reason to complain. He had been given castles and a pension; he dined with the King, drank with the King, and received every possible consideration. But he was tired of having expended so much effort over a period of three years on people who refused to take a risk, on a young man to whom he was offering a crown! – and what a crown – and who failed to seize it. Besides, he was lonely. His exile, comfortable though it might be, weighed on him. What could he talk to young Queen Philippa about, unless it was of her grandfather Charles of Valois or her grandmother of Anjou-Sicily? At times he felt as if he were an ancestor himself.

He would have liked to see Queen Isabella, who was really the only person in England with whom he had memories in common. But the Queen Mother no longer appeared at Court; she lived at Castle Rising in Norfolk, where her son very occasionally went to visit her. Since Mortimer's execution she no longer took any interest in anything.[38]

Robert was suffering from the nostalgia of exile. He thought of Madame de Beaumont; how would she look, when he saw her again after so many years of imprisonment if he ever did see her again? Would he recognize his sons? Would he ever see his house in Paris, his Castle of Conches or France again? At the rate the war he had taken so much trouble to foment was going, he would have to wait till he was a hundred before he had any hope of seeing his country once more.

Irritated and depressed, he had gone off hawking by himself this morning to pass the time and to forget. But the thick soft grass under his horse's hooves, the English grass, was denser and more luxuriant than the grass of the Ouche countryside. The sky was pale blue, with little, high and ragged clouds; the May breeze was blowing through the hawthorn and the white apple blossom, which reminded him of the hawthorn and apple blossom of Normandy.

Robert was nearly fifty, and what had he done with his life? He had eaten, drunk, whored, hunted, travelled, worked hard for himself and at State business, taken part in tournaments, and gone to law more than any other man of his time. No single life could have encompassed greater vicissitudes and tribulations, none been more turbulent. But he had never enjoyed the present. He had never really stopped in what he was doing to savour the passing moment. He had always been concerned with tomorrow and the future. His wine had gone sour because of his desire to drink it in Artois; in his mistress' bed his thoughts had been concerned with defeating Mahaut; and even in the most enjoyable tournament his jousting had been governed by his diplomacy. Throughout his travels as an exile the food at the inn and the beer in the tavern had always had the bitter savour of hate and vengeance. And now he was still thinking of tomorrow and the future. His angry impatience prevented his appreciating the fine morning, the splendid countryside, the soft air he breathed, and the savage yet docile bird whose grip he could feel on his wrist. Was this what was called living, and was there nothing to show for the fifty years he had spent on earth but the ashes of his hopes?

He was startled out of his bitter reflections by his equerry, who was posted on a hill a little way ahead, crying:

'Mark, Monseigneur! Mark! A heron!'

Robert sat up straight in the saddle and screwed up his eyes. The falcon in its leather hood, from which only the beak emerged, was trembling on his wrist; it, too, recognized the cry. There was a sound of reeds rustling and a heron rose from the river bank.

'Mark, Monseigneur! Mark!' the equerry repeated.

The great bird was flying straight towards Robert, low against the wind. He let it fly on past him a hundred yards and then, freeing the falcon from its hood, he threw it into the air with a wide sweep of his arm.

The falcon circled its master's head three times, came low, skimming the ground, saw its prey and streaked away like a bolt from a crossbow. Seeing it was being pursued, the heron stretched its neck and, so as to lighten itself, disgorged the fish it had just eaten in the river. But the falcon was closer now and soaring upwards in a spiral. To prevent the falcon getting above it, the heron gained height with a great beating of wings. Though it continued to rise and grow smaller to the eye, it was nevertheless losing distance, since it was rising against the wind and was slowed by its own wing-spread. Then it turned downwind, but the falcon turned above it and stooped. The heron jinked and the talons failed to gain a hold, but the shock of the impact made the heron fall like a stone for fifty feet before it recovered and flew on. The falcon stooped again.

Robert and his equerry stared up at the battle in which

speed of manoeuvre and sheer lust to kill counted for more than size and pacific strength.

'Look at that heron,' cried Robert angrily; 'It's really the cowardliest of birds! It's four times the size of my little falcon; it could kill it with a single thrust of its great beak; but the damned coward runs away! Go on, my brave little bird, strike! Ah, that's the way! There! The heron's given up. It's taken!'

He put his horse into a gallop towards the spot where the birds would fall. The falcon's talons were round the heron's neck, strangling it; its great wings were beating more and more feebly as it carried its conqueror down in its fall. A few feet from the ground, the falcon released its hold to let its victim fall alone, and then hurled itself on it again to kill it by pecking at its head and eyes. Robert and his equerry had already come up.

'To the lure, to the lure!' said Robert.

The equerry took a dead pigeon from his saddle-bow and threw it to the falcon to lure it away. But a well-trained falcon knows it must accept its reward in this form and not touch its prey. And the brave little bird, its head all bloody, devoured the dead pigeon, one foot still on the heron. A few grey feathers, torn out during the fight, were drifting slowly down out of the sky.

The equerry dismounted, picked up the heron and handed it to Robert: it was a splendid bird and, when he held it out at arm's length, was from beak to feet almost as tall as a man.

'What a damned coward of a bird!' Robert repeated. 'There's almost no sport in taking it. These herons are noisy birds, but afraid of their own shadows, and start bawling when they see them. They're really fit game only for villeins.'

The falcon was satiated and, obedient to the whistle, came

to Robert's wrist. When he had replaced its hood, they trotted back towards the castle.

Suddenly the equerry heard Robert of Artois utter a short loud laugh, for which there was no apparent cause. It made the horses shy.

The horns had already sounded for dinner when they reached the postern.

'The King is going to dinner,' said the groom who came to take Robert's horse in the courtyard.

'What shall I do with the heron, Monseigneur?' asked the equerry.

Robert glanced up at the royal standard flying over the keep of Windsor and there was a wickedly mocking expression on his face.

'Bring it along and we'll go to the kitchens,' he said. 'Then you'll go to find me one or two of the castle minstrels.'

5

The Heron and the Oath

DINNER HAD REACHED THE fourth of its six courses, but the Count of Artois' place on Queen Philippa's left was still empty.

'Has our Cousin Robert not come home?' asked Edward III, who had been surprised at his absence when they went into dinner.

One of the pages waiting on the diners replied that Count Robert had been seen returning from hawking over an hour ago. What could have happened? Surely, if Robert had been tired or ill, he would have sent a servant to make his excuses to the King.

'Robert treats your Court, Sire, my nephew, as if it were an hotel. Though, I must admit, it doesn't surprise me,' said Jean of Hainaut, Queen Philippa's uncle.

Jean of Hainaut, who prided himself on being a paragon of knightly courtesy, did not like Robert, in whom he could not help seeing the perjurer banished from the Court of France for forging seals; and he blamed Edward III for placing so much faith in him. Moreover, like Robert, Jean of Hainaut had in the past been attracted by Queen Isabella, and with no greater success; but he was shocked by the loose way in which Robert talked to the Queen Mother in private.

Edward made no answer and lowered his long lashes till he had mastered his irritation. He was always afraid of making some remark which would give people an opportunity of saying later: 'The King spoke without knowing the facts; the King was unjust.' Then he looked up at the Countess of Salisbury, who was undoubtedly the most attractive woman at his Court.

Tall, pale-complexioned, with a pure oval face, beautiful black tresses and wide, mauve-shadowed eyes, the Countess of Salisbury seemed always to be dreaming. Such women are dangerous for, though they look as if they are dreaming, they are in fact thinking. Her dark-shadowed eyes frequently met those of the King.

Salisbury paid no attention to this exchange of glances, in the first place because he considered his wife's virtue as unquestionable as the King's fidelity to the Queen, and secondly because he was himself at the moment captivated by the laughter, vivacity and bird-like pipings of the Earl of Derby's daughter, who was sitting next to him. Honours were raining on Salisbury; he had just been made Warden of the Cinque Ports and Marshal of England.

But Queen Philippa was rather disturbed. A woman is always anxious when she is pregnant and sees her husband's glances turning too frequently towards another's face. For, indeed, Philippa was pregnant again, but she had not this time noticed in Edward that amazed gratitude that he had shown when she had first become a mother.

Edward was now twenty-five; for some weeks past he had been growing a little fair beard that covered no more than his chin. Was it to please the Countess of Salisbury? Or was it merely to give his youthful face a look of authority? The beard made him look a little like his father; the Plantagenet in him seemed to be struggling with the Capet. Merely by living, man becomes degraded and loses in purity what he gains in power. However clear a spring may be, when it becomes a river it cannot help being polluted by mud and slime. Madam Philippa had reason to be anxious.

Suddenly, from outside the doors, came the sound of glee-singing and the prim, sharp notes of lute and viol. The doors were thrown open and two little maids, of no more than fourteen years of age, crowned with leaves and wearing long white dresses, came in and scattered irises, daisies and eglantines from a basket. As they did so, they sang: 'I am going to the woods as my love has taught me ...' Two minstrels followed, playing the accompaniment. Behind them came Robert of Artois, taller by half than his little choir, holding aloft a roasted heron on a great silver platter.

The whole Court smiled, and then burst out laughing at this farcical entrance. Robert of Artois was playing the part of a page. What a charming and delightful way of making one's excuses for being late!

The pages ceased serving and, carving-knife or ewer in hand, joined the procession to take part in the joke.

Suddenly the giant's voice was heard, drowning glee, lute and viol.

'Make way, you wretched lily-livers! This is for your King!'

Everyone was still laughing. 'You wretched lily-livers' seemed merely an amusing jest. Robert came to a halt in front of Edward III, and, beginning to go down on one knee, presented him with the platter.

'Sire,' he cried, 'I have here a heron taken by my falcon. The heron is the most cowardly bird in the world, for it flees before all others. I think the people of England should adopt it, and I should like to see it in the arms of England instead of the leopards. And it is to you, King Edward, that I offer it, for it belongs of right to the most cowardly and craven prince in the world who, disinherited of his Kingdom of France, lacks the courage to conquer that which is his.'

Everyone was silent. For some it was a silence of anxiety, for others of indignation. There was no more laughter. The insult was plain. Salisbury, Suffolk, Guillaume de Mauny and Jean of Hainaut half rose from their seats, waiting for a sign from the King to hurl themselves on the Count of Artois. Robert seemed sober enough. Had he gone mad? What other explanation could there be? Nothing like this had ever been heard before in any Court in the world, particularly from an exiled foreigner.

The young King blushed. He looked Robert straight in the eyes. Was he going to have him thrown out of the hall, and out of the kingdom?

Edward always waited a few seconds before speaking; he knew that every word a king said mattered, even if it was only 'goodnight' to an equerry. To silence a man by force does not remove the outrage he has committed. Edward was wise and loyal. He realized that to deprive, in a moment of anger, a relative you have made welcome and who has served you of the gifts you have made him is no way to prove your courage; nor could you do so by throwing a lonely man who has accused you of weakness into prison.

You proved your courage by showing that the accusation was false. He rose to his feet.

'Since you call me a coward in the presence of the ladies and of my barons, I had best tell you my intentions; and to assure you, my cousin, that you have judged me ill, and that it is not cowardice that restrains me. I give you my oath that before the year is out I shall have crossed the sea to defy the King of France, and to join battle with him, even if he comes against me with ten to one. I am grateful to you for this heron you have taken for me, and I accept it with much thanks.'

The diners still sat silent; but their emotions had undergone a profound change. Their chests heaved as if they felt the need for more air. Someone dropped a spoon and its clatter seemed curiously loud in the silence. There was a gleam of triumph in Robert's eyes. He bowed and said: 'Sire, my young and valiant cousin, I expected no other answer from you. Your noble heart has spoken. It gives me great joy for the sake of your glory; and for myself, Sire Edward, I am filled with hope that I may see my wife and children again. By God above, I give you my oath that I shall precede you everywhere in battle, and I pray that I may be accorded a long enough life to serve you as you deserve and avenge myself on my enemies according to their deserts.'

Then, addressing the whole company, he said: 'My noble lords, are you not all eager to take an oath as your beloved Lord the King has done?'

Still carrying the roasted heron, in whose wings and tail the cook had replaced some of the feathers, Robert went to Salisbury.

'Noble Montacute, I call upon you first!'

'Count Robert, it shall be as you wish,' said Salisbury, who a few seconds before had been ready to hurl himself on him.

Rising to his feet, he said: 'Since our Lord the King has named his enemy, I shall select mine. As Marshal of England, I take my oath never to rest till I have defeated in battle the Marshal of Philippe, the false King of France.'

The whole table applauded enthusiastically.

'I, too, want to make an oath,' cried the Earl of Derby's daughter, clapping her hands. 'Why should the ladies not have the right to make an oath?'

'But they have, my dear lady,' replied Robert, 'and it will be much to everyone's advantage, for it will make the men more loyal to their word. Go on, my girls,' he added, turning to the two garlanded children, 'sing in honour of the lady who wants to make an oath.'

The minstrels and the girls began singing again: 'I am going to the woods as my love has taught me . . .' And then, in front of the silver platter on which the heron was cooling in its gravy, the Earl of Derby's daughter said in a high voice: 'I vow and promise to God in Paradise, that I shall take no husband, whether he be prince, earl or baron, before the oath noble Lord Salisbury has taken is accomplished. And when he returns, if he escapes alive, I shall give him my body, and with a grateful heart.'

The oath caused considerable surprise and Salisbury blushed.

The Countess of Salisbury's beautiful black tresses did not even quiver; there was merely an ironic curl to her lips and her mauve-shadowed eyes sought King Edward's, as if she wished to say to him: 'After that, we really need not worry overmuch.'

Robert halted in front of each diner in turn, while the viol played and the girls sang a little to give the knight time to prepare his oath and select his enemy. The Earl of Derby, the father of the young woman who had made so daring a vow, promised to defy the Count of Flanders; the new Earl of Suffolk selected the King of Bohemia. Young Gautier de Mauny, in his excitement at having recently been dubbed knight, much impressed the assembly by promising to reduce to ashes all the cities in the neighbourhood of Hainaut belonging to Philippe of Valois, even if he was to see the light with only one eye till his vow was accomplished.

'Be it so,' said the Countess of Salisbury, who was sitting next to him; and she covered his right eye with two fingers. 'And when you have fulfilled your oath, then my love will be his who loves me most; that is my oath.'

As she said this, she looked at the King. But the ingenuous Gautier, who thought the promise made for his benefit, kept his eye shut when she had removed her fingers, and then took a red handkerchief from his pocket and fastened it round his forehead over his eyes.

The moment of true grandeur had passed. Laughter was already breaking into this competition in brave words. The heron had now reached Messire Jean of Hainaut, who had hoped that the provocation would turn out otherwise for its author. He disliked being given lessons in matters of honour, and his chubby face reflected his annoyance.

'When we are sitting round drinking wine,' he said to Robert, 'it costs us little to make oaths and acquire the approbation of the ladies. We are all Olivers, Rolands and Lancelots then. But when we are campaigning, charging on our war horses, our shields slung and our lances in rest, and we feel a great, icy cold as the enemy approaches, how many boasters would prefer then to be in the safety of a cellar! The King of Bohemia, the Count of Flanders, and Bertrand, the Marshal, are as good knights as we, Cousin Robert, as you well know; for exiled though we both may be from the Court of France, though for different reasons, we have known them; and their ransoms are not in our pockets yet! For my part, I vow simply that if King Edward decides to pass through Hainaut, I shall always be at his side to sustain his cause. And this will be the third war in which I shall have served him.'

Robert then went to Queen Philippa. He went down on one knee. Stout Philippa turned her freckled face to Edward.

'I can take no oath,' she said, 'without the permission of my lord.'

She was tactfully giving the ladies of her Court a lesson.

'Vow anything you wish, my dear, vow bravely; I agree to it in advance, and may God help you!' said the King.

'In that case, my dear Sire, if I may vow as I please,' said Philippa, 'since I am big with child and can even feel it stirring, I vow that it shall not be born unless you take me across the sea to accomplish your oath ...' There was a quaver in her voice as on her wedding day ... 'For should it so happen,' she added, 'that you leave me here and go overseas with others, then I shall kill myself with a big steel knife and lose both my life and the fruit of my womb!'

She said it without emphasis, but in a clear voice all could hear. Everyone took care not to look at the Countess of Salisbury. The King lowered his long lashes, took the Queen's hand, raised it to his lips and then, to break the embarrassed silence, said: 'My dear, you give us all a lesson in duty. No one shall take an oath after you.'

Then, turning to Robert, he said: 'My cousin of Artois, take your place beside Madam the Queen.'

A page carved the heron, whose flesh was tough from having been cooked too soon, and cold from having had to wait so long. Nevertheless, everyone ate a mouthful. For Robert it had an exquisite savour: the war had really begun that day.

6

The Walls of Vannes

THE VOWS TAKEN AT Windsor were kept.

On July 16th of that same year, 1338, Edward III set sail from Yarmouth with a fleet of four hundred vessels. He landed at Antwerp the next day. Queen Philippa accompanied him. Many of the knights, emulating Gautier de Mauny, had covered one eye with a patch of red cloth.

The time for fighting had not yet arrived and negotiations were in train. On September 5th Edward met the Emperor of Germany at Coblenz.

For the occasion, Louis of Bavaria appeared in a strange costume, which was half emperor's and half pope's; he wore a pontiff's dalmatic over a king's tunic, and a crown with fleurons scintillated about a tiara. In one hand he held a sceptre, in the other an orb surmounted by a cross. It was thus that he asserted his sovereignty over the whole of Christendom.

Seated on this throne, he pronounced Philippe VI to be an imposter, recognized Edward as King of France and handed him the golden staff which made him the Imperial Vicar. This was another idea of Robert of Artois, who remembered how Charles of Valois, before engaging in his personal campaigns, had always taken care to have himself appointed Pontifical Vicar. Louis of Bavaria swore to defend Edward's rights for seven years, and all the German princes in the Emperor's train confirmed the oath.

In the meantime, Jakob Van Artevelde was rousing to rebellion the population of the County of Flanders, from which Louis of Nevers had fled for good and all. Edward III moved from city to city, holding great assemblies at which he had himself recognized as King of France. He promised to attach Douai, Lille, and even Artois, to Flanders, so as to make one nation of all these territories with common interests. It was not difficult to guess who was responsible for the inclusion of Artois, nor who would benefit from it under England's auspices.

At the same time, Edward decided to increase the commercial privileges of the various cities and, instead of demanding subsidies from them, he made them grants. He sealed his promises with a seal on which the arms of England and France were jointly engraved.

Queen Philippa was brought to bed of her second son, Lionel, in Antwerp.

Pope Benedict XII, in Avignon, was vainly doing all he could to preserve peace. He had forbidden the crusade in order to prevent a war between England and France. Nevertheless it now looked all too certain.

There had already been skirmishes on some scale between the English advance-guards and the French garrisons in Vermandois and Thiérache. Philippe VI replied by sending troops into Guyenne, and others to Scotland to foment rebellion in the name of young David Bruce.

Edward III was going to and fro between Flanders and London, pawning his crown jewels with the Italian banks so as to be able to maintain his troops and meet the demands of his new vassals.

Philippe VI, having raised his army, took the oriflamme at Saint-Denis, and advanced just beyond Saint-Quentin. Then, when only a day's march from the English, he turned his army about and took the oriflamme back to the altar at Saint-Denis. What could be the reason for this extraordinary turning-tail by the famous jousting King? Everyone wondered. Did Philippe think the weather too wet to engage battle? Or had the sinister predictions of his Uncle Robert the Astrologer suddenly influenced his decisions? He declared that he had determined on a different strategy. As he lay anxiously awake one night, he had conceived another plan. He was going to conquer the Kingdom of England. It would not be the first time the French had set foot in that country. Had not a Duke of Normandy conquered England three centuries ago? Very well! He, Philippe, would land on that very same coast at Hastings; and another Duke of Normandy, his son, would be at his side. Both Kings were hoping to conquer the other's kingdom.

But any expedition of the sort had first to have command of the sea. Since Edward had the greater part of his army on the Continent, Philippe determined to cut his lines of communication and prevent his supplying his troops or reinforcing them. He proposed to destroy the English fleet.

On June 22nd, 1340, off L'Eclus, two hundred ships sailed into the wide estuary between Flanders and Zeeland. The

French ensign floated from their mainmasts and they rejoiced in the most charming names: *La Pèlerine, La Nef-Dieu, La Miquolette, L'Amoureuse, La Faraude, La Sainte-Marie-Porte-Joye.* The ships were manned by twenty thousand sailors and soldiers, to which had been added a whole corps of crossbowmen; but there were scarcely a hundred and fifty gentlemen along them. The French chivalry had no liking for the sea.

Captain Barbavera, who was in command of the fifty Genoese galleys leased by the King of France, said to Admiral Béhuchet: 'Monseigneur, the King of England and his fleet are coming down on us. Make out to sea with your ships, for if you stay here enclosed between these great dykes, the English, who have the wind, the tide and the sun with them, will hem you in and you will be unable to manoeuvre.'

His advice should have been taken, for he had thirty years' experience of naval warfare; and, what was more, only the year before he had burnt and sacked Southampton for the French. But Admiral Béhuchet, a former Master of the Royal Rivers and Forests, replied proudly: 'Shame on whoever retreats from here!'

He ordered his ships to form up in three lines of battle. In the first were the sailors of the Seine, in the second those from Picardy and Dieppe, and in the third those from Caen and the Cotentin. He then ordered the ships to be made fast to each other by cables, and he disposed his men as if they were in castles.

King Edward, who had left London two days before, commanded a fleet of about the same size. He had no more fighting men than the French; but in his ships were two thousand gentlemen, among whom was Robert of Artois despite his great dislike of the sea.

Among the English fleet there was also a ship, protected by eight hundred soldiers, for Queen Philippa's ladies.

By the time evening fell, France had bidden farewell to the command of the sea.

So great was the light from the burning French ships that the coming of night was scarcely noticed.

The fishermen from Normandy and Picardy and the sailors from the Seine had been shot to pieces by the English archers and by the Flemish, who had come to the rescue in their flat-bottomed boats from higher up the estuary, and took the floating castles in the rear. The air was filled with the cracking of masts, the clank of arms and the cries of the wounded. The battle was fought out with swords and axes amid heaps of wreckage. The survivors of the massacre, diving into the sea among the corpses, could scarcely tell whether they were swimming in water or in blood. There were hundreds of dismembered hands floating on the sea.

Admiral Béhuchet's body was hanging from the yard-arm of Edward's ship. Barbavera had long ago stood out to sea with his Genoese galleys.

The English, though they had had losses, were triumphant. Their greatest disaster was the loss of the ship full of ladies which had sunk amid heartrending cries. Dresses floated like dead birds in the great charnel-house of the sea.

Young King Edward had been wounded in the thigh and his blood was trickling down over his white leather boot; but from now on the war was to take place on French soil.[39]

Edward III at once sent Philippe VI new letters of defiance. 'In order to avoid grave destruction to town and countryside, and great mortality among Christians, which every prince should do his best to avoid,' the English King challenged his cousin of France to meet him in single combat, since the quarrel over the inheritance of France was their personal affair. And if Philippe of Valois refused to accept this 'challenge between their bodies', he offered to meet him in the lists with only a hundred knights a side. In fact, it was to be a tournament, but with pointed lances and sharp swords, with no stewards to supervise the mêlée, and for which the prize would be no ornamental brooch or hawk but the crown of Saint Louis itself.

But the jousting King replied that he could not accept his cousin's proposal, since it had been addressed to Philippe of Valois and not to the King of France, of whom Edward was the treasonably rebelling vassal.

The Pope once again negotiated a truce. The Papal legates worked hard and took the credit for a precarious peace which the two princes had, in fact, accepted only to give themselves a breathing space.

Nevertheless, this second truce might have had some chance of lasting, if the Duke of Brittany had not chosen that moment to die.

He left no legitimate son nor direct heir. The duchy was claimed both by his youngest brother the Count of Montfort-l'Amaury, and by his nephew Charles of Blois, who was a Valois by marriage. Edward III immediately took the side of Jean de Montfort. The result was that there were two Kings of France, each with his own Duke of Brittany, as each already had his own King of Scotland.

The question of Brittany closely affected Robert, since his mother was sister to the late Duke Jean. Edward III could do no less, nor indeed better, than give Robert the command of the army that was to disembark on the coast of Brittany.

Robert of Artois' great hour had come.

Robert was now fifty-six. The muscles of his face had grown hard with a lifetime of hate, and the hair that framed it had turned the curious colour of cider mixed with water common to red-headed men when they start going grey. He was no longer the bad lot who thought he was making war when he sacked his Aunt Mahaut's castles. He knew now what war was. He planned his campaign with great care; and he had all the authority conferred by age and the accumulated experience of a turbulent life. He was held in great respect. Who remembered now that he was a forger, a perjurer, a murderer and something of a sorcerer? Who would have dared remind him of it? He was Monseigneur Robert, a giant beginning to grow old but still possessed of surprising strength and immense self-assurance who, invariably dressed in red, was leading an English army into France. Nor did it matter to him that his soldiers were foreigners. Indeed, this was not the sort of thing to which any count, baron or knight gave a thought. Their campaigns were family matters; their battles quarrels over inheritance; the enemy was a cousin, the ally another. It was to the population who would be massacred, whose houses would be burnt, barns looted and women raped, that the word foreigner meant enemy; not to the princes who were defending their titles and asserting their rights.

For Robert this war between France and England was *his* war; he had wanted it, preached it, created it, it represented ten years of unceasing effort. It was as if he had been born and had lived only for this. He had once lamented that he had never been able to enjoy the passing moment; now, at last, he could savour it to the full. He breathed the very air as if it had some peculiarly delectable quality. Each moment was a happy one. From the back of his great chestnut, his head bare and his helm hanging from the saddle-bow, he cracked terrifying jokes with his entourage. He had twenty-two thousand knights and soldiers under his command and, when he looked back, he could see his lances, like some death-dealing crop, rippling away to the horizon. The poor Bretons fled before him, some in carts, but most trudging along in their cloth or bark boots. The women dragged their children by the hand, while the men carried a sack of black flour on their shoulders.

Though Robert of Artois was fifty-six, he could still ride stages of fifteen leagues, and he could still dream. Tomorrow he would take Brest; then he would take Vannes, then Rennes; after that, he would enter Normandy and seize Alençon, which belonged to Philippe of Valois' brother; from Alençon he would go on to Evreux, and then to Conches, his own Conches! He would hasten to Château Gaillard and free Madame de Beaumont. Then he would fall irresistibly on Paris; he would go to the Louvre, to Vincennes, to Saint-Germain, seize Philippe of Valois, remove him from the throne and hand the crown to Edward, who would make him Lieutenant-General of the Kingdom of France. His destiny had already known less probable ups and downs, and never before had he had a whole army raising the dust of the roads behind him.

And, indeed, Robert took Brest, where he relieved the Countess de Montfort, a robust and spirited woman who, though her husband was held prisoner by the King of France, had continued to resist with her back to the sea at this extreme end of her duchy. And Robert crossed Brittany in triumph and besieged Vannes; he set up his perriers and catapults, and sited his bombards, whose smoke dissolved among the November clouds, to breach the walls. There was a strong garrison in Vannes but it did not appear to be particularly resolute and was merely awaiting the first assault so as to be able to surrender honourably. A few men on both sides would have to be sacrificed so that the decencies might be preserved.

Robert had his steel helm laced up and mounted his huge war-horse which seemed to sag a little beneath his weight. He shouted his last orders, lowered his visor, and waved his six-pound mace round his head. The heralds held his banner to the breeze and shouted at the tops of their voices: 'Artois into battle!'

Footmen ran beside the horses, some carrying long ladders between six of them, others parcels of burning tow attached to the ends of rods; and the army thundered forward towards the heap of stones where the rampart had been breached, while Monseigneur of Artois' steaming surcoat flashed like lightning under the heavy grey clouds.

A crossbow bolt fired from a loophole pierced the silk surcoat, the armour, the leather jerkin, and the linen of his shirt. The shock was no greater than that of a lance in a joust. Robert of Artois pulled out the bolt himself; but a few strides farther on, though he did not understand what was happening to him, why the sky had suddenly turned so black and why his legs were no longer gripping his horse, he fell into the mud.

While his troops were taking Vannes, the giant, whose helm had been removed, was being carried back to the camp on a ladder; his blood was dripping down between the rungs.

Robert had never been wounded before. Throughout his

two campaigns in Flanders, his own expedition into Artois, and the war in Aquitaine, Robert had never received so much as a scratch. In fifty tournaments no broken lance had ever touched him, nor had any wild boar when hunting.

Why should this have happened before Vannes, a town that was making no more than a show of resistance, and was only a minor stage in his epic progress? Robert of Artois had heard no sinister prophecies about either Vannes or Brittany. The hand that had released the bolt was that of an unknown man who did not even know whom he was shooting at.

Robert fought for four days, but now it was not against princes and parliaments, against the laws of succession, the customs of counties, or the greed and ambition of royal families; he was fighting his own body. Death had entered into him through a wound whose black lips stood open between the heart that had beaten so ardently and the stomach that had feasted so well; nor was it the death that freezes, but that which burns. The fire was in his veins. In four days death was to burn up the strength of that body which was good for another twenty years of living.

He refused to make a will, shouting that tomorrow he would be on horseback again. He had to be tied down to receive the last sacraments, for he wanted to attack the chaplain whom he believed to be Thierry d'Hirson. He was delirious.

Robert of Artois had always hated the sea; but now a ship was made ready to take him to England. Throughout the night, to the tossing of the waves, he seemed to be pleading in some strange court of justice, addressing the barons of France, calling them 'my noble lords', and demanding of Philip the Fair that he should order the seizure of all Philippe of Valois' possessions, his royal robe, his sceptre and his crown, in conformity with a Papal Bull of Excommunication. His voice, from where he lay in the sterncastle, could be heard in the bows and even by the lookouts at the mastheads.

He grew a little quieter just before dawn and asked that his mattress be placed near the door, so that he might gaze at the last stars. But he never saw the sun rise. Till the moment he died, he still believed he would get well. The last word he uttered was: 'Never' And no one could tell whether he was speaking to the kings, to the sea or to God.

Every man born into the world has his own function which, whether trivial or important, is usually unknown to himself, but which, unawares and apparently of his own free will, he is forced by his nature, his relations with his fellow men and the chances of life to fulfil. Robert of Artois had set the Western world on fire: his task was done.

When King Edward III, in Flanders, heard of his death, his eyelashes became moist, and he wrote a letter to Queen Philippa in which he said:

'Dearest Heart, Robert of Artois, our cousin, has been called to God; because of the affection in which we held him and for our honour, we have written to our chancellor and our treasurer and have ordered them to have him buried in our city of London. We wish you, dearest Heart, to see that our will is properly carried out. May God keep you. Given under our private seal in the town of Grandchamp, on Saint Catherine's day, in the sixteenth year of our reign over England, and in the third over France.'

At the beginning of January, 1343, the crypt of St Paul's Cathedral, in London, received the heaviest coffin ever to be carried into it.

AT THIS POINT THE AUTHOR, COMPELLED BY HISTORY TO KILL OFF HIS FAVOURITE CHARACTER, WITH WHOM HE HAS LIVED FOR SIX YEARS, IS MOVED TO A SORROW COMPARABLE TO THAT OF KING EDWARD OF ENGLAND; THE PEN, AS THE OLD CHRONICLERS SAY, FALLS FROM HIS HAND, AND HE HAS NO DESIRE TO CONTINUE, AT LEAST FOR THE PRESENT, EXCEPT TO INFORM THE READER OF THE DESTINIES OF SOME OF THE PRINCIPAL CHARACTERS IN THIS STORY.

WE NOW MOVE ON ELEVEN YEARS AND CROSS THE ALPS.

EPILOGUE:
1354–62

I

The Road to Rome

ON MONDAY, SEPTEMBER 22nd, 1354, in Siena, Giannino Baglioni, an important man of that city, received at the Tolomei Palace, where his family held its bank, a letter from the famous Cola di Rienzi who had seized the Government of Rome and assumed the ancient title of Tribune. The letter, which was dated from the Capitol on the preceding Thursday, ran as follows:

'My very dear friend, we have sent messengers to seek you out and, if they found you, to pray you to be good enough to come to us in Rome. They have reported that they found you in Siena, but were unable to persuade you to come to see us. Since it was uncertain whether they would be able to find you, we did not write to you; but now that we know where you are, we pray you to come to see us in all haste as soon as you receive this letter, and in the greatest secrecy, about a matter which concerns the Kingdom of France.'

Why did the Tribune, who had grown up in a tavern in the Trastevere, but asserted that he was the illegitimate son of the Emperor Henry VII of Germany – and therefore half-brother to King John of Bohemia – and whom Petrarch celebrated as having restored to Italy her ancient grandeur, wish to converse so urgently and so secretly with Giannino Baglioni? This, indeed, was the question Giannino was pondering as he journeyed towards Rome with his friend the notary Angelo Guidarelli, whom he had asked to accompany him both because a journey seems less long when you are travelling with a friend and also because the notary was a clever man of affairs and knew the banking business.

The sun still beats down warmly over the Sienese country-side in September, and the stubble left by harvest covers the fields with a sort of animal fur. It is one of the most beautiful countrysides in the world: God has drawn the curve of its hills with an exquisite freedom, and has given it a rich and varied vegetation among which the cypresses stand out like lords. Man has worked this earth to advantage and has spread his dwellings over it; but from the most princely villa to the humblest cottage they all have a similar grace and harmony with their ochre walls and curved tiles. The road is never monotonous; it winds and rises, only to descend into another valley between terraced fields and age-old olive groves. Both God and man have shown their genius at Siena.

What was this matter that concerned France and about which the Tribune of Rome wished to talk to the Sienese banker? Why had he approached him twice, sending him this pressing letter in which he addressed him as 'very dear friend'? No doubt it must be some question of a further loan to the

King of Paris, or of ransoms to pay for great lords held prisoner in England. Giannino Baglioni had been unaware that Cola di Rienzi took so much interest in the fate of the French.

If this was so, why had the Tribune not approached the more senior members of the company, Tolomeo Tolomei, for instance, or Andrea, or Giaccomo, who were much more expert in matters of this kind and had gone to Paris in the past to liquidate the affairs of old Uncle Spinello, when the French branches had been closed? Of course, Giannino's mother had been French, a daughter of the nobility, who figured in his earliest memories as beautiful, young and rather melancholy, living in an old manor lost in a rainswept countryside. And of course, his father, Guccio Baglioni, who had died fourteen years ago, the dear man, during a journey in Campania – and Giannino crossed himself discreetly as he swayed to the motion of his horse – had been mixed up with great and secret affairs between the Courts of Paris, London and Naples, at the period he lived in France; he had known very high personages indeed, even kings and queens, and in days gone by had told Giannino of these matters.

But Giannino did not care to remember France, just because of the mother he had never seen again – he did not even know whether she was alive or dead – and also because of his birth which, though legitimate according to his father, had always been held to be illegitimate by the other members of the family whom he had never met till he was nine years old: grandfather Mino Baglioni, the Tolomei uncles, and innumerable cousins. For a long time Giannino had felt that he was a stranger to them and different from them. He had done all he could to obliterate this difference, to become part of the community he had entered so late, in a country in which he had not been born.

Among the many diverse activities of the Tolomei Company he had specialized in the wool trade; perhaps he had a deep longing for sheep, green fields and mist. Two years after his father's death he had married an heiress of a good Sienese family, Giovanna Vivoli, by whom he had had three sons, and with whom he had lived very happily for six years; but she had died of the Black Death in 1348. The following year he had married Francesca Agazzano, who had given him two more sons and was now expecting her third child.

He conducted his affairs with integrity, was much respected by his fellow citizens and had been appointed, owing to the consideration in which he was held, Administrator of the Hospital of Our Lady of Mercy.

They passed by San Quirico d'Orcia, Radicofani, Acquapendente, the lake of Bolsena and Montefiascone, spent the nights in hostelries with great porticos, and took the road again next morning. Giannino and Guidarelli had now left Tuscany. The farther they journeyed, the more decided Giannino became to tell the Tribune Cola, with all possible courtesy, that he had no wish to be mixed up in transactions with France. The notary Guidarelli wholly approved his resolve; there was really very little to be said for a country in which the Italian companies had been so often despoiled, and whose affairs since the outbreak of war with England had been going far too ill to encourage risking money. How much more agreeable it was to live in a little republic like Siena, where the arts and commerce prospered, rather than in one of these great kingdoms governed by madmen![40]

From the Tolomei Palace, Giannino had kept in touch with

French affairs during these last years; indeed, there were many debts there which would no doubt never be collected. The French really seemed to be demented, and Valois the worst of all, for he had succeeded first in losing Brittany, then Flanders, then Normandy, then Saintonge, only to be brought to bay like a roe-deer by the English armies encircling Paris. The tournament hero, who wanted to lead the world on a crusade, had refused to accept the challenge by which his enemies offered him battle in the plain of Vaugirard, almost at the doors of his palace; and then, believing the English to be in flight because they were withdrawing northwards – and, after all, why should they have been in flight when they had been everywhere victorious? – Philippe had suddenly hurried off in pursuit, exhausting his troops by forced marches, had caught up with Edward, beyond the Somme and been heavily defeated.

The echoes of Crécy had reached Siena. It was known that the King of France had ordered his infantry straight into the attack after a march of five leagues, without giving them time to rest, and that the French chivalry, irritated by the slowness of the infantry's advance, had charged through the ranks of their own footmen, spreading chaos and trampling them beneath their horses' hooves, only to be shot to pieces by the cross-fire of the English archers.

'They explained away their defeat by claiming that it was the gunpowder artillery, supplied to the English by Italy, which had sown disorder and panic in their ranks by the noise it made. But it was not the gunpowder artillery, Guidarelli; it was their own stupidity.'

And what splendid feats of arms had been performed that day! For instance, John of Bohemia, now fifty and blind, had insisted on being led into the battle; his war-horse had been attached to those of two of his knights, one on either side; and the blind King had charged into the mêlée, brandishing his mace. Unfortunately it had fallen on the heads of the two unlucky knights who were escorting him. He had been picked up dead, still linked to his battered companions.

And this might well stand for a symbol of the French chivalry who, enclosed in the dark of their helms and despising the people, wantonly destroyed themselves.

On the evening of Crécy, when Philippe VI was wandering about the countryside with an escort of no more than six men, he had knocked on the door of a little manor house and cried: 'Open, open to the unhappy King of France!'

Nor must it be overlooked that Messer Dante had cursed the whole race of Valois because the first of them, Count Charles, had once sacked Siena and Florence. All the enemies of the *divino poeta* had come to a bad end.

And after Crécy had come the Black Death, brought by the Genoese. You could never expect anything good from them either! Their ships had brought the foul disease from the Orient; it had gained a hold in Provence, had fallen on Avignon, that vicious and debauched city, and had ravaged it as a punishment for its sins. Merely to have heard Messer Petrarch's descriptions of the stinking infamy of that latter-day Babylon was to know it was marked out for avenging calamities.[41]

The Tuscan is never pleased with anything or anybody, except himself. Disparagement is the breath of life to him. In this Giannino was very much a Tuscan. He and Guidarelli were still busy criticizing the world in general when they reached Viterbo.

Why, for instance, was the Pope reigning in Avignon instead of in Rome, as Saint Peter had intended? Why were French popes always elected like this Pierre Roger, former Bishop of Arras, who had succeeded Benedict XII and was now reigning under the name of Clement VI? And why did he always appoint French cardinals and refuse to return to Italy? God had punished them all. During a single summer seven thousand houses had been shut up in Avignon; corpses were being picked up by the wagon-load. Then the scourge had moved north into the districts exhausted by the war. The plague had reached Paris where it had killed a thousand people a day, sparing no one, the great no more than the humble. The Duke of Normandy's wife, who was the daughter of the King of Bohemia, had died of the plague. Queen Jeanne of Navarre had died of the plague. Even the Queen of France herself, Jeanne the Lame, had died of the plague; and the French, who hated her, said that her death was a just punishment for her crimes.

But why had Giovanna Baglioni, Giannino's first wife, Giovanna whose neck was like the shaft of an alabaster column and whose eyes were like almonds, been carried off by it? Was that justice? Was it fair that the epidemic should have devastated Siena? God really showed very little discernment and too often taxed the good to pay for the sins of the wicked.

How lucky some people were to have escaped the plague! Messer Boccaccio, for instance, the son of a friend of the Tolomei, whose mother had been French like Giannino's, had taken refuge in a fine Florentine villa as the guest of a rich lord. During the period of the epidemic, to amuse the refugees in the Villa Palmieri and help them to forget that

death was at their gates, Boccaccio had written those delight-
fully entertaining stories the whole of Italy was now repeating.
Had not Count Palmieri and Messer Boccaccio shown more
courage in the face of death than those idiotic French knights?
Notary Guidarelli was certainly of that opinion.

King Philippe had remarried only thirty days after the
death of the wicked Queen. Giannino criticized him, not
exactly for having married again, since he had done so
himself, but for his indecent haste. Thirty days! And whom
had Philippe VI chosen? This was where the story gained
relish. He had carried off his eldest son's fiancée, for the
son was a widower too and was intending to marry his
Cousin Blanche, daughter of the King of Navarre, who was
nicknamed Belle Sagesse.

On this girl of eighteen appearing at Court, Philippe had
been so dazzled by her that he had at once made advances.
Jean of Normandy had had to give her up to his father and
submit to being married to the Countess of Boulogne, a
widow of twenty-four, for whom he showed no great liking
– not, indeed, that he showed much liking for any woman, his
tastes being directed more towards the pages.

The King, who was now fifty-six, seemed to have regained
all the ardour of youth in the arms of Belle Sagesse. Beautiful
and chaste – how well the name became her! Giannino and
Guidarelli shook with laughter as they rode along. Really,
Messer Boccaccio might well have put her into one of his
tales. Within three months the wench had killed off the
jousting King, and the ineffable fool, who during the third of
a century he had reigned had reduced his realm from wealth
to ruin, was taken to Saint-Denis.

Jean II, the new King, who was now thirty-six and called

the Good, though no one quite knew why, appeared from what travellers reported to have qualities as outstanding as those of his father and to be blessed with a similar good fortune in his undertakings. He was merely perhaps a trifle more extravagant, futile and unstable; and to these traits he seemed to have added by inheritance his mother's cruelty and hypocrisy. Believing that he was beset by treason, he had already beheaded his constable.

When in Calais, which he had recently captured, King Edward III had instituted the Order of the Garter, on the occasion of his having himself fastened the stocking of the beautiful Countess of Salisbury with whom he was in love. King Jean II, determined not to be outdone in chivalry, immediately founded the Order of the Etoile to honour his Spanish favourite, young Charles de la Cerda. But that was as far as his prowess went.

The people were starving; both agriculture and industry were short of labour owing to the war and the Black Death; food was scarce and prices were continually rising; trades were being forced out of existence; and a tax of one sol in the livre had been imposed on all transactions.

Errant bands, similar to the *pastoureaux* of the past, but more demented still, were roaming over the country; thousands of ragged men and women flagellated each other with cords and chains as they sang lugubrious psalms along the roads; and then, suddenly seized with crazy fury, turned inevitably to massacring the Jews and the Italians.

And yet the Court of France still displayed an insolent luxury, and spent on a single tournament money enough to feed the poor of a whole county for a year; while the courtiers dressed in a far from Christian manner, the men adorning themselves with more jewels than the women, and wearing narrow-waisted tunics so short that they revealed the buttocks, and shoes with such immensely long points to the toes that they impeded their wearer in walking.

Could a sensible banking company lend money or supply wool to such people? Clearly not. And Giannino Baglioni, as he entered Rome, on October 2nd, by the Ponte Malvio, was determined to tell the Tribune Cola di Rienzi so.

2

The Night at the Capitol

THE TRAVELLERS WENT TO an *osteria* in the Campo dei Fiori; it was the hour at which the flower-sellers were disposing of their bunches of roses at reduced prices and starting to free the square of their fragrant, multi-coloured stalls.

When night began to fall, Giannino Baglioni set out for the Capitol taking the innkeeper as guide.

What a marvellous city Rome was! This was his first visit to it, and he regretted that he had not the time to stand and stare at every step he took. It was so huge compared to Siena and Florence, larger so it seemed to him – if his vague memories were correct – even than Paris. It was certainly more crowded and lively than Lyons, which he had visited in the past. The maze-like alleys would open suddenly on to some splendid palace, its courts and porches bright with torches and lanterns. Boys strolled singing, arm in arm across the streets. But there was much good-humoured jostling, and everyone smiled at foreigners; there were innumerable taverns and from them came the delicious odours of hot oil, saffron, frying fish and roasting meat. Life here did not stop at nightfall.

Giannino climbed the Capitoline hill by the light of the stars. There was grass sprouting in front of a church porch; fallen columns and a statue holding up a mutilated arm bore witness to Imperial Rome.

Cola di Rienzi was at supper with a numerous company in a great hall that had been raised on the foundations of the Temple of Jupiter. Giannino had Cola di Rienzi pointed out to him, went to him, fell on one knee and introduced himself. The Tribune immediately took him by the hand and raised him. Then he had him conducted to a neighbouring room, where he joined him a few minutes later.

Rienzi had assumed the title of Tribune, but in face and bearing he was more like an emperor. Purple was his colour and he draped his robe about him like a toga. The collar of his robe enclosed a bull-neck; there was a massive quality about his face; and he had large bright eyes, short hair and a firm chin. Indeed, he might well have found a place among the busts of the Caesars. The Tribune had a slight nervous tic, a quivering of the right nostril, which made him look impatient. There was authority in his step, and it was clear, even on first sight, that he was born to command. He had great plans for the improvement of his people's lot; and there could be no doubt that it would be wise both to understand and conform to his ideas. He made Giannino sit down beside him and told the servants to close the doors and see they were not disturbed. He at once began asking questions that had nothing whatever to do with the banking business.

He was not interested in the wool trade, money-lending, or bills of exchange. It was Giannino himself, Giannino in his own right, in whom he was interested. How old had Giannino been when he came from France? Where had he spent his early years? Who had brought him up? Had he always borne the same name? And, after each question, Rienzi waited for the answer, listened, nodded and began questioning him again.

So Giannino had been born, or so he had been told, in a convent in Paris. His mother, Marie de Cressay, had brought him up till he was nine, in the Ile-de-France, near a village called Neauphle-le-Vieux. Did he know whether his mother had ever been at the Court of France? Yes, she had spent a short time there. Giannino remembered what his father, Guccio, had told him of it; having given birth to him, Marie de Cressay had been summoned to the Court as wet-nurse to Queen Clémence of Hungary's child; but she had stayed there only a very short time, since the Queen's child had died almost at once, poisoned so it was said.

Giannino smiled. He had been foster-brother to a king of France; but he scarcely ever thought of it and now it suddenly seemed an incredible, almost laughable thing to have happened in the tranquil life of a citizen of Siena who was approaching his forties.

But why was Rienzi asking him all these questions? Why was the Tribune, the bastard of the Emperor before last, gazing at him so attentively out of his wide bright eyes?

'It's you,' said Cola di Rienzi. 'It's most certainly you!'

Giannino had no idea what he meant by this remark. He was even more surprised when the imposing Tribune went down on his knees and kissed his right foot.

'You are the King of France,' Rienzi said, 'and this is how everyone must treat you from now on.'

The lights seemed to waver a little before Giannino's eyes.

When the house in which you are peacefully dining suddenly collapses in an earthquake, or the ship in which you are sleeping suddenly hits a reef, for a moment or two you are necessarily at a loss to grasp what has happened.

Giannino Baglioni was sitting in a room in the Capitol, and the master of Rome was kneeling at his feet, assuring him that he was the King of France!

'Marie de Cressay died nine years ago last June.'

'You mean my mother's dead?' cried Giannino.

'Yes, my most gracious lord, the woman you thought to be your mother is dead. But before dying she confessed.'

It was the first time that anyone had called Giannino 'most gracious lord' and he sat there with his mouth hanging open, more surprised at it even than at having his foot kissed.

When Marie de Cressay knew she was dying, it appeared that she had summoned to her bedside an Augustine monk from a neighbouring monastery, Brother Jourdain d'Espagne, and had made her confession to him.

Giannino was recollecting his earliest memories. He could see the room at Cressay and his fair and beautiful mother. And so she had been dead nine years, and he had not known it! She must have died in 1345. And now, so it appeared, she had not been his mother at all.

Brother Jourdain, at the dying woman's request, had put her confession down in writing. It was the revelation of a most extraordinary State secret and of a no less extraordinary crime.

'I shall show you the confession, together with Brother Jourdain's letter; they are both in my possession,' said Cola di Rienzi.

The Tribune talked for four hours and more. No less was required to instruct Giannino in those events of forty years ago which formed part of the history of the Kingdom of France: the death of Marguerite of Burgundy, and King Louis X's second marriage with Clémence of Hungary.

'My father was part of the embassy that went to fetch the Queen of Naples; he often told me about it,' Giannino said. 'He was a member of the suite of a certain Count de Bouville.'

'The Count de Bouville, did you say? It all fits in. Bouville was Curator of Queen Clémence's stomach, and she was your mother, my most gracious lord; and it was he who sent for the Dame de Cressay to the convent, where she had just been brought to bed, so that she might be your wet-nurse. Of all this she gave a detailed account.'

As the Tribune went on talking, Giannino felt as if he were losing his reason. The whole world seemed topsy-turvy; shadows were turning bright, and day into night. He continually asked Rienzi to repeat things, as if to revise some over-complicated arithmetical calculation. He was not the foster-brother of a king of France, who had died in the cradle; it was the foster-brother who had died. He was learning all at once that his father was not his father, that his mother was not his mother and that his real father, a king of France, had murdered his first wife, only to be later murdered himself. Was it that man's memory he must venerate from now on?

'You were always called Jean, weren't you? The Queen, your mother, gave you that name because of a vow. Jean or Giovanni, of which the diminutives are Giovannino or Giannino ... You are Jean I, the Posthumous.'

The Posthumous! A sinister name, one of those words that were redolent of the cemetery, and which no Tuscan could hear without warding off the evil eye with his left hand.

And then, one after the other, Count Robert of Artois, Countess Mahaut, and all the other names which had appeared in his father's reminiscences – no, not his father's, the other man's, Guccio Baglioni's – played their terrible parts in the Tribune's story. Countess Mahaut, who had poisoned Giannino's father – yes, that was right, King Louis – had then murdered the newborn child.

But the Count de Bouville had prudently exchanged the Queen's child for the wet-nurse's, who was also called Jean. It was he who had died, and the son of a Sienese merchant had been buried at Saint-Denis.

Giannino felt very uncomfortable indeed, because he could not help thinking of himself as Giannino Baglioni, the son of the Sienese merchant; it was rather as if he were being told that he had died at the age of five days and that the whole of his life since then had been a figment; his body, his memories and his family mere illusion. He was become his own ghost. This night at the Capitol was a nightmare!

'She sometimes called me: "My little prince", when we were alone,' Giannino murmured.

'Who did?'

'My mother – I mean to say the Dame de Cressay. I thought it was merely an ordinary term of endearment French mothers used towards their children; and she used to kiss my hands and weep. Oh, how it all comes back to me! The allowance the Count de Bouville used to send; and how the Cressay uncles, the bearded one and the other, were so much nicer to me on the days the money arrived.'

What had happened to them all? No doubt most of them had long been dead: Mahaut, Bouville, Robert of Artois. And the Cressay brothers had been knighted on the eve of the Battle of Crécy, simply because King Philippe VI had made a pun on their name.

'They must be quite old now, too.'

And if Marie de Cressay had always refused to see Guccio Baglioni again, it was therefore not because she hated him, as he had so bitterly imagined, but in order to keep the oath she had been almost physically compelled to take, when the little King had been handed over to her.

'And for fear of reprisals, both to herself and to her husband,' Cola di Rienzi explained; 'for they had been married, properly though secretly, by a monk. She confirmed it in her confession. And then, when you were nine years old, Baglioni came and took you away.'

'Did she never marry again?'

'Never.'

'Poor woman! What an appalling life. He never married again either.'

Giannino looked thoughtful for a moment. He was trying to think of the woman who had died at Cressay and the man who had died in Campania as foster-parents.

'Could I have a mirror?' he asked suddenly.

'Of course,' the Tribune said in some surprise.

He clapped his hands and gave the order to a servant.

'I saw Queen Clémence once; it was when my father had taken me from Cressay and I was spending a few days in Paris at Uncle Spinello's. My father – my foster-father, I should say – was very proud of having known her and took me to see her. He wanted to give me something to remember. She gave me sugared almonds. She was very beautiful. And so she was my real mother?'

He suddenly felt much moved. He put his hand into his robe and brought out a little reliquary he wore round his neck on a silk cord. 'This relic of Saint John came from her.'

He was trying desperately to remember exactly how the Queen had looked to him as a child. He recalled the gesture with which she had absent-mindedly placed her beautiful hand on his head. And he had not known it was his mother's hand! She had been dressed entirely in white, as were all widowed queens. And she had died without ever knowing that her only son was alive.

What a ruthless criminal the Countess Mahaut must have been to assassinate an innocent newborn child and create such havoc and distress in the lives of so many people.

Giannino's feeling of his own unreality had now disappeared to give place to a sensation of being two people at once, which was just as unnerving. He was both himself and another, the son of a Sienese banker and the son of the King of France.

And what of his wife, Francesca? He suddenly thought of her. Whom had she married? And what of his children? It seemed that they were the descendants of Hugues Capet, Saint Louis and Philip the Fair.

'Pope John XXII must have got wind of this business,' Cola di Rienzi went on. 'It has been reported to me that certain cardinals in his entourage were whispering at one time that he had doubts about the death of King Louis' son. People thought it a mere rumour like so many others. Indeed no one really believed it till your foster-mother – your wet-nurse – made her confession *in extremis*. She extracted a promise from the Augustine monk to seek you out and to tell you the truth. Throughout her life she obeyed men's orders to keep silence; but at the moment she was to appear before God, and since those who had imposed this silence on her had died without relieving her of her vow, she felt the need to share the secret.'

Brother Jourdain d'Espagne had been true to his promise and had set out to look for Giannino; but the war and the Black Death had prevented his travelling farther than Paris. The Tolomei no longer had a branch there by then; and Brother Jourdain had felt too old to undertake long journeys.

'He therefore handed the confession and his own account of it,' went on Rienzi, 'to another monk belonging to his order, Brother Antoine, a most saintly man who had made several pilgrimages to Rome and had come to see me on previous journeys. And it was Brother Antoine, when he had fallen ill at Porte Venere, who told me about all this, and sent me the documents together with his own account of the circumstances. I must admit that, at first, I hesitated to credit the facts. On reflection, however, they seemed to me far too extraordinary and fantastic to have been invented; human imagination could not go as far as that. Indeed, it is the truth that so often takes us by surprise. I checked the dates, collected a few more facts, and sent to find you. First, I merely sent you messengers who had no letter from me and therefore were unable to persuade you to come to see me. But then, in the end, I sent you the letter due to which, my most gracious lord, you are now here. If you wish to claim your rights to the crown of France, I am prepared to help you to do so.'

A silver mirror had been brought. Giannino took it over to the great candelabra and looked at himself for a long moment.

He had never cared for his face; it was round and rather flaccid, his nose was straight but lacked character, his eyes were blue but beneath eyebrows that were too pale. It was the face of a busy banker engaged in the wool trade – could it really be the face of the King of France?

And yet, when he remembered Queen Clémence of Hungary, he could not deny that there was a certain resemblance. Great beauty in a woman often becomes transformed into a sort of insipidity in her male offspring. And what had Louis X looked like?

The Tribune placed his hand on the banker's shoulder.

'For many years my birth was also impenetrably mysterious,' he said gravely. 'I was brought up in a tavern in this city. I served wine to street-porters. It was only later I discovered whose son I was.'

The formidable and imperial profile, where only the right nostril quivered a little, seemed suddenly a little drawn.

3

'We, Cola di Rienzi . . .'

BY THE TIME GIANNINO left the Capitol the first rays of
dawn were beginning to turn the ruins of the Palatine to gold.
He did not go back to the Campo dei Fiori to sleep, for the
Tribune had provided a guard of honour which led him across
the Tiber to the Castle of Saint Angelo, where an apartment
had been prepared for him.

The next day he spent several hours in prayer in a neighbouring church, seeking God's help in his greatly perturbed
state; then he returned to the Castle of Saint Angelo. He had
asked to see his friend Guidarelli; but he was requested to
hold no converse with anyone before seeing the Tribune
again. He waited all alone till evening, when they came to
fetch him. It seemed that Cola di Rienzi dealt with affairs only
at night.

Giannino therefore returned to the Capitol, where the
Tribune showed him even greater deference than the day
before, and once again interviewed him privately.

Cola di Rienzi had made a plan of campaign and now told

him of it; he was writing immediately to the Pope, the Emperor, and all the sovereigns of Christendom, inviting them to send him ambassadors to receive a communication of the first importance, though he gave them no indication of its nature. And when the ambassadors had assembled in solemn audience, he proposed that Giannino should appear before them, clothed in all the insignia of royalty, while he informed them he was the true King of France – all this, of course, if his most gracious Lord agreed.

Giannino had been King of France only since the night before, but he had been a Sienese banker for twenty years; and he was wondering what advantage Rienzi hoped to derive from adopting his cause with such enthusiasm, with a nervous impatience, indeed, that set the potentate's huge body quivering. Why, when four kings had already succeeded to the throne of France since Louis X's death, was he so eager to engage in such a dispute now? Was it simply, as he asserted, to right a monstrous injustice and restore a prince who had been despoiled to his heritage? The Tribune soon made his basic thought clear.

'The true King of France could bring the Pope back to Rome. These false kings have false popes.'

Rienzi was far-sighted. The war between France and England, which was gradually becoming a struggle of one half of the Western world against the other, had, if not for origin, at least as its legal basis, a dynastic quarrel of succession. By producing the legitimate heir to the throne of France, the other two kings would be deprived of all basis for their claims. The sovereigns of Europe, at least those who were not engaged in the war, would assemble in Rome, remove King Jean II and give King Jean I his crown. And Jean I would bring the Holy Father back to the Eternal City. The Court of France would cease to have designs on the Imperial territories in Italy; there would be no more fighting between the Guelphs and the Ghibellines; Italy would be united again and could aspire to the recovery of her lost greatness; and the Pope and the King of France, if they so wished, could even make Cola di Rienzi, who was after all an emperor's son and would be the architect of the peace and regained greatness, Emperor, and not a German emperor either, but a classical one. Cola's mother was of the Trastevere, where the shades of Augustus, Trajan and Marcus Aurelius still walked, even in the taverns, and could still set minds dreaming.

The next day, October 4th, during the course of a third conversation, which this time took place in daylight, Rienzi gave Giannino, whom he now called Giovanni di Francia, all the documents in his extraordinary case: his foster-mother's confession, Brother Jourdain d'Espagne's account, and Brother Antoine's letter. Then, summoning a secretary, he began dictating a declaration of their authenticity.

'We, Cola di Rienzi, Knight of Grace of the Apostolic Throne, Illustrious Senator of the Holy City, Judge, Captain and Tribune of the Roman people, have carefully examined the documents which have been delivered to us by Brother Antoine, and all that we have learned and heard has merely served to increase our faith in them, for it is indeed by the will of God that the Kingdom of France has been a prey for many long years to war and calamities of every kind, and all these things have been permitted by God, we believe, in expiation of the fraud of which this man is the victim, and which has resulted in his living a long while in lowliness and poverty . . .'

The Tribune seemed more nervous than the day before; he

stopped dictating whenever he heard an unusual sound, and again when there was an unwonted silence. His large eyes were often turned towards the open windows; it was as if he were keeping watch on the city.

'Giannino, on our invitation, presented himself before us, on Thursday, October 2nd. Before explaining to him what we had to tell him, we asked him who he was, his condition, his name, his father's name, and about everything that concerned him. All that he told us agreed with the information contained in Brother Antoine's letters. We then respectfully revealed to him everything we had learned. But since we know that a conspiracy is being set on foot against us in Rome . . .'

Giannino started. Was Cola di Rienzi, who was so powerful that he could talk of sending ambassadors to the Pope and all the princes of the world, really in fear for his life? He stared at the Tribune; and Rienzi confirmed the fact by slowly lowering his lids over his bright eyes; his right nostril quivered.

'The Colonna,' he said gravely; then he began dictating again: '. . . and as we fear we may die before being able to give him our support or the means of recovering his kingdom, we have had these documents copied and have given them into his hand, this Saturday, October 4th, 1354, having sealed them with our seal and engraved with the great star surrounded by eight little stars, and with the little circle in the centre, as well as with the arms of the Holy Church and of the Roman people, so that the truths they contain shall be the better guaranteed and that they may be recognized by all the faithful. May our Most Pious and Most Gracious Lord Jesus Christ accord us a sufficiently long life to see so just a cause triumph in this world. Amen, Amen.'

This done, Rienzi went to the open window and, taking Jean I by the shoulder with an almost paternal gesture, showed him the great ruins of the ancient Forum a hundred feet below, the triumphal arches and the fallen temples. The setting sun was turning the fabulous quarry, from which Vandals and popes had drawn their marble for nearly ten centuries, and which was not yet exhausted, to rose and gold. From the Temple of Jupiter they could see the House of the Vestal Virgins, and the laurel growing in the Temple of Venus.

'It was there,' said the Tribune pointing to the site of the ancient Roman Curia, 'that Caesar was assassinated. Will you do me a very great service, my noble lord? No one yet knows who you are, and you can travel peacefully like a simple citizen of Siena. I want to do everything in my power to help you; but to do so I must be alive. I know there is a conspiracy being set on foot against me. I know my enemies want to put me to death. I know that the messengers I send out of Rome are watched. Set out for Montefiascone, go and find Cardinal Albornez on my behalf, and ask him to send me troops with all speed.'

In what an extraordinary adventure Giannino had become involved during the last few hours! Hardly had he become the claimant, the Prince Pretender to the throne of France, than he was to set off as the Tribune's emissary to get him help. So far he had agreed to nothing, and yet how could he possibly say no?

The next day, October 5th, after twelve hours on the road, he reached Montefiascone, through which he had passed five days earlier cursing France and the French. He had an interview with Cardinal Albornez who at once decided to march on Rome with the troops at his disposal: but it was already too late. On Tuesday, October 7th, Cola di Rienzi was assassinated.

4

Jean I, the Unknown

GIOVANNI DI FRANCIA RETURNED to Siena, where he lived quietly for two years, continuing his banking and wool business. He merely looked at himself rather often in the mirror. However, he never went to sleep without thinking he was the son of Queen Clémence of Hungary, the cousin of the sovereigns of Naples, and the great-grandson of Saint Louis. But he was not naturally very audacious. It was difficult to leave Siena abruptly at the age of forty, and announce to the world: 'I am the King of France,' without incurring the risk of being thought mad. The assassination of Cola di Rienzi, his protector for three days, had given him seriously to think. Besides, to whom could he turn for help?

All the same, he had not kept the matter entirely secret. He had told something of it to his wife Francesca who, like all women, was curious, and to his friend Guidarelli who, like all notaries, was curious too; above all, he had spoken of it to his confessor, Fra Bartolomeo, a Dominican.

Fra Bartolomeo was an excitable and talkative Italian

monk, and he immediately saw himself as confessor to a king. Giannino had shown him all the documents Rienzi had given him; and the Dominican began to gossip about them in the town. Soon the Sienese began to whisper to each other about the fabulous circumstances of the legitimate King of France being their fellow citizen. People gathered in front of the Palazzo Tolomei to stare. Customers bowed very low when ordering wool from Giannino; they considered it an honour to sign a contract with him; and they pointed him out as he walked through the narrow streets. The commercial travellers who had visited France asserted that he bore a great facial resemblance to the French princes, since he was fair, round-cheeked, and had a wide gap between his eyebrows.

The Sienese merchants began spreading the news to their correspondents in the commercial houses of all Europe. It was then discovered that Brother Jourdain d'Espagne and Brother Antoine, the Augustines everyone thought dead, since they had both given an impression in their accounts of the affair of being old and ill, were in fact still alive and even on the point of setting out on a pilgrimage to the Holy Land. The two monks wrote to the Council of the Republic of Siena and confirmed all the declarations they had made; and Brother Jourdain even wrote to Giannino, pointing out all the misfortunes that had fallen on France and exhorting him to take courage.

Indeed, these misfortunes were grave. King Jean II, 'the False King' as the Sienese now called him, had given the measure of his genius in a great battle fought in the west of his kingdom, not far from Poitiers. Since his father, Philippe VI, had been defeated at Crécy by infantry, it had occurred to him to dismount his knights, though he had neglected to make them discard their armour when throwing them into the assault against an enemy established on the crest of a hill. They had been cut to pieces in their grey shells like so many live lobsters.

The King's eldest son, Charles – who was known as the Dauphin since the House of France, towards the end of the previous reign, had bought back the Dauphiné from the Count of Viennois – had been in command of a section of the army, but had quitted the battlefield, so it was asserted, on his father's orders, though there could be no question of the alacrity he had displayed in obeying them. It was also said that the Dauphin's hands had a tendency to swell and that he therefore could not hold a sword for long. In any case, his discretion had saved a few knights for France, while Jean II, cut off with his youngest son, Philippe, who kept shouting: 'Father, guard your right! Father, guard your left!' when it was a whole army he had to guard against, had in the end surrendered to a knight from Picardy who had taken service with the English.

The Valois was now King Edward III's prisoner. And the fabulous sum of a million florins was being asked for his ransom. There was certainly no question of the Sienese bankers coming to his aid.

One morning in October 1356 these events were being discussed with a great deal of excitement in front of the Siena Municipio, in that fine square which is like an amphitheatre, surrounded by rose and ochre palaces. Indeed, the discussion was so animated and the accompanying gestures so emphatic that the pigeons had taken fright. Fra Bartolomeo, in his white habit, suddenly joined the largest group and, justifying his renown as a predicant friar, began speaking as if he were in the pulpit.

'We shall now see at last what kind of a man this prisoner king really is and what right he has to the crown of Saint Louis! The time for justice has come; the calamities that have overtaken France during these last twenty-five years are a punishment for her sins. Jean of Valois is merely an usurper! *Usurpatore! Usurpatore!*' cried Fra Bartolomeo to the rapidly growing crowd. 'He has no right to the throne he occupies. The true, the legitimate King of France is here in Siena. Everyone knows him as Giannino Baglioni!'

He pointed across the roofs towards the Tolomei Palace.

'He is thought to be the son of Guccio, who was the son of Mino; but he was in fact born in France, the son of King Louis and Queen Clémence of Hungary.'

The city was so stirred by this speech that the Council of the Republic met at once in the Municipio, summoned Fra Bartolomeo to bring the documents, examined them, and after a long discussion decided to recognize Giannino as King of France. They were prepared to help him recover his kingdom; and they appointed a Council of Six from among the wisest and richest citizens to watch over his interests and inform the Pope, the Emperor, the sovereigns and the Parliament of Paris that there was a son of Louis X in existence, who was legitimate though dispossessed. They also voted Giannino a guard of honour and a pension.

Giannino was rather frightened by all this to-do and began by refusing everything. But the Council insisted; it waved his own documents in his face and refused to take no for an answer. In the end, he told them of his interviews with Cola di Rienzi, whose death still obsessed him. After that, there was no limit to the Council's enthusiasm. The most noble among the Sienese quarrelled for places in his bodyguard. Indeed, the various districts of the city almost came to blows as on the day of the Palio.

The enthusiasm lasted for something under a month, during which Giannino walked the streets of his city with a princely suite. His wife could not quite make up her mind as to what attitude she should adopt and she wondered whether, mere bourgeoise that she was, she could ever be anointed in Reims. As for his children, they had to wear their Sunday suits every day of the week. The eldest by Giannino's first marriage, Gabriele, wondered whether he should be considered heir to the throne? Gabriele Primo, King of France, sounded a little odd. Or again (and poor Francesca Agazzano trembled at the thought), would the Pope not have to annul the marriage, which was clearly a most unsuitable one for so august a person as her husband, so that he might contract another with a king's daughter?

The enthusiasm of the merchants and bankers was soon quieted by their correspondents, who represented to them that business in France was bad enough, and that the Italians had quite sufficient difficulty already in maintaining their establishments there and in England without anyone putting forward a new king. The Bardi of Florence laughed at the very idea of the legitimate sovereign being a Sienese. France had a Valois king, at the moment a prisoner in London, where he enjoyed a luxurious captivity in Savoy House on the Thames, with all his household complete, and the freedom to console himself for the assassination of his darling La Cerda with the young pages. France had too, an English king, who was demanding that the crown should be recognized as his by right. And now the new King of Navarre, grandson of Marguerite of Burgundy, and Giannino's nephew, if it came to that, already known as Charles the Bad, was also claiming the throne. And the whole lot of them were in debt to the Italian bankers. This was clearly no moment for the Sienese to support the claims of their Giannino.

As a result, the Council of the Republic forbore to write to the sovereigns, send an ambassador to the Pope, or represent-atives to the Parliament of Paris. Giannino's pension and guard of honour were soon withdrawn.

Nevertheless, having been drawn into the adventure almost against his will, he was himself now anxious to pursue it. His honour was at stake and his ambition – if somewhat belatedly – had at last been aroused. His having been received in the Capitol, having slept in the Castle of Saint Angelo and having marched on Rome in company with a cardinal could not all, surely, be allowed to go for nothing. Besides, for a whole month he had never walked out without a guard of honour. Nor was he disposed to listen any longer to the whisperings – 'Do look, that's the man who said he was King of France' – when he went on Sundays to the Duomo, of which the splendid black and white façade had just been completed. Since it had been decided that he was a king, he proposed to continue behaving as such. He wrote, on his own account, to Pope Innocent VI, who had succeeded Pierre Roger in 1352; he wrote to the King of England; he wrote to the King of Navarre; and he wrote to the King of Hungary. He sent them copies of his documents and asked them for their support. And there the matter might have rested, if the King of Hungary, alone of all his relations, had not replied. The King was Queen Clémence's nephew, and, in his letter to

Giannino, he gave him the title of King and congratulated him on his birth.

On October 2nd, 1357, therefore, three years to the day after his first interview with Cola di Rienzi, Giannino, taking with him his documents, together with two hundred and fifty gold crowns and two thousand six hundred ducats sewn into his clothes, left for Buda, accompanied by four equerries who believed in his star, to seek out the distant cousin who had consented to recognize him.

But when Giannino reached Buda two months later, Louis of Hungary was absent: he returned only in March. Giannino had had to wait all winter, spending his ducats. He had met a Sienese there, Francesco del Contado, who had become a bishop.

Eventually his cousin of Hungary returned to his capital, but he gave no audience to Giovanni di Francia. He sent a number of his lords to interview him. At first they declared their conviction of his legitimacy, but within a week they had changed front and asserted the whole story to be nothing but an imposture. Giannino protested; he refused to leave Hungary; and he set up his own Council presided over by the Sienese Bishop. He even managed to recruit from the gullible Hungarian nobles, who were always ready for adventure, fifty-six gentlemen who engaged themselves to support him with a thousand horsemen and four thousand archers. They even carried their misguided generosity so far as to offer to serve him at their own expense until he was in a position to reimburse them.

Nevertheless, to equip themselves and set out, they needed the authorization of the King of Hungary. But the King, though he liked being called 'the Great', was far from remarkable for consistency, and he demanded to be allowed to re-examine personally Giannino's documents. He decided they were genuine and announced that he would help him conquer his throne; yet, a week later, he declared that he had now thought the matter over and proposed to have nothing to do with it.

Nevertheless, on May 15th, 1359, Bishop Francesco del Contado gave the Pretender a letter dated that same day, and sealed with the seal of Hungary, in which Louis the Great, 'finally enlightened by the sun of truth', certified that the Lord Giannino di Francia, who had been brought up in the city of Siena, was undoubtedly a scion of the royal family of his ancestors, and the son of King Louis of France and Queen Clémence of Hungary, of happy memory. The letter also confirmed that divine Providence had made good use of the royal wet-nurse by arranging that another child should be substituted for the young Prince, and that this child's death had saved the Prince's life, 'as once the Virgin Mary, when flying into Egypt, had saved the life of her child by pretending that he was dead . . .'

However, Bishop Francesco advised the Pretender to leave at once, before the King of Hungary could change his mind again, particularly since it was not absolutely sure that the letter had been dictated by him, nor the seal applied to it by his order.

The next day Giannino left Buda, without having had the time to assemble all the troops who had offered for his service, but nevertheless with a fine enough train for a prince who had no lands.

Giovanni di Francia then went to Venice where he had royal robes made for himself, then to Treviso, Padua, Ferrara,

Bologna, and finally home to Siena, after a journey lasting sixteen months, to present himself as a candidate at the elections for the Council of the Republic.

But, though his name came third in the ballot, the Council invalidated his election precisely on the grounds that he was the son of Louis X, had been recognized as such by the King of Hungary, and was therefore not a native of the city. His Sienese citizenship was taken from him.

It so happened that the Grand Seneschal of the Kingdom of Naples was passing through Tuscany on his way to Avignon. Giannino hurried off to see him; after all, Naples was the cradle of his mother's family. The Seneschal prudently advised him to go and see the Pope.

Without an escort now, for the Hungarian nobles had grown weary, he reached the Papal City in the spring of 1360, dressed as a simple pilgrim. Innocent VI obstinately refused to give him audience. The Holy Father was already having quite enough trouble with France without becoming embroiled with Jean I, the Posthumous.

Jean II, the Good, was still a prisoner; and there had been bloody riots in Paris in which the Provost of the merchants, Etienne Marcel, had been assassinated following an attempt to establish a popular régime. There were also risings in the provinces where poverty had led to rebellion on the part of the so-called 'Jacques'. Everyone seemed to be killing each other, and no one knew who was friend or foe. The Dauphin with the swollen hands, and without troops or money, was fighting against the English, the Navarrese, and even the Parisians, with the help of du Guesclin, the Breton, to whom he had handed the sword he could not wield himself, and he was endeavouring also to raise his father's ransom.

There was utter confusion and all the factions were equally exhausted; companies, who called themselves soldiers but were in fact merely brigands under the command of adventurers, made the roads unsafe by robbing travellers and making a profession of murder.

Avignon, as a residence for the Pontiff, was becoming as insecure as Rome, even with the Colonna. It was essential to set negotiations on foot as quickly as possible, impose peace on the exhausted combatants, and persuade the King of England to renounce the throne of France, even if it meant his keeping half the country by right of conquest. What on earth could a pilgrim who claimed to be King of France expect one to do about him?

So Giannino wandered about, seeking support and subsidies, trying to interest in his story anyone who would listen to him for an hour at a tavern table between a couple of flagons of wine. He ascribed influence to people who had none, talked to adventurers, down-and-outs, commercial travellers from the big companies, and the leaders of the English bands which had come as far south as Provence and were scouring the countryside. People said he was mad and, indeed, he was becoming so.

One day in January 1361 the notables of Aix had him arrested in that town on a charge of sedition. Since they did not know what to do with him, they handed him over to the Provost of Marseilles, who put him in prison. Eight months later he escaped but was recaptured at once; and since he so insistently claimed kinship with the royal family of Naples, asserting stubbornly that he was the son of Madame Clémence of Hungary, the Provost sent him to Naples.

At this very time the marriage of Queen Jeanne, heiress to Robert the Astrologer, was being negotiated with Jean II's youngest son. Jean II had scarcely returned from his luxurious captivity, and the peace of Brétigny had scarcely been concluded by the Dauphin, when the King hurried to Avignon where Innocent VI had just died. And King Jean II proposed to the new Pope, Urban V, a most splendid project: the famous crusade which neither his father nor his grandfather had succeeded in getting under way.

In Naples, Jean I, the Posthumous, was imprisoned in Castel Uovo; from the window of his dungeon he could see the Castel Nuovo, the Maschio Angiono, from which his mother had set out so happily to become Queen of France forty-six years before.

And it was there he died, that same year, having suffered, in the most curiously roundabout way, the fate that had so relentlessly pursued the Accursed Kings.

When Jacques de Molay uttered his anathema from the stake, did he know, through those sciences of divination in which the Templars were adepts, of the future that lay in store for Philip the Fair and all his race? Or did he see a prophetic vision amid the smoke in which he died?

Peoples bear the weight of curses longer than the princes who incur them.

Of Philip the Fair's male descendants not one had escaped a tragic fate, not one had survived, except King Edward III of England, who never reigned over France.

But the people were to suffer for a long time to come. There were still to be a wise king, a mad king, a weak king, and seventy years of calamity before another pyre, lit at the farther end of the Seine to punish a French girl for having loved her country too well, at last dissipated its smoke, as if in reply to the pyre on the Ile de la Cité, the curse of the Grand Master.

Rome, 1949.
Paris, 1954–60.

Historical Notes

1. The Roman Church has never imposed any fixed and uniform legislation on the marriage rite, indeed has tended to be content with confirming peculiar usages.

The diversity of rites and the tolerance of the Church with regard to them are based on the fact that marriage is essentially a contract between individuals and a sacrament in which the contracting parties are ministers towards each other. The presence of a priest, or even a witness, was not required in the primitive Christian Churches.

The blessing became obligatory as a result only of a decree of Charlemagne. Until the reforms made by the Council of Trent in the sixteenth century, betrothal, by the fact of being a pledge, had almost as much importance as marriage itself.

Every region had its peculiar usage which might vary from diocese to diocese. For instance, the Hereford rite was different from that of York. But in general the exchange of vows which constituted the sacrament proper took place in public outside the church. It was thus that King Edward I married Margaret of France, in September 1299, at the door of Canterbury Cathedral. The modern obligation to keep the doors of the church open during the marriage ceremony, non-observance of which may constitute grounds for annulment, is a survival of this tradition.

The marriage rite of the archdiocese of York had a certain resemblance to that of Reims, in particular the placing of the ring successively on each of the four fingers (as will be seen later in the chapter), but at Reims the rite was accompanied by the following formula:

> *Par cet anel l'Eglise enjoint*
> *Que nos deux coeurs en ung soient joints*
> *Par vray amour, loyale foy;*
> *Pour tant je te mets en ce doy.*

2. Jeanne of Evreux, third wife of Charles IV.

It will be remembered that after the annulling of his marriage to Blanche of Burgundy (see *The She-wolf of France*) Charles IV had married successively Marie of Luxembourg, who had died in childbirth, and Jeanne of Evreux. Jeanne of Evreux was the niece of Philip the Fair through her father Louis of France, Count of Evreux, and also the niece of Robert of Artois through her mother, Marguerite of Artois, Robert's sister.

3. The passing of the County of La Marche into the possession of the first Duke of Bourbon was the result of an

exchange made at the end of 1327, when Charles IV handed over the fief which had previously been his apanage to Duke Louis I in exchange for the County of Clermont in Beauvais, which he had inherited from his father, Robert of Clermont.

4. During this year 1328 Mahaut of Artois was often ill. Her household accounts show that she was bled two days after this council, on February 6th, 1328, and again on May 9th, September 18th and October 19th.

5. 'A gold hat' *(chapeau d'or)*: this term was used in the Middle Ages as a synonym for a crown.

6. Pierre Roger, previously Abbé of Fécamp, had been a member of the mission charged with the negotiations between the Court of Paris and the Court of London before the homage at Amiens. He was appointed to the diocese of Arras on December 3rd, 1328, replacing Thierry d'Hirson; then he successively became Archbishop of Sens, Archbishop of Rouen – where, as we shall see later on, he preached Philippe VI's crusade – and, finally, Pope at the death of Benedict XII in 1342; he reigned under the name of Clement VI.

7. Until the sixteenth century there were no full-length or even half-length mirrors; whether they were intended to hang on the wall, stand on the furniture or be carried in the pocket, they were all small. Mirrors were either of polished metal, as in classical times, or, from the thirteenth century onwards, of glass with a backing of tin-foil attached with transparent glue. Silvering with an amalgam of mercury and tin was not invented till the sixteenth century.

8. The Hôtel de la Malmaison, which was of palatial size,

was eventually to become the Amiens Hôtel de Ville.

9. *Hortillons*: Market-gardeners who practised then, as now, a form of cultivation peculiar to the wide marshy valley of the Somme. These gardens, called *hortillannages*, are artificially raised with alluvium dredged from the valley and intersected by canals which drain the subsoil. The *hortillons* move about the canals and bring their produce to the Marché d'Eau in Amiens in long black flat-bottomed boats, which they propel by punting.

The *hortillonages* cover an area of some seven hundred acres. From the Latin derivation of the word (*hortus*: a garden) one may infer that these market-gardens date back to the period of Roman colonization.

10. All the members of the Capet royal family were known as 'Princes à la Fleur de Lis', because their arms consisted of a semy of France (azure semy de lis or) with a bordure varying with their apanages or fiefs.

11. Guillaume de la Planche, bailiff of Béthune, and later of Calais, was in prison for the over-hasty execution of a certain Tassard le Chien, whom he had condemned to be drawn and hanged on his own authority.

La Division went to see him in prison and promised that if he gave evidence in accordance with instructions the Count of Artois would save him by persuading Mille de Noyers to intervene on his behalf. Guillaume de la Planche, at the time of the second inquiry, retracted and declared that he had given his evidence 'under threats and because of his fear of remaining long in prison and dying there, if he refused to obey Monseigneur Robert who was so great and powerful, and so much about the King'.

12. 'Mesquine' or 'meschine' (from the Walloon *eskène*, or *méquène* in Hainaut, or again *mesquin* in Provençal), signifies: weak, poor, wretched or miserable. It was a common epithet applied to women servants.

13. In June 1320, Mahaut commissioned Pierre de Bruxelles, a painter living in Paris, to decorate with frescoes the great gallery of her Castle of Conflans, which lay at the confluence of the Marne and the Seine. The agreement gave precise instructions about the subjects of the frescoes – portraits of Count Robert II and his knights in land and sea battles – the clothes the figures were to wear, the colours, and the quality of the materials to be used.

     The paintings were completed on July 26th, 1320.

14. These witches' practices, whose origins go back to the earliest Middle Ages, were still in use at the time of Charles IX and even under Louis XIV; this magic unguent, consisting of these disgusting ingredients, was in fact made during a black mass celebrated on Madame de Montespan's stomach.

     The prescriptions for love philtres, given further on, are quoted from the miscellanies of the Petit and the Grand Albert.

15. We remind the reader that Blanche of Burgundy, after being imprisoned for eleven years at Château Gaillard, was transferred to the Château de Gouray, near Coutances, and ultimately took the veil in the Abbey of Maubuisson, where she died in 1326. Mahaut, her mother, was also to be buried at Maubuisson; her remains were only transferred to Saint-Denis later, where her effigy still is – the only one, so far as we know, to be made from black marble.

16. From Candlemas 1329 till October 23rd, Mahaut seems to have enjoyed excellent health and to have scarcely had need to call in her ordinary doctors. From October 23rd, the date of her interview with Philippe VI at Maubuisson, until November 26th, the eve of her death, the progress of her illness can be traced almost day by day in the payments made by her treasurer to doctors, physicians, barber-surgeons, herbalists, apothecaries and spice-makers for attendance or supplies.

17. The body of Edmund of Kent was buried, on the orders of Edward III, in the Church of the Dominicans in London, for this order was openly hostile to Mortimer's government.

18. The eldest of the twelve children of Edward III and Philippa of Hainaut was Edward of Woodstock, Prince of Wales, who was known as the Black Prince because of the colour of his armour.

   It was he who won the victory of Poitiers against the son of Philippe VI, Jean II, and took him prisoner.

   He was a great soldier and spent most of his life on the Continent, being one of the dominant leaders at the beginning of the Hundred Years War. He died in 1376, a year before his father.

19. The keep was an essential feature of Norman castles, and was built round a courtyard open to the sky.

20. The original text of the judgement against Roger Mortimer was drawn up in French.

21. London's Common Gallows, on which most common criminals were executed, were at Tyburn. They stood approximately on the site of Marble Arch and were in use till the middle of the eighteenth century.

22. These robes appear in the inventory drawn up a few years later when Robert of Artois' possessions were seized.

23. Watriquet Brasseniex, known as de Couvin from the name of his native village near Namur in Hainaut, was minstrel to all the great Valois houses. He acquired considerable celebrity for the lays he composed between 1319 and 1329. His works were preserved in handsome illuminated manuscripts, which were executed under his personal supervision for the princesses of the time.

24. The official year began at Easter, but the feast of the New Year was traditionally celebrated on January 1st, when people exchanged good wishes and presents.

25. The number of serving-men in the household, both noble and plebeian, the *livrées du roi* as they were called, increased enormously under Philippe VI; it would seem that for every function that existed under Philip the Fair, there were three or four under the first Valois. Among the names of the clerks attached to the King's person, that is to say the members of his private office, are to be found Robert Mulet, Seigneur de la Bruyère, Robert le Coq, Jacques la Vache, Hugues de Pommard, Simon de Bucy, Pierre des Essarts, Geoffroy de Fleury – and this list is far from exhaustive.

It was the same with the chamberlains, pages and cupbearers among whom were Michel de Recourt, Robert Frétard, Trouillard d'Usages, Vidame du Mans, Thibaud de Mathefelon, Jean de Beaumont, Hérouart de Belleperche, Pierre Trousseau, Jean d'Andresel, and many more.

Many of these people moreover, besides their functions in the King's service, also held administrative appointments in the Council, Parliament, the Exchequer or the Chancellory.

The clerks were all clergy, having often entered the Church less from vocation than in order to acquire the education necessary for such employment.

26. Queen Jeanne the Lame would go to any lengths to gratify her hatred for any of her husband's friends, counsellors or servants.

When she wanted to get rid of the Marshal Robert Bertrand, known as the Knight of the Green Lion, she sent a letter 'in the King's name' to the Provost of Paris, ordering him to arrest the Marshal for treason, and to send him to the gallows of Montfaucon forthwith. She sealed the letter with her husband's private seal, which she had stolen from him when he was asleep. The Provost was the Marshal's intimate friend; he was astounded by the order, which had been preceded by no trial of any kind. Instead of sending Robert Bertrand to Montfaucon, he took him straight to the King, who welcomed him warmly, embraced him and could not make out why his visitors were so concerned. When they showed him the warrant, he realized at once that it had been issued by his wife, and he took her, says the chronicler, into a room apart and beat her so severely with a stick 'that he nearly killed her'.

Bishop Jean de Marigny was also very close to becoming a victim of Jeanne the Lame's criminal tendencies. Though he was unaware of it, he had managed to displease her. On his return from a journey into Guyenne, the Queen pretended to welcome him with a great show of friendship, and to take the weariness from his limbs had a bath prepared for him in the palace. The Bishop, seeing no urgent necessity, at first refused to bathe; but the Queen insisted and told him that her son Jean, Duke of Normandy (the future Jean II), was going to take a bath too. She accompanied him to the baths. The two baths had been made ready; the Duke of Normandy inadvertently made for the bath intended for the Bishop and was about to get into it, when his mother stopped him with a show of panic. Her demeanour caused considerable surprise and Jean of Normandy, who was a great friend of Marigny, immediately suspected a trap. He seized a dog that happened to be prowling about and threw it into the bath; upon which the dog died. When King Philippe VI heard of the incident, he beat her once again 'with torches'.

As for the Hôtel de Nesle, Philippe had given it to his wife in 1332, two years after he had bought the house from the executors of Mahaut's daughter's will. This was Jeanne of Burgundy, the Widow, who had been left it by her husband Philippe V.

As a result of a clause in Jeanne's will, the proceeds of the sale, a thousand livres in cash, plus an income of two hundred livres, were put to the founding and maintaining of a school which was set up in part of the property. This is the origin of the famous Collège de Bourgogne; it is also the basis for the confusion in the popular mind between the two sisters-in-law, Marguerite and Jeanne of Burgundy. The debauching of schoolboys of which Marguerite was accused, and which existed only in the popular imagination, can also be explained in this way.

27. The lance-rest (*fautre* or *faucre*) was a hook fixed to the

brest-plate of the armour in such a way that it supported the wooden shaft of the lance and prevented its recoil at the moment of impact. Till the end of the fourteenth century it was fixed immovably; but later was hinged or sprung to prevent its projection being an embarrassment when fighting with a sword.

28. Edward III's secret stay in France at Saint-Christophe-en-Halatte lasted four days, from April 12th to 16th, 1331.

29. The King-at-Arms was the master of ceremonies and presided over all the formalities of a tournament.

30. The Tolomei Company was the most important of the Sienese companies after the Buonsignori. It had been founded by Tolomeo Tolomei, the friend or at any rate the familiar of Alexander III, Pope from 1159 to 1181, who was himself Sienese and the opponent of Frederick Barbarossa. The Tolomei Palace in Siena was built in 1205. The Tolomei were often bankers to the Holy See; they established their business in France about the middle of the thirteenth century, first in the fairs in Champagne and then in a number of branch houses, of which Neauphle was one, with the head office in Paris.

When Philippe VI issued his decrees and many of the Italian businessmen were imprisoned for three weeks, having to purchase their liberty at very high rates, the Tolomei left secretly, taking with them all the funds deposited by other Italian companies and by their French clients, which created considerable difficulties for the French Treasury.

31. The 'remonstrances' had been carried to very great lengths since John of Luxemburg, to oblige Philippe VI, had organized a coalition and was threatening the Duke

of Brabant with invasion of his territory. The Duke of Brabant preferred to expel Robert of Artois, but not without taking advantage of the occasion to negotiate a satisfactory alliance in the marriage of his eldest son to the daughter of the King of France. As for the King of Bohemia, he received as a reward for his intervention an agreement to the marriage of his daughter Bonne of Luxemburg with the heir to France, Jean of Normandy. She was, therefore, after Marie of Luxemburg who had been sister to King John and the wife of Charles IV, the second daughter of Luxemburg-Bohemia to be Queen of France within two generations.

32. On October 2nd, 1332. The oath Philippe VI demanded from his barons was one of loyalty to the Duke of Normandy. Since he had not himself been the direct heir to the throne but had come to it by choice of the peers, Philippe VI reverted to the tradition of the elected monarchy of the first Capets, who had always had their eldest sons recognized by the peers as heir to the throne. This tradition continued till Philip Augustus.

33. Old King Robert the Bruce, who was a leper, and had held Edward II and Edward III in check so long, had died in 1329, leaving his crown to a boy of seven, David Bruce. David's minority was an opportunity for the different factions to renew their quarrelling. To ensure his safety, young David was taken by barons of his party to the refuge of the Court of France, while Edward III supported the claims of a French noble of Norman origin, Edward de Baliol, who was related to the ancient Scottish kings and was agreeable to the crown of Scotland being placed under English suzerainty.

34. Jean Buridan, born about 1295 at Béthune in Artois, was a disciple of William of Occam. His learning in philosophy and theology gained him a considerable reputation; at the age of thirty or thirty-two he became Rector of the University of Paris. His controversy with old Pope John XXII, and the schism that nearly resulted from it, served merely to increase his fame. In the latter part of his life he retired to Germany where he taught principally in Vienna. He died in 1360.

    The part attributed to him by popular imagination in the affair of the Tower of Nesle was pure fantasy and, indeed, only made its first appearance in the writings of two centuries later.

35. In the Exchequer accounts are to be found the following payments made in the first months of 1337: in March, an order to pay Robert of Artois 200 pounds as a gift from the King; in April, a gift of 383 pounds, another of 54 pounds, and the grant of the castles of Guildford, Wallingford and Somerton; in May, the grant of an annual pension of 1,200 marcs sterling; in June, the payment of 15 pounds due by Robert to the Bardi Company, etc.

36. If it were not that historical fact compels its acceptance, the novelist would hesitate at so absurd and unlikely a coincidence. Nor did the presentation of Edward III's defiance, which legally began the Hundred Years War, put a term to the strange fate of the Tower of Nesle as the scene of tragedy.

    The Constable Raoul de Brienne, Count d'Eu, was living in the Hôtel de Nesle when he was arrested in 1350 on the order of Jean the Good. He was condemned to death and beheaded.

And it was from this house that Charles the Bad, King of Navarre (the grandson of Marguerite of Burgundy) took up arms against the House of France.

Later, Charles VI, the Mad, gave it to his maniacal wife, the sinister Isabeau of Bavaria, who handed France over by treaty to the English, and denounced her own son, the Dauphin, as illegitimate.

Hardly had the Hôtel de Nesle been given to Charles the Bold by Charles VII, when the latter died, and Charles the Bold took up arms against the new King, Louis XI.

The monks of Saint-Germain-des-Prés then occupied it temporarily.

Francis I gave part of it to Benvenuto Cellini, but since the Provost of Paris objected, Cellini had to resort to force to gain occupation of it.

Henri II installed a mint in it. The Monnaie de Paris is still on the site, by which the great extent of the property and buildings may be judged.

Charles IX sold the house to pay his Swiss guards. It was bought by the Duke of Nevers, Louis of Gonzaga, who had it demolished and built the Hôtel de Nevers on the site; and it was at this time that the Tower was pulled down.

Mazarin acquired the Hôtel de Nevers and built on the site of the old buildings the Collège de Quatre Nations, which still exists, and is today the home of the Institut de France.

37. Henry de Burghersh seems to have been a sort of English Talleyrand of the Middle Ages; he was an extremely able man and knew how to make himself indispensable to each successive prince. He had, too, a sense of the right

moment at which to abandon the powerful of yesterday to join those of tomorrow. He had served King Edward II and had been sent by him to Queen Isabella to persuade her to return from her exile in France. He had joined Isabella and Mortimer as soon as they disembarked in England, and Mortimer had appointed him Chancellor. He suffered only a temporary eclipse at Mortimer's downfall. In 1334 Edward III recalled him to be Treasurer, having meanwhile consistently sent him on embassies abroad. It was he who was fundamentally responsible for organizing the great coalition of the English, the Germans and the Flemish against France. As with Talleyrand, moral integrity was not the outstanding feature of his character; on the other hand, he had a high and effective regard for the real interests of his country.

38. Queen Isabella still had another twenty years to live, but she took no further part in affairs. The daughter of Philip the Fair died on August 23rd, 1358, at Hertford Castle and was buried in the Franciscan Church of Newgate in London.

39. L'Eclus was not the last battle France lost on equal terms through making poor use of her forces. We have seen equally remarkable examples of the folly of the strategists in our own day. Though the contrary has continually been asserted to excuse the defeat of 1940, the French army at the time was equipped with as many tanks as the German army, and their fire-power was equivalent if not superior to the German. The French High Command was responsible for the defeat by its conception of the tactical use of tanks, despite notable warnings. With a gap of six centuries – L'Eclus in June 1340, Flanders in June

1940 – the same ridiculous obstinacy was responsible for similar results. The breed of Béhuchets is a tenacious one, but it never conquers anything but staffs.

40. In spite of political struggles, risings, and rivalry between social classes or with neighbouring cities, all of which were the common lot of the Italian republics at this period, Siena nevertheless was at the height of its prosperity and fame, both in commerce and in the arts, during the fourteenth century. Between the occupation of the town by Charles of Valois in 1301 and its conquest by Giovanni Galeazzo Visconti, Duke of Milan, in 1399, its only real disaster was the Black Death in 1347–8.

41. 'I am now living in France, in the Babylon of the West, amid everything that is most hideous under the sun, on the banks of the untamed Rhône, which is like the Cocytus or the Acheron of Tartarus, where reign the Fisherman's successors, who were once poor, but have forgotten their origin. Instead of saintly solitude, one is confounded to find a gathering of criminals and bands of infamous satellites on every hand; instead of austere fasting, there is luxurious feasting; instead of pious pilgrimage, a cruel lewd idleness; instead of the bare feet of the apostles, the fast steeds of thieves, white as snow, apparelled in gold, lodged in gold, eating gold, and soon to be shod with gold. In short, it makes one think of the kings of the Persians or the Parthians, whom one must worship and can visit only with an offering of gifts . . .' (Letter V).

'Today Avignon is no longer a city, but the country of ghosts and phantoms; and to sum it up in a word, it is the sink of every crime and every infamy; it is the hell of the living prophesied by David ...' (Letter VIII).

'I know from experience that there is here no piety, charity, faith, or respect, no fear of God, nothing saintly, just, equitable or sacred, in fact nothing human ... Welcoming hands, cruel actions; angel voices, devilish deeds; sweet chanting, hearts of steel ...' (Letter XIV).

'It is the only spot on earth where reason has no place, where everything happens at hazard and without reflection, and of all the plagues of this place, of which there are an infinite number, the most harassing is that it is full of snares and grapnels, so that when one thinks to escape one finds oneself yet more strictly bound and chained. Moreover, there is no light and no guide ... And, to quote Lucan, "it is a black night of crime" ... You would not think these were people, but particles of dust blown hither and thither by the wind ...' (Letter XVI).

'Satan looks on laughing at this spectacle and takes pleasure in the unequal dance, sitting as arbiter between the decrepit old men and the young girls ... Among them [the cardinals] there was a little old man capable of fecundating no matter what animal; he was as lascivious as a goat or as whatever there may be which is more lascivious and more stinking than a goat. Whether it was that he was afraid of rats or ghosts, he dared not sleep alone. He considered that there was nothing more melancholy or unfortunate than to be celibate. He officiated to Hymen every day, though he had long passed his seventieth year and had at the most seven teeth left ...' (Letter XVIII). (Petrarch: *Letters without Title*, to Cola di Rienzi, Tribune of Rome, and others.)

Bibliography

For the benefit of the many readers whose interest in the last of the Capet kings of the direct line has been aroused by *The Accursed Kings*, a list of the principal sources on which this historical panorama has been based is given below.

This bibliography has been drawn up by Pierre de Lacretelle.

Chroniclers

FRENCH

Les grandes chroniques de France.

Les chroniques de Saint-Denis.

Chronique parisienne anonyme.

Chroniques des quatre premiers Valois.

The continuator of *Guillaume de Nangis.*

Pierre Cochon: *Chronique normande.*

Geoffroy de Paris: *Chronique métrique.*

Jehan le Bel: *Les vrayes chroniques*.
Jean Froissart: *Les Chroniques*.

ENGLISH

Adam of Murimuth: *Chronica sui temporis*.
William of Malmesbury: *De gestis regum anglorum*.
Holinshed: *Chronicles of England*.

Contemporary Sources

Recueil des Ordonnances des Rois de France (Publ 1770 et seq).
Itinéraires des Rois de France (Recueil des Historiens de la France XVIIIe et XIXe siècles).
Calendar of Close rolls (for the reigns of Edward II and Edward III). London 1893–1900.
Archives of the Record Office.
Rymer, Thomas: *Foedera, conventiones, litterae, acta publica inter reges Angliae et alias . . .* (Vol II, London, 1739).

General

Anselme, le Père: *Histoire générale de la maison de France et des grands officiers de la couronne* (1726–33).
Cokayne, J. E.: *Complete peerage of England* (London, 1893–1900).
Dictionary of National Biography (London, 1885–1901).
Giry, A.: *Manuel de diplomatique* (1894).
Berty, A.: *Topographie historique du vieux Paris* (1888 et seq).
Calmette, J.: *Le monde féodal* (1934).
Deprez, E.: *Les préliminaires de la guerre de Cent Ans* (1902).
Lafaurie, J.: *Les monnaies des rois de la France* (Vol I, 1951).

Franklin, A.: *Les rois et les gouvernements de France* (1960).
   Les rues et les cris de Paris au Moyen Age (1874).

Viollet le Duc, E. E.: *Dictionnaire de l'architecture au Moyen
   Age. Dictionnaire du mobilier de la France au Moyen Age.*

Enlart, C.: *Manuel d'architecture française au Moyen Age*
   (Vol III: *Le costume*).

Lacroix, P.: *L'ancienne France* (1886). *Les Arts au Moyen Age*
   (1869). *Moeurs, usages et costumes au Moyen Age* (1873). *Vie
   militaire et religieuse au Moyen Age* (1873). *Science et Lettres
   au Moyen Age* (1877).

Michelet, Jules: *Histoire de France* (17 vols, 1833–56).

Sismondi, J. C. L. de: *Histoire des républiques italiennes au
   Moyen Age* (1840).

Langlois, C. V.: *Histoire de France*, dirigée par E. Lavisse
   (Vol III-2). *La vie en France au Moyen Age* (1924).

Coville, A.: *Histoire de France*, dirigée par E. Lavisse
   (Vol IV-1 & 2).

Fawtier, R. and Coville, A.: *L'Europe occidentale de 1270 à 1380*
   (Histoire générale, dirigée par Glotz, Vol IV-1 & 2).

Gautier, L.: *La chevalerie* (1884).

Dupouy, E.: *La Moyen Age médical* (1888).

Gauzons, T. de: *La magie en France au Moyen Age* (1910).

Gilbert, E.: *Les plantes magiques* (1899).

Brachet, A.: *Pathologie mentale des rois de France* (1903).

Dodu, G.: *Les Valois* (1934).

Belleval, Marquis de: *Les bâtards de la maison de France*
   (1901).

Fournel, V.: *Les rues du vieux Paris* (1879).

Le Goff, J.: *Les intellectuels au Moyen Age* (1957).

Mollat, G.: *Les papes d'Avignon* (1912).

Léonard, E. G.: *Les Angevins de Naples* (1954).

Richard, J.: *Les ducs de Bourgogne et la formation du duché du XIe au XIVe siècle* (1954).

Garetta, J. C.: *Les quartier Saint-André-des-Arts des origines à 1660* (Position des thèses, 1957).

Parmentier, A.: *Album historique* (Vol II, 1897).

Gams, P. F.: *Series episcoporum ecclesae catholicae* (Regensburg, 1873).

Particular

ARTEVELDE, JAKOB VAN

Lettenhove, Kervyn de: *Jacques d'Artevelde* (Ghent, 1863).

ARTOIS, MAHAUT D'

Richard, J.: *Une petite-nièce de Saint Louis: Mahaut d'Artois, comtess d'Artois et de Bourgogne* (1897). *La bibliothèque de Mahaut d'Artois* (Revue des questions historiques, 1886).

Le Roux de Lincy, A. J. V.: *Inventaire des biens meubles et immeubles de la comtesse Mahaut, pillés par son neveu Robert* (Bibl de l'École des Chartes, 1861).

ARTOIS, ROBERT D'

Frondeville, H. de: *Le comté de Beaumont le Roger* (1937). *Inventaire des biens saisis après l'arrestation de la comtesse de Beaumont* (Actes normands de la Chambre des Comptes).

Lancelot, C.: *Mémoires pour servir à l'histoire de Robert d'Artois* (Mémoire de l'Academie des Inscriptions et Belles Lettres, 1736). *Les voeux du Héron.* (The two known manuscripts of this fourteenth-century poem are preserved in the Berne Library and the Royal Library in Brussels.)

CHARLES IV, King of France

Journal du Trésor de Charles IV, published by Jules Viard (1917). *Information de l'Annulation du marriage de Charles IV* (Arch. Nat. J 682–2). (This document has never been published.) *Testament de Charles IV*. (A copy taken from the original, then preserved in the archives of the Chambre des Comptes, is now in the Manuscript Department of the Bibliothèque Nationale: fds. fr. nouv. acqu. 7600).

CHATILLON, GAUCHER DE

Du Chesne, A.: *Histoire de la maison de Chastillon-sur-Marne* (1621).

CLÉMENCE OF HUNGARY, Queen of France

Lettres secrètes et curiales de Jean XXII relatives à la cour de France (1900–13). *Inventaire et vente après décès des biens meubles et immeubles, bijoux, etc, de la reine Clémence* (Nouveau recueil des comptes de l'argenterie des rois de France, published by L. C. Douet d'Arcq, Vol II, 1874).

CRESSAY, family of
See JEAN I.

EDWARD II AND EDWARD III, Kings of England

More, Thomas de la: *Vita et mors Edwardi secundi* (A contemporary chronicle published for the first time in 1603).

Marlowe, C.: *Edward the Second*.

Barnes, J.: *The History of Edward the Third* (Cambridge, 1688).

Mackinnon, J. P.: *The History of Edward the Third* (London, 1900).

Ramsay, J. H.: *Genesis of Lancaster* (London, 1913).

Longman, N.: *History of the Life and Times of Edward the Third* (London, 1869).

Pons, C.: *L'Edouard II de Marlowe* (Thèse complémentaire, 1959).

HIRSON, THIERRY D'
Richard, J. M.: *Thierry d'Hirson* (1892).

ISABELLA OF FRANCE, *Queen of England*
Strickland, Agnes: *Lives of the Queens of England* (1889).

Rhodes, W. E.: *The Inventory of the Jewels and Wardrobe of Queen Isabella* (*English Review*, 1897).

JEAN I, King of France (Giannino)
Monmerque, L. J. N.: *Dissertation historique sur Jean Ier, roi de France et de Navarre, suivie d'une charte par laquelle Nicholas de Rienzi reconnaît Giannino, fils supposé de Guccio Baglioni comme roi de France et d'autres documents relatifs à ce fait singulier* (1844). *Doutes historiques sur le sort du petit roi Jean Ier*; lecture delivered on Friday, August 9th, 1844, at the Institut Royal. *Lettre du frère Antoine à Nicolas de Rienzi, suivie de deux lettres de Rienzi addressées à Giannino* (1845).

Bréhaut, L.: *Giannino Baglioni, roi de France (Revue contemporaine*, 1860).

Tavernier, E.: *Le roi Giannino* (Mém. de l'Ac. d'Aix, 1882).

Maccari, L.: *Istoria del re Giannino di Francia* (Siena, 1893).

JOHN XXII, Pope
Bachelet (X): *Étude critique de la vie et des oeuvres de Jean XXII*, in: *Dictionnaire de théologie catholique; Lettres secrètes et curiales de Jean XXII, relatives à la cour de France* (1900–13).

Verlacque, Abbé V.: *Jean XXII.*

Albe, E.: *Autour de Jean XXII* (1904).

Labande, L. H.: *Le palais des Papes au XIVe siècle.*

Pétrarch: *Epistolae sine titulo* (French tran, 1885).

Bertrandy-La Cabane, M.: *Recherches historiques sur l'origine de l'élection et le couronnement de Jean XXII* (1854).

Valon, L. de: *Le service de table à la cour de Jean XXII.*

Principal works of John XXII: *Thesaurus pauperum. L'art transmutatoire. L'elixir des philosophes* (attributed).

JOINVILLE, le sire de
Paris, Gaston: *Jean, sire de Joinville* (1897).

LOUIS X HUTIN, King of France
Dufayard, C.: *Le réaction féodale sous les fils de Philippe le Bel* (Revue historique, 1894). *Obsèques et pompe funèbre de Louis X et du petit roi Jean* (in: *Comptes de l'argenterie des rois de France au XIVe siècle*, published by L. C. Douet d'Arcq, Vol. II, 1874).

MORTIMER, ROGER
Chronicon Galfredi Le Baker.
Planché, R.: *Genealogy of the Mortimers* (Journal of the British Archaeological Association, 1868).

PHILIP IV THE FAIR, King of France
Lévis-Mirepoix, duc de: *Philippe le Bel* (1912).
Baldrich: *Maladie et mort de Philippe le Bel,* rapport au roi de Marjorque, daté du 7 décembre 1314 (Bibl de l'École des Chartes, 1897).
Douet d'Arcq, L. C.: *Notes sur la mort de Philippe le Bel et son codicille* (Revue des Soc. savantes, 1876).

PHILIPPE V THE LONG, King of France

Leghugeur, P.: *Le règne de Philippe le Long* (1931).

Comptes du trésor de Philippe le Long, published by Douet
    d'Arcq (1857).

Olivier-Martin, F.: *Études sur les régences* (Vol I, 1931).

PHILIPPE VI OF VALOIS, King of France

Viard, J.: *La France sous Philippe VI* (1899). *Documents parisiens
    pour servir à l'historie de Philippe VI* (1899). *L'Hôtel de
    Philippe VI* (1895).

La Roncière, C. de: *La guerre navale entre la France et
    l'Angleterre* (1898).

Cazelles, R.: *La société politique et la crise de la royauté sous
    Philippe de Valois* (1958).

THE TEMPLARS

Michelet, J.: *Le procès des Templiers* (1841–51).

TOLOMEI, Family of the

Piton, C.: *Les Lombards en France* (1882).

Van Roon, Basserman: *Les Tolomei au XIVe siècle.*

Bautier, R. H.: *Les Tolomei aux foires de Champagne* (1955).

VALOIS, CHARLES OF

Petit, J.: *Charles de Valois* (1900).

Testaments de Charles de Valois (authentic copies made in the
    seventeenth century and preserved in the Manuscript
    Department of the Bibliothèque Nationale: fds. fr. nouv.
    acq. 7600).